Snow & Sanity

Book 3 of Dust & Cannibals

Bruce I Schindler

ISBN: 0-9914627-3-4
ISBN-13: 978-0-9914627-3-5

This is a work of fiction. All the characters and events portrayed in this book are fictional, and any resemblance to real people or incidents is purely coincidental.

Other novels by

By Bruce I. Schindler

Dust & Cannibals

Mud & Horizons
(Book 2 of Dust & Cannibals)

The LaGrange Legacy

Touch Stones

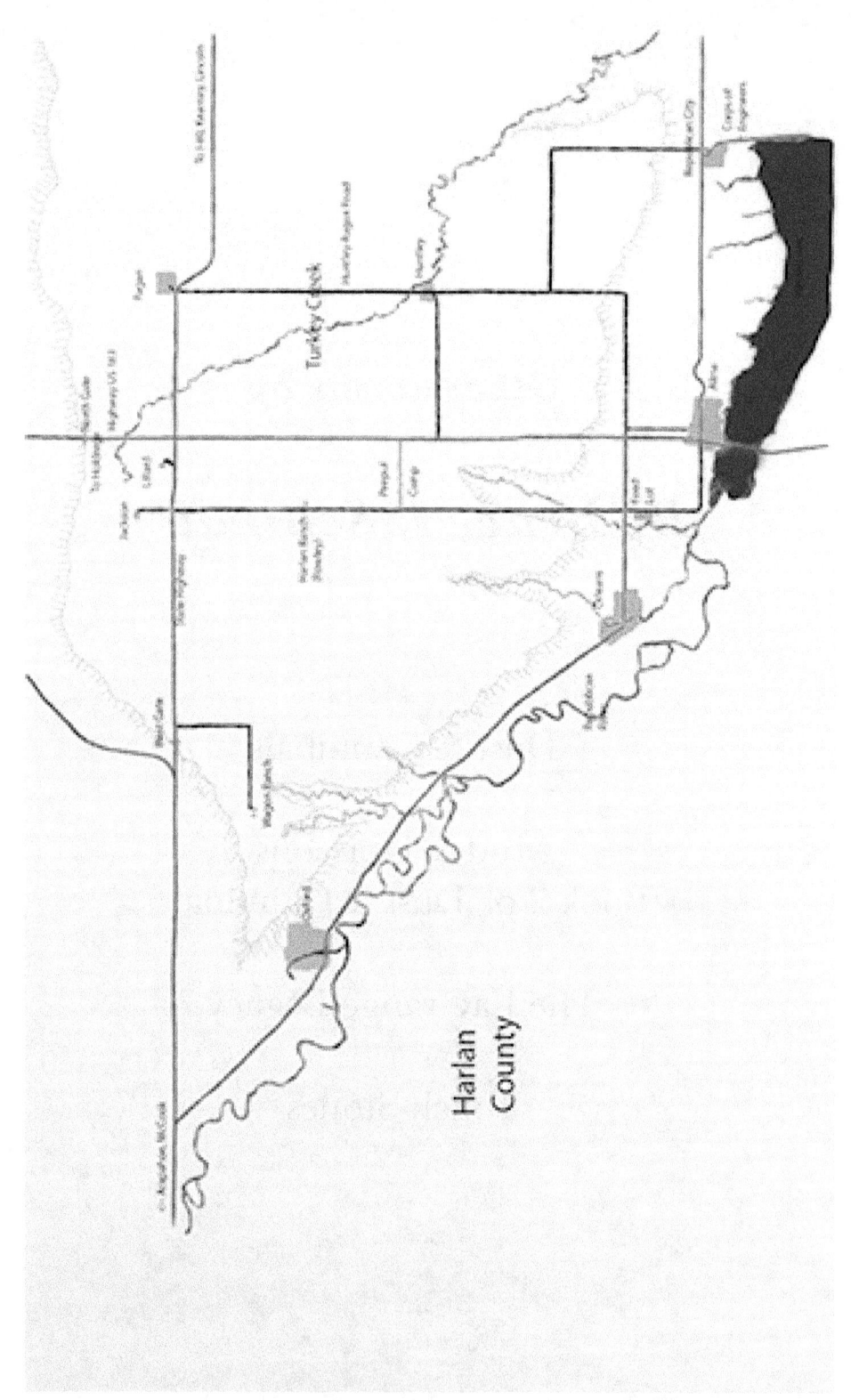

Chapter 1

Mystery in Ragan

"Hey, Rick, you'd better pick up the pace. This frigid weather will kill both you and your horse."

Rick glanced at Vince with empty eyes. "The cold could be the death of me. It feels like a vacation in spite of Nebraska looking like Antarctica. You might say I'm prolonging the coolness between the frying pan and the fire."

Vince's law enforcement mentality clicked into fact-finding mode, although perfectly aware of Rick's situation. "How's that?"

"Kevin wants to run me off. He always gives me every crap job he can think of. There are a couple of reasons he'd let me go on this. Mainly, it's because Mark told him to. In addition, Kevin knows Don Rowley hates me, too. Mark has me going because Don Rowley wants somebody to fix his computer and I'm the only living computer geek. No doubt Mr. Rowley will take one look at me and throw me out."

That confirmed what Vince heard a number of other places. "Behind you, there is a new storm coming in. Old Don Rowley won't throw you anywhere until the storm is over. It isn't about you. There is no way he wants to give Mark any advantage. The worst would be for Mark to tell Lyle Lillard that Don mistreated a horse."

Vince saw Rick look at the approaching storm and shudder, followed by urging his horse ahead at a faster pace. Rick, of all people, would get the point about having anybody say he mistreated a horse. It was a certain way to end up walking. Kevin was the ranch manager, but Mark could take a horse from anyone in Harlan. If he took a horse, it would be gone forever.

They rode into Ragan, once tiny and barely existing, but now the largest population center anywhere.

Vince looked around and mentioned, "I'm off duty. My horse lives at the Rowley livery stable, so we're going to the same place. Maybe I can help grease your entrance."

Rick lapsed back into his usual taciturn mode by that time. Vince was surprised he got that little bit of information.

The big door to the stable opened just as they approached. Vince was amazed since Don Rowley was not big on service. Then he saw the reason. Mrs. Rowley was pushing it open while Don Rowley drove a one-horse sleigh. Vince recognized Mrs. Stamford in the back of the sleigh, and thought it was very strange for her to associate with mere working-class people. Even stranger was what appeared to be a rag bag next to her. It was as tall as Mrs. Stamford.

"I brought your computer guy, Don," Vince called to him.

Don didn't even look. "I have to get these ladies home before the storm. Computers can wait."

Vince caught what Don said. There were two women in the back of the sleigh. The rag bag contained a lady? Immediately, Vince's law enforcement antennae focused on the situation. Including the refugees from McCook who lived in Orleans, the total population of Harlan was four hundred fifty. Vince knew all of them, at least by face. Why take anyone like that? The only reason to be in a bag was for anonymity. That pointed to the hundred fifty tribal members living just outside Harlan. On one hand, Vince needed to go home. At the same time, he absolutely had to find out what the story was.

Nancy Rowley kept the door open so the two men could get their horses inside.

Inside, Vince dismounted, but waited with his horse while Nancy closed the door.

"I see you and Don have moved into high society. A visit from Mrs. Stamford is a big deal."

Nancy laughed nervously. "I don't know about the high society part. Still, Mrs. Stamford seems like a nice person."

"Are you acquainted with the other three families in their group?"

"No, it has only been her. I've met the other three families, but I don't really know them. Nell Stamford shared a few recipes and cooking tips with me. Can you stay for dinner, Vince?"

Vince noted that Nancy avoided any mention of the second woman in the sleigh. She also downplayed whatever was going on between the four families and the Rowleys.

"I really can't, Nancy. My wife expects me home. I should have been there before now, actually, but got delayed. I think Rick will volunteer to sample your new recipes, though."

Vince turned to put his horse away. At the same time, he saw Rick still had his horse saddled, like he planned to make a quick getaway.

"You'd better find a stall and take care of your horse, Rick. There's no way you're going home tonight. There's always heat from the forge in the back room to warm the stable. Sometimes it can get too hot, especially when he is working on a big project. I don't know how Clay stands it. If there's an empty stall, just pile up some straw. It is pretty comfortable."

Rick jerked involuntarily at Vince's comment. Then, without a word, he turned to start getting the saddle off his horse.

Nancy smiled brightly. "We hoped you would get here sooner, Rick. I'm sure Don will appreciate whatever you can do to get his computer going. He wants to put his inventory on it, you see."

Vince, well aware of the arctic conditions outside, made sure his coat was buttoned and his hat pulled low over his eyes. "I'll just go out the office door, Mrs. Rowley. Say hello to Don for me, will you?"

Snow started falling. Fortunately, there wasn't much wind with it. Vince took a shortcut, and thanks to the small size of the town, got to the corner as Don left off his passengers. The rag bag came to life, and walked beside Mrs. Stamford up to the front door of her house. Mrs. Stamford looked around nervously before going inside. She didn't notice Vince, standing behind a tree trunk.

Vince saw the rag bag was a woman. She uncovered her head as she went inside. That made him wonder if she was a tribal member who snuck in to work. If that was the case, why did Mrs. Stamford make such a secret of it? Come to think of it, Mrs. Rowley was not forthcoming about it, either. This was a situation he felt compelled to look into further.

He really was not lying when he told Nancy Rowley he should have already been home. Vince was late for dinner. At the same time, Beth knew better than to have a problem with it. After all, he was now the senior law enforcement officer in Harlan. Technically, he was the only law enforcement officer. Lyle Lillard, his nominal boss, was an honorary under-sheriff, appointed by Sheriff Crichton, who, like nearly everyone else on the planet, died in the Omega dust.

At the same time, Vince was one of very few who still had an intact family, for which he was continually grateful. As such, he tried to share his daily experiences with them whenever possible. The main time it wouldn't be possible was if a principle in an ongoing case was on hand. Since the Rowleys, Stamfords, and the woman dressed up like a rag bag weren't there, that wasn't the case. It also gave him an excuse for being late, so as they ate, he talked about bringing Rick to the Rowley stable and then picking up on their attempt to hide a woman in the sleigh going back to the Stamford house. Vince mentioned how he was certain it was a woman.

The reaction from the kids wasn't what he expected. His youngest started to giggle. The two older kids first tried to hush their younger sibling, only to end up laughing themselves. Vince just had to explore the situation a bit more. It turned out they had been spying on the four families ever since Vince's family moved to Ragan. When their mother went to call on one of the families, it was normal for the kids to see a mousy-looking girl trudging across the backyard to another house. Keeping track of her had become a major game.

Vince tried to keep his composure even while he was perfectly aware of the fact there was no way he could pass up a break like this.

"I would like to play your game, kids. Would that be okay with you?"

"It has to be a secret, Dad, just between us."

"Would it be all right if Mom knows about it?" he asked, looking at his wife across the table.

The three kids looked at each other in confusion and panic. After a moment, his daughter looked at him with a straight face, and said, "Of course Mom knows about it. Mom knows everything."

Vince grinned at his wife, Beth, and she smiled modestly.

"Will you be spying on them tomorrow?"

"We do it almost every day," his oldest son stated. "It is all part of doing a stake-out, just like you told us."

Chapter 2

Rick and the Rowleys

Rick shook off the cold, looking around inside the brick building. It was built just after 1900 as a livery, and now returned to its original function. He then went to help Nancy Rowley close the big door while deputy Vince went out through the office. Vince departed with a very curious sense of urgency, but Rick had no idea why. After all, the only people in the street were Don and his passengers. Rick recognized Mrs. Stamford, the grande dame of the four upper crust families in town. That view was according to those families, not that any of them deigned to communicate with him.

Nancy Rowley must now be part of that group. It was only right since Don was now the resident tycoon. The livery stable seemed an odd choice for their home, but Don's claim to fame was his freight business, consisting of horses and freight wagons. The two seemed happy with it as a home since they moved to town.

"Don't just stand there. Come on inside and tell me about yourself, Rick. How do you like working at Harlan Ranch?"

Rick went into the living area, but stopped just inside the door.

"I'm hardly ever at Harlan Ranch. Most of the time, I'm at what they call Wagon Ranch."

"Is Mark pretty good to work with?"

"Kevin is my boss these days. I was with Mark during the evacuation, and that was okay."

"Oh, I see. Do you like working for Kevin?"

Rick let the question hang in the air for a minute. Then he replied, "Kevin's the boss," and let it drop.

Nancy didn't pursue that. She also did not press him to move beyond where he stood. Fortunately for both of them, Don returned soon, and Rick went back into the stable when he came in. Don only now focused on who he was.

"You're who they sent?"

"Mr. Lillard told Mark to send me. Kevin is kissing up to Mark and Lyle, and he hates me. Playing the big man while he pisses you off is his idea of a good time. In our vast population of four hundred people, how many computer people could there would be? I'm it."

Rick had a reputation of being of few words. That speech was far and away the longest ever said in Don's presence. The combination of internal heat from the irritation of the whole situation, combined with the arctic conditions outside conspired to set off Rick's wise-ass response machine. It shocked Don and granted Rick a moment of silence.

Finally, Don got cranked up again. "Damn! You actually have a pair of balls. Who'd have thought it? Well, lets get in the door before the heat escapes. Don't you have any sense?"

"I didn't want to impose on your hospitality. There was always the hope you'd just throw me out and I could avoid any further aspersions being cast on my character."

Don just growled in response, telling Rick that old Don had no idea what he just said other than being aware that it wasn't a compliment. He followed Mr. Rowley into the living quarters, where he got down to why he was here. "What high-tech device do you have that couldn't be repaired with a blacksmith's hammer?"

"Clay owns the hammer. I may borrow it to repair your skull if you continue being such a smart ass."

"Pardon me, oh great one. What's your computer problem? Other than Mr. Lillard, I didn't think anybody in Harlan had a computer."

"That shows what you know. I need to keep track of my inventory, but the stupid computer doesn't work. It has to work."

Don enunciated every syllable of the last sentence just to make sure Rick got the message.

"What kind of computer is it?"

"What do you mean, what kind? It's a broken computer. It's a damn busted computer."

"Can you show it to me?"

"I thought you'd never ask."

Don Rowley led Rick into the office area at the front of the living quarters. He pointed at an ancient desktop computer in the corner. Rick could only stare.

"Is that it?"

Don nodded, and Rick took a closer look, shaking his head.

"This qualifies as an antique. With all the computers on the planet available, I can't believe you'd even try to use a relic like this."

Don's wife, Nancy, came up then. "Ten years ago, our children thought we could use it to stay in touch with everyone. We never figured out how to do much with it. It was several years before we could send an e-mail. Our children tried to get us to do social networking, but the satellites and power went down before that could happen."

"Can you show me the trouble, Mr. Rowley?"

It did not take Rick long to track down the source of the trouble. "This machine was past its life expectancy when you first got it. You're lucky it worked this long. I might be able to restore most of the files and transfer them to your other computers."

"I never bothered to get additional computers. There was no reason since there was no power. Now that we hooked up the solar panels, I thought it would be a good way to do my inventory."

Rick was puzzled now. "How much inventory do you have on it?" Don's face acquired a distinctly sour look. "There's just about none. I thought about it during the last snow storm, and drug it out. I found something called a spreadsheet program that might do the job. I was still figuring out how to make it work when the whole thing died."

Rick smiled to himself but kept a look of professional concern on his face. "Let's not worry about this old box. I'll check around and see if there's something that might actually take care of what you want to do. It might take several days. I'll even try to show you how to use it. Before you ask, though, I am not keying in the information. That part is up to you, or whoever you bring in here to be a clerk. How would that be?"

Don appeared to suddenly be on the borderline of enthusiastic. "That would sure work for me. I'll owe you."

"You saying that you owe me beats the heck out of offering to pay me dollars or something. I could quote some number of the play money the banker calls Loups, and is busy promoting, but who would take them from me?"

Don actually chuckled then. "He thought I could take them for hauling freight instead of taking produce and other stuff. Like you said, though, what could I swap Loups for?"

Rick tried to keep a professional look on his face. "At the moment, computer services are the only thing under discussion. Your people can get in touch with my people about that."

"Could we offer you some dinner, Rick? Mrs. Stamford showed me some of her recipes, and we ended up with far too much food for just Don and me." Nancy added. "The way it is snowing, you'll never get back. We can put you up for the night."

Rick expected to be sent on his way the moment his services weren't specifically required, whatever the weather. When they met several months earlier, he and Don decided not to like each other at the first glance. All this hospitality was beyond belief, and he tried to remember his manners. "Thank you, ma'am. I really appreciate it. If my horse got into trouble along the way, I'd never hear the end of it. I should go check on it, anyway."

Then a bit of his snark snuck back, and he added, "Vince reminded me about the weather on the way in. For all I know, Kevin may have planned it this way. If he was in charge of the weather, this is exactly what he would order. As for dinner, I'm sure whatever you're having is better than what they're eating at the ranch."

Nancy beamed in spite of his comments. "Go see to your horse. There's water, plenty of hay, and a place for your tack. Take care of what you need to, and come back in. While you're in the stable, I'll put Mr. Rowley on his best behavior. You won't have to worry about him biting — not too hard, anyway."

Rick took care of his horse, wondering about the hospitality. Don having him look at a computer that served no purpose sounded more like an excuse than a reason. It all appeared to be something that Nancy Rowley wanted to do. Since he was staying overnight, Rick figured she had plenty of time for whatever she had in mind.

They were soon eating, and Rick knew Nancy Rowley planned on his being there. The meal they had was not what two people had at home. In addition, there was more than enough food for a fourth person, as well. For additional clues, Rick soon noticed a trend in the conversation.

Don didn't say much, for a start. On the other hand, Nancy was not only far more chatty than he was comfortable with, it was on subjects he didn't want to discuss. More than that, it was about people he didn't want to discuss, not that Rick liked talking about people at all. He figured Nancy picked up on that.

"How is Kevin getting along with Susie?" Nancy inquired sweetly.

"Okay, I guess. Kevin doesn't talk about that. Anything to do with Susie is not open for discussion at the ranch."

"We heard how her father, Dennis Maguire tried to split them up. Now, he not only allows them to see each other, he insists on it."

Rick knew about all of that. Susie got a good deal more frisky than Kevin could deal with. From all reports, Susie now had a baby on board. It happened a few months ago while everyone escorted the last vial of Omega bugs to their eternal rest. Kevin's sanity came more and more into question as his affair with Susie twisted and turned. Rick managed to stay in Kevin's good graces for a while, by knowing when to keep his mouth shut. Rick also knew better than to try to lie, especially with an inquiring mind like Nancy Rowley on the case.

"Kevin never said much about it, ma'am. He's got everybody working pretty hard all day, and then he's gone to Huntley every chance he gets." That was information he knew already spread across Harlan.

"I have no doubt that he's gone on Susie Maguire business. What do all the guys at the ranch say about it?"

"Nobody says anything. It's the best job in Harlan, and nobody wants to mess it up." Rick now spoke the gospel truth. The trouble was that he said it in the wrong house, Don Rowley was Harlan's largest employer. Rick knew he blew it the moment the words were out of his mouth.

"Are you saying nobody wants to work for me?" Don snarled at Rick.

Yeah, that was it, all right. Since he was sitting in Don's house and eating his food, Rick tried for something more like a peaceable response.

"Plenty of folks around Harlan like working for you, sir. Having any occupation these days is a precious thing. It's just that everybody isn't suited for every occupation. That's all I'm saying."

Don growled, but couldn't find anything in what Rick just said to fight about. Rick could only hope Nancy would come to the rescue, even though he knew any such rescue would come with a price.

She came riding to the rescue right on time and with a smile. Yes, there was a price. Taking advantage of Don's inability to immediately come up with a scathing rebuttal, Nancy quickly stepped in.

"So, Rick, how many young ladies are you seeing these days?"

That question was both a blessing and a curse. On the plus side, it changed the subject so Don could not start the other line again. It also was not about anybody Rick felt obligated to keep some level of privacy in this small, increasingly tight-knit society. On the other hand, it was about his own love life, which sucked, and that was putting it mildly.

"Yeah, well, I needed to put the social scene on the back burner while I got my feet on the ground. My experience and training was in areas that simply don't exist any more. You know?"

"I'm amazed you aren't having to fight off all the girls. After all, you're one of the heroes who got the McCook people safely to Harlan." Rick saw Don look daggers at his wife, and she quickly added, "Of course, Don was the big hero, but he's not available. I've got him," as she patted Don's arm gently.

Nancy kept going, "There was Mark, as well, but he's well and duly wedded. I cannot see any way you could go anywhere without every gal in Harlan stringing along after you, hoping for you to favor them with even a glance."

Rick shook his head and chuckled. "I'd have noticed if such a thing was going on. If I missed it, everybody else would call it to my attention. Back in the day, I became a nerd because that was suddenly cool. It was also a socially acceptable version of what I was doing anyway. Being the only nerd left standing is not cool. It's just embarrassing."

"There may be more to the young ladies around here than you think. All of them may not be simple farmer's daughters."

Rick thought Nancy's eyes glittered as she added, "You might even find a soul mate. Who knows?"

Rick sat back, wiping his chin with the napkin carefully positioned with each place setting. "Should I expect all the eligible single women, somewhere between puberty and ninety-seven to come waltzing through the door about now? How many would that be? Two?"

Nancy sat back in what Rick took to be amazement and shock. At the same time, Don leaned forward as though he was ready to attack right through the table. Okay, social interactions weren't his forte. He thought he'd better see if he could get out the hole he'd just dug. If he couldn't do that, maybe he could at least quit digging it deeper.

"I'm sorry. You've been really nice, letting me stay overnight and feeding me and all. I shouldn't have gone off like that."

"Oh, that's quite all right, dear. I understand. Really, I do. There are no ladies in a line outside the door. You can be certain of that. They'd have all frozen to death by now. At the moment, I wouldn't have a clue about anyone available, much less whether such a person and you would be interested in each other."

Nancy held up her hands as if fending off an invisible opponent. "I am not a match maker. Still, if I should happen upon somebody, would you at least talk to her once, just for me?"

Rick tried to keep a straight face. The long list of denials by notable people came to mind. I am not a candidate. I did not come to praise Caesar, I came to bury him. Yeah, she's a match maker.

He remembered Mark's wife, Ellen, going on about bringing back the old traditional ways. Computer dating sites were more to his taste. They were gone, and match makers were back. In addition, Nancy had someone specific in mind. Who that might be escaped Rick completely, but there it was.

"Sure, I could do that," he responded, attempting a nonchalant shrug. "It would be nice if there was some arrangement to be sure there wasn't a proud pappy with a shotgun behind the tree or around the corner."

Don suddenly chortled. "That sounds like where Kevin finds himself these days. When Kevin takes off each day, does he have a haunted look? Maybe like he's afraid that somebody's coming after him?"

Rick considered that. When he was on the evacuation runs, Mark commented about his military background, and a lot of interrogation involved getting the subject to talk about anything. Once a person's jaw got lubricated, usable intelligence was certain to come out eventually. This conversation was going exactly like that, and it was a bummer.

"I couldn't say anything about that. We're expected to get work done. We're not expected to look at Kevin."

That really tickled Don. "Kevin is somebody I could get to like. He knows how to keep a bunch of guys going. Good for him."

Nancy broke in, "I'll keep all your reservations in mind, Rick. You prefer orphans between puberty and ninety-seven."

Other than the uneasy thought that she had already found somebody, Rick felt secure in not having to deal with anyone that Nancy would ever find. "That would work. If they had a pacifist father, that might be all right, too."

Don was really laughing, now. "Rick, when it comes to daughters, no man is a pacifist. Since you rode with Mark, you're aware of how rough and ready weddings have gotten lately."

Rick was acutely aware of that fact. Since the Omega dust killed off nearly all of humanity, greater Harlan, to include the McCook group now living in Orleans, had seen four weddings. Only one resembled a traditional wedding. The rest were more simple declarations of status than anything else. For Mark and Ellen, it resembled more of a wishful forecast. The fact that they seemed to be getting along now was a source of wonder around the county.

There was another thing keeping Rick's sexual urges in check, at least to a degree. That was the likelihood of a one-night stand turning into a permanent marriage. It might be by force, if necessary. That was the story with Jimmy and Vickie.

"That's a really good point, Don. Yeah, let's keep it to orphans if at all possible." Then, to try to keep the feeling light, he added, "Oh, and female, please, and a member of the human species."

Now Don was nearly falling off his chair, laughing. Nancy looked at both of them and shook her head. "I got that part. It's a good thing you specified all of that for the big man, though. There's no telling what kind of creature Don might come dragging in otherwise."

Don was feeling so good that he opened up what turned out to be a very well-filled liquor cabinet.

Rick felt a little more confidant in asking about their history. "You used to live where Mark and Ellen are staying now, isn't that right?"

Don nodded, suddenly moody. "We lived there and I was born there. Everybody calls it the Harlan Ranch now, but to me, it will always be the Rowley Ranch."

Nancy was quick to add, "Still, it was nice of them to have us out there for three days over Thanksgiving. I never ate so much in my entire life. We spent our lives in that place. Still, Lyle did save us from those cannibals."

Don growled, "Yes he did, and he will never let us forget about it, either. It was dumb luck he had us go by to see Adeline before we left."

Don thought about it a moment, and his mood brightened a bit. "On the other hand, his luck didn't give him a comfortable ride on that horse of his. The saddle was too small, with one stirrup adjusted shorter than the other. He had saddle sores by the time he got to our place, and he still had ten miles to get to Alma. When we saw him that night, he was a complete mess."

Nancy smiled, and Rick congratulated himself that the two of them were off down memory lane, where his love life was not likely to get mentioned. "Speaking of luck, there had to be something going on with Lyle's horse getting him away from the cannibals. Not to mention his meeting Josh and Mark in Alma. The two of them, with their military backgrounds really saved the day."

"Josh and I got along just fine," Don mused. "Lyle took one look at Mark and decided he could be a horseman. Not only that, he set him up at the ranch, renamed it Harlan Ranch, and proceeded to get a fat head."

"That's not quite right, dear," Nancy returned. "Mark got a number of projects done that you'd just talked about for several years. On the other hand, you thought it was so funny when Ellen set her cap for Mark the moment she saw him. That was you drove her and the two kids out there to help him."

"Mark was the only person in Harlan who didn't know what was going on. He was done the moment she set eyes on him."

The stories about Mark and Ellen became nearly the stuff of legend just in the few months it was going on. That made Rick a less reticent about pursuing the subject. "Mark never talked about it while we were doing the evacuation, but it seemed like the two of them were touch and go for a while."

"That's putting it mildly," Don chortled. "There in Arapahoe, Lyle was going to marry them. The two of them were on the outs at the time, and he ended up sentencing them to be together for life. Whether they did it as a married couple or some other way was up to them, but they had three days at the castle to figure it out."

He reflected for a moment, and then continued, "My man Dave was driving the carriage, and he said it was the strangest newlywed operation he'd ever seen. First she was screaming at Mark. Then Mark crawled up on the seat with Dave and told him to stop. Lyle and Adeline caught up with them a few minutes later for an intervention."

"An intervention for a couple married only a few minutes sounds pretty strange."

"Oh, it was. Ellen screamed that they weren't married. Just before Lyle caught up to them, Mark told her to shut up, and she did. Mark was about to hit the road after they got to the castle, but Tom and Sammie talked him out of it just as he was getting ready to jump over the fence. Mark and Ellen have practiced wedded bliss ever since."

"I heard that a couple of places, but it sounded too strange to believe. Neither Mark nor Ellen want to tell me about it, not that I really pushed for details."

Don snorted. "I can just see how you'd ask about that kind of thing. If they didn't immediately make a full confession when you cleared your throat, you'd write them off. That's a great approach to romance, sucker."

Rick reflected that's how it always went. Just when he thought things were going his way, something would turn around and slap him. Well, this time he had firmly in mind that he was the guest, and really didn't want to go out with the snow continuing to fall. In any case, when it came to being a bullshit artist, Rick knew he wasn't even in the same league as Don Rowley. "You've been married a long time, and I'm single. I obviously bow to your wisdom, sir."

Nancy smiled brightly. "I think you handled that quite well, Rick. You listened to what he said and engaged your brain before starting your mouth. I think you can do just fine. One thing always puzzled, me, though. That's how we got in contact with McCook in the first place. Not only that, but now they say we need to be friends with those horrid cannibals."

Rick nodded. That was one thing Mark talked about quite a bit. "Mark said Deputy Vince got him in on it after he brought Dr. Dover back from Lincoln to give away Alicia at the wedding. Vince and his posse had seen bicycle tracks around Harlan County ever since the thing with Morgan Carr when we went down to open the spillway."

Don chuckled. "I remember that kid. He acted like a spoiled teenager the whole time he was in Harlan. It was just an act. When Lyle cornered him down at the Corps of Engineers building, he came out shooting, and wearing a bullet-proof vest from what Josh said later."

"That's him, all right. Anyway, it turned out the whole thing had more audience than anybody knew at the time. The posse found bicycle tracks at a point overlooking Republican City, or Rep City as you call it."

"Those guys were watching us that long?" Nancy wondered.

"They were watching us a lot longer than that. The four guys and a gal were the official invisible chaperones for the cannibals from when they were in St. Louis. After Harlan, the gal claimed credit for getting them to quit the cannibalism gig."

Nancy acted stunned. "The cannibals were from St. Louis?"

Rick couldn't believe anybody hadn't heard about that. "They were mostly drug addicts, and Willy was their drug supplier. When the New Madrid earthquakes ended everything from St. Louis to Memphis, it also put an end to drug availability. Willy turned them to cannibalism. I heard Willy was your stable boy for a while."

Don snarled, "Yeah, he was. I just called him Towny, but that's who we're talking about, and he lived under my roof and ate my food. He didn't do squat, either."

Nancy immediately changed the subject. "What made the people on bicycles decide to contact us after just watching us all that time?"

Rick nodded, happy to get away from such a sore subject with Don. "Vince and Mark found where they came into Harlan. The day before Josh and Alicia got married, the bicycle bunch peddled in. Soon, the whole posse was around them, although staying out of sight. The idea was to make sure they didn't do anything. The strangest part was that an older gentleman was with them. It turned out to be Alex Thomas, Alicia's father."

Nancy shook her head. "I thought he and his wife only came the day we dumped the Omega vial."

"That was how it was supposed to look. The group followed Lyle and Adeline to the church here in Ragan. After the wedding, but before the reception, Vince and the posse let the bicycle people know their party was over. They took them to the old school and kept them in a basement storeroom. After the Wedding House fiasco, Vince took Mark and Ellen over to the school. The group claimed to be from McCook and Vince wanted to see if Ellen recognized any of them. Alex was the only one."

"What happened then?"

"Mark made a deal with Sammie, the gal leading the group. She and her buddies would go back to McCook and return openly through the Oxford gate, with both Alicia's mother and gifts of pork. Alex would stay as Mark's guest. The relationship between the bunch and the cannibals would not come out if they did it. If not, then stories would be told."

Don suddenly jolted upright. "Wait a minute. Kevin was at the ranch until Josh and Alicia's wedding night. That night, Mark had him take possession of Wagon Ranch, beating me out. It was really because if Kevin saw Alex, he'd have blabbed about it everywhere. I sent my guy first thing the next day. Kevin was already squatting in the middle of the place like a great ugly toad. They talk about Mark and his luck. I'm just now figuring out how much luck he has."

Rick recalled Mark having a glint in his eye as he described his side of that gambit, as he termed it. Mark commented about the whole thing, saying he probably outsmarted himself. Still, getting one on Don Rowley definitely weighed in his sense of how the scale of things went. Rick had enough control over his mouth not to bring up any of that, and elected to get back to the story.

"Nobody found out about Alex being in Harlan, and the day of the great procession to dump the last vial of Omega, Ellen stayed behind, supposedly to take care of the ranch. Actually, it was to get Alex to Orleans, where they would wait until later in the day. The bicycle people kept their word and brought Cordelia — that's Mrs. Thomas, along with a load of pork. They showed up together during the barbecue."

"They managed an entrance. I'll give them that," Don allowed. "It was all too pat, though. We were all wondering about it at the time. I can't believe Lyle bought it."

"Mark wondered about that side of it. Later, after getting their guests bedded down, Lyle cornered Mark and Ellen. He advised that he enjoyed the production, but it was show and tell time for both of them. Mark had to confess how he arranged the whole thing. He expected Lyle would throw him out then, but instead, Lyle enlisted him to help try and find out just what the dark lady and the ghosts were up to."

Nancy looked at Rick. "Did they ever figure it out?"

"Mark worked on it all the way through the evacuation. The only conclusion he reached was that St. Louis was their last military mission. Following the tribe was supposed to be temporary, until their boss found something else for them to do. Mark finally put them to work in Oxford at the meat processing plant, sorting out priorities for processing wild game and feral pigs as opposed to cattle, and acting as game wardens to keep them from hunting the local wildlife into extinction."

"That's an awfully simple solution for what they'd spent all that time doing," Nancy said doubtfully.

Rick thought about it for a moment. He agreed it seemed too good to be true. "I think so, too. It's working for now, and that's all anybody asks. At least the former cannibals are providing us with meat products, not to mention that they seem quite willing to help defend Harlan from the terrorists. From what I hear, they've taken care of more terrorists than anybody else."

"I can't argue about the cannibals doing some good," Don said. "Hell, they pitched in with the corral at Arapahoe and took good care of my equipment when I was there. One thing bugs me is not the cannibals so much as the way Lyle Lillard acts like a dictator. Nothing matters in Harlan unless Lyle thinks it does. If he wants to do it, heaven and hell are supposed to get relocated while he takes care of it."

"You know, dear, an example would be nice," Nancy suggested.

Don harumphed. "Okay, how about when Lyle ordered me to drop everything important I was doing and to go help build that overnight stop or lodge at Arapahoe. Not only that, but he made me haul a lot of good merchandise out there and get absolutely nothing for my effort. I no sooner got that done, but he abandoned the place. There's still food in the refrigerators, for crying out loud."

Rick considered how Don described the great Arapahoe Inn project was the gospel truth. On the other hand, while Lyle called the shots in Harlan, he didn't act very much like a dictator. "Would you want to run Harlan, sir?" Rick asked cautiously.

Don nearly snorted his drink out his nose. "Are you kidding? It's nothing but a pain in the ass. Why would I want to?"

Nancy smiled graciously. "I think that's Rick's point, dear. I recall Lyle wanted deputy Vince to take over when it turned out he survived, but Vince declined."

Don tried to maintain his grumpy mood. "Okay, I get your drift. He still seems to be pushing it."

"Not only that, ever since all those poor people from McCook moved to Orleans, you are always taking deliveries to what used to be a ghost town. I remember you talking about how much more we're making from that," Nancy observed.

The conversation ran down at that point, and the three sat there and watched the snow continue to fall for quite some time after that. Rick wouldn't need to worry about an early start the next day. Don and Nancy talked about being stuck in the building during the great rain for two weeks. At least now the only problem had to do with getting through the snow. As had been the case for the last several storms, there wasn't much wind. That was good, since it would keep the drifting to a minimum.

Chapter 3

Stable Raid

At breakfast, Beth looked at Vince and the kids through narrowed eyes. "If you are all dead set on going out in that arctic blast and sitting in the snow, all of you had better wear enough clothes so you don't get sick. It seemed like we had summer until a month ago. Ever since, it feels like we moved to Siberia."

Vince felt a great deal of conflict about the whole thing. Using his own kids as street informers didn't set right with him. The fact that they did this every day and called it fun caused even more confusion. At least the snow quit just as the sun came up, not that the sun would provide much warmth that day. Billy, his oldest, demonstrated his enthusiasm for the project. He shoveled all the snow from the front door without anybody saying anything.

With the kids duly suited up, Vince let Billy lead their little group to where the three watched the four families. The location was an empty shed across a side street on a slight rise. It gave them a view of the four backyards, peering through knotholes and cracks in the side. It made for a tight fit with an adult joining three kids, but it was definitely warmer than laying in a snowdrift.

"Does this happen on a regular schedule?" Vince wondered.

"She makes breakfast at each place," came from Rachel, his eight year old daughter. "She is in the far house on the left now, and will be going to the nearest house on the right."

"That is a lot of information, Rachel. How do you know all that?"

"We've watched a long time. She does the same thing every day. Sometimes the girl carries covered dishes from one place to the next. She never wears a coat, and she is always barefoot. Mom would never let me go outside barefoot, even when the weather was warm. Why do these rich people make her do it?"

"How do you know they make her do it?"

"Sometimes the ladies yell rude things at her, like she's not going fast enough. Why doesn't she run away, Daddy?"

"That is a very good question, Rachel."

The back door opened, and the woman Vince saw momentarily the previous afternoon, emerged. She was dressed in rags and barefoot. She was carrying something that appeared to be a platter, but it was hard to tell, since it was wrapped. She stumbled a few feet into the yard. The door of the house immediately opened, and the woman screamed at her. The raggedy woman recovered her footing and continued across the yard, following a path visible even after the fresh snowfall. Even dressed for the weather, Vince felt cold, and couldn't imagine going as far as the girl.

Since she was moving in a direction that enabled him to see her face, Vince confirmed this was the same person he'd seen the night before. One thing was certain. Yesterday was the first time he had ever seen her. The only other survivors were the farmers from McCook, who were living together in the southern end of the county, around Orleans. That wasn't quite right. There were other survivors besides the terrorists. They were in the tribe of former cannibals. A few of them were in Harlan County, but Vince knew them very well.

The four families somehow got a tribal member to work for them. None of the families left Ragan very often and the tribe only recently moved close to Harlan, Vince had a hard time figuring out how they had managed to get her. One thing he had to do was to interview her and find out whether she wanted to be a servant. Knowing the attitude Don and Nancy had about the Peepul tribe, as they called themselves, Vince couldn't imagine Nancy, much less Don, having anything to do with one of them being in the Rowley living quarters.

"Okay, guys, was this something that happens all the time?"

"She does this every morning, noon, and we think she must do it in the evening, as well, Daddy."

"You wouldn't know about the evening part, since you are all home. Is that right?"

All three of them nodded.

"I don't know about you guys, but I think it is about time to go get warm and have a cup of cocoa. What do you think?"

That got immediate agreement from everyone, and they headed for home.

Once they had some privacy, Vince asked his wife, "Beth, those times you went over to visit the four families, did you ever see anybody besides the families themselves?"

"No, but there were times they were pushing something or someone out the back as I was coming in the front. This was going on even before the dust came. I didn't want to seem too nosy, but none of the ladies ever seemed to do any cleaning or cooking. On the other hand, the houses were always spotless, and if it was near meal time, it was obvious that cooking was going on. Do you think they are making some poor girl do all the work?"

"It is looking that way. I can't imagine what their hold over her could be. I've never seen her before, and the only people I don't know by sight are members of the Peepul tribe. I'm going to have to talk to Mark or Lyle about this."

Vince wasn't quite sure what to do next, planning while he walked toward the Rowley stable and his horse. A little farther down the street, he noticed the Harlan Ranch wagon as well as Mark's palomino at the Co-op. That was when he realized he didn't need to saddle up to take care of the situation.

The Co-op had become the general store and coffee shop for Ragan. It had always been where farmers bought and sold grain and bought supplies and some parts. In addition, the Co-op always sold sandwiches. Bread was now baked in house. There were ongoing discussions about what they would do when the flour was no longer usable.

There was talk of sending people to whatever elevators held wheat. In the meantime, the smell of fresh-baked bread along with coffee was very inviting, in spite of the fact that his wife just fed him breakfast.

Mark and Ellen were at a table in the back, sipping coffee. When Vince's eyes adjusted to the indoor dimness, he saw Mark waving at him, and beckoning him.

"I figured that if you were in Ragan, you'd be holding court or some other official function, Mark."

"That would be a reasonable guess, but Lyle sent us on a job."

Vince already knew there was nothing in the wagon, and the coffee cups were the only objects on the table. "Lyle sent you to Ragan to drink coffee?"

"He said I needed to keep my ear to the ground, and that I should come here and listen to what everybody says."

Vince chuckled. "What are you hearing, other than how bad the weather is?"

"The weather qualifies as breaking news. The in-depth reporting concerns how long anybody can keep making bread. The closest thing to consensus is that cornbread does not work well if you want a sandwich. There is also general agreement that any expedition to find wheat storage will have to wait for warmer weather. That, in turn took us back to the state of the weather."

"I can't argue with any of that. Are you ready to hear some really juicy stuff?"

"From the estimable Deputy Vince? I know what you managed to do with a few bicycle tracks, getting my advice as a purely technical matter. That really makes me nervous when you think something's juicy. In spite of that, lay it on me."

Vince sat down and told the two of them what he saw personally, as well as what his kids told him. He was very careful to keep it quiet so that all the large ears in the place wouldn't pick up on it. Vince concluded with, "I don't know who it could be unless they got hold of one of the Peepul tribe somehow. I have no idea how they could have done that. The kids remembered first seeing her during the dust and before the rain. My wife has the impression something was going on even before that."

Mark thought about it and replied, "I agree with you. I also think Don and Nancy wouldn't have anything to do with any tribal members in their house. Could you keep some posse members around here to see when Don brings the girl? I'd like to have a chat with her, and the only way that will happen is if she is at the livery stable."

"The table by the window has a view of the Rowley stable. This is one job the posse members will compete to get. I'll probably take a few shifts myself. I'll let you know when a bag of rags rolls inside."

Mark nodded. "I'll need to let Lyle know about this, but I'd better make sure I can take information and not just a reaction."

Ellen grinned. "It sounds like that much got through to you. There may be hope for you yet."

"It is clear to me that keeping information from Lyle is nothing I want to do. Did you notice the wind has switched around out of the south. Maybe we will have some better weather for a while. Who knows? It might warm up enough for us to see a bit of bare ground."

Two days later, the warm breeze melted most of the snow. Vince was having a late breakfast with his bride. The kids roared back into the house.

"Daddy, Mr. Rowley just picked up the lady. She is the only one in the carriage."

That qualified as real news. Vince quickly grabbed his gear and kissed Beth as he went out the door. He walked quickly along the street, soon catching sight of the carriage with Don driving and what appeared to be the rag bag sitting behind him. Nancy was opening the stable door as Don pulled up, so the carriage only slowed slightly as he drove into the livery stable. If there were grounds for suspicion before, Vince knew he had probable cause now.

The posse member was coming out of the Co-op as Vince got there. The posse member's horse was saddled and tied in front of the store, where people would have parked cars at one time.

Vince collared him and said quietly, "Look normal as you leave town, but once you are out on the road move at your best pace to Harlan Ranch. Tell Mark and Ellen the show is on."

The guy nodded and mounted. Vince went inside and immediately occupied the table his posse member just vacated. It was a pretty good deal. Hell, the chair was still warm. A fresh cup of coffee presently made its appearance.

"What's the big deal over at the Rowley stable, anyway?" the manager of the Co-op wanted to know.

"That's nothing you need to worry about right now. What makes you think I'd tell you anything you haven't already heard from my posse members?"

"They haven't said squat. Maybe you can give them awards for that."

"Maybe I will. Maybe we're just sitting here admiring the view. Back when they had railroad tracks into Ragan, the livery was right across from where the train stopped."

"That's what they tell me. It quit being a livery stable long before I moved here. They tore out the tracks a year or two after I came, but they hadn't been doing much with the line anyway. Trucks were doing nearly all the hauling by then."

"Now there are no trucks. There is also no market."

"Yeah, Don Rowley thinks we'll be back to chipping flint pretty soon."

"I hear that one couple likes to make their own flour by grinding seeds between two rocks. Maybe they can supply you with flour for bread."

"Yeah, I tried some of it that they made up. It tasted okay, but they admitted themselves a decent sandwich loaf needs white flour."

"Well, maybe you could switch over to flat bread for sandwiches."

The owner mumbled something as he wandered off. Vince wondered what he just contributed to the local rumor mill. Offhand, he couldn't think what it could be, but then, if something he said got twisted around some, who knew what would end up being attributed to him?

A cup of coffee later, Don drove a single freight wagon out of the stable. He looked even more grumpy than his sour normal, and Vince wondered if the rag bag girl messed up his plans for the day. Whatever it meant for Don's attitude, the girl and Nancy Rowley were the only ones inside, which would simplify the situation when Mark got there. If Ellen came as well, Vince considered the likelihood of making some sense of all of this might improve.

Come to think of it, they wouldn't have the place to themselves. There was the blacksmith and farrier, Clay, but he only came out of his smithy when he had to. Clay claimed he had several lifetimes worth of work lined up, and didn't have time for anything else. Thinking about it, the rare occasions Vince had seen Clay lately, that was the sum total of his conversation. It was funny, really, how everybody wanted a good steady job, but nobody wanted to be Clay's apprentice.

Mid-morning, Mark and Ellen rode in, with his posse member right behind them. All their horses were lathered up, showing how hard they pushed to get into Ragan. Vince reflected that he must have found an issue Mark was concerned about. One thing was certain. Vince would not just run into the street and give this flock of crows anything more to screech about than they already had. What did they call a flock of crows, anyway? It was a murder of crows. Yeah, that seemed about right.

Outside, Mark said something briefly to the posse member, and then smiled at Ellen. The posse member slowly dismounted, as though he had all the time in the world. He tied his horse to the rail and strolled inside.

"Vince, thanks for taking over for me. I really appreciate it. By the way, I ran into Mark and Ellen. Mark said he heard something about the tribe down at Oxford."

"Anything the tribe does is interesting. Thanks for letting me know."

Vince got up and pulled on his coat like it was just another day in the neighborhood. For him, that's exactly what it was, except this had suddenly turned into the cop's neighborhood. It appeared he was going to have the opportunity to rain on somebody's parade. If the members of that parade happened to be the denizens of the local snob's hollow, so much the better. At the same time, he'd be giving the farmers something to talk about all winter.

Vince joined Mark and Ellen, strolling across the street toward the stable. The pair acted as though they had just come on a pleasure ride. The snow having mostly melted, it was a nice change from the arctic conditions of a couple of days before. Vince walked a couple of steps ahead and opened the stable door for them to bring in their horses. Vince heard a bit of noise from the living quarters as the three entered.

For the moment, they acted like everything was normal rather than the raid it actually was. City boys would have brought the SWAT team and acted like they were going to war. Sheriff Crichton never bought into that, preferring to treat people like the neighbors they were. Of course, if somebody insisted on being an idiot, there were ways to deal with it.

They walked into the living quarters and office. There, they found Nancy Rowley standing behind a twenty-something female, holding her in place.

"I think these people may be able to help you, dear," Nancy told her softly.

Nancy then looked up at them. "This is Gwendolyn. She is in a bad situation. Can you help her?"

Vince was prepared for any number of reactions to their arrival. This was not one of them, and nothing like any of them.

Ellen recovered first. "What kind of bad situation, Nancy? Can you tell us about it, Gwendolyn?"

Gwendolyn stared at the floor, so that Vince found himself looking at unkempt brown hair instead of a face.

Nancy finally answered for her. "The four families have kept this sweet girl as a community drudge. They wanted what Don has stored around here, and finally agreed to exchange some of her services for a piece of the action. They want us to give them some of what we have in our warehouses."

Ellen walked up to Gwendolyn, bent slightly and picked up the girl's chin with a finger so she could look at her face. "Did you go to work for the families voluntarily?"

Gwendolyn shook her head without looking up.

"How long have they been using you like this?"

Gwendolyn finally looked up just a little and whispered, "I've been working for them since last spring. I was traveling to a job when some guys grabbed me. I was able to get away from them when a semi ran us off the road. I could see Ragan and started walking. The families said they would give me shelter and help me find a ride, but it turned into this."

She appeared to start sobbing, but there were no tears and no sound.

Mark nodded. "We are talking about people who are always going on about self-reliance and the American way. I always wondered how they were able to do so much for Josh and Alicia's wedding. Gwendolyn, would you like to stay away from those people?"

Gwendolyn nodded. "I'd like to, but I'm afraid they'll come after me and beat me."

Vince was on point now. "Did they beat you while you were with them?"

Gwendolyn simply nodded again.

The situation was now completely within Vince's jurisdiction. "Gwendolyn, I'm the deputy sheriff. These people are not going to do anything to you. From now on, they can clean their own houses and cook their own food."

She looked up then. "What can I do? Where can I go?"

Nancy looked at the three of them. "When I knew she was coming the last time, I got Don to ask for somebody to repair his computer. I knew Rick Forbes was the only one around, and hoped he would show up while Gwendolyn was still here. It seems they both have backgrounds in the computer business."

Vince looked at Mark for guidance. Mark thought for a moment and nodded to him. "Vince, ride out to the Wagon Ranch. Tell Kevin to get Rick's butt over to my place. We had better keep moving, because the wind is switching around again, and another storm may be coming. We'll wait for Don to come back. He can take Nancy and Gwendolyn out to Harlan Ranch. I think Don can tend to other business for a while before he comes back to get his lady. Nancy, I want you to take care of the introductions when everybody gets there."

Chapter 4

Blind Date

Rick felt good, having found a way to get along with Don Rowley a little better. He knew that was with a great deal of help from Nancy. He suspected she orchestrated the entire encounter. At the same time, what she hoped to get out of it or why she bothered was completely beyond his understanding. The only thing that didn't happen like she wanted was that he hadn't gotten there sooner. That appeared to irritate her. It was all very strange.

Getting along with Don on any basis didn't help his relationship with his boss, Kevin, who counted on Rick having a really rotten time. That being the case, Rick kept his mouth shut when he returned to the ranch. Kevin had become largely insufferable with anybody he considered his inferior. Speculation about this centered on problems with Kevin's love life.

Kevin soon picked up on Rick's not following his plan. It was clear to Kevin the encounter neither caused Rick great pain nor left any obvious scars. After finding that Rick would need to do more things for Don Rowley and was not dreading the prospect, Kevin had become an even larger piece of shit toward Rick. Two days later, the weather cleared off and warmed up somewhat. Kevin insisted a corner post had to be put in a specific spot immediately.

The job had nothing to do with building fences. No fence lines were anywhere near here, neither now nor the future. The whole exercise was more to do with it being the most frozen patch of rocky soil in the area. Still, a job was a job. So, Rick cleared the snow off the area, and attacked the frozen ground with a digging bar. After several feet of listening to the digging bar ring from encounters with stones, and feeling it vibrate in his hands, Rick finally won through to more easily dug ground, and carefully continued to dig, being certain the sides were as straight as possible. He became aware of a shadow over him, but did not look up. Suddenly there was a harsh laugh from above and behind him.

"Time to wake up, sleeping beauty. A messenger came. You've got an appointment to see Mark Tahner at Harlan Ranch."

Rick knew Kevin was just pulling his chain and kept working. "The only messenger was Deputy Vince. That was a long time ago," he said between strokes. "Whatever he came about, it wasn't for my sorry ass."

"Oh, but it was. The message was for you to be at Harlan Ranch. As a matter of fact, Vince said you are supposed to be there right now. You're always running off, hanging out with all these important people. Well, I'm damn sure going to get the share of work you owe me. Now your butt had better get moving so you can make a grand entrance."

Rick looked up as Kevin wheeled his horse around. The horse went a step before Kevin turned around in the saddle, looking at Rick. "Oh, you had better take your bedroll. The way he talked, it didn't sound like you are going to make it back here tonight. Enjoy your time off, because you're damn sure going to make up for it when you get back." Another harsh, cackling sort of laugh completed the announcement.

Walking quickly to the cot in the hallway where he bunked, Rick reflected that Kevin's personality continued to change, and none of the change was for the better. It was like he'd gone over to the dark side. He worked as quickly as possible, getting his horse saddled, and tying his bedroll behind the saddle. It was not that far to Harlan Ranch, but the hour or so on the horse would stress his packing skills as much as a full day's ride.

Arriving at Harlan Ranch, he unsaddled and turned his horse into the area for short-term stays. His tack taken care of, Rick went into the bunkhouse to get cleaned up, only to find the two apprentice wannabes waiting for him.

"You know the rule," the one informed him. "The newest guy cleans out the bunkhouse."

Yeah, he knew the rule. He'd been one of the apprentices who made that rule. That made him doubly obligated to abide by it, no matter what else might be going on. Rick grabbed the broom and started sweeping. One of the guys took a look out the window.

"Mark and three women are coming this way," he commented to his buddy. "The two of us had better get scarce."

Rick could not imagine what Mark coming toward the bunkhouse had to do with them needing to leave. Becoming real apprentices with the chance to get their own horses depended on a recommendation from Mark. Disappearing with work to do was not how anybody got such a recommendation. The two didn't stick around to explain. Instead, they were out the side door. A moment later came a knock on the door. That was another rule. Mark always knocked on the bunkhouse door. It was his way of being polite. Whoever was inside was obligated to open the door without delay, so Rick opened it, broom in hand. He figured that he presented a wonderful picture of grunge, disgust, and domesticity.

The wannabes had the VIP party right. Mark stood there, looking distinctly irritated. With him was his wife, Ellen. Then there was Nancy Rowley, of all people. There was also a mousy-looking girl with them. Rick had never seen her before. As a matter of fact, he barely saw her now, since she was doing her best to hide behind the other two women.

"What took you so long to get here, Rick? We expected you quite a while ago," Mark asked.

Rick decided he'd better be straight. "It was Kevin's opinion that I was not doing my fair share over at Wagon Ranch. He deferred giving me the message Vince brought for well over an hour so I could finish punching a corner posthole."

"Is that right?"

When Rick nodded, Mark asked, "Is Kevin doing this sort of thing more than he used to?"

"I really shouldn't say, Mark."

"Rick, this is me. Remember how we rode and worked together to get the evacuation done? If you're concerned about retribution from Kevin, I can guarantee nothing will come from that end."

"If he can't get me in a straightforward way, he'll do it under-handed."

"Oh, so our boy Kevin is full of himself, is he?"

Rick sighed, glancing nervously at Nancy Rowley. She was totally focused on the conversation, as was Ellen. Rick finally shook his head, "There's an observed correlation between how things go at Wagon Ranch and how pleasant things are at the Maguire hacienda. I believe happiness and the Maguire family are on opposite sides of the world."

Mark pursed his lips, seeming almost amused. "That bad, eh? Lyle Lillard says part of my job is to keep my ear to the ground. I heard a few rumblings, but nothing about things getting this far. It appears that I'd better update him about this."

Rick noticed Nancy and Ellen glance at each other. Suddenly, Ellen's boot swung around sharply, impacting Mark's ankle with a thud.

Mark flinched, but kept his gaze on Rick. "That is something we need to handle, but it isn't why we came out here. Rick, this is Gwendolyn Fuller. She's been working as a housekeeper and nanny for a number of the families in Ragan since before the dust came through."

As he said that, Ellen and Nancy both grabbed the girl's shoulders, and forced her front and center. She stood there, staring at him like a puppy that's been beaten too many times for too few reasons. Rick stared back at her, almost in shock. He became aware of Ellen standing beside the two of them, a hand on his shoulder. He suddenly noticed her other hand was on Gwendolyn's shoulder.

"Why don't you two get acquainted?" Ellen suggested. "We're letting all the warm air out of the bunkhouse. We'll head back to the house. You two come on over when you get sorted out, Rick. We can eat any time."

With that, Ellen softly pushed Gwendolyn through the door, closing it softly while Rick tried to figure out what just happened. Okay, he knew exactly what happened. This was why he got the assignment to work on the Rowley computer which no longer computed.

Nancy Rowley knew about Gwendolyn, and wanted them to meet there. He flashed back on Don driving Mrs. Stamford home just as they arrived. The bag beside her in the sleigh had to have been this girl. Rick recalled promising to talk to whoever she found. He promised to talk to her one time, and that was all. Either she would find him intolerable or else he wouldn't be able to stand being around her. On the other hand, something about this Gwendolyn suddenly brought out protective urges he had no idea existed. Okay, he knew they existed. He just didn't have any idea that they existed in him.

He finally stammered, "You've been living in Ragan? I lived there until I got on with the ranch. There's only a hundred people in Ragan. There is no way you could live there. I'd have seen you."

She just looked at him with those eyes. "If you like, sir, I could take care of sweeping so you can do whatever you need to do."

Rick had completely forgotten he was still holding the broom, and he stared at it for a moment, trying to remember what he was going to do with it.

"Yeah, sure, if you don't mind."

He obviously wasn't going to get cleaned up just then, so all Rick needed to do was move in. That amounted to finding an empty bed and throwing his bedroll on it. He was able to pay close attention when Gwendolyn started softly talking as she swept. It seemed like she was talking in rhythm to her sweeping. "I have been in Ragan all this time. I was there and nobody except the four families ever saw me. They moved me from one house to the next. Nobody outside the group was supposed to know. Now Nancy Rowley parades me all around like a trophy. The deputy talks about protecting me. I guess I'm out of a job now. Maybe I'm free. I don't know."

Rick was even more astounded. "I lived south of Railway Street. The Stamford family and their friends live north of there."

"That's where I was," she murmured.

"I heard those people carry on about freedom, and all that time, they had you as a private drudge and servant. You weren't much more than a slave."

She stopped sweeping momentarily and looked at Rick. "A slave is exactly what I am, or was. I don't know what I am now. Would they take me back, do you think?"

"Why would you want them to?"

"They gave me food and shelter. They gave me a place to sleep. Where will I find that now?" Gwendolyn suddenly seemed nearly hysterical.

Rick cocked his head. "Did you hear about us bringing everybody from McCook? How do you suppose they get food, shelter, and a place to sleep?"

"The families talked about it a lot. I didn't think about it. There was something about them occupying an entire town. The town was vacant because the Omega dust wiped out the population."

"Your information is right on. Let me tell you something. They're doing just fine. If it comes down to it, you could stay with them. They're really nice folks." Rick came to a full stop then. "On the other hand, I thought all the folks in Ragan were nice, too. Maybe going to Orleans is not such a good idea. That is the name of the town, by the way. How did they manage to take such advantage of you?"

"Last spring, before the power and fuel went away, I was trying to get to Silicon Valley. I heard there were still computer jobs out there. I was riding my thumb. A van stopped to pick me up. There were four guys in it, kind of nasty looking. I decided riding with them wasn't a good idea and backed away. Two of them jumped out and grabbed me. The van got off the Interstate and headed south on US 183. They stopped in Holdrege for gas. I couldn't do anything because there were always two of them with knives in my back telling me to smile and not say anything. When we got to the state highway intersection, a semi came at us at high speed down the middle of the highway. The guy driving the van swerved to get out of its way, ran off the road and hit a power pole. I got away and hid in the brush and trees. The four didn't look for me very hard or very long. They got the van running, and took off."

Now Rick was completely astonished. "Do you remember seeing a car right behind the semi?"

Gwendolyn had to think about that. "Now that you mention it, I do remember something like that." She swept the dust out the side door, leaned the broom against the wall, and came over and sat on a bunk across from Rick. "In any case, as I walked toward the grain elevators at Ragan, one of the families picked me up, and almost immediately turned me into this drudge or slave thing." She studied him for a moment. "Were you in that other car?"

Rick nodded. "I was driving to Boston. It was the same story as you, only I was going the other way. I picked up these three guys. They said they'd help out with gas and driving. Once I let them in the car, they kept looking at me in weird ways, you know? I was keeping my guard up. We got in behind the semi, and couldn't ever get around it."

The memory of it suddenly flashed back through his mind. "All of a sudden, this van came roaring by going the other way, and trying to head right toward me. I managed to steer clear of the van, but my three riders took advantage of the situation, and clubbed me. They dumped me a short way up the road, and took off with my car, like that would do them much good. I walked into Ragan, and lived where I could, doing whatever odd jobs would feed me. Finally, I got on at the ranch."

She suddenly looked at him more intently. "We very nearly met that day. I've always wondered what became of those creeps in the van."

"You did better than they did. I could show you the van. It's in the ditch down by the old cannibal camp. They only lived for five miles after you escaped. The cannibals had their people flag down cars like they needed help or a ride. Whenever a car stopped, the cannibals attacked the occupants with knives, with the plan to have them for supper." After a moment, Rick added, "Did you say that you were after a computer job out in California?"

"That's right, although it seems like several lifetimes ago. You wouldn't know it to look at me now, but I was into social networking, e-zines, and things like that. When you said your story was the same as mine, were you talking about being in the industry, too?"

"I was. My end was programming. It was just beginning to pay off when there was suddenly nothing left to program."

"Nancy said you were helping Don with his computer."

"I was going to try. I'll need to find a decent computer, along with inventory software or some kind of data base. He wants to keep track of all the stuff in his several warehouses."

Gwendolyn raised a thoughtful finger. "The families made many jokes about the computer at the Co-op. They said its only function was to collect dust. That should have point of sale and inventory software already installed. Whether the equipment is simple enough for Don to use is another matter."

"You're a genius. I could kiss you."

She nodded, and Rick noticed some life had come into her eyes. "Yes, you could. It would certainly validate Nancy's judgment of the situation. By now, the three are sitting around the table at the house, thinking warm thoughts of our presumed romantic reaction to each other. At the same time, they must be in despair for my presumed virtue. Frankly, now that you've revived my inner nerd, I can't imagine going back to that small circle of self-styled patricians. Are you prepared to defend my virtue from all attackers, Sir Galahad?"

Rick tapped his cheekbone thoughtfully with a forefinger. "You're giving me a choice between defending you from attackers or joining them. Can I get back to you on that? Whatever the status of your virtue, maybe we could talk computer now and again. There are enough solar collectors up, we might even be able to use a computer periodically. I'm in no mood to drill more post holes for Kevin. What say we go join the others for dinner, and see if there's a place for nerds around here?"

They strolled across to the house. A light wind had sprung up, and snow was in it. From the look of the sky, there was a lot more to come. Rick looked at Gwendolyn out of the corner of his eye. The hard times showed in her features, but in spite of it, he thought she was not bad looking.

"How can it be that every time I see Nancy Rowley, there's also a pile of snow?" he wondered.

"From what I hear, there's been a sit-down meal each time, too," came her response.

"You got me there. Now that I think about it, I was breathing on both occasions, as well."

They walked into the house. Gwendolyn's prediction was right on time. The three were sitting at the table, smiling in their direction.

"Your point, Gwendolyn," Rick commented.

Mark sat back in his chair. "The two ladies were having all kinds of warm feelings about how you two were getting along. They were also despairing over your virtue, Gwendolyn."

Nancy gave Mark a dirty look, and Mark suddenly jolted, probably from Ellen kicking his shin. That, Rick thought, appeared to be a regular thing. It made him wonder if Mark's cowboy boots had padding in them.

Gwendolyn broke into his thoughts just then. "Just one point, Rick? I count three, anyway."

Rick nodded. "Three points it is, plus another point for nailing it so precisely."

Ellen grinned. "You two act like you've known each other forever."

Rick shrugged it off. "It comes from common backgrounds. Mark and those snipers from McCook could communicate more with two words than most people could get done in a day."

"True statement, Rick," Mark replied.

"Well, you two," Ellen piped up. "Why don't we have something to eat? We might have a few other things to talk about, don't you think?"

While they were eating, Nancy Rowley observed, "You two look very comfortable together, even beyond just getting along remarkably well for two people who just met."

Rick glanced over at Gwendolyn, and saw she was looking at him as well. He then cocked his head, looking at Nancy. "That makes the second comment in as many minutes about how comfortable we seem with each other. There hasn't been much conversation about anything else. That comes across as something more than exclamations standing on the rim of the Grand Canyon. This smells like a road going someplace."

Rick saw Gwendolyn nodding in agreement with what he just said.

Mark fidgeted momentarily, faked a cough, and finally sat back. "We find ourselves with a situation, guys. It's like when Vince and I figured out what the bicycle tracks all around Harlan were about. We need Lyle Lillard to make the final call on at least some of this."

He tapped nervously on the table before continuing. "In the first place, Gwendolyn, there's no way you're going back to Ragan. You're not going back today. You may never go back. Wherever you go, it will not be to play servant. Tonight you'll stay in our guest bedroom."

Rick saw waves of relief sweep across Gwendolyn's face. "Thank you so much," she murmured.

Mark looked at Nancy. "I don't know how much trouble you'll have with your four friendly families because of this. They shared their secret with you, and you betrayed their trust."

"That shouldn't be a problem, Mark. We're a business more than a residence, after all. I have no idea who might have seen her and told you guys about it. I'm just as upset about it as anybody else. After all, didn't I trek all the way out to Harlan Ranch to plead my case to you?"

Mark laughed. "Your husband doesn't know how you operate, does he?"

Nancy sat and beamed, basking in her victory, not saying anything.

After a moment, Mark looked directly at Rick. "Now, with you, it gets sticky. I was getting hints about Kevin. He hauls guys over here all the time. I see him and I talk to them. Just how bad it's gotten only became more evident today with him playing silly games with you. Something has to be done, but that will be Lyle's call, like I said. Meanwhile, nothing can get back to Kevin to make him think anything's amiss. It's getting dark and the snow is getting heavier. I told the two candidates this was a romantic rendezvous, and to bring your bedroll if they didn't see you by now. Their presumption is that it must have been love at first sight."

"Is this the mail-order bride kind of thing? Is that another thing from the old days we're bringing back?" Rick asked.

"I'm getting really tired of getting blamed every time somebody tries doing things some way beside the old straight up and at them approach," Ellen growled.

"Be at ease, you two. Ellen, you of all people should recognize my venting. Rick, I told you it was a sticky situation. I don't want to force you two into an instant decision about a permanent situation. You can sleep on the couch. Just make sure your boots never get on it."

Just then came a light knock on the front door. Mark immediately answered it, opening the door just wide enough to take Mark's bedroll, waving to the figures outside, and closing the door again. Rick followed everybody into the front room, and stood behind Mark, who placed the bedroll beside the door. A large number of snowflakes adorned both the bedroll and the area of the floor where the opening had been.

Before any other conversation could begin, they heard the sound of sleigh bells outside. Nancy immediately got her coat and boots, knowing that was her ride. Don had already switched from the carriage to the sleigh, and wanted his lady home before the storm got any worse. Most likely, he wanted some supper, as well, Rick reflected. After the sound of the sleigh faded away, the four looked at each other for a while. Finally, Ellen grabbed Mark's hand and towed him into their bedroom.

Now being together with Gwendolyn felt really uncomfortable to Rick. He wandered over to the front window, parted the drapes, and stared at the snow, now falling at a considerable rate. After a while, he felt her come up beside him.

Trying to think of what to say, Rick temporized with, "All I've heard anyone call you is Gwendolyn. How do you want to be called?"

The response was immediate. "Call me Gwendolyn. Shortening a name is shortening an identity. Whatever you do, never, ever call me 'Gwen dear.' That's what those old bats in Ragan all called me. Are you actually Rick?"

"I'm officially Richard, but everyone called me Rick my whole life to differentiate me from my father of the same name."

After a while, they went over and sat on the couch.

Chapter 5

Assigned Marriage

Rick's eyes popped open at what passed for first light. The snow was still falling, and he was still sitting on the couch. Gwendolyn never went to the guest bedroom. She was asleep, her head on Rick's shoulder. He thought it felt pretty good. A few minutes later, Mark and Ellen quietly came out of their room. They took one look at the situation, nodded at Rick, and both tip-toed into the kitchen. A minute later, Gwendolyn woke up with a start.

"Oh, I'm sorry," she said, once again the timid person Rick first met.

She jumped up, straightening her clothes and hair. "I must go and do my job."

"You being here didn't bother me in the least," Rick replied. He saw she didn't understand her location or situation. Rick decided to added, "I think the only job you have right now is to realize that you're among friends."

Ellen and Mark came out of the kitchen as he said that, and got the impression they approved of his approach. All at once, Gwendolyn's eyes took on a sharper, more meaningful focus. She blinked, and looked around at everyone.

"Oh, good morning, everyone," she said in a normal conversational tone. Then she looked right at Rick, the slightest hint of a smile on her face. "You are my Galahad. Thank you, sir knight, for rescuing me from the dragon. You should know, though, the dragon has not been slain, and will almost certainly be back."

As Rick stood up, he noticed that with them both in stocking feet, Gwendolyn was only two or three inches shorter. He looked in her dark eyes as he said, "I fight for your honor, my lady, not because I wear your favor, but because it is the chivalrous thing to do."

Ellen shook her head in mock dismay. "You are Sir Galahad, indeed. Come on, you two. We've got victuals by means of which we may break our fast. Damn! Now you've got me talking like that. Just come on."

Over breakfast, Ellen was the first one to get to the subject. "What is this dragon of yours, Gwendolyn?"

"I'm not sure. It might be like having a split personality, although I remember what I was doing, slaving away for those people. It's as though all those people, from the guys in the van to the people I worked for in Ragan, expected me to be the mousy little thing. They expected it, so that's what I gave them. It was the only way I could protect my true self."

Mark nodded. "What you're saying is that if those Ragan people saw you and treated you in the old way, as a servant, you would automatically react as a servant?"

"I think so."

"That certainly takes care of any doubt I had last night. If any of those people show up here, we will not allow them anywhere near you. What Rick did to bring you out of it … would that work all the time?"

"I don't know. I can only hope so. If one of the Ragan people was here, I don't know whether it would or not."

Mark shook his head. "On to our other subject: did you reach any agreement about what to do now? You realize the guys in the bunkhouse have whipped themselves into a lather, imagining the hot and steamy night you two had."

"There is plenty of snow. They could certainly use that to cool their engines," Gwendolyn replied. "The fact is that they'll spread the news as soon as they can find an ear to listen. Everyone will think we might have married, and certainly mated, no matter what actually happened."

All at once, she put down her fork, and studied Rick. Then, she reached out and stroked his upper arm. Soon, her hand slid across to his chest, which Rick found intensely embarrassing, and he felt his face reddening.

"You've got an exceptional body for a nerd," she said finally. "On top of it, you're modest. What do you say, Rick? We've already been cast as a married couple. Should we try playing the part?"

Rick was not normally a person of many words. At the moment, he couldn't think of any words at all. His tongue was unaccountably dry. He took a gulp of coffee, which scorched the inside of his mouth and got him working once more. "Am I supposed to propose?"

Mark grinned. "It sounds like Gwendolyn already did. I never heard of a rule against it. There was always Sadie Hawkins day."

Rick had to let that soak in. He finally responded, "If they're going to hang us for murder, we might as well go kill somebody. Is that about it?"

"I guess you could think of it that way."

"Gwendolyn, when I first met you yesterday, I suddenly felt a need to protect you. That would be a lot easier if we were married. Why don't we go for the gusto? Would you marry me?"

That made Gwendolyn blink. "For real?"

Rick nodded.

"Wow. What about my dragon?"

"I'll do my best to slay the sorry thing. Anybody causing it to appear will incur my wrath, or at least my unhappy face. I might even unfriend them."

"Ooh, you have laid on some brave words, indeed. You make my maiden's heart go all aflutter. Sure, let's do it."

Rick looked at Mark and Ellen. "So what do we do now? Nobody issues marriage licenses any more. There are no more entries in a church register."

"The two of you deciding to be married is nearly all of it. The only other thing would be Harlan people accepting you as a married couple. I suppose we could get somebody official to say a word. That would be the only other thing. Lyle will be over here as soon as the snow stops. Can you wait until then?"

"With marriage, we're in the age of instant gratification. You're Mr. Lillard's Special Assistant," Ellen commented. "Isn't that official enough? Your word was enough to pry Gwendolyn from the grasp of the folks in Ragan."

Mark nodded. "You're right, Ellen. Okay, Rick and Gwendolyn, you have decided to be married. On behalf of Lyle Lillard and all the citizens of Harlan, I declare you two are husband and wife. Now, in the spirit of what Ellen and I did, let's all stand up. Rick, stand by the back door. Gwendolyn, stand by the door to the living room, and face each other, please."

"Your common interests are a big thing. Each of you take two steps toward each other. You are already only a step apart. Take that last little step, and look in each other's eyes."

Rick was mainly conscious of her eyes, but felt Ellen's hand on one side, and Mark's on the other, as each softly guided his hand into that of Gwendolyn.

"Why don't you two kiss? You know you want to."

He did want to kiss her, and her eyes invited him.

Rick's normally acute sense of time disappeared. He finally became aware of a hand other than Gwendolyn's on his shoulder, and looked that direction. Ellen looked at them quizzically.

"How many times have you two kissed before this?"

Rick caught his breath, and finally replied, "That was the first time."

Gwendolyn nodded, whispering, "That's right," breathlessly.

"Damn," came from Mark. "If you want to see a passionate kiss, just throw two people together one afternoon and declare they're married the next morning. Why don't the two of you take some time? Go into the guest bedroom and get acquainted or something?"

That sounded good to Rick. He smiled hopefully at Gwendolyn, and she both smiled back and squeezed his hand.

As they left the kitchen, Rick heard Mark comment to Ellen, "That certainly wasn't anything like our wedding kiss, was it?"

"It was more like the kiss we had for our second wedding," she agreed. "I still claim that first wedding didn't count."

Rick heard the story from a number of sources, but Mark never talked about it when they did the runs between Harlan and Arapahoe. Wherever that conversation was going, Gwendolyn softly closed the bedroom door, marking an end to their hosts' married talk.

"They said you would sleep on the couch last night. It turned out we both slept in what was supposed to be your bedroom. Now, we're both in my bedroom. What do you think of it?"

"I think anyplace I can hold you is just dandy, Gwendolyn," Rick responded.

She smiled and came into his arms. "You have that nasty old dragon shivering in fright now."

Rick thought about saying something more, but the second kiss they shared suddenly occupied all of his attention. All at once, she drew back a little, looking at him.

"So, we're married," she murmured. "What happens now?"

Rick grinned. "After those last kisses, I could tear your clothes off."

"I might not fight it."

Rick thought that was a very strange comment, but then a jigsaw puzzle piece fell into place. He nodded. "You might not resist. You didn't waste energy fighting those people in Ragan. All they got was the little mouse. That might be all I'd get, too, because I'd be acting like them."

"Are you the same as them?"

"If all people are basically the same, it's possible. At the same time, I hope there are differences. Even if there aren't, I could hope to improve."

Gwendolyn nodded. "You're a lot smarter than any of that bunch. None of them ever had a clue the whole time I was there. By the time they started lending me to Nancy Rowley, they were certain I was just a good little mouse, and could be trusted to just clean Nancy's place. When I was done, my instructions were to stand quietly in a corner, waiting for them to come around for me, however long that might take."

"I assume Nancy saw through all of that and started conversations with you."

Gwendolyn picked something off her shirt. "It went the other way, actually. I thought she might be different and occasionally asked odd little questions. That got her attention, eventually, and at that point the conversations started. It got me everything I wanted, and a good deal more, besides." She reached up and stroked her fingertips across Rick's chest. It was like the previous time, only now, she stopped at the top snap of his western-style shirt, and popped it open.

Rick licked his lips nervously. Another piece of the puzzle fell into place suddenly. Gwendolyn admitted that she was a head case, with this multiple personality thing. The trouble was he'd looked up some of that and knew when people had that disorder, they could not remember what they did as the other personality. Now, there were plenty of psychiatrist's couches available but no psychiatrists. What could he do? Gwendolyn opened another snap on his shirt and softly hummed to herself.

Rick fell back on his normal reactions. He could keep his mouth shut, and figure out ways through the situation. Gwendolyn appeared to like what she was seeing. If she was crazy enough to want to be with him, then he'd be crazy if he didn't just hang on and enjoy the ride. That, Rick thought, would certainly be Mark's point of view.

His shirt now hung open, and Gwendolyn was rubbing his chest softly with both hands. He felt himself reacting to her even while he looked out the window at the snow, which now appeared to have some wind with it. It appeared that whatever happened, he was on his own with her. Mark declared himself a Gwendolyn supporter. Ellen seemed more neutral on the subject of Gwendolyn, but Rick never knew what women really thought of one another.

Gwendolyn finally looked at Rick's face. "Is this bothering you?"

"You bothering me in more ways than I can count," Rick replied truthfully. "Is there any way I can bother you that you wouldn't take wrong?"

She smiled. "You already bother me with the way you look and smell. That's not to mention how easily you get goosebumps when I stroke your chest just to watch your muscles ripple. All those fence posts you've done turned you into a real hunk. You're that rarest of creatures, a nerd hunk. Being this close to you bothers me more than I can tell."

"It's strange. I've been on any number of dates, and nobody ever gave any inkling they thought anything about me, one way or another."

She looked at him seriously. "That's because in dating, everybody thinks they are the prize, and everyone in the world has to compete to win. Of course, some of the rules are out in the open, but the important rules are never disclosed."

"I would imagine one of the undisclosed rules is what each person thinks is romantic."

Gwendolyn's eyebrows raised. "Ah, yes, the old bards and poets really released a monster into the world when they invented that, didn't they? That search for romantic love was so successful that half of all marriages ended in divorce. I never heard how many of those staying together were still in love, or whether they stayed together for some other reason."

"I heard that, too. I also heard stories of arranged marriages, from back when they did such things, where the couple became quite happy being together."

"Is what we have an arranged marriage?"

"Not really," Rick replied, finding his fingers stroking Gwendolyn's hair. "If I had to put a term to it, I think assigned marriage would be closer. Maybe we can make a good thing of it, whatever it is."

She led him to the bed, where they lay facing one another. Rick's shirt was open, but otherwise, both were fully clothed. Rick saw Gwendolyn had something on her mind. Not knowing what to say, he reached over and stroked her hair a little more. She didn't seem to find that a problem. Finally, she seemed to have framed her thoughts a bit better.

"The Ragan ladies were all in a tizzy about something that guy out at Arapahoe said. I have no idea if it actually happened."

"What thing was that?" Rick thought he knew, but let her tell the story. "Are you talking about Jimmy?"

"Yeah, that's the name they said. He did the marriage ceremony for the people from the castle. Anyway, he commented that people were still getting married, but since there was no government or church, there was no longer any way to be divorced. Did he really say that?"

Rick nodded. "Mark swears that's exactly what he said. It sure got Mark's attention. There's no longer a priest or a justice of the peace to handle getting married. There also isn't anybody to say people aren't married. The way everybody keeps carrying on, people are married just about when they decide that's what they are."

"I hear that may not apply to Kevin and Susie."

"A girl's parents would weigh in on such matters. The parents of a younger girl will be even more certain to make their opinions known. Susie is one of very few single girls lucky enough to have living parents. Whether either Kevin or Susie would define that as lucky could be a rather large question."

Gwendolyn stroked Rick's cheek with a finger. "What would you do if Susie was your daughter."

"Now there's a leading question. My experience with Kevin would have been quite different were I the prospective father-in-law as opposed to an employee. The big consideration is just how conflicted I might be, knowing Susie is making up her own mind. At the same time, I would be quite certain neither Kevin nor any other man born could possibly be good enough for her."

Now she completely changed the subject, asking, "Would you ever leave me, Rick? Mark almost left Ellen."

Rick gave that one some thought. Finally, "You are talking about what Mark thought about doing. If I was the type to bug out when things got bad, I wouldn't have been digging a post hole like a fool when Kevin finally got around to delivering the message for me to come over here. As far as that goes, if I had any sense whatever, I'd have shoved the digging bar up Kevin's rectum quite a few days ago. I am far more likely to stick around until the bitter end. If you pushed hard enough, I might leave. It would take such a shove that nobody would want to be friends later on."

Gwendolyn nodded. "You're thinking of the old 'let's just be friends' gig. Yeah, okay, I understand what you're saying."

Rick shook his head. "You don't understand. Not really. Hanging in there at Wagon Ranch wasn't just a job. It was a duty. It didn't matter that I didn't ask for it. It was what I was supposed to do. Today, we're married. At least, that's what Mark and Ellen say. That means we need to figure out some way to tolerate all the little quirks each other has. No doubt, you've already enumerated a long list of bad things I do."

Her entire hand now stroked the stubble on Rick's face. Gwendolyn suddenly giggled. "They brought me here yesterday wearing my chore clothes. You came loping in direct from working on a fence line. Neither of us got cleaned up since then, and it's my wedding day. To top it off, you just made a vow like I could have never imagined. Are you really okay with us being married?"

"That's what I said. If it's anything important, should I plan on saying it at least twice?"

"There are things a girl doesn't mind hearing over and over. Vows to be true are right at the top of the list. While ours is not a marriage based on romantic love, there's no reason we couldn't see about getting some romance into the mix. I guess I should probably find out what my last name is, now that I'm married."

"That depends on whether you want to take mine."

"From what I hear, that seems to be what all the gals are doing."

"Okay, my last name is Forbes. Rick Forbes."

She grinned. "I am pleased to meet you, Rick Forbes. I used to be Gwendolyn Fuller. Now, I'm Gwendolyn Forbes. That's easy enough. I think I like it."

At that point, her hand circled around behind his head, and she kissed him deeply. After hesitating just slightly, he returned the kiss, and found her very receptive. Gwendolyn's response became quite passionate shortly after that. Their clothing suddenly went in all directions.

Some time later, they lay tight against each other. She looked at him with a sly little smile. "I don't think I'd mind being in love with you."

"So being in love with me might be as appealing as bamboo splinters shoved under your fingernails, or hot pokers jabbing your skin?"

"Oh, I might go for the hot poker, as long as it's yours."

Rick scratched his ear. "This brave new world we're in seems to do things in random order. Mark and Ellen fell in love, but got married at a point when they hated each other. You and I got married before we even got acquainted. Next thing you know, somebody will get married in absentia."

"I can't see it happening. There's a practical reason. It would be really tough to consummate the marriage that way."

A soft knock came just then, followed by Ellen's voice. "Excuse me, guys, but if you'd like some lunch, come on out. The snow is about to quit, if you're interested."

They looked at each other and agreed they were indeed interested in food. As they were getting dressed, Rick looked at Gwendolyn and grinned. "It's going to be a real challenge for those Ragan ladies. They're going to have to do their own cleaning."

"Perish the thought. Who knows? My dishpan hands might even get a break."

Rick walked around the bed and took her hand. "I could kiss your hands until they get all soft and supple."

"That might work. Then again, I might use them to slap you until you're all silly."

"It's way too late for that. Whatever's in the kitchen smells good." Rick felt he should be a little gallant, and whispered in Gwendolyn's ear as they walked out the door, "I'll bet your cooking is better."

Rick recalled locals comparing the local weather to a battle between giants. The one with snow and cold retreated for now, leaving Harlan to the giant with fair skies and soft warm breezes. Saying it would be warm was more relative than absolute, though. Rick's mind freewheeled as he attempted to make sense of everything that had happened.

After lunch, both couples moved to the living room, talking about nothing in particular. By mid-afternoon, the snowplow crew went past, their job made easier by the fact that they were not trying to remove the snow. They just made a level, well-packed surface that now served as the road. The snowplow teams came from the north, and headed toward Orleans and Oxford.

Rick and Gwendolyn both suggested to their hosts that they would really wanted to spend more time getting acquainted with one another. These suggestions were brushed off without comment. A bit later, when they got insistent, Mark had enough.

"Lyle is coming," he informed them. "I wanted him here when the two of you came. He wasn't able to do that, but sent word that he would be over here just as soon as he could. With the road plowed, Lyle should be arriving any time now. You need to prepare to meet your public. At the same time, remember that experts say that if you resist these urges, when you do satisfy them, the feeling will be much more meaningful."

Rick didn't think Mark spoke from personal experience when he gave advice about putting off sexual urges. On the other hand, Rick wondered about Mark's psychic abilities, because it wasn't five minutes before they heard Lyle yell hello toward the house. His wife, Adeline, was with him, and they both had bedrolls and bags of provisions tied behind their saddles. This was not a short social call. Rick considered the small house would be crowded. He looked at Gwendolyn, but she seemed lost in her own thoughts just then.

Coming into the house, Lyle and Adeline acted like it was a party. "Mark and Ellen have an increasing list of matches for which they claim either credit or blame. We came to inspect their latest effort."

Gwendolyn blinked. "They got us married. Then we met. These past couple of hours, we've been trying to get acquainted."

Adeline's eyebrows arched high, and they both immediately turned their attention to Rick.

"That summarizes it perfectly," was Rick's supporting comment.

Lyle now turned to Mark and Ellen, who both seemed quite relaxed. "You two set a new record with this one. I hope you've got something that even partially smells like a reason."

Mark nodded. "We did it to save them both. I'll bet neither of you ever saw Gwendolyn before, even though she has lived in Ragan since before the dust. Several families used her as a community drudge."

Mark pursed his lips. "They must not have considered her human, since the times we specifically got everybody in town together, she was not included. The one time even Willy the Rat showed up. Of course that's when Josh and I exposed his true identity as the organizer of the cannibals."

Lyle nodded. "I remember Willy well enough. Adeline, those times you talked with the Ragan ladies, did they ever mention this young lady?"

Adeline shook her head. "When everybody was working on Josh and Alicia's wedding, it did seem that an extraordinary amount of work got done. Was some of that really you, Gwendolyn?"

"Yes, ma'am, they had me racing around doing all kinds of things for that wedding."

"How were you able to escape, dear?"

"They decided I could help Mrs. Rowley. After Nancy figured out my situation, she thought Rick could help. Then Deputy Vince also figured it out and brought Mark and Ellen into it. They got me over here."

"Well, good for you. That terrorist is the only person in Harlan who needs to do involuntary work. Maybe he should take her place doing drudge work. It would serve him right."

Lyle rubbed his neck. "I agree that Gwendolyn does not need to go back to Ragan. What's your story, Rick?"

Rick related his situation as simply as possible, with both Lyle and Adeline paying extraordinarily close attention. When Rick finished, Lyle did not ask any questions of him. Instead, he turned to Mark.

"What is your plan to handle this?"

Rick noticed that Mark still seemed comfortable. "I have no reason to doubt what Rick says. It's unfortunate that Kevin seems to be going off the deep end. If we go to Kevin with what we have now, that young man will have a parade of excuses, and maybe a marching band to go with it. We have to go check it out for ourselves."

Lyle considered that. "How would you do that? Kevin's people saw Adeline and me come in. They not only know Rick is here, but also why you brought him."

"That is true. Kevin will bring replacements for his candidates, and not too long from now. With Rick in here, he will want to get an eyeball on the situation. He only swaps out his candidates a couple of times a week, so we'll wait a little while after he leaves, and head out ourselves. That reminds me, Ellen, could you keep an eye out that direction, and let us know if Kevin shows up?"

Ellen nodded, and stood discreetly by the curtains. Rick started to feel the pressures of the past several weeks start to lift.

Lyle nodded. "I think you have a good plan, Mark. I'm going to throw in a small addition, though. I want Rick to go with us. We need additional information about the situation that only he can give. In the meantime, Rick, you and Gwendolyn go into your room. You'll have to be very quiet, because when Kevin checks in, we'll tell him you two are sound asleep. Don't get too comfortable, though. We'll be leaving very soon after he disappears."

Rick grinned as Gwendolyn grabbed his hand without another word and towed him into the room. They kept their clothes on, but crawled under the covers, and embraced as though they were exhausted on the one hand, but deeply in love on the other. Rick then gave Mark's psychic powers another vote as he heard Ellen comment that Kevin arrived. A few minutes later came a knock on the front door.

"Mark, where's Rick? His ass needs to be working … oh, I'm sorry, I didn't know you were here, Mr. Lillard."

Lyle's unmistakeable voice replied. "Rick's ass has been working, Kevin. His bride wiped out whatever energy he had. They're both asleep right now."

"Bride? He's married?"

"Like you and Susie should be."

"There's no way."

"Take a look."

Rick lay there, his eyes closed, smelling Gwendolyn's breath, and a slight smile on his face as the door softly opened.

Rick heard the door close, not so softly this time. There followed an even longer silence. He presumed everybody in the living room was watching Kevin. With an eye half open, he studied Gwendolyn. Rick felt very comfortable holding her, and was in no hurry to go anywhere or discover anything that wasn't next to him in the bed. All too soon, there was the sound of boots on the living room floor. A moment later, the bedroom door opened, and he knew the good times were over.

Mark was laughing. "Kevin looked like a dog that just lost his big meaty bone. His candidates may have an interesting ride back."

"I think you're right," Lyle returned. "So far, Kevin confirmed everything you guys told me. Nonetheless, we need to get moving. For one thing, we need to verify some other points. Also, we may need to rescue the guys over at Wagon Ranch. Rise and shine, Rick. We have to interrupt your honeymoon. With any luck, you can pick up where you left off tomorrow."

The group moved into the living room while Rick and Gwendolyn got up. Rick held her close for a moment.

"Will you be okay for a day or so? How's the thing with the dragon?"

"Ellen and Adeline will do their best to keep me out of danger. In any case, you got the dragon on the run. I survived all these months with no hope. Being here with friends and having the hope that you will come back, I just may make it."

She paused, and then, "You are coming back, aren't you?"

"If you want me back, I'll be back."

Gwendolyn gave him a squeeze and a kiss. "I want you back, big guy. Hurry every chance you get."

Rick suddenly had an inspiration. "Yes, Mrs. Forbes, I'll do that."

Gwendolyn froze for a moment, and then grinned. "Mrs. Forbes. Gwendolyn Forbes. I'll practice that while you're gone."

The two candidates helped with the horses as much as they could, though it was clear that neither of them knew what needed to happen. Rick saw they hindered more than helped the effort. It was also clear the two of them were far more interested in figuring out what was going on, especially with all three men carrying bedrolls. Neither Mark nor Lyle made any effort to enlighten them, so Rick kept his mouth closed, as well.

Once they were out of sight of Harlan Ranch, Mark turned to Rick. "Do you know those two?"

"I've seen them a couple of times, but never talked to them. From what they just demonstrated, I have to wonder how well the chores at Harlan Ranch will get done."

Lyle grunted. "There's another discussion point. It should be a major item but from the look of things, it may be fairly minor. We'll check the stock at Harlan Ranch when we get done with Wagon Ranch."

As they rode, Rick discovered he was the target of endless questions from Lyle. Many were about training horses and riders. More were about caring for livestock, especially horses. Facility maintenance came up, too. All the while, Lyle kept them moving at a brisk pace. Rick figured they would catch up to Kevin before he turned onto the state highway. A quarter of a mile from the state highway, Mark pointed ahead.

"There they are."

"Let's pull over to the side of the road," Lyle ordered. "Are there any shortcuts to Wagon Ranch, Rick?"

"There are some other ways, but nothing you'd want to do with this deep snow."

"What will Kevin do now?"

"He'll drop off the candidates, yell at everybody for a few minutes, and then take off for Huntley."

Lyle considered that and asked, "What he should be doing?"

Rick rubbed two days worth of whiskers on his chin. "He should tell Susie it is time to move to Wagon Ranch. There's too much to do for him to be playing games all the time. If Mom and Pop want to tag along, that's their call. If they all come out, her parents could help with all the chores, too. That's just my opinion, of course."

There was still an hour's daylight when they saw Kevin ride by the opposite direction on the state highway, covering ground at a lope, and not looking around. The three men watched until Kevin went past the turnoff to the Lillard Ranch before they went out on the state highway.

"Who at Wagon Ranch would be on Kevin's side?"

Rick shook his head. "There are a few who might cover for him, but they'd do it more out of fear than anything else."

"I guess we'll see how accurate that assessment might be. In case you're interested, I have no intention of roughing it. We'll stay over at Wagon Ranch."

Mark nodded. "We might have some interviews this evening."

"There might well be a few interviews." After a moment, Lyle added, "Okay, there will be, Mark."

At Wagon Ranch, Rick showed them the hallway and cot where he bunked. Fortunately, nobody had gotten around to destroying it. His sleeping arrangement was a mark of Kevin's esteem for Rick. People Kevin considered worthwhile had private rooms. Some of the guys came out to give Rick a hard time, but stopped when they saw Lyle and Mark. At that point, they faded away.

Lyle didn't say anything, but Mark came by Rick's cot. "Some of these folks just figured out they've been kissing the wrong ass. This could be an interesting evening. Do you want to participate?"

"I should stay away. It wouldn't do to let anybody to say I tried to influence what anybody says. They'll say it anyway, but why give them ammunition? Mr. Lillard only wanted to quiz me along the way. I still don't know what that was all about. Here, it's his show."

Mark nodded. "I wondered about that myself. Lyle plays a deep game. With us here, you could move to a real room."

"I'll just stay here. It'll make getting back to Gwendolyn all that much more appealing."

"Punching post holes didn't slow your mind in the least. What do you think of Gwendolyn?"

"For all that you assigned us to be married, it was a good deal. We have more in common than I had any right to expect."

Mark grinned. "Your pile of lemons may make some good lemonade after all."

Chapter 6

New Boss at Wagon Ranch

Everybody left Rick alone in that brief time before dark. Lyle and Mark walked back and forth between interviews. When either went by, they nodded and said a few words. Early on, it looked like a couple of the guys thought about approaching him, but the longer Mark and Lyle interviewed, the more everybody simply avoided him. The only reason Rick could imagine was that these guys saw their jobs were in jeopardy, and decided he was to blame.

As it got toward dark, the guys all took off to do chores. Lyle and Mark collected Rick, and they trooped into the kitchen where they dipped into a stew pot. With nobody else around, Rick thought he'd try to find out what was going on.

"Were you able to find out much?" he asked Lyle.

"There were a few additions to what I'd already figured out. Did you know that Kevin feels threatened by you?"

"Threatened? He's afraid I'll shoot him or something?"

"He's certain that you're after his job."

Rick nearly choked on his bite. "Why would I want it? What would I do with it? Do the guys think their jobs are connected to his?"

Lyle grinned at Rick's discomfort. "The guys have the impression that if Kevin went away, their job security would become zero. There's only one place they could have gotten such an impression, and that's from Kevin. Kevin's insecurity constitutes as good a recommendation of your abilities as anybody could ask for. Unfortunately for him, it could also become a self-fulfilling prophecy. The descriptions of what's going on both agrees with and extends what you and Mark already told me. I hear that Kevin hasn't actually slept here in some time. Where's his room?"

"It's the one with padlocks on the doors and windows."

"We could send for some bolt cutters, boss," Mark commented.

"Why ruin perfectly good padlocks when the key person will deliver them to us?" came Lyle's response. "He'll be here before we could get a pair of bolt cutters anyway. Rick, what do you think Kevin is likely to do since you've been out of his grasp for a day and a half?"

"He'll heap as much abuse on me as he can, and believes I'll tolerate."

"Would that include physical abuse?"

"It hasn't so far, but he's gotten increasingly erratic recently."

Lyle nodded. "Okay, Rick, here's what I want you to do …"

His cot had never been comfortable, but that night, Rick recalled he spent the previous night sitting up in the sofa with Gwendolyn. Neither the position nor the situation had been at all restful. All in all, it had been one hell of a day, so much so that he was asleep almost the instant he laid down. The next thing Rick was aware of was his cot abruptly turning on its side, and him hitting the floor. He rose up on one elbow, blinking, and trying to see what was going on. A large shadowed outline stood above him.

It was no mystery who the voice belonged to. That cackling, jeering laughter could only be Kevin. "You are a lazy piece of shit, taking off two days, and now can't even drag your sorry ass out of bed."

There was intense pain as Kevin stepped on Rick's fingers. "Oh, did I accidentally step on your hand? Well, here's something to make you forget all about your stupid fingers."

Kevin aimed a vicious kick at Rick's chest. Rick tried to avoid the kick, but he was already against the wall, and could only partially deflect the sharp-toed boot.

"You're worse than some flea-bitten dog coming around chasing chickens. Did that feel good? I've got a bunch more for you," Kevin roared.

Rick tried to untangle himself from the bedroll and get up, but knew there was no way he could do it fast enough. Even while he was trying to get out of the way, Rick braced himself for more. The next kick never arrived. Instead, two more shadows joined Kevin's shadow and pulled him backwards.

The next voice was Lyle's. "The beatings will continue until morale improves. Isn't that how it works, Kevin?"

"Mr. Lillard, I didn't know you were here. If I knew you were coming, we could have ridden together this morning. You just don't know what I've been having to put up with here."

Rick finally got to his feet, still rubbing his fingers and chest. Mark and Lyle both kept a firm grip on Kevin's arms and shoulders. "I wasn't at the house, Kevin. Nobody was there. I was here, taking care of business. There is plenty around here to take care of. You needed to be here taking care of it instead of galluping to Huntley to court Susie."

"When did you get here?"

"Mark, Rick and I got here yesterday afternoon. I've been finding out what's going on. The things going on are exceeded only by all the things that should be happening but aren't. The real question is not what you've had to put up with around here. It's what I've been putting up with by having you pretend to be the manager."

There was a pause, as though Kevin might have a rebuttal. There wasn't, and Lyle continued, "In case you weren't aware of it, there are lots of things considered best management practices. Injuring employees has never been one of them. By the way, your infamous mouth suddenly seems to be malfunctioning. I haven't heard a great deal, and believe me, you have a great deal of explaining to do."

Kevin hung his head. "When I go to the Maguire place, I never have any romantic moments with Susie. They hardly let me see her."

"So what are you doing over there?"

"Mr. Maguire said I committed a sin and a crime when I violated his daughter's virginity in the first place, and got her pregnant in the second place. He says I have to pay a large penance. Part of it is that I cannot physically touch her for a year. After the child is born and is healthy, I must marry her and publicly announce that I adopt the child."

Rick could see Mark's interest increase at that point. "What happens if the child is not healthy?"

"Mr. Maguire says that would mean the sin and the crime is beyond forgiveness. I think he might kill me. If I don't get over there promptly every day, he swears he'll hunt me down like a rabid dog."

Lyle shook his head. "I think I see what's going on now. What I don't see is what to do about it, or at least about the Maguire part of it."

Everybody just stood in place at that point, looking at each other for something approximating inspiration. Lyle finally nodded.

"Okay, Kevin, effective right now, you are no longer the manager here. Give me the keys to your room, and clear out your stuff this very minute. Your assignment is to go do your penance with Mr. Maguire."

There wasn't much in the room, and it only took a moment for Kevin to grab his stuff. Rick stayed well back of Mark and Lyle. It didn't seem to matter. Kevin's attention was completely on his own misery.

Rick was in complete shock at the speed events were moving. If he could believe what he'd heard, Lyle Lillard seemed to have him in mind to run Wagon Ranch. That was, of course, totally nuts. Still, nobody had looked at him cross-eyed and told him to go away, so there he stood, watching as Kevin, slump-shouldered, drug his few possessions out the door and rode away.

Lyle asked over his shoulder, "How would you have handled this, Rick?"

Rick couldn't think of anything and just snorted. "The only way Kevin would pay attention is if Vince and all his gun-toting deputies were behind me. Even then, he wouldn't have listened to anything I said."

After reflecting a moment, Rick added, "He most certainly wouldn't bring up Mr. Maguire having him do something called paying penance."

"I'm quite amazed he told it to me. The situation with Susie and her family must be pretty bad for him to need to get it off his chest like that. Mark, you and I need to pay a visit to Huntley."

Mark nodded. "Our wives should go with us. I have a feeling there are several sides to the situation. Susie must have really wanted to get away from her daddy. The ladies of the house may have something to say, but I have a feeling they would be more likely to say it to other women."

"That sounds right, and we need to do it sooner rather than later. Now, Mark, go round up all the folks pretending to work. We need a staff meeting. Bring them into the kitchen."

The room was soon packed. Mark looked in the kitchen doorway, nodding to Lyle, who cleared his throat and called for attention.

"I'll start by confirming two of your worst fears," Lyle announced. "First, Kevin is no longer the manager here at Wagon Ranch. Second, Rick is the new manager."

That earned a great deal of nervous coughing and shuffling of feet. Rick thought it was a testimony of their respect for Lyle that everyone kept their mouths shut.

"The rumor is that a lot of you would be sent packing as well. That is most specifically not the case. Nobody gets fired without my say-so. Rick will be on a very short leash. Mark and I will be giving him a great deal of guidance, both now, and probably for a considerable amount of time. The other side of the coin is that Mark and I will be watching all of you. If anybody thinks they can undermine Rick, and get rid of him, they'd better think twice. That would be a guaranteed ticket out of here."

Lyle then did the standard handshake and shoulder slap with Rick. Mark then came over and repeated the process.

"Rick," Lyle then commented loudly, "take your bedroll into the manager's room and get settled. Mark, get back to Harlan Ranch. Bring all the ladies. I'm sure Gwendolyn has little or no experience on a horse. You may have to ride double with her."

Lyle glanced around the room, and pointing at random. "Help Mark saddle up unless you want to register a complaint with me first."

The selected guys shook their heads and followed Mark out of the house. Lyle gave Rick a significant look like it was time for him to take care of the small amount of business he'd been assigned, so Rick turned and went down the hallway, where his tangled bedroll was still on the floor beside the cot. Rick made his first management decision. There would be no more cots in the hallway, so he folded it up. Bedroll in hand, he went by the kitchen on his way to his new digs while Lyle conducted close supervision with the group.

As he straightened his bedroll, Rick realized he broke a promise to Gwendolyn. He said he'd go right back to her, and he didn't go. That was not a good way to start, even if it was for a good purpose. Over here, Gwendolyn would be the lady of the manor, with all these guys doing her bidding. At least he hoped it would work that way. There was no way in hell he'd let her become the community drudge for this bunch.

Lyle knocked on the open door to the room.

"May I come in?"

"Yes, sir."

Lyle handed Rick a piece of paper. "This is what those guys say they were doing. A fair amount of it makes sense. Some of it makes no sense at all. Take a look at it and see what you think."

Rick studied it a little while, and then pointed to a couple of lines. "These two items have nothing to do with anything I've ever seen around here. Who says that's what they're doing?"

Lyle described the men, and Rick shrugged. "I don't know either of them. As for the rest, I'm not sure they'll pay any attention to me unless you're physically standing beside me. If Gwendolyn is in the picture, they might go out of their way to make her life just as miserable as possible."

"At least you're not underestimating the challenge you've got." Lyle sighed. "You know, Rick, none of this around Harlan is turning out to be like I hoped it might go."

Rick nodded. "Mark told me how you talked about creating some kind of utopia."

"Yeah, I promoted that. I still want it, but I keep it to myself. Our little group of survivors retained many good qualities, like cooperation, invention, and productivity. On the other hand, we've also brought with us all the seeds of destruction that nearly spelled an end to the human race. It may be the end of us yet, if we're not really lucky."

"That sounds like the old Indian story about the two wolves inside each of us, fighting for our souls. The one that wins is the one we feed."

Lyle approved that response. "The problem is that folks feed the wrong wolf, thinking that's how they will bring other people to their way of thinking." After a momentary pause, "Are you moved in yet?"

"I finished moving thirty seconds after I walked in."

"Splendid. What say we practice a little management by walking around. I'm curious about how these jobs are going."

A few moments later, dressed for winter, the two crunched out through the crusted snow, hoping to find proof of productive workers.

A bit of horse wisdom Rick learned was that when a horse looks at something with both eyes, they are really paying attention. When they only have one eye on it, it can mean a number of things. One possibility is that they aren't sure whether the thing is a danger, so they'll keep track of it while at the same time looking for an escape route. Rick noticed a great deal of horse training applied directly to working with people. Making the rounds with Lyle, nearly everybody regarded Lyle with the full focus and attention he associated with a horse giving a trainer both eyes. With him, hardly anyone looked at him directly. At the same time, they kept track of him in their peripheral vision. To become a manager, Rick knew he had to figure out how to change the situation. Lyle and Mark would invest some time, effort, and energy with him. In the end, it was going to be up to him to make it work.

One thing was certain from that morning: beating wouldn't gain the trust of men or horses.

When they got back to the house, Lyle asked Rick, "What's your take on the situation?"

"It is pretty much as I expected, and it follows the old saying that trust comes slowly and painfully. It can be lost in a moment and might never be regained."

"I never heard it expressed exactly that way, but it matches the idea, certainly. Are you getting some ideas on how to proceed?"

"A couple of the guys may need to find a new home. Several others may or may not come around. In the meantime, about all I can do is to treat everybody as fairly as possible."

"I hope that's how you really intend to do it, and not just trying to give me warm and fuzzy feelings."

Rick shrugged. "Driving with Mark, he told me how you see through attempts to pull the wool over your eyes. Being clever is not something I'm awfully good at anyway."

"From everything I've seen and heard, you're very clever working with computers."

"Computers either work or they don't. Software functions as it should, or it doesn't. People are hardly ever one or the other. The best are screwed up, and the nastiest of them sometimes make their problems into some kind of strange gift."

"What about Gwendolyn?"

Rick was not ready for that. It made him blink as he sorted out a response. "She talks like she has two personalities. She's aware of what she's doing either way, so it doesn't match up with what I've read on the subject of multiple personalities. It is more like having divergent ways to deal with different challenges. One thing seems certain. If Gwendolyn suddenly gets passive, I know she's feeling a very negative kind of stress. With her, that could be a really bad thing."

Lyle nodded. "I think that's a good analysis. The reason I asked is because Mark and the ladies are coming up to the house right now, and Gwendolyn is riding double with Mark."

Rick wasn't sure why Lyle found that last worthy of comment, since it was how he told Mark to handle it. In any case, they were both out the door almost immediately. Rick helped Gwendolyn off Mark's horse, noticing she was now wearing clothes that didn't come from a dust bin.

"Was that your first time on a horse?" he asked her as he got her on the ground.

"Yes, it was. It was exciting at first, but really tiring as I tried to keep my balance the whole time."

Rick looked up at Mark. "Your horse make it okay?"

"Yeah, my filly is just fine. I wouldn't want to make a habit of it."

They got to the door, and Rick had a thought. "Gwendolyn, you look really nice. I'm sorry that I haven't gotten cleaned up. Still, this is our first home as husband and wife. In the spirit of tradition, I should carry you over the threshold."

Gwendolyn wasn't sure about it, and Ellen giggled. Rick cracked the door open, picked her up, and took her inside. Everybody followed them in, and Rick placed her feet back on the floor a couple of steps inside. She rewarded him with a short but passionate kiss.

"Where is our room?"

"I'll take you there now."

She looked at the room and shook her head. "It needs a woman's touch."

"It's warm and has a door for privacy. There's a bed to sleep in. Most important, it has you. That makes it perfect, as far as I'm concerned."

She looked at him. "Well, aren't you the romantic."

"I sat on a couch two nights ago. Last night, I was on a cot in the hall. Being here with you is the lap of luxury."

"Well, that's nice to hear, although it isn't much of a comparison."

Rick nodded. "I was just hoping to distract you from the fact that I already broke the only promise I ever made to you."

Gwendolyn looked puzzled. "What promise?"

"I promised I would be right back to you, and I didn't do it."

"I'll forgive you this time. You managed to up the ante enough to cover your losses."

"You talk like a poker player. I could be in real trouble. Everybody tells me they can read my mind just by watching my face."

The group now showed up to inspect the manager's quarters, and Gwendolyn whispered in Rick's ear, "We can try some strip poker later. Then I will be able to read your mind without having to look at your face."

Rick whispered back, "My virgin ears have undoubtedly turned crimson, hearing such things."

Ellen shook her head in mock disbelief. "You two have had four hours of married life. You've known each other less time than that. Yet here the two of you are, publicly sharing secrets of a prurient nature. I am absolutely astonished."

Gwendolyn smiled modestly. "We are doing everything in reverse. You should have been there for our golden anniversary. It was quite a bash. I must admit, though, that un-having children was most difficult."

Lyle cleared his throat. "Why don't we go to the kitchen? I believe there's still a pot of coffee on."

Adeline looked at Lyle doubtfully. "The pot may be there. There may be something in it. The question is whether it is drinkable."

Rick thought he'd better put on his newly acquired manager hat. "Ma'am, the fluid in that pot is cowboy coffee. We use it for lots of things. Drinking it might be just about the last thing on the list."

Adeline looked over at Lyle then. "At the very least you got an honest manager out of the deal."

Lyle shook his head. "All that tells me is that he doesn't lie all the time. If he'd lie about the coffee here, he'd lie about anything."

Adeline shuddered. "Ladies, let's go make some coffee that everyone can drink, not just use to patch the roof."

It wasn't long before everybody was in the kitchen. Rick admitted what the ladies made definitely tasted better than anything they'd had before.

"Since you got into a talkative mood, Rick, why don't you lay out the place for the benefit of Gwendolyn, if nobody else. We need to figure out a plan of attack here."

Rick nodded, and grabbed a piece of paper. "This house is situated like this with the road running by over here. What we call Wagon Ranch used to be two separate operations, set back-to-back. It must have been an extended family operation. It works out well for us, having a house on either side of the pens. A lane goes between the two sides. The barn over there has stalls, while the one over here is more for storage. I understand Mr. Rowley's freight wagon was stored over here."

"What are you going to do with your guests, Rick?"

That made Rick blink. "We have enough rooms for everyone here. A worthwhile winter project for the guys would be to build a bunkhouse, possibly in the equipment building near the stock barn. It might be a larger version of the bunkhouse at Harlan Ranch. In the meantime, they can make do with the house over there, and if they want privacy, they can go to the barn."

"Damn," Mark chuckled. "It didn't take much to turn you into a hard ass, did it?"

Rick shook his head. "When company comes for Thanksgiving, the kids all bunk together. It's all part of being a family."

"I'll take your word for that, Rick. I can hardly remember having a family, but living as a foster kid, I was definitely the first one moved out and the last one moved back."

Lyle nodded. "In this family, when will Thanksgiving be over?"

Rick shrugged. "When the relatives leave, of course. Meanwhile, the hands will be busy building better digs anyway. It will be work they will use personally, and doing that kind of work will beat being out in the weather. Speaking of which, training in this kind of weather is going to be really nasty. Does anybody know of an available arena?"

Lyle chuckled. "Moving like that, you'll never have moss growing on your back. By the way, your people are coming in. I'll let you take care of the arrangements."

The guys in the house looked nervously at the group as they passed the kitchen. Rick stood up and walked out into the hallway.

"Mark Tahner is here with his wife. Mr. Lillard is also here, and his wife is with him. Lyle and Mark agreed to room together before their wives showed up. Now they each need a room. You guys need to find places over in the other house."

The one guy was Kevin's chief ass kisser, and one Rick figured would find employment elsewhere. He snarled, "Says who? I don't take orders from any wimpy nerd boy."

Rick kept his composure. "You've usually taken orders from the Wagon Ranch manager, and that's who is telling you this now. Pick up your stuff and remove it from that room. If you don't want to go to the other house, you can bed in one of the other buildings. If you don't want to take orders from me, the road is just outside the door."

"You'd just love to see me leave, wouldn't you?"

"That will be a problem either way. You know your job. If you leave, it'll be pain in the ass to train somebody else. If you stay, you'll spend all your time being a pain in my ass anyway. That makes it all the same to me."

"You got rid of Kevin. You're not getting rid of me. I'm staying even if I have to sleep in a snowdrift."

"Well, great. You can go to the other house and improve morale there. I can hardly wait to see all the smiling faces."

The guy, whose name Rick had never known, glared at him, and stomped into the room to collect his belongings. The two guys in the other room decided they'd just follow directions. It was already obvious to them who was setting himself up to get slapped silly. In the meantime, Rick didn't need eyes in the back of his head to know that he was being closely watched and evaluated by both Mark and Lyle. For all Rick knew, the three women might weigh in on it, too.

After the house became quiet and the residence of the three couples, Rick went into both of what were now guest rooms to see if they were suitable for his VIPs. They were grungy, but not too badly maintained, all in all. Back in the kitchen, everyone looked at him expectantly.

"I'm sorry the rooms I can offer aren't in the best condition," Rick advised. "From everything I've heard, the guys at the other house eat pretty good. The coffee over there still wouldn't meet the standards you ladies would expect, though."

Lyle smiled. "You did everything extremely well. Just out of curiosity, why did you handle that one gentleman like you did?"

"All he knows is how the hot air blows. The truth is not something he knows how to deal with, so that's what I gave him. If I had asked him to stay, he would have been out the door and down the road in a flash. The fact is that he does know his job. More than that, he's quite good at it. He'll make my life as miserable as he can manage. I simply told him that I knew all of that. The pain for me is about equal whatever he does. For him, being a burr under my saddle just became a challenge."

Ellen grinned wickedly. "You do pretty well handling men. How are you with women?"

"I can't say that I know anything at all, ma'am."

Mark was nodding. "Kevin said you mostly kept your mouth shut. That was how he described you to me. Now, you give entire seminars without a second thought. I find that very interesting."

"When it's clear the other person isn't listening, talking is a waste of energy. People jabber endlessly about rumors, but you never hear good rumors. Why hand somebody a weapon to use against other people? I understand that people do it. The guy I sent across to the other house is taking my name in vain right now, and I'll have to deal with it. What I don't get is the joy they get from it. They had me doing the cooking. Should I start making some supper?"

"Not on your life," came from Gwendolyn.

Rick found himself being herded out of the kitchen, along with Mark and Lyle.

"Is it something I said?" Rick asked Mark.

Lyle answered from just behind as they walked into the living room. "You just proved your worth as a manager. Gwendolyn feels she needs to prove her worth, as well. Adeline and Ellen will help out, of course."

Rick shook his head. "Since the cowboy coffee didn't meet their standards, I shudder to think about what they'll say about the pantry. It's pretty basic."

"It's no secret that Wagon Ranch is all working men," Mark offered. "The flow of trainees getting horses has slowed markedly recently."

The three found facing chairs, and Mark continued thinking out loud. "The snow and cold weather have a great deal to do with it. I think your idea of moving the training into an indoor arena would be a good thing. What do you think, Lyle?"

"It's a fact that working with horses gets really questionable during the winter when you don't have someplace indoors for them. Even with a large barn, about the most you hear about is simply trying to keep horses trained to the same level they were before the weather turned bad. Do either of you have any ideas where to do that kind of training?"

"We could use that building down in Orleans where we dropped off the McCook people. I don't know if any of them are still camped there," Rick suggested.

"Some were still there a week ago," Mark confirmed. "They don't want to move Vicky until there's a place ready for her and Jimmy. That will be the old school, and Don hasn't gotten the solar equipment and refrigerators there yet. He's been really dragging his feet on that project."

"What about the auction barn in Alma?" Lyle wanted to know. "Did Don take that?"

Mark nodded. "It's a large, roofed area with a big door. Why wouldn't he take it? I heard a couple of his people talking about him using it."

"The possibilities of an arena don't look good," Rick observed. "We may not get much training done this winter. Maybe next spring, we could build a pole barn here that we could use as an arena. It could cover over some of the pens between here and the other house."

"That's good, Rick. As a matter of fact, that's a great idea."

"I can't take any credit for it. Nearly everyone that's been out here for any amount of time has suggested the same thing. We could use power poles for the uprights and the major framing. The sides could be hinged for ventilation during the summer. Building it would require a huge amount of manpower, and a not insignificant amount of horsepower. That is the really big problem, since when we get good enough weather to build, everyone will want to be off farming."

Lyle nodded. "I see you've looked at both sides of the question. It sounds like something we should consider some more. Do you have any ideas what worthwhile things you can do over the winter here, other than build a bunkhouse?"

"I don't know of anything offhand. We need to develop some kind of plan before everybody rushes off madly to punch holes in the ground. For example, the corner post Kevin wanted me to dig the hole for didn't seem to be part of any kind of plan."

Mark laughed. "That hole had more to do with you, and less to do with fencing."

"If I'd put it that way, you two would have accused me of whining. I've heard farms always have a backlog of projects. Some can be done no matter what the weather is like. Feeding stock and fixing fences has to be done anyway."

"You've learned that much, anyway," Lyle observed. "How does it feel, to have camped in the hallway last night, and own the house this afternoon?"

"It may take a while to get used to. Being married is totally out of the box for me. Having both things happen at the same time is beyond belief."

They sat there for a little bit, and Rick recalled some old business. "I heard you guys say you might be heading over toward Huntley. If you happen to run into Mr. Rowley, could you tell him that I will get him a computer just as soon as I can?"

"Your number one troublemaker did call you a nerd," Lyle said with a smile.

"Coming from him, I decided to take it as a compliment."

"You're our one and only nerd. Wear the badge proudly. Sure, we'll let him know. I don't know what Don will make of you running Wagon Ranch now. You know he had his sights set on taking the place, but Mark beat him to it."

"Yeah, that story made the rounds. Mr. Rowley may have been the only one in Harlan pretending it never happened. I think he managed to put it all together when I ended up over there trying to make polite conversation," Rick commented.

"Don does not take kindly to not coming in first. That's for sure," Mark agreed.

Lyle evidently did not approve of the turn of conversation. He cleared his throat and said, "At least your marriage started out with a good omen, Rick. You carried Gwendolyn over the threshold without having an accident."

Rick wasn't so dense as to miss that rather pointed comment. "I was stepping very carefully, and made a point of not trying to do it for too long," he offered.

Mark seemed to have figured it out as well. "Whatever they found in the pantry is really starting to smell good."

"You're right," Rick agreed. "I don't recall anything in there smelling anywhere near as good as that."

It wasn't long before the ladies declared that they should come in to eat. Rick decided that his comments about Gwendolyn being able to cook extremely well fell short of the mark. Both Ellen and Adeline gave all the credit to her, although it did feel like they were smearing it on a little too thick. There were also off-hand comments circling between the three women that led Rick to be quite certain they'd been discussing a lot more than recipes in the kitchen. Well, he thought, that was probably just human behavior at work.

After dinner, Gwendolyn decided the excitement of the past several days had completely worn her out. Ellen and Adeline encouraged that thought, going so far as to volunteer to clean up the kitchen so she could rest. Rick was alert to those particular signals, and gallantly volunteered to take her to the room.

In the room, Gwendolyn turned to Rick. "Are you going to tuck me in, Rick?"

"Certainly, my lady."

"You do know, fair sir, that I require your body heat to be really tucked in."

"You should have it no other way."

Chapter 7

Learning the Ropes

Rick and Gwendolyn stumbled out of their room the next morning, only to find all four of their guests already up and waiting for them.

"You two survived your first argument, I see," Lyle remarked.

Rick shrugged. "I wouldn't call it an argument, exactly. We did have a discussion about how to share the room."

"Make that a heated discussion which lasted quite a long time," Mark added. "Ellen and I are no strangers to those kinds of discussions, and we both agreed yours was a doozy."

"We need to talk about this marriage some more, guys," Lyle advised. "Maybe it wasn't such a good idea after all. I agreed with Mark that both of you needed a better situation. From what we heard last night, this doesn't seem to be the way to have gone with it. What we're thinking is that if you two don't think it will work, we can simply say it was never a marriage in the first place."

"We agreed to be married. You all agreed that we became husband and wife," Rick stated. "That means it is up to us to make it work."

"Still, it's not right to force people to be together when they shouldn't be," Lyle replied.

Adeline spoke up then. "Why don't we have some breakfast? Then, Rick, perhaps you could show Gwendolyn some of the basics of horses and horsemanship. It looks like a pretty nice day. You two can talk about horses for a few hours. If you feel comfortable enough to talk about other things as well, that will be good. We can discuss this situation a bit more at lunch."

Nobody could think of anything better to do, so they all moved into the kitchen. Ellen and Adeline sat Rick and Gwendolyn together. They placed Lyle on one side of the two, sitting next to Gwendolyn. Mark on the other side of the couple, next to Rick.

Mark kept his voice pitched low but clear. "I know what I heard last night. Why don't you two tell me what it was all about?"

Rick shook his head tiredly. "I always wanted to find somebody like me. You guys talked about how we seem to be pretty much the same. Last night, we found out we might be too much the same. This is all pretty embarrassing, but you might as well hear it. As long as the side of the bed we wanted to be on was the middle, everything was fine. Then, when we wanted to actually get to sleep, we found out we still wanted the same side of the bed. It all sounds stupid now, but it seemed pretty important then."

"Just out of curiosity, who won?"

"She did. I was going to just put my bedroll on the floor, but that didn't suit her either. I ended up with about six inches on the wrong side of the bed."

Gwendolyn glared at Rick. "That's not true. You had almost half the bed. Anyway, you farted and snored the whole damn night. I can see why they made you sleep in the hall. I'm surprised they didn't send you out to the barn."

Lyle shook his head. "You got one thing right, Rick. All of that is really petty stuff. It is also what every couple has had to work their way through. Back when couples wanted to think of themselves as being in love before they started living together, one or the other would typically give in on the basis that since they loved their partner, they needed to love everything their partner did."

Rick returned Lyle's gaze. "We don't have that situation. As I see it, we either make accommodation for everything or pretend none of this ever happened. Arranging for Kevin to see us, supposedly blissfully in love, would make all of that pretending really difficult. With Nancy Rowley busy promoting her abilities as a matchmaker, it would be close to impossible."

"It would be difficult to sell," Lyle replied. "I never said it wouldn't be. I just thought it prudent to offer a possible way out of this. If you want to go that way, you need to do it now. The longer you wait, the harder it will be."

Breakfast served then, which Rick considered good timing, since he really needed to think about all of it. Other than the one comment, Gwendolyn hadn't said anything, and Rick wondered if she might retreat into the mouse persona. One thing he found out the previous evening was that she would argue almost anything if anybody would listen to her side of it.

After breakfast, the two went out to the barn, and Rick selected a horse he thought might work for her. It was one that might have carried children previously, and tolerated almost anything. The downside was that the horse would not move at anything more than a slow walk when anybody was mounted. It would not have mattered if the barn was on fire. That horse just wouldn't move. The consensus was the horse was for beginners only, and would never be assigned as a working animal. In this way, new people could obtain some idea about horses before they began the real work of ground training a more spirited mount.

It wasn't long before they were both mounted, and riding around the area. When they got to a fairly private spot, Rick looked over at her.

"Gwendolyn, you're awfully quiet. Did the dragon get you?"

"No," she replied, "I've been working on the logic of the situation. First they said we ought to get married. Then they thought it was a good thing we agreed to get married. Now, they are saying we aren't good enough to get married."

"I agree with your analysis. There is a flaw. In all those statements, the governing opinion originates with somebody besides the two people closest to the subject, namely you and me."

Gwendolyn nodded. "It's like Lyle Lillard is challenging us to be a happy couple."

"If we can't be a happy couple, he's challenging us to act as though we are. You bring out a protective urge in me, although that urge is to protect you from others. You say I help keep your dragon away. None of that kept us from snarling at each other like a pair of alley cats last night. I've got to admit, my arguments were pretty silly."

"I'll tell you what, Rick, we can take turns sleeping on that side of the bed. Now that I think about it, both of us sleeping in the middle of the bed suited me pretty well."

Rick thought about that a moment. "Okay, we can take turns. How about this, Gwendolyn, you can be in charge of assigning whose night it is on that side. I'll just take your word for it."

"You want us to stay together as a married couple, then?"

"Yes, I do."

At lunch, Rick and Gwendolyn relayed their decision. Rick expected to see Lyle Lillard leading the charge to talk them out of it. Instead, it was Mark who spoke up.

"You both realize, of course, that what you just smoothed out was really trivial. What happens when you come across things that are really important, and you can neither agree nor compromise?"

Rick nodded. "I remember a guy who maintained his marriage kept right side up because he and his wife had agreed that she would make all minor decisions, and he would get the major ones."

Mark shook his head. "I can see endless squabbling what kind of decision anything might be."

"No, there were no disagreements of that sort. In over twenty years of marriage, there had never been any truly major decisions to make."

Adeline and Lyle were both nodding knowingly. Ellen had her head cocked to one side, like she was considering the situation. Mark seemed inclined to bark at that squirrel some more.

"What are you going to do? You spout wise sayings from somebody the dust took. That's supposing you didn't just make it all up."

Rick shrugged. "I don't think it started with that guy. I think it's been around as long as men and women have attempted to share anything. It looks pretty simple to me. You and Mr. Lillard will tell me what to do around Wagon Ranch. Gwendolyn will tell me what to do when I walk in here. That little bit of a ride cleared my head, as you can tell."

"What about the guys working for you?"

"I have to learn how to translate what you guys tell me to do into specific things I tell them to do."

"What if they don't treat you or your wife with respect?"

"I'll do what I can to earn personal respect from the guys. If they don't treat Gwendolyn with respect, it is a whole other ballgame. It will be personal and have, as they say, consequences."

"That sounds like pretty tough talk for a nerd."

Rick shook his head. "It isn't tough talk. It's horse talk. Anybody dumb enough to get between a stallion and his mare has to deal with the consequences. The stallion will not apologize afterward, either."

All three women were suddenly looking at Rick intently. Of the three, Gwendolyn's look might have been the most intense. Adeline nodded agreement with Rick after a moment.

Lyle leaned back. "Mark, I believe we have a manager at Wagon Ranch. As a matter of fact, the ranch has a married manager. What do you think?"

"Rick impressed me from the beginning. I think he'll do just fine."

Mark turned to Rick then. "I'll take care of the candidates at Harlan Ranch and the Lillard place. It makes no sense for you to have to do it. By the way, where is the list of everybody who signed up to get a horse?"

Rick shook his head. "I've heard of such a list, but nobody's actually seen it."

Mark and Lyle looked at each other. "That makes another reason to go over to Huntley, Mark. You did give him the list when he took over here, didn't you?"

"He was the keeper of the list even before then, Lyle. I wonder what he did with it? Come to think of it, I don't think some of the people we've seen around here were even on the list. I know we didn't go through the whole thing. There should have been as many women out here learning to ride as men. Now there aren't any. What has he been doing?"

"He's been passing out favors, and no doubt used the list to start a fire. It probably happened quite a while ago. However, we'll have to verify that."

Lyle's attention came back to Rick. "Would you be opposed to the list staying with Mark for the time being? We need to get this favoritism thing taken care of right away."

"You send the people and horses for me to train, and I'll do my best for all of them. That reminds me — our bunkhouse needs to separate men and women, with as much privacy for both sides as we can manage. Maybe it would be best for the men to be in the bunkhouse, and the women to be in the house itself."

Mark laughed. "You won't get any objection from whatever women you get. I suppose I should start trying to remember who was on that list, and in what order. That's going to be a real pain to reconstruct."

Rick looked at both of them. "As we've already discussed, though, the really big pain is going to be trying to get any meaningful training done with these weather conditions. I can use the guys already here as a labor pool. Maybe we can get things put together so that we can really get after it when the weather conditions allow."

Lyle stood up. "Thank you for the hospitality, Rick. I think you made some excellent points. Mark, you'd better plan on reconstructing the list, while hoping for the best. We'd all better get back to our own places now. Mark, maybe we can head over to Huntley tomorrow. Then you could stop by here on your way home. I'll try to get up here the next day. That's if the weather cooperates, of course."

Adeline looked over at Gwendolyn. "We should help with the dishes before we go."

Gwendolyn shook her head emphatically. "Mr. Lillard is right. You all need to be back at your own places. Lord knows I've done enough dishes in the past several months. This is almost a vacation after that."

Ellen came around the table and gave Gwendolyn a hug. "Are you guys going to be all right?"

Gwendolyn nodded with a smile. "Yes, we'll be just fine. I'm tempted to make a joke about us killing each other, but you guys would take it all wrong. Rick and I have decided that we'll work this out, and that's how it's going to be."

By the front door, Mark turned to Rick. "You do realize that when your motley crew sees us ride off, you'll be in for a major test. How good a shot are you, by the way?"

"From what they tell me, I could become a crack shot after a mere ten thousand rounds down range. I fired a gun five or ten times."

"Well, that won't be on your side. We'll just hope your abilities as a nerd can keep this bunch down to a dull roar. They went along with you earlier, but that was with Lyle and me listening in the other room. I'll see if Vince can put you on his regular route."

After their guests disappeared from sight, Gwendolyn turned to Rick. "Well, we're on our own."

Rick thought about that a minute, and then replied, "Not really. This is two kinds of probation. One is to see if we belong together and the other is to see if I can run this place. They'll take care of you in any case. They'll protect you any way they can, and by whatever means they have to. That's going to include protecting you from me, if it comes to that."

"From what I've seen of you, there isn't anything about that I'd be afraid of."

"If you had any reservations about how I'd act alone with you, they'd have picked up on it, and I'd have watched you ride off with them just now. When the knot heads around here decide what they're going to try to do to me, you may end up wishing you were with them instead of with me."

Rick kept on looking out the window, but he felt Gwendolyn looking at him. "You make it sound really grim," she said finally.

He finally turned to her. "Then I must have gotten the message across. This won't look like a honeymoon, and I'm really sorry for that. Hell, neither of us asked for this. Maybe I should have spent my time this morning trying to talk you out of being married. Mark even asked me how good I am with a gun."

"What did you tell him?"

"I told him the truth. I might be able to learn, but it would take more practice than I'm likely to get in the immediate future. Do you shoot?"

An odd look crossed her face, immediately gone. "Me? I've never even handled a gun. What can we do if these guys decide to come after us?"

Rick's brow furrowed as he thought about it. "They aren't organized, and there was never a lot of courage going on around here before. I have to include myself in that comment. They might organize eventually. They might also get the courage to do something, most likely with the help of fermented beverages. Before that, I think it would be more like minor bits of harassment. They might try to intimidate you as a way to get at me."

"What about that guy who was the manager here? What was his name?"

"Kevin is his name. That's hard to say. It almost sounded like Mr. Maguire would use Kevin like those people in Ragan used you."

They walked into the kitchen, where Gwendolyn pushed Rick into a chair and then headed over to start taking care of the dishes.

"Do you want me to help with those?" Rick inquired.

"I recall you saying that in this house, I would be in charge. Well, you can sit in that chair, drink some coffee, and tell me something to make me smile."

"Okay. I think you're the prettiest nerd I've seen in six months. How's that?"

"Well, now, it's not like I have a whole lot of competition. I'll take that back. If I see you swooning as you look in the mirror, it could cause me a great deal of pain."

"I may look in the mirror now and then. I might even swoon, but it will be from fright more than anything."

Gwendolyn turned around, looked at Rick, and grinned. "There, did you see that? You made me smile. You did good. That keeps the dragon away. When you say things that make me worried or sad, the nasty old dragon starts creeping up close."

Rick saw the work crew approaching. "As much as I'd like to do my famous comedy routine, the guys are coming. I'm going to have to go tell them what we're doing now. Your knight gets to fight a dragon with one hand, and keep the ravening hordes at bay with the other. I don't recall reading about this in King Arthur. Wish me luck, my lady."

Out on the back porch, most of the guys were there, including the two guys who had been in the house, but left quietly the previous day. Counting up, Rick thought the only one missing was the loudmouth from yesterday.

One guy took a step forward. "Kevin being gone has been a breath of fresh air," he said. "So far, we like what we see of you. If old Duane gives you any trouble, just let us know. There are a couple of us who have a score to settle with him anyway. We saw Mark and Mr. Lillard leave, and from what we've seen, figured they must have given you our marching orders."

Rick was both amazed and relieved. "Now at least I have a name to go with his face. Duane doesn't really describe him."

That got a couple of chuckles, as well as low-voiced opinions of names that might describe him better.

"Our new project is to build a bunkhouse for all you guys, out in that big empty shed. Mark will start the list again, and we'll train women as well as men in the basics of horsemanship. The plan right now is for the women to be in the house, and the guys in the bunkhouse. We'll need to build accordingly. Yes, I said, 'we.' I plan on being out there swinging a hammer with all of you."

That got some approving nods.

"Speaking of the list, did any of you ever see it? We couldn't find it after Kevin left."

Everybody looked at each other and shook their heads. Gwendolyn came to the back door just then.

"Gentlemen, meet my wife, Gwendolyn. Please don't give her a bad time, okay?"

Gwendolyn smiled. "Maybe I could sometimes make up a treat or something for you guys. Would that be all right with you?"

The guy who had been the spokesman for the group spoke up. "Do you cook better than Rick?"

"I've never tasted his cooking, but they say I put out some pretty good stuff."

"You couldn't cook any worse than him. Oh, never, ever, let him make coffee. It reeks!"

That got laughter.

Gwendolyn grinned. "Rick offered to make coffee for Mr. Lillard, Mark, and their wives. I think it might have been a good thing that I made it instead. The way you guys talk, that could have gotten Rick a one-way ticket away from here."

Rick felt his face redden. "It's funny, but I never heard any of you volunteer to make it instead."

The response of, "We hoped it would poison Kevin and Duane," was greeted with whoops and laughter.

"Okay," Rick said after it quieted down a bit. "Mark will also take care of the candidates over at Harlan Ranch and the Lillard Place. If you guys could take care of the chores, that'll be it for the night. We'll hit it in the morning."

"What should we tell Duane?"

"I don't want anybody going around uninformed, so you guys will have to let him know. When and how much is up to you."

That evening went rather well, Rick thought. After the comments from the guys, Gwendolyn made it clear that the only thing Rick would do in the kitchen was eat. He was specifically to stay away from food preparation.

"You know," Rick told her, "it's very strange how the only comments I heard before this afternoon were along the lines of there not being enough, and it wasn't done soon enough. Anything about quality never saw the light of day."

Gwendolyn pointed a wooden spoon in his direction. "Maybe they were telling the truth about how they were hoping you'd poison Kevin and Duane."

After dinner, they moved into the living room, where they cuddled on the couch, each contributing a bit more about their past, some of the things that irritated them, along with their hopes for the future. There were exceptions, of course, but generally, their attitudes seemed to mesh rather well. Of course, Rick considered, that was only if they were telling each other the truth rather than what they thought the other wanted to hear.

Later, in bed, they did indeed harmonize in the center of the bed. Rick was true to his word, and when Gwendolyn later aimed him to a particular side of the bed, he simply went. Soon, however, she was over cuddling next to him. It wasn't long before the center of the bed included that side as well. When it was all done, Rick decided he didn't really care what side of the bed he was on, as long as Gwendolyn was there, too. Lyle had called that issue of the bed a trivial one. Whatever it had been, Rick was glad to be past it.

In the morning, Rick had to wander the house until Gwendolyn invited him into the kitchen for breakfast. He had to admit that what Gwendolyn cooked was infinitely better than the slop he'd put out. With food like this under his belt, Rick felt he was miles ahead of the rest of the guys, getting by on whatever slop the new cook gave them.

"I'd better get out there. I promised them I'd swing a hammer along with them, and I intend to keep my word. By the way, the breakfast you fixed was wonderful. Thank you. Oh, I have no idea what the others are doing for lunch, but I'm coming here." He gave her a deep kiss before he put on his coat and headed out the door to the job site. Gwendolyn favored him with a bright smile as he left. Even that smile promised to keep him warm for a while.

In the shed, Rick made sure everyone had a chance to express their opinion. One opinion, along with the mouth to express it, was missing. That was Duane. His absence didn't surprise Rick much. Several guys were quite specific that they passed the information along to him, but he shrugged it off like a light dusting of snow. He ate by himself and disappeared. There was some discussion and no agreement about what Duane's malfunction might be. There would have been more discussion, but Rick decided they'd better get moving on the bunkhouse.

By lunch time, they had the basic layout sketched on the floor of the shed. Several guys already left to locate lumber and other necessities for the project. Rick walked back up to his house for his first private married lunch, and felt pretty good about the whole thing. Inside, Gwendolyn had been busy, and the house looked cleaner than in quite some time. She also had lunch ready and waiting. It was quite miraculous, actually.

He gave her another deep kiss, along with the comment, "I think I could get used to this married life stuff."

She smiled as she reached up and ran a finger down his nose. "Any more kisses like that and your crew may have to get along without you this afternoon."

"I just might take you up on that, Mrs. Forbes."

She then pushed him toward the back door. "You'd better go do some great deeds for me then, sir knight."

That afternoon, they got some framing for the outer structure in place. The idea was to get a weather-tight shell with heat, and then they could work through whatever the weather threw at them. Rick thought that part alone might take the better part of a week. It wasn't like they could just call up the lumber yard and get materials, after all. Much of it was a case of making whatever they found work in spite of the fact that it wasn't exactly right. They had swiftly gone from 'build it right' back to the older concept of 'make do or do without.'

When it was time for chores, Rick left the guys to take care of that business, and headed for the house. Suddenly, he saw several horses next to it. That's when Rick recalled that Mark was going to stop by after they went to Huntley. Getting closer, he recognized Mark by the corner of the house next to the kitchen and back door. Vince, the deputy, was there as well, and it looked like they were discussing something. That's when Rick heard a confrontation inside.

Mark saw Rick coming, and even at that distance, Rick could see Mark had a relieved look on the one hand, and additional concern on the other. He motioned Rick over to where they were standing.

"We thought you two were having a major fight, and were trying to decide what to do next. Now it looks like you've got an intruder. Are any of your people not accounted for?"

"Duane is the only one. He's been missing all day."

"That sounds like him, Vince. How do we do this?"

Vince immediately went into tactical mode. "Mark, you take the front. Rick, we'll go in the back door. I don't care what we see inside, you stay behind me. Got that? Mark, go in whenever you're ready. We'll wait until you are through the front door before we enter."

Standing on the step by the back door, Rick could hear Duane inside, yelling, "This is my house. My house! Do you hear me? You don't belong here. Get out of here."

Rick heard Mark noisily open the front door and stomp inside. Just then, Vince hit the back door, his pistol drawn and cocked. Shocked, Duane turned toward the back door.

"What the …?" was all he got out, because the second he turned, Gwendolyn grabbed a cast-iron fry pan. It was on the stove, and red-hot. She hit the side of his head like a home run hitter swinging for the fences. A massive 'whomp' echoed through the kitchen as Duane dropped like a rock.

Duane finally came to, only to find Vince and Mark both nearby with weapons leveled at him.

Mark asked, "Do you have a word of wisdom for him, Rick?"

"Yes, I do. Duane, you're fired."

Mark nodded. "That sounds pretty wise to me. Since our sleeping beauty is conscious again, Gwendolyn, could you tell us what happened, please?"

"I was starting supper, and he burst through the kitchen door. He stopped and stared at me. Then he yelled, 'Who are you? Get out. This is my house. I'm in charge here. It's my house. Kevin told me.' I told him it wasn't his house any more, and that he needed to leave right then. He didn't want to hear anything I said."

Rick spoke up then, but there was some venom in his voice. "Did he touch you, Gwendolyn?"

"No, Rick, he didn't. I think he was going to grab me. Suddenly, he started coughing. It was a really violent cough. After he caught his breath, he started shouting again, repeating the same stuff. He took a couple of steps toward me. I backed up, kind of looking around for what might be here that I could use to defend myself. After those couple of steps, though, he stopped, and just started sobbing. While that was going on, he said a couple of things, but I couldn't make out what he was saying."

Gwendolyn thought for a moment, and added, "I don't know how long it went on. It might have been five or ten minutes. After the crying jag, he was suddenly back yelling at me again. It was like he was on drugs or something."

Vince looked down at Duane. "Is that it Duane? There are plenty of prescription drugs around yet. They're old enough that there's no telling what they might do. Have you been swallowing a bunch of pills, Duane?"

"No sir," came from Duane. The words had respect but the tone was sullen, Rick thought.

Duane turned so the injured part of his face became visible. Vince chuckled. "That was a pretty good slap with that frying pan. Duane, I believe you'll be carrying the brand of that frying pan manufacturer for quite a while."

"I didn't do anything," Duane whined. "I live here. This is my place. Nobody can take it away from me. Kevin told me so."

Mark shook his head. "Kevin worked for Mr. Lillard and he also worked for me. He no longer works here. What he told you doesn't count any more. I'm not even sure he told you anything like that, Duane. From what I'm hearing, you could have just thought he said something like that. Maybe you wished he said that."

Vince looked at Mark. "Could Duane be confused? Is it possible he thought he still lived here?"

Mark shook his head. "Lyle Lillard introduced Rick to everybody as the new manager here. Rick did not stutter when he said Duane and the other two guys had to move out of the house. The two other guys weren't confused. Lyle and I were not confused when we heard him tell Duane. We also heard Duane threaten to get back at Rick."

Vince looked at Duane, still on the floor. "Duane, old son, you're in it up to your eyeballs. Your crimes include breaking and entering, assault with intent to commit bodily harm, and maybe even terroristic threats."

"I want a lawyer."

"There are no such animals any more, Duane. Also, since we're still under martial law, it will be up to Lyle Lillard what happens to your sorry ass. Now roll over on your stomach. I have a pair of handcuffs just your size. For the record, you do have the right to remain silent. I'd recommend you use that right, since if you start talking, everybody will know you're an idiot."

Vince got Duane cuffed, and then looked at Rick. "We thought we might have to handle a case of wife beating. After seeing Gwendolyn handle that frying pan, I no longer have any such fears."

He drug Duane up onto his feet at the same time. "Gwendolyn, we'll let you and Rick get on with your evening. Mark and I have more than enough information to give Lyle Lillard. That's our next stop. We're going to have to get moving to get it done before dark."

Rick heard chuckles and whispers outside the kitchen window. He glanced over in time to see a couple of heads ducking down. News about this would be at the other house within minutes, inflating with every telling. Rick could only hope that he would not suffer too greatly in the retellings. He glanced over at Mark, who apparently saw the same thing. Mark grinned and shook his head. Evidently he and Mark were on the same page for that one.

Rick crossed the room to Gwendolyn, who still had the frying pan. He gently took it from her, and set it back on the stove, hoping she never felt the need to use it on him. The side of Duane's face was still red, and a couple of blisters were starting to show. As to having the manufacturer's name branded on him, Rick couldn't see it. As far as that went, he didn't think there was any kind of logo on the bottom of the pan. At the same time, it might help the story gain momentum, and might even make some people stare at Duane a bit longer than they might otherwise.

Mark and Vince took Duane out the front door. Rick followed, watching them leave. As he shut the front door, Duane stumbled as they forced him to lead them on foot down the muddy, half-frozen road, it suddenly occurred to Rick that Duane lost more than his job. He also lost his license to have and use a horse. He had some sympathy for that kind of thing. Then he looked at Gwendolyn and decided that whatever Duane got would be pretty easy compared to some of the things Rick could have come up with himself.

"I think he's crazy, Rick," Gwendolyn said softly but assertively. "He must be insane. What would make him act like that, do you think?"

"Beats me. You were more into the social networking thing. There were people I tried to work with over the internet, and I swear there were times I would have loved to have a way to reach through the computer and just shake them really hard."

Gwendolyn reached around to give him a hug. "Yeah, there were plenty like that. So, you said you'd unfriend anybody messing with me. Are you going to do it?"

"From what I can see, the network administrator will cancel his Facebook account. That saves me from having to worry about it."

"Ooh. That would be the ultimate punishment. I just remembered I was going to fix something fancy tonight, but all this happened. I'll just have to throw something together. What are you in the mood for?"

"Kisses from Gwendolyn," Rick promptly replied.

"You are a romantic devil, aren't you. Well, you can have those for dessert. Come in the kitchen and tell me about your day."

Chapter 8

Duane Takes a Walk

Vince and Mark, both mounted, walked Duane down the road, his handcuffs attached to a lasso. They had Duane walk in front of them, and he kept up a pretty good pace, considering that a cold north wind was blowing and the snow was picking up. Every few minutes, Mark rode up beside Duane and tried to get him to talk. As Vince listened, Duane's ability to speak coherently improved as they got farther from Wagon Ranch. That was in spite of his having to deal with a forced march and frigid air.

By the time they got to the Lillard place, Duane was stumbling. Part of it was because of pushing through the fresh powder that got deeper as the snow continued to fall. Another issue was that he appeared to be nearing exhaustion. There was also the possibility of a concussion from the mean frying pan that Gwendolyn laid on him. In spite of all that, he appeared to be in better shape mentally now than at any time since they burst into the house.

It all made Vince's mind focus on the ranch itself. As a deputy, it was common knowledge the previous residents of the place were into drug trafficking of some kind, but even with State and Federal assistance, they had never been able to pin anything on them. They were certain the freight wagon and horses, which the group hauled around the country and displayed in parades was connected. They checked the equipment and property closely a number of times, often with drug dogs. The dogs seemed to pick up something, but there nothing made them actually alert. It was as though the dogs were puzzled.

Was it possible that whatever they brought in was still there? If so, what kind of drug could it be? It apparently drove Duane temporarily insane. Why didn't the substance have that effect on everyone else?

Inside, Mr. Lillard had Vince remove the shackles, and instructed Duane to sit on a straight wooden chair facing the sofa. Mark then told what he'd seen and done. After that, Vince added additional details. When he finished, Vince asked for permission to get a bit of additional information from Duane.

"Where did you stay the last several days?"

"When they threw me out of the house, I went to the other house and stayed in a back room. Rick was certain that I was going to put together a mutiny. He thought I was dumb enough to try. It wasn't so. I knew there was no way to win doing that kind of thing. I stayed in the room and didn't talk to anybody. There was no way to keep the room warm, so I stuffed paper and rags into every crack to keep the wind out. Pretty soon I heard through the door about what a great guy Rick was, so I stuffed rags under the door, as well. Something about the stale air made me sleepy. I had really strange dreams."

Lyle leaned forward. "What made you go to the main house?"

Duane shook his head and looked at the floor. "I halfway woke up. The place was quiet and the sun was up. I didn't know where I was or what was going on. I staggered out of the room and went outside. The guys were doing chores, so I headed for where I knew I lived. The rest of it is like Mark and Vince told it."

Duane suddenly started to shake and sob. After a few moments of that, he had a coughing fit. Vince and Mark looked at each other. This was just like he did in the house. They both moved to just behind his shoulders. Sure enough, he finally got his coughing under control, only to look around, wild-eyed. Mark and Vince immediately each grabbed a shoulder.

"Calm down, Duane," Vince told him, squeezing his shoulder hard to ensure he got the point.

Vince thought it was interesting that Duane managed to calm down at that point. Part of it might have been seeing that he was in the Lillard house. Lyle looked at all three of them.

"Is this how he acted at Wagon Ranch?"

Mark nodded. "Yes, but he was doing a lot more of it."

Mark then looked down at Duane. "What is going on when you have those fits?"

"I get completely angry. It doesn't feel like I have any control over it. Then I can't breathe and I get a coughing fit. About then, I just think what a worthless piece of shit I am. After that, something tells me that's not right, and it starts all over again."

"That isn't what happened just now, though, is it?" Lyle observed.

"Not exactly. When you made me think about what I did, that made me think how worthless I was. Then I lost my breath. After that, I wanted to hit anybody around."

A number of emotions ran across his face at that point. Finally he added, "I'm really sorry I messed things up."

Lyle stood up, staring out the window at the snow, which continued to get heavier. Then he turned around and faced Duane.

"There could be a good argument for keeping you under observation for several days at a minimum. The outburst I just saw certainly votes in that direction. Just like it happened with the McCook evacuation, the weather is forcing actions we're not ready for. There is no place suitable to hold you in any case."

Vince wasn't sure where he was going. Lyle continued, "There are plenty of jobs around here, and nowhere near enough people to do them. Clay needs an apprentice for his farrier and blacksmith shop. That couple we found who are experts on how to use our native plants are another case. Which would you prefer, Mr. Walsh?"

Duane seemed shocked that Lyle called him by his last name, but managed to stammer, "I'd rather not do the blacksmith stuff. I can try to learn about the plants and all that."

Lyle nodded. "We'll try you with them. Keep this in mind, Duane. You will work at something. If Charles and Marcie do not find your work satisfactory in all respects, you will work with Clay. Do you understand me, sir?"

Duane nodded.

Lyle looked at Vince. "Take him into Ragan. Put him in a storeroom in the school basement until the weather clears. Keep a posse member nearby. When he goes, I want you to personally escort him to his new employment."

"I'll do that, Lyle. How should I take him?"

"You had better not make him walk in this weather. I'll have one of my apprentices take him in my farm wagon. To remind Mr. Walsh not to have any more episodes, put those cuffs back on him. Secure him in the wagon so that he won't bother the driver."

When he finally got home, Vince had quite a tale to tell when Beth asked how his day went. She knew he was going to check on Gwendolyn, and was really interested in how she was getting along. When Vince got to the part where Gwendolyn defended herself with a red-hot cast-iron skillet, Beth giggled a little.

"Just imagine," she said, "that gal could have cold-cocked all four families quite easily. I can't imagine why she didn't."

"From what Mark told me, the four families decided how they thought Madeleine should be, and she played the role as expected. That was why she could only put together an escape plan once they turned her over to Nancy Rowley. The real Gwendolyn stood up when confronted by a raving lunatic."

She cocked her head, which Vince knew meant she was announcing a new subject. "Did you say something about the possibility of drugs hidden in or around Wagon Ranch?"

"Yeah, and what bothers me is what could happen if we get really deep snow so the houses don't have any circulation. It may hit people differently, depending on their personality and health. Gwendolyn being over there under those conditions might be a real problem, considering how she reacted to the four families."

"Did you warn them about that?"

"It didn't occur to me until later. I will be sure to tell them after this storm. Have the kids been behaving themselves today?"

"Spying on the four families has become such a way of life for them, they were doing it again today. Rachel says she and her brothers want to see how the families get by without Gwendolyn around to do everything for them."

"What have they found out?"

"So far, the ladies from the other three families were at the Stamford house most of the morning. They may be trying to remember how to get things done. The group may also be plotting revenge, but that's my personal take on it."

"What do you think about trying to be friends with them now?"

"I am going to leave them alone for now. They would undoubtedly hold the fact that we're married against me. Even if they didn't, there are other issues. If I took a covered dish over to them at this point, I'm afraid they'd hit me up to do their cooking all the time, and that isn't about to happen."

The snow quit for a short time the next day, so Vince bulled his way through knee-deep snow to the schoolhouse to collect Duane. This time, both were on foot, with a couple of posse members accompanying them. Fortunately, Charles and Marcie were in a small place not very far from there. The pair insisted on staying in their tent until the snow got too deep. Now, at least, they were in a house that was halfway air-tight.

The pair came from Holdrege, trying to stay away from civil unrest which happened not long before the Omega dust went through. Mark and Josh found them. They were camped with another couple. The other couple's tent was a short distance down the hill from them. The slight difference in elevation turned out to be a matter of life and death, as they watched their friends evaporate in the Omega dust.

Neither were anywhere close to being past the experience, but seemed to be doing better the last couple of months. They had expertise in knowing what plants in the area could be used for food, as well as what other uses they might have. Vince thought Duane's place was in the blacksmith's shop, but Lyle was calling the shots. There was also the fact that Lyle had quite a track record of success.

Vince tried to explain to Charles and Marcie what they could do with Duane. There was quite a long time when he wasn't sure whether he'd managed to get the idea across to them. Finally, the light came on in Marcie's eyes.

She took Duane to a counter and showed him some seeds. Whether Duane, in turn, was absorbing the information she was putting out was unclear, but when she indicated that he should grind up the seeds with a mortar and pestle, he set to work. Vince got the impression that his efforts were not what Marcie was looking for, but she seemed satisfied in the results of his first effort.

Outside, Vince told his posse members to stop by several times a day to make sure Duane wasn't flying off the handle, and to do a basic welfare check on everybody in the house. That task complete, Vince considered his next project had better start with heading for home to be a husband and father for the duration of the storm.

Chapter 9

Honey Moon

As the snow kept falling, Rick was quite happy to stay inside the main house at Wagon Ranch. To pass the time, he described what they planned to do with the bunkhouse. Gwendolyn brought up a couple of additional points that Rick decided to pursue them when he could. That opportunity was not going to be right away, he knew.

They sat close to each other at the table during dinner, rubbing knees which thoroughly distracted Rick. All at once, Gwendolyn brought up another point.

"You know, Rick, Mark came straight here from Huntley. We never heard a word about what he and Lyle found out about Kevin's situation with the Maguire family."

"That's right. Maybe it just wasn't the time or occasion."

"It might also be that he didn't think about it. Say, didn't Mr. Lillard say something about coming tomorrow?"

A gust of wind brought Rick back into the present tense with a vengeance. He glanced at the kitchen window. "It looks like a major snow storm. How's the supply of wood?"

Gwendolyn shrugged. "What would I know? You're closer to the door. The immediate wood pile is under the little shed roof. What did you think it was for, a place to wait for the bus?"

Rick nodded. "That makes sense to have it there. They always made me go all the way over to the main wood pile, even with the snow. Come to think of it, they made me go more often in the snow."

Opening the door slightly, he looked to the side where a shed roof came away from the house. "The shed is nearly full of wood. Maybe that's what the two guys were doing this afternoon. The snow never started this time of day before. Does that bode good or ill for how much we'll get?"

As he shut the door, Gwendolyn came over and wrapped her arms around his neck. "Maybe what we're seeing is that since Mark and Lyle Lillard didn't see fit to give us time for a honeymoon, the weather gods took pity on our situation and gave us the best possible excuse to have one."

"That works for me," Rick replied. "If I can't get out to supervise the guys and pass along your great ideas, you're going to need to refresh my memory. You'll probably need to do it a number of times."

"I wouldn't do that. You might get the impression that I was nagging."

Rick bent forward slightly and rubbed noses with her. "Coming from you, it could never be nagging. It could only be wise wifely advice."

"There is no doubt in my mind that I'll need to remind you that you made that statement. Not only did you make it, but you did it voluntarily, and with no gun pointed at you."

"We won't mention pans alongside the head."

"No, we won't mention that. You should try to remember. I noticed it impressed deputy Vince a great deal."

"I think it made a deeper impression on Duane. Speaking of Vince, he lives in Ragan. Why didn't he rescue you himself?"

Gwendolyn nodded. "Nobody outside the four families was allowed to know about me. Vince and his family were at the very top of the list of people kept in the dark. They didn't have much trouble avoiding Vince since he was always traveling around Harlan.

"His wife was more of a problem, since she kept trying to be the good neighbor. She often showed up with small gifts of things she had made. It nearly got out of control after the dust came through but before they found Vince. Still, they had a strategy. They escorted me out the back door when she came to the front door. The families had adjoining back yards, so that worked just fine."

Gwendolyn came to a full stop at that point. "Here I am, carrying on like I agreed with what they were doing. Anyway, Vince's kids were the really big problem. They showed up at the strangest times and for little or no reason at all. At least, that was the opinion of the families I so willingly served."

"I have to think that made your going to work for Mrs. Rowley even more problematic."

"Indeed it did. A couple of things tipped the scale. They knew Mr. Rowley was always running around with his freight wagons. When he wasn't hauling stuff for other people, he was collecting items for himself. They knew he had accumulated a great many things. My families knew about quite a bit of it, especially what he had stored in Ragan. When my ladies heard about what was there, they naturally lusted after it. Also, Mr. Rowley made a point of grousing about how hard his poor wife had to work to keep their livery stable and home at all livable. My families saw a way to make a trade that could make everyone happy. That way was little old me."

Rick grinned. "Little, quiet as a mouse, and saving your powder for a battle you could win."

"You got it." Gwendolyn gave him a kiss. "Well, maybe not all that little, but I'll allow the rest of your statement. Come on, let's go into the living room, and cuddle on the couch. We can still keep an eye on the weather from there."

"Did Don Rowley ever give them anything?"

"My families had no idea how fast Don could accept favors, or just how slow he might be about returning them. He hadn't gotten around to computing the value my presence added to his well-being when Nancy Rowley did her thing. If Mr. Rowley gave them anything, he did it purely out of the goodness of his heart."

They were on the couch, and starting to share body heat by that time. Rick chuckled, "Ah, yes. The goodness of Don Rowley's heart is truly a marvel to behold."

"It would be a marvel if there was anything to behold. What interests me right now is the hardness of your muscles, Mr. Forbes."

"Yes, indeed, my biceps are really looking good," Rick said flexing his free arm.

"That's a nice muscle, but that isn't the one I'm working on."

"How about my triceps or my deltoids?"

"None of them, although you're going the right direction."

The discussion about Rick's anatomy proceeded. Outside, the snow piled up while the wind crafted the snow into incredible drifts that would take several days to plow. Rick might have considered the weather gods Gwendolyn talked about were indeed worthy of his worship. He would have, but had neither a clue or a care about anything happening beyond what his wife had in mind to do next.

They awoke to a morning so dark, it was hard to tell if the sun had come up. Rick's main clue was that he always got up the same time, and his internal clock told him it was half past time for him to be moving. Voting against was the warmth under the comforters. As he hesitated, Gwendolyn decided it was time to act, throwing back the covers and hitting the floor. Rick shivered, but considered that since he gave her the house, her making the decision was only right and proper. He just wished she hadn't made it so soon.

One point about the absence of central heating, together with the tendency for even the best wood stoves to finally die out overnight, was the fact that floors were incredibly cold, and sub-freezing temperatures inside the house made it imperative to dress quickly. There was no way anybody would run around the house naked. At least it wouldn't happen until after the high-efficiency stove in the living room and the cook stove in the kitchen were both not only revived but roaring.

The reason for Gwendolyn getting up became apparent after Rick considered how fast she not only dressed, but also donned her outdoors clothing. It was only twenty feet outside the door to the outhouse, and most times, the consensus was that it needed to be farther away. Now, as he watched Gwendolyn push out through the door, Rick decided it was already too far. With her taking her life in her hands to relieve herself, Rick started to work getting the fires in both stoves going again.

Fortunately, since there were still live coals in the heating stove, he rebuilt it without much trouble. He soon transported some fire into the kitchen. The place was still cold, but at least there was the promise of warmer times to come when Gwendolyn got back. On the other hand, those warmer times took a great deal longer to arrive than he wanted. Curiously, she seemed in good spirits, and her eyes were sparkling as she shook the snow off her coat and boots.

"How could you possibly have a good time going to the outhouse in a blizzard?"

"If I was still working for the families in Ragan, they would make me trek coatless and barefoot between all of the houses. It's a hundred feet from one back door to the next. Not only that, they had me choring away in all four homes each day, complaining the whole time that I did things far too slowly. This was just twenty feet, and I only went because I wanted to."

Rick nodded. "I guess that if you've gotten accustomed to people shoving two by fours under your fingernails, putting up with bamboo splinters isn't too bad. It's still a shame that we are in a house with an indoor bathroom, and all we can do with it is store stuff there."

"Do you need to go?"

"Me? I did what I needed to do by the wood pile. Speaking of which, I need to bring in some more wood and stoke both fires."

It wasn't long before Gwendolyn started to work her magic in the kitchen. Rick knew no construction would happen until the storm was over. That left him wondering what he could do that would justify the faith Lyle Lillard and Mark Tahner had bestowed upon him by making him manager at Wagon Ranch.

Sitting at the kitchen table, nursing a cup of coffee, Rick became aware of a tapping at the back door. There were two of the guys.

"Come on in out of the snow, guys," Rick invited.

"Thank you, sir," the one said. "We just moved wood up to the shed outside the door, and wanted to make sure you all were okay." Rick was astonished. "You guys came all the way up here through that storm? You must be crazy."

"We saw you go to the wood pile through worse weather than this. Anyway, we know where the snowdrifts are, and just route around them. We took a break from working on the bunkhouse to come up here."

"How are you able to do anything there?"

"Some of the wood we needed came in yesterday. We're just doing what we can with what we've got. There were too many people and too few supplies for us to make much of a difference, anyway. Chores are getting done, by the way."

Gwendolyn came over to them. "Would you gentlemen like some coffee? How about something to eat?"

"Oh, we wouldn't want to be a bother, ma'am. We just wanted to make sure you were both okay."

Rick couldn't help himself. "Did I see the two of you yesterday when Vince and Mark resolved Duane's problem?"

They both grinned. Rick nodded and asked, "What did the guys think about all of that? I'm sure you told them."

"They all thought it was funny as hell. Duane sure bought his ticket, doing that. The best part was the way you punched his ticket, ma'am. Do you think it realigned his brain?"

Gwendolyn smiled slightly. "I'm sure I did. The trouble is that once you've got scrambled eggs, you can hit them all day, and they'll never be one bit less scrambled. About all you can do is cook the damn things."

That got both of them laughing and snorting.

Rick was still working on what they were doing. "I'm glad we were able to brighten your day. So, what brought you up here this morning?"

"We thought you're already such an improvement over Duane that everybody agreed we need to do what we can to make sure you're okay."

"This was a welfare check?"

"Yeah, kind of like that. We'd better head back before the guys decide they need to rescue us."

"Well, let them know that I appreciate them pushing ahead with the bunkhouse. If you like me being the manager here, that will count for more than almost anything."

The two took off then, and a couple of minutes later, Rick realized he didn't know their names. That wasn't a good indicator among managers. At least, that's what he'd heard.

Gwendolyn tapped on his shoulder, as he stood there looking at the closed back door.

"Can I offer you something to eat sir? Would it offend your high moral standards if I helped you eat it?"

"Gwendolyn, you can sit on my lap and help me eat it if you want." "Ooh. Goody." She walked over to the window and stared out through the snow.

"Now what?" Rick inquired.

"Those two made me realize our privacy may not be what I'd like. If I'm going to sit on your lap, I want to feel where I'm sitting, and I don't need any witnesses."

She dished up breakfast and then pulled down both her pants and his like it was part of the menu.

After breakfast, Rick couldn't remember what he ate but he knew every detail about what he had. Gwendolyn sent him out for buckets of clean snow that she could melt. The hand pump outside was buried, and more snow was coming in. Rick agreed her solution made perfect sense. He made sure that he didn't pick up any yellow snow.

When Gwendolyn declared him persona non grata in the kitchen, Rick wandered into the former bathroom and wondered how they could get water in there. They did it in Arapahoe, and he heard they wanted to move the equipment to Orleans. That made the question one of what he would have to offer Don Rowley to get solar panels and the special water pump he'd need? Come to think of it, he'd heard some of the guys talk about some solar-powered wells for agriculture.

Since he had this crew, maybe they could find wells like that, grab the equipment, and use it here, both for this house and the bunkhouse as well.

He wandered into the living room, recalling a notepad there, and started a to do list. It might be something to talk about with Mark and Lyle at some point.

Since both of them had solar power and running water, maybe he could get a sympathetic ear. Having those reminders of civilization for the bunkhouse should make the prospect of coming to Wagon Ranch even more desirable than it already was.

"Hey!" came from Gwendolyn in the kitchen. "What's going on? What are you doing?"

Rick was about to answer when he heard scraping and hammering from the back of the house. That brought him running into the kitchen. Gwendolyn was a few feet away from the back door, where all the racket originated. She looked at him, almost in a panic. Rick's thought it might be a bear, but realized they would be in hibernation. The sound didn't go with dogs or wolves.

He took a deep breath and pulled open the door, only to find himself totally dumbfounded. A covered walkway headed toward the woodpile and outhouse. It gave access to the wood storage next to the house. Rick tried to imagine what effort the guys had made to get this done so fast. On top of it, the snow in the passage was gone.

A panel opened a little way down the passage, and the two guys from before breakfast stepped in, grinning.

"You look surprised, Rick. I guess we did our job, then."

Gwendolyn was beside Rick by that time. "You did that, for sure," she told them. "By the way, Rick never told me your names."

"I'm John Parkhurst, and this is Dan Goble. It's likely Rick didn't know our names. Kevin and Duane isolated him from everyone else. Kevin seemed to like Rick until the McCook evacuation. When Rick came back with congratulations and praise from Mark and Mr. Lillard, it was like Kevin felt obligated to destroy him. Dan and I came out here less than a week before the evacuation began, so we knew about him."

"What's the deal with the walkway?" Rick wondered.

"Oh, we figured your lady would have to make a lot more trips to the outhouse than you would. We also thought the snow would get worse before it got any better. We thought this was a better use for the lumber we scrounged than what we could manage starting on a bunkhouse. Call it a wedding present."

Gwendolyn shook her head. "I'm flattered you thought about my problems. Come on in. While that area is enclosed, I don't think we can keep it warm. Get everybody else working on this, and get them inside as well. Dan, fetch all the people. John, get your butt in the kitchen."

John grinned. "If it's okay with you, ma'am, I'll go with Dan. We'll get them inside a lot quicker that way."

"Don't bother knocking this time. Just open the door and come on in," Gwendolyn ordered.

When the door closed, she looked at Rick. "Did they see us?"

"I don't know. I don't think so. If they did, they had the good sense to not smirk. Did you want to do it again, in case they missed something?"

"I was never into public exhibitions, especially involving too much of me showing. Let's wait a little while. It was fun, though, wasn't it?"

Rick grinned at her, and gave her a kiss. That's all the time he had in any case since the crew started piling on into the kitchen just then. Somehow, Gwendolyn managed to get enough coffee together. Even that drew rave reviews, which inspired her to whip up some really delightful things she was pleased to call snacks.

Rick decided this might as well be a meeting. "I really appreciate what you guys did. The bunkhouse project is still on, though, and we need to get after it. As fast as you built the walkway, the bunkhouse should be no problem. I realize that won't happen until we lose enough snow to be able to find more lumber. I've got another idea to run past you guys. Would it be possible to find some solar-powered agricultural wells and put them in our wells?"

Dan perked up when Rick said that. "I used to install those. I even know where a number of them are. Old Mr. Rowley does not own them all, not by any means. They're not hard to put in."

John was nodding, listening to Dan. "Having running water has been on our wet dream list, if you'll pardon the expression, ma'am. Do you think we could do something like that, Rick?"

Rick considered the situation for a moment. "I was going to clear it through Mark and Lyle Lillard. I will, anyway, but this is a project we can do on our own. We can probably rig the existing sinks and toilets. I don't imagine the water pressure would be all that great, but just being able to turn on a tap or flush a toilet would be a great deal."

"You'd like that better than getting buckets of snow, would you?" John commented.

Rick took a deep breath on that one, and decided that playing straight man was his only way out. "When the hand pump is buried in snow, buckets of the stuff get the job done."

"Well, when you get about two-thirds of the way to the outhouse, you'll see the hand pump in a sort of alcove. I think we'd better get going for the other place while we can still do it."

They shuffled on out.

It wasn't long before Gwendolyn decided she'd test out the great new addition, and headed for the outhouse. When she got back, Rick glanced at her.

"Was it everything you hoped for?"

She pursed her lips. "It was everything I hoped for and more. As a matter of fact, there's something you just have to see."

Now she really had his curiosity stirred up. She led him straight out the kitchen door ten feet.

"Now, turn around and look at the wood storage next to the house."

Rick saw a definite opening in the wall. Not only that, but the wood wasn't stacked there. There was enough room for one or two people to peer through the hole. On closer inspection, Rick saw it was an existing hole, but recently enlarged. Looking through it gave a good view of most of the kitchen.

"We've been giving peep shows. I don't recall getting a share of the money usually required for such things," Rick told her.

"Those were my thoughts as well. What should we do about it?"

"What say we go back inside and figure out exactly how to handle this."

By early afternoon, a fine wire led to a tiny bell. They had tested it several times, and Gwendolyn volunteered to play a special part. The weather was clearing, and Rick dug a trail from the front door around the house to the covered walkway, being careful to avoid the existing path. Then they waited to see who might come to the party.

That waiting was not easy. "You know, if I'd trained to be a hunter, this waiting might feel more natural," Rick told Gwendolyn.

"Ha!" she replied. "Just try being the bait in your own trap for a while. This is really the pits. There is one thing, though. This is the first thing you and I have decided to do together, other than be married."

Rick nodded. "Okay, except that getting married was not something you and I decided. It was only afterward we chose to make a go of it."

Gwendolyn grinned at him. "You picked up on that. You really are a bright boy, aren't you?"

Just then there came a tinkling sound from the kitchen.

"It must be show time, Gwendolyn. Give me a minute to get around the house. You really don't mind doing this?"

"Maybe there is a little exhibitionist to go with my modesty. I'll act like I'm doing something at the stove, and then wander over to the spot we picked."

Rick gave her a kiss and took off out the front door, circling the house as fast as he could. At the covered walkway, he caught his breath and made sure the one panel would actually open. He only did a fraction of an inch, and then stopped, listening intently. When it came, there was no confusing what Gwendolyn was doing.

"How do you like this?" he heard her say clearly.

The plan was for Gwendolyn to drop her pants and moon whoever was behind the hole in the wall. Rick heard a couple of sharp intakes of air inside the walkway. That was his cue. He threw open the panel, throwing bright daylight on the two figures crouched next to the wall in the wood bin. They stared at his silhouette in the doorway.

"Hello, John. Hello, Dan. Did you get a really good show? I hope so, because now you owe us a show of your own. You two will start by repairing the hole in the wall. It is a safety and health issue. After all, there's no telling what could get through there. Also, the cold outside air creates a real draft in the kitchen. Bugs and mice could go right on into the house. For all I know, peeping toms might take advantage of the situation."

John and Dan both scrambled to their feet. "Right, Rick. We'll get right on it. We just noticed it ourselves and were about to do something about it. We didn't want to disturb you guys, what with you having just gotten married and all."

Gwendolyn opened the kitchen door, crossed her arms, and smirked as she leaned against the door jam. "Are you really buying any of this, Rick?"

Rick snorted. "I think the bullshit is deeper than the snow right now. You looked really stupid, with both of you trying to stare through the same knothole. When I go to take care of the Rowley's computer, I'll mention to Nancy Rowley about a couple of young studs who really need matched up with suitable females."

Gwendolyn looked at him appraisingly. "Are you declaring yourself a satisfied customer?"

"I can't complain. Our first meeting went a good deal further than simply getting acquainted. However, you two are burning daylight. I'm glad you volunteered to take care of it. Find something to fill the hole, and then seal it, both on the inside and the outside. If you find any other holes in my house, you can take care of them, as well. Also, that area in the wood bin next to the house needs to be filled with firewood, if you don't mind."

John's embarrassment morphed into nervousness. "Are you serious about getting us instant wives?"

"Instant marriage seems to be the 'in' thing right now."

"If we get this fixed really well and really fast, could you put off that talk with Mrs. Rowley for a while?"

"I'll think about it. Right now, the only thing that's working is your jaw. I'm not impressed."

They patched the hole. They were able to fill the hole quite well, and both the exterior and interior repairs looked good. Rick thought they seemed really interested in getting excused at that point. Later, Rick and Gwendolyn talked about it.

"I'm glad there were just two of them. I had visions of opening that panel to find the entire congregation lined up for a look."

"How do you know they didn't already have their look, and John and Dan were the last ones?"

"I don't, but I'll take the existing evidence for the time being. That must have been quite a moon you shot them. They were drooling all over the wall when I opened the panel."

"Well, dearest husband, there are moons and then there are moons."

"Maybe I should have joined them at the knothole, then."

"Why don't you come with me, and I'll show you what I did."

"Oh, ho. A private show. That's cool."

"That's what marriage gives you, sir. You get your very own private shows. You may get more of a show than you want or can handle. On the other hand, you're going to get them anyway."

Rick joined her in the doorway. "I can hardly wait. It's for the rest of my life, you say. I believe I will lock the doors as we go, though. As you said, it is private."

After two days of clear weather, the snow plows got out to Wagon Ranch. Since they only compacted and smoothed the snow, rather than trying to remove it, the driveway was now halfway up the windows. Rick devoted time and effort to cut and compact a stairway that now went up three steps instead of down two steps to the ground. It was a lot of snow. The level dropped as the direct sunshine compacted the snow level and settled it further. Rick supposed some of it might get absorbed by the soil, as well.

When the snow plow teams got to the house, Gwendolyn invited them all in for coffee and conversation. They said that Lyle specifically asked them to clear the road to the Harlan Ranch, and from there to the Wagon Ranch. They said they would now work on the roads to Oxford and Orleans. Rick inquired if they could clear the road over to the other place on Wagon Ranch before they left, and they agreed to do that.

After the snow plow teams departed, Rick looked at Gwendolyn. "My guess is company is coming, and it will most likely be tomorrow."

"Do you think you need to work over at the other place, or do you think you could help me put this house together a little better?"

"It behooves me to help you out. The guys at the other place have proven they can think up enough stuff. They don't need any additional help from me. Mark and Lyle will want another little bit of management by wandering around, or MBWO. We'll all find out together what they've been up to."

True to form, the two couples constituting the first families of Harlan showed up the next day. Rick watched for them, and concluded that if the snow got any deeper, he'd need a periscope to see anybody coming to call. Rick and Gwendolyn were able to get their coats on, and were standing in front of their half-buried house when their distinguished guests arrived. Out of the corner of his eye, Rick saw two riders coming from the other place. Obviously, they'd figured it out as well.

Lyle took one look at everything and burst out laughing. "What did you do with your house? I almost rode right by it."

"It's become a basement apartment."

"How on Earth do you get to your woodpile, pump, and outhouse?"

"The guys were kind enough to take care of that for us. You can't tell much from the outside now."

"This I've got to see. You two haven't killed each other yet. That's a really good sign."

Rick gave Gwendolyn a hug, and felt her answer him in kind. "I'm sure there are a lot of things we'll end up disagreeing about. One thing we've agreed is that we want to be together."

Rick blinked, almost astonished to hear himself say it that way. He looked at Gwendolyn, who favored him with a smile, and then back at their visitors. "Well, the guys are just about here. They'll take care of your horses. Come on in and make yourselves comfortable."

One thing Rick was not going to bring up or even talk about if at all possible was the way he'd handled the situation with John and Dan. He hadn't discussed it with Gwendolyn, but supposed that, given her self-proclaimed modesty, she'd be disinclined to bring it up. In the house, the three ladies headed for the kitchen, and Gwendolyn advised Rick that the men should just stay in the living room.

It wasn't long before there was the sound of giggles coming from the kitchen, along with the comment from Ellen, "You didn't!"

Nearly hysterical laughter followed. Rick found Mark and Lyle both looking him.

"What's that about, I wonder?" Mark commented.

Rick had a pretty good idea, but responded, "It's probably a woman thing. If they choose to talk about it, there's little doubt I'll be sitting here with a red face."

Lyle nodded. "That's a fair amount of wisdom, coming from one so young. I'm also reading that there's been more than a honeymoon in the snow drift happening around here."

Rick felt his face flush slightly. "Yeah, well, there's a lot of snow, but that didn't mean things ever got boring."

The ladies came out with coffee then. That kept Rick from saying anything more incriminating. On the other hand, it greatly expanded his opportunities to put his foot in his mouth. He knew he had a tendency to be that way around women anyway. Cups of coffee got passed around, and all the couples reunited. Gwendolyn sat very close to Rick, looking like she was really fighting back a need to laugh. So did the other two ladies, for that matter. Adeline got her composure first.

"Rick, Gwendolyn tells me that you managed to take care of a small personnel problem here. Gwendolyn was able to help, and did it in a rather unique manner."

Ellen burst out laughing while Gwendolyn grinned at him. Rick just shook his head.

"Gwendolyn came up with a way to take care of what you termed a small personnel problem. I did some grunt work for it. Judging from the laughter we heard in the kitchen, Gwendolyn told it a great deal better than I could ever hope to."

Ellen got her laughter under control for a moment. "From what Gwendolyn said, when she showed you how she distracted those two, she had your undivided attention as well."

"That's the absolute truth," Rick said, nodding. "At least we got a hole in the wall sealed up. Oh, and you all haven't seen the covered walkway. That was a pretty neat thing they did, even if the two of them did have ulterior motives. At least they weren't selling tickets."

"That we know of," Gwendolyn added.

Adeline clapped delightedly. "You're already finishing each other's sentences. That's perfect. Come to think of it, I would like to take a look at the covered walkway. I suddenly have a need to check out the ladies' room."

The three women trooped off through the kitchen. Rick looked at his guests.

"Would you like to take a look at the patch job, anyway?"

Lyle and Mark approved the maintenance job. Mark whistled when he looked at the small amount of room the two men had for the peeping tom operation.

"They were really both in there?"

"Yeah, and it looked completely stupid, I'd have loved to have gotten a picture of it, their heads together peering though that small hole. It's the sort of thing that would have been a big hit on the internet, back when there was such a thing."

Mark chuckled. "If your eye had been up to that hole, all three of you would probably still be there."

Chapter 10

Snowed In

Once everyone was back together, Rick's need to change the subject together with his curiosity prompted the next question.

"What happened with Kevin and Duane?"

Mark looked at Lyle, who leaned back and folded his hands. "Kevin is indeed doing Mr. Maguire's bidding. He keeps trying to prove how much he loves Susie. Mr. Maguire pronounced his judgment of the situation. It is what Kevin told us before he left. The idea is that Kevin forced Susie to commit a great sin. That sin is so great that Mr. Maguire is keeping Susie confined for the entire period of her pregnancy. Since Kevin deprived Mr. Maguire of his daughter, Kevin must do the work that Susie should be doing. In short, Kevin is required to do women's work."

Gwendolyn shook her head. "Poor Susie. Is there any way to get her away from Mr. Maguire?"

Mark nodded his head and pointed at Gwendolyn. "You see, Lyle? I told you that would be her reaction."

"That particular prediction doesn't get you any points, whatever, Mark. What's your reaction, Rick?"

Rick shook his head. "It doesn't sound right. I agree with Gwendolyn about Susie. Mr. Maguire is going out of his way to make life miserable for Kevin. On the other hand, while you told Kevin to go over there, he could have done any number of things besides what he did. While Mr. Maguire is using emotional blackmail, Kevin did go voluntarily. Susie is another situation. She might insist that she is happy and her whole focus in life is to be her father's good girl. At the same time, her actions with Kevin fly in the face of any such statements."

Lyle's eyebrows elevated. "For a computer programmer, your analysis of a purely behavioral situation goes beyond merely remarkable. It may even be miraculous. Standing in Gwendolyn's light has done you a lot of good. Now comes the hard part, Rick. What should we do about it?"

Rick rubbed his chin while he considered. Finally, "It is tough not to rub my hands together with glee, thinking about how Kevin is getting his comeuppance. On the other hand, Mr. Maguire sounds more like the terrorists, whose whole purpose in life is to kill all of us. His idea of being righteous doesn't agree with anything I've ever known or been taught."

"You put out a bunch of philosophy there. It goes along with what I think, but does nothing to solve the situation. Neither Kevin nor Susie are twenty-one. They may both be eighteen. I haven't checked. If they are minors, do we treat the situation differently than if they're both adults?"

"The last I heard, we are still under martial law. In the absence of either military people or military lawyers, justice is whatever you say it is, Mr. Lillard. One thing Mark talked about some on our rides back and forth to Arapahoe included experiences he had growing up in foster care. We're not looking at Mark's situation, but there's a larger question about how wise it is to allow the government to decide what makes up acceptable parenting."

"So you send the monkey back home to my back," Lyle commented. "At the same time, you want a hands-off policy about the situation. Is that what I understand?"

"I don't see any way out of this. Vince and his deputies could easily liberate both Susie and Kevin. Maybe Susie is the only one they should set free. What's the situation with Mr. Maguire after that? Riding herd on that single terrorist we call a prisoner stretches our capabilities to the breaking point, from what I hear."

Lyle applauded. "You hit all the main points, Rick. Congratulations on pointing out everything we've argued about. For the moment, we're not taking action, even though it's the source of a great deal of anguish.

Now, you also asked about Duane. We're still trying to figure out the best thing for him. There was that couple who Josh and Mark rescued just after the final wave of dust went through. Charles and Marcie are not right in the head themselves, but they do have a remarkable command of all the wild plants around here. We made him an apprentice to them, to learn what plants we can eat, and what other things we can use them for."

"What can Duane learn, when all the plants are under three feet of snow?"

"They have several reference books. In addition, they have supplies of seeds, roots, and herbs. They claim that cedar bark and needles are good as a tea, although in moderation." Lyle looked at Adeline sitting next to him then. "I suspect some of the cedar found its way into what we're pleased to call coffee these days."

Adeline smiled slightly, but didn't say anything.

Rick considered that statement. "We'll do many things to stay alive that we wouldn't have even considered a year or two ago. What does Duane think of the arrangement?"

"Vince's posse checks several times a day. The three of them get along. Maybe we've found him a new home. At least, we can hope so."

Mark was getting restless. "Rick, do you know an easy way to get over to the other place? I'd like to see what they're doing. We didn't get a chance the last time I was here."

Lyle looked at Mark and then over at Gwendolyn. "Don't you just love how he said that with a dead pan expression? Maybe you should go grab the famous skillet, and liven up his features a little bit."

Ellen put an arm up in front of Mark, as though to protect him. "Please don't do it, Gwendolyn. Mark's already too silly, and you'd just slap him even sillier."

Rick shook his head. "Mark, we should exit stage right. They'll be throwing rotten produce next. Worse yet, they'll be competing to see who can deliver the line getting the loudest groan."

"I owe you, partner."

"It's duly noted, and added to your account."

"You didn't say anything about being in that groan competition. That isn't fair. I understand your people not only had the bunkhouse done, but had also finished the arena, right? I can hardly wait to see it."

"You turned it around, Mark. Nobody will top that groaner. By the way, the guys know the path. I don't, and only hope we can survive the maze of snowdrifts going to the other place."

They carefully wound their way over to the other side of Wagon Ranch, following the route taken by multiple boot prints. On the way, Rick described his ideas about solar-powered wells for the two houses. If he thought it might be a hard sell, he was mistaken.

"You've got the people. You've got the talent. They know where to find the gear to make it all happen. You should go ahead and do it," was Mark's response.

"I didn't want to use them for that, only to find out that you and Lyle wanted them working on something else. I thought I'd better clear it through you guys first."

"I appreciate your concern, Rick. Our concern ... that is to say, Lyle's concern, which I share, is to see what the guys have been doing down here lately."

Rick shook his head. "The last day I was down here was when you and Vince rode out. That's when we did the layout for the bunkhouse. They used the wood they got for the bunkhouse to build the walkway for Gwendolyn. Of course, we found out they had ulterior motives, or at least some of them did. The site of the future bunkhouse may be a pile of trash for all I know."

Mark laughed. "At least you're being honest about it. Some people would try to keep me on a mushroom plantation about now."

"Yeah, I know. They might try keeping you in the dark and feeding you bullshit. It wouldn't work with you, and it is certain not to work with Mr. Lillard. Except with him, he might play the situation for a while just to see where it all goes. We'll both know the truth very soon."

Mark was chuckling. "You really were listening when I talked about him when we were on the road together. There should be some points awarded for that. Maybe I can find a gold star to stick on your forehead."

"That might be a good idea. If what we find down here turns out to be a complete disaster, it will give you a good target when you shoot me."

"Didn't you read about how you should have positive expectations?"

"It works better to expect the worst. I'm never disappointed and hardly ever surprised."

"Oh, Rick, I can't believe all this negativity. We need motivational speakers. Where are they?"

"They expected the best and became part of the dust. For a good outcome, I should rely on that famous luck that you and Josh and Mr. Lillard all have. Some of it rubbed off already, since you guys put me with Gwendolyn."

"Ah, I hear that nasty old negative attitude draining away as we speak. All it took was the right woman to cure you. Well, it looks like we survived the trek. On a good day, we could have done this in a couple of minutes. At least we didn't get lost in the snowdrifts."

The only person in the house was the guy currently playing cook. He said everyone else was out in the big shed, working on the bunkhouse.

"I thought they used all the wood on the walkway," Rick commented.

"Nah. A couple of the guys came across a good stash of lumber, and have made pretty good progress. I hope they aren't looking forward to my cooking as a reward. When they taste it, they're going to know it's a punishment."

Rick nodded. "Are you trying to get out of cooking by demonstrating extreme incompetence?"

"No sir. I'm doing the best I can. Really I am. My talent runs more in other areas, that's all."

It wasn't hard to find the way to the big shed, as he called it. The trampled snow showed the way, with a trail wide enough that Mark and Rick walked side by side.

"Well, Rick, I didn't see a total disaster in there. From what I smelled at the lower house, the guy we talked to was creating one."

"The day is young. There are lots of opportunities yet."

The shed was originally for equipment, a structure known as a pole barn with two large sliding doors. Both doors were open, letting in the bright if vague winter sunlight. Inside was evidence of a great deal of construction. It was obvious the work effort that went into the covered walkway had simply transferred down here. One good thing was that the building was still weather-tight. That meant they didn't have to worry about a roof, or very much about the outside walls.

"Where did you come up with all the supplies?" Rick wanted to know.

"The people living here were accumulating it. We guess they were going to build something, though nobody knows what. It was awfully nice of them to include all this insulation, don't you think?"

"It really was. Do you think the outer shell is still weather-tight?"

"There was no sign of water on the concrete, even with the big rain. We're all pleased with the situation."

"You have set it up to use the passage door over there. What's your ideas for the big doors?"

"We want to install a door in the inside wall. That's part of the public area right there. It will leave a couple of feet between the wall and the door. It would be good to have a bolt hole just in case we need to get out in a hurry."

Mark looked over the situation while the conversation was going on.

"In your wanderings, like to find parts for solar wells, you ought to collect all the firearms you find, as well as ammunition. This group could represent quite a collection of fire power if the terrorists come calling. For firearms, I'm thinking thirty aught six caliber or larger if you guys have experience."

"We can do that. Did you just say that we can go ahead with the solar power for the wells?"

Mark grinned. "Rick brought it up; I think it's great. Having solar power at Harlan Ranch has been wonderful. I can't imagine massaging a pump handle every time I want a drink any more."

"Okay, Dan, you're back in the solar well business. There are two wells here for the people, along with the wells for the livestock. Consider Wagon Ranch your first customer. All we can pay is three hots and a flop, but it's a start."

Dan smiled then. "Oh, there's another way you can pay me. What's a horse worth?"

That got Mark laughing. "We've got a wheeler and a dealer here. I think we might work out something, actually."

Mark wandered off at that point, and Rick bent over to keep what he said private. "Dan, Mark might make you a deal for a horse. You've already collected a couple of eyes full of my wife, and you owe me big time for that. You hear what I'm saying?"

"I hear you, boss."

Just then, one of the guys hustled in from outside, and pulled Dan off to the side. Rick thought the guy looked concerned, and maybe even worried. Whatever he had to say generated a fair bit of conversation. Well, they'd just managed to sweeten everyone's attitude. Anything sweet tended to attract flies, as well. Maybe a fly just landed. Dan nodded to the guy, who took off toward the nearest group of workers. Then he turned to Rick.

"We won't be powering wells very soon. A major storm's moving in right now. You and Mark had better get back to the main house. We're going to build a covered walkway from this building over to the current bunkhouse, so we can keep working. After that, we'll build a walkway of some kind up the alley to the main house."

Rick was shocked. "You think the storm will be that bad?"

"Think about it. Each one has been worse than the one before. Take a look toward the west."

It was quite clear what Dan was talking about. Rick turned around and nodded, but it was to empty space, since Dan was already moving rapidly toward Mark. Rick wondered if Dan was trying to make up for his faux pas earlier. Well, he didn't need to wonder very much. It was clear that was exactly what Dan was trying to do, along with whatever other agenda he was working on.

Mark got up to Rick, standing in the big double-door.

"I see what they're talking about. Looking at that storm coming, I'm amazed and honored you stuck around for me, Rick."

"You're the boss. I take care of you, and you take care of me. I'm sure we'd be fine down here with the guys, other than having to suffer through the cooking. On the other hand, Mr. Lillard is up there by himself with three women. That could be awfully good, or it might just be awful."

"Now that shows some wisdom, Rick. Let's move."

The edge of the storm came rapidly. The crew shut the double doors even as they left at a fast walk. Their pace slowed as they left the beaten path, heading back up the alley. It wasn't far, but snow started falling just as they got into the alley, and the wind kicked up a minute later. For a while, they could see the trail they made going the other way. As they neared the other end of the alley, both the snow and wind picked up even more. They couldn't see the main house, and it was right in front of them.

Rick and Mark had no choice but to stick very close together, and head for where the house was, or at least where they remembered it. Rick let Mark do most of the steering, and he finally figured out that Mark was basically keeping the wind out of the same quarter. That seemed reasonable. In the last storm, the wind blew the same direction until the clouds cleared off. All Rick could do was keep moving forward, hoping each time he took a step, it truly was forward.

Pushing through waist-deep snow took an extraordinary amount of energy, Rick thought. It suddenly came to him that he'd heard about people surviving things like this, and they did it by focusing on someone they loved. That kind of realization a week ago would have left him with more questions than answers. Now, his main question was whether his connection with Gwendolyn was strong enough to get him through this. He got thinking about their several days together and wondered whether it was a week already.

Was he in love with her? It seemed a strange to get married first and worry about love later, but there it was. There was that strange protective instinct he felt when he first met her. There was her willingness to do things that were almost certainly far beyond anything her mother might have talked to her about. She was a sexy nerd beyond the end of human time. Not only that, she seemed happy to be with him. How good was that? That was more than good, it was excellent, but did it qualify as love?

After what seemed like an eternity of struggling to make headway, Rick suddenly noticed the wind changed. It not only changed, it began to swirl. Maybe they were close to a building. With a whole bunch of luck, they might have found the house. Two steps later, Rick nearly hit the back corner of the house with his nose, the snow was that heavy. Mark was right there with him, and together, they worked their way down the back wall to the covered walkway. After some effort, they were able to dig out enough snow to open the same panel Rick had used to nab the peeping toms.

They were still re-sealing the panel when Gwendolyn opened the back door. She took one look and nearly jumped into Rick's arms.

"We hoped you guys found shelter down there. We discussed the situation and knew it was really dumb to try to make it back." She pulled back from him slightly. "I'm sure happy you made it, though. Come into the kitchen and warm up."

Mark had to wait until he was in the kitchen for his reunion, and then, Ellen took one look at him, and shook her head.

"I'll give you a welcoming hug," she said. "However, there is no way I will embrace a bunch of snow and ice. Come with me, Mr. Tahner. You have to rejoin the human race before I welcome you home."

Rick defrosted in front of the cook stove for a few minutes, and as the snow and ice transformed to ice water, decided he had better take his sogginess off to the bedroom to get changed into dry clothes. A couple of feet behind him, Gwendolyn followed, towels in hand.

When they were alone, she wanted to know, "What did you think about when you were out there?"

"At first, I just thought about making tracks. When I couldn't see anything any more, I started thinking about you."

"What was on your mind?"

"I wondered whether we were in love, and how I could know."

"What did you decide?"

"I didn't. I ran into the back corner of the house. I couldn't see the house from a foot away."

Rick was undressed by that time, and Gwendolyn was covering him with towels. "Well, aren't you the romantic rogue? I'll bet you just sweep all the girls off their feet with talk like that."

"The times we were both off our feet were pretty neat. Besides you, computer code is the only thing I ever got along with, and I never thought of it as being particularly feminine."

With everybody together, discussion of how to get through this in one piece commenced.

"When the dust went around us, somebody took to calling our area of high ground 'lifeboat Harlan.' With all horses, that means that we're adrift in a wagon instead of a boat," Lyle considered. "They did build wagons that floated, I understand, but it's still not very reassuring."

"So far, at least," Rick reported, daring to interrupt Lyle's flight of fancy, "the roof has taken the snow load without any problem. That's not to say it will do so well with this one, though."

Mark shook his head. "There you go again, expecting the worst."

Rick shrugged. "You saw how it went with the other place. Whatever I expected didn't happen."

Mark chuckled. "That means weather disasters should be at the top of your list of expectations. Your guys already did a huge amount of work down there. For the moment, I think we mostly need to see how much food we have, and figure out how far we can make it stretch."

"Do you need hard numbers on the food, like how many calories we've got?" Gwendolyn asked.

Rick shook his head. "First, we have to figure out a couple of other things. There are six of us, so that's a given. How long we're liable to be here is the really big one. The last storm lasted a day and a half. If this one's twice as bad, it could hang around for three days. Then, it will take several days to get the roads cleared. We could be stuck here for a week, other things being equal. Oh, and by the way, we probably should keep an eye on the roof, just in case."

Lyle just looked at Rick. "It's your house. Take a lantern into the attic and look around. That might not be a bad idea, actually."

Gwendolyn got up. "I'd better do a real inventory on what we have. I may have to get pretty creative to put anything resembling real meals together, especially after a few days of feeding all of us."

Ellen and Adeline got up at the same time, both offering assistance. Rick looked at the movement, and blinked.

"I would offer to help, but unless you've got a specific task for me, I'd do better by staying out of the way."

Gwendolyn nodded, and the three headed into the kitchen.

Lyle looked over at Rick. "You're getting trained very quickly, my friend. You ducked the domestic job while appearing to volunteer. That was very well done, sir."

"We agreed it's her house, and while I'm in it, I'll do what she says. At least, I'll try to do what she says."

Lyle grinned. "The key word there is 'try.' You do know you'll never succeed, don't you?"

"If I don't succeed in minor details, but manage to keep the two of us together, then it counts as win anyway, doesn't it?"

"It does, indeed. Are you listening to him, Mark? He has a negative attitude, but Rick shows wisdom in spite of it."

Mark grunted. "He talks the talk, sure enough. Time will tell if he walks the walk."

Rick peered out the living room window. He shook his head and went to the door. Opening it slightly, he saw the snow was two-thirds of the way to the top of the door. Shutting the door quickly and firmly, he put another log in the high-efficiency stove.

"When they try to get to everybody, I hope everybody has really tall landmarks. If this goes anything like we were just talking, it won't be possible for anyone to even see the roof of the house. This is one hell of a lot of snow, guys."

"Maybe we should take a look up in the attic, Rick. You've got my interest now," Lyle said as he got up.

Instead of taking a kerosene lantern into the attic, they gathered hand-held mirrors, and did a survey without the dangers that went along with an open flame up there. It appeared the roof structure was stout, and holding its own. Many of the long-time residents in the area were originally from Scandinavia, and brought those building sensibilities to the New World with them. A roof built this well would have usually been considered over-engineered, but at the moment, it was just right.

Mark looked at Rick when he crawled down from the attic. "Are you happy with the roof now?"

"I am happier than I was. Still, every structure has its limits. It's something to keep an eye on."

"Since Gwendolyn is in charge of the house, maybe she should keep an eye on it."

Lyle chuckled. "More likely, as the one in charge of the house, she will tell Rick to go do it."

The attic access now re-sealed, Rick led the way back into the living room. The three women just got back themselves.

"That didn't take long. For an inventory to be done so quickly is not reassuring," Lyle informed them.

"There's not as much as we'd like. On the other hand, it went quickly because Gwendolyn had it organized so well," Adeline informed them.

"If we're looking at a week, meals will be near normal. If it goes longer than a week, it could get pretty skinny, but we aren't going to starve."

Gwendolyn looked around the room. "The biggest challenge we'll face will be how we can keep from being on each other's nerves."

"That's not a problem," Rick replied. "Lyle and Adeline will tell us how it will be, and the rest of us will figure out some way to make it happen."

Lyle shook his head. "Gwendolyn, I see your point. Fortunately, with three couples and three bedrooms, we will all have privacy. I think the key is that if a couple or an individual wants some time, the rest of us ought to honor that desire where possible. That assumes there isn't something else to override the desire. Does that sound reasonable?"

Everybody nodded. Rick raised a finger, then. "I can bring up wood and pump water, but if you guys want to help out now and then, that would be great. It's not like that is a full-time job anyway. One thing all of us guys might want to do is to build steps to the surface, and also to check the covered walkway now and then. The people who put that in are not the same people who built the house. I think we'll want to ration our use of kerosene, too. When the house gets covered with snow, we'll need light all the time."

They agreed to have only one lamp burning at a time, and to keep the wick as low as possible without losing the flame. In addition, they would cut back on the wood they used, but would keep the fires burning at all times. With three cords of wood, they were in no danger. Still, it made sense to do it that way.

A group decision that puzzled Rick was when Adeline promoted the notion that the first thing they should do was to have a substantial meal. What really struck him as strange was her reasoning.

"If you're going to fast," Adeline stated, "you should do it on a full stomach. This way, we have a good meal to think about later when things get thin."

Rick considered that must be a folk thing she'd picked up somewhere. It did make sense, though, and Adeline had become the wise woman of Harlan. That meant that if he had to say anything against her proposal, he'd better have his ducks in a perfect line. Since he didn't have very strong feelings on the subject, one way or the other, he decided to just let it go.

In any case, after the effort to push through the snow, together with being warm and dry again, his belly demanded attention. His stomach ganging up with Adeline against Rick's brain was an uneven contest. He knew his brain would lose. Everybody put out lamps, and took the last lit lamp into the kitchen, where they tried to be positive.

Rick knew in his heart of hearts that he was not now, never had been, and never would be a positive thinker. That being the case, he took the next best approach, and kept his mouth shut most of the time. In return, nobody asked his opinion of things, which also helped. The meal, with the three women augmenting one another's expertise, was superb, and more than satisfied his hunger. Afterward, things got cleaned up, and everybody moved with the lamp into the living room, where the flame was turned down.

"Seeing how the two of you got worn out getting back here, Adeline and I can take the first watch," Lyle said. "We'll keep the fires going and the lamp burning. There's no rush on you replacing us."

Mark looked at Rick significantly. The boss saying there was no rush meant they'd better keep it really short. Rick saw Mark point at himself with his thumb, while mouthing, "We'll get it."

Rick thought that was awfully nice of them. Then, when he got in the bedroom, Gwendolyn undressed him in the dark, and pushed him into the bed.

"Everybody was worried about how bad you looked when you came in. You don't look a whole lot better now," she told him.

"That's strange. I feel okay, pretty much. Do you think I look that bad?"

Whatever Gwendolyn replied didn't register. Rick was out as soon as his head hit the pillow. When he awoke, it was still dark, which didn't mean much, considering the snow had to be above the windows.

"Are you awake, Gwendolyn?"

"I have been for some time now. How are you doing?"

"I'm feeling better. How long was I asleep?"

"It's hard to say. I think it has been eight or ten hours, anyway."

"Damn. I should have been out there standing watch before now."

"You're waking up when you need to. Mark and Ellen took over a while ago, but I'm sure they're ready for a break."

Out in the living room, Mark and Ellen welcomed them.

"Sorry to wuss out on you, Mark," Rick said.

"Wuss? You? My God, Rick, you played snowplow the whole way back. All I had to do was tag along behind you. I kept trying to take the lead to give you a break, but you just moved that much faster. You're the man."

"Is that what I did? I was just trying to get back to the house. I didn't think I was moving fast enough."

Lyle and Adeline came out of their room. "We heard everybody was up. Don't you feed guests around here, Rick?"

That started the next meal. Afterward, Rick and Gwendolyn took care of the lamp and the stoves. The snow was so deep, they couldn't hear the wind any more. It seemed the snow encasing the house made for great insulation, so a little heat went a long way. The covered walkway out back was groaning some, but holding its own. The stoves running all the time helped, as well. If the snow did overtop the chimneys, the hot smoke should still keep a way open out into the air. Since they weren't getting any back drafts, that idea seemed to be correct.

The three couples settled into a sort of rhythm. There wasn't much conversation, and actual discussion was nonexistent. Rick considered they might run out of breathable air. He mentioned it to Gwendolyn in passing, but decided not to bring it up anywhere else. How much time passed was a complete unknown, but it seemed forever.

While a meal was being prepared, Rick went out into the covered walkway for some more firewood. Just as he closed the back door, he thought he heard a scraping sound on the outside of the panel he and Mark came in. A moment later, there was more scraping. That followed almost immediately by somebody saying, "We did it! We're there!"

Rick opened the back door, and called everyone. Within minutes, the panel opened outward, and the crew from the other place stood there grinning. Behind them was something like a mine shaft, with candles in holders every ten to twenty feet.

"Welcome, guys! How on Earth did you do it?"

"Dan said he promised you that we'd punch a covered pathway up here. Well, we've done it. He knew Kevin and Duane had stripped a lot of the supplies from up here. The other place had beaucoup stuff by the time they were done. We figured with six people here, you'd be running out of just about everything pretty soon. By the way, the storm finally passed. While we're here, we'll punch a stairway out the front door, and check your chimneys to make sure they're clear. We passed the word back, and supplies should be up here soon."

"Where did you take all the snow?" Rick asked.

"We found a good gully, and built a tunnel out to it. It's been quite a circus trying to keep a tunnel two wheelbarrows wide this whole way, and bracing it, but here we are."

Chapter 11

Hijacked House

"Do you guys want to come in and take a load off?"

"We'll take a rain check on that. Can somebody help us find the corner of the house? We don't want to send wheelbarrows through the house to take out the snow. Anyway, it will get our digging crew out of the thoroughfare when the supplies come up the line."

Rick went with them. They cleared the tunnel all the way to the ground, so he was able to study the impressions and recall where everything went. "The corner of the house should be about here. It may actually stick out another foot or so."

"That's what we thought, but we needed some confirmation. Okay, let's move this panel. Everybody knows the drill. Let's get them some sunlight while it's still around."

Rick shook his head. He headed back in the house, his help obviously neither wanted nor needed.

Mark looked at him. "Who the hell are they trying to impress, Rick?"

"Beats me. I don't inspire that much love or fear in any of them. It must have been you guys being here that kept them moving."

Mark chuckled. "Maybe you're such a relief to be around after Kevin, they're willing to do almost anything."

"You make it sound like the Dennis Maguire insane asylum is just where Kevin needs to be."

Mark shook his head sadly. "There might be a benefit to it for a while. Just how long remains to be seen."

"Considering how things were for the six of us here, I can't imagine the pressure cooker the Maguire household must be, where nobody even wants to get along with each other."

"That's an excellent point, Rick."

"What point is that, Mark?" came from Lyle Lillard, who had just joined them.

"Rick was saying how bad it must be over at the Maguire hacienda."

Lyle nodded. "I agree. They may need another visit. Vince should do a welfare check on the families in Huntley. The Maguire family would be a required place to check. With his background in law enforcement, he'd have a feel for the situation. If immediate action is needed, he can do something. Otherwise, he can update us about how things are over there."

Rick went back into the new passage, and took the few steps to where the new intersection was. Wheelbarrows full of snow went down the outgoing lane, and the tunnel was already to the corner of the house. Coming toward him were loads of additional lumber. In the candlelight, he saw the first load of food. They were really serious about this. Rick wondered if he could act as traffic cop and direct traffic, but the guy pushing the food was John Parkhurst, Dan's cohort. He grinned at Rick as he went by, heading directly for the kitchen door.

The way these guys were going, Rick concluded the only thing he'd accomplish by trying to help would be to gum up the works altogether. He finally followed John, but had to step over the wheelbarrow handles to approach the kitchen. As it was, he ended up occupying space in the walkway for the several minutes it took to hand the supplies in the back door. He did notice a gallon of kerosene along with everything else. The guys were really thoughtful.

John was soon on his way, heading back for another load. Rick went on into the kitchen, where the three women were occupied with adding these new and unexpected items to the inventory.

"Did they haul up much good stuff, Gwendolyn?"

"It was like they had a crew of mind readers down at the other end, Rick," she replied. "Of course, they knew what Kevin and Duane had stripped from here. I think they're basically just bringing some of that back. There may be some guilty consciences down there."

"It's very strange that Duane would strip this place when he was sleeping here. Kevin's room was here, too."

"Kevin only stayed around here during the day. That leaves Duane. Did he eat here?"

"Not a lot, as I recall. Now that you mention it, he always seemed to have some duty or other down at the other place at meal time. It was just the other two guys and me up here. Come to think of it, the other two guys weren't here that much at meal time either."

"It sounds like Kevin and Duane had gone beyond merely harassing you, and were busy starving you."

Rick glanced up to see Lyle and Mark standing by the doorway. Both of them looked very thoughtful.

"I didn't recall you mentioning that, Rick," Mark commented. "They were trying to run you off. Did either of them say where they'd prefer you went?"

"I got the impression they'd have preferred I was far, far away. If I'd managed to go play in the Omega dust, that would have suited them just fine. I don't know that either of them would have put it exactly that way."

"So, from their point of view, you refused to cooperate with their wishes."

Lyle spoke up then. "At the same time, you insist on showing some concern for their welfare. That would mean you won't even sink to their level. An attitude like that could really irritate them."

Rick cocked his head and pursed his lips. "I'm not about to tell them. Maybe we don't have to let them know. By the way, the crew nearly got across the end of the house. Rumor has it some daylight is happening outside. I'm sure that can't be the case, but it's nice to think about."

Lyle chuckled at the obvious change of subject. "I must admit a little fresh daylight would be awfully nice. Having a supply of kerosene in the meantime is pretty nice, too. For right now, we're taking up real estate in the kitchen. I suggest we move someplace healthier for us man-type people."

"I guess you guys are looking forward to getting home again," Rick commented as they got into the living room.

"It'll sure be nice, that's for sure," Lyle replied. "At the same time, our time here has reassured me that we've got the right guy running Wagon Ranch. You've managed to overcome a great deal to get this far. I must congratulate you, Rick."

Rick grinned. "Thanks for the vote of confidence, but Gwendolyn deciding to put up with me helped more than anything I could imagine. Then, the two of you backed me up with the little bit that's happened so far. A good part of it is the crew deciding to vote for me. I still haven't figured that part out."

Rick was sitting with his back to the kitchen. Suddenly, he felt two arms on either side of his head.

"You mentioned me first. I think I like that."

"That's how it's supposed to be, Gwendolyn."

All at once, they heard noise up on the roof. Mark and Rick looked at each other.

"They decided to do that sooner instead of later," Mark observed.

"It may be they want to dig the snow once instead of twice. That is what they'd be doing if they cleared it first and then went up on the roof."

"Good point," Lyle nodded. "So do we feel more like we'll survive this thing? Evidently they'll be able to keep the roof from crashing in on us."

Just then, they all heard another load of supplies arrive. "The guys are truly serious about all of this," both Rick and Mark said in unison.

Lyle shook his head. "I swear, you two are becoming the Bobbsey twins."

"That wouldn't work very well, sir, unless one of us suddenly became female."

"That's an accurate observation, even if it wasn't the point."

They listened to the sounds of organization in the kitchen along with scraping across the roof. The sound on the roof continued toward the eaves, and finally stopped. Then came sounds of things happening along the front of the house.

"I remember houses with enough soundproofing in the walls that we wouldn't be able to hear most of this," Mark said.

"When you're old and gray, you can tell that to your grandchildren at the fire in front of your teepee," Lyle grinned.

"We'll be doing that well, will we?" Mark cracked back.

Rick thought the sound was getting closer, and walked back to look into his bedroom. "Come take a look at this. There's actually daylight coming in the window. Here's a preview of what's coming to a living room window near you."

The two other men joined Rick over at the bedroom door, gazing at the bright afternoon sun coming through the window. In a moment, the three women joined them. Everybody squeezed through the door for a better view.

"I used to think the moon could be romantic, but all of a sudden, I find the sunlight is really wonderful," Gwendolyn said.

"Does that mean you two need privacy all of a sudden?" came from Ellen.

Just then a couple of the snow-digging crew went by the window and glanced in.

"I believe I can restrain my romantic impulses for a little bit, now that I think about it."

They drifted back into the living room, where the front windows were beginning to show light. Pretty soon, they were able to put out the lamp, although it was quite clear they'd be relighting it shortly. Other than light, there wasn't much of a view, since the snow outside blocked everything. The crew was making steps to the top. They needed far more than the three steps Rick had carved after the previous snow.

One of the crew finally knocked politely on the front door. When Rick answered it, he simply said, "We hope this helped you guys. We've got to get back over to the other side now."

He gave something resembling a salute, and took off at that point. There was no doubt a great deal more needed doing, but the roof was clear, along with the chimneys. They had some daylight. The trade-off was that they could feel the cold air infiltrating the walls now, and Rick knew he'd better make sure they had plenty of wood close to the back door.

Rick looked at his guests. "At least now, when they come looking for you guys, there's half a chance they'll find you."

Lyle laughed. "The funny thing is that they'll be trying to find Mark, the best tracker in Harlan. How does that compute?"

They had a great meal a little later, and the sun setting shortly after they saw a little daylight did little to dampen their spirits. It had been quite a day. Later on, everyone retired for the evening, after agreeing they would simply rebuild the fires the next morning. Gwendolyn walked over to the window.

"Oh, I can see some stars."

Rick came over with her, and she pointed out stars. It didn't take long before Rick was seeing stars that Gwendolyn generated. Evidently, having even a little view outside helped her romantic impulses. On his part, Rick didn't mind at all.

Early the next afternoon, the snowplow crews found their way to Wagon Ranch. Their four guests decided that the following morning would be soon enough to head home. That thought was affirmed when the snowplow crews described conditions around the county. Their main hope was for the storms to stay away for as long as possible, and for the temperatures to come up for a while. They'd seen several houses severely damaged by the snow. Fortunately, none of them were occupied.

The next day, everybody trooped over to the other side. One purpose was to check the horses and other livestock. The main reason was to see what had been done to allow them to ride home that day.

Rick hesitated to say it, but finally spit it out anyway as they headed to the other side. "Considering the work we know has been done, I am fairly certain that everybody will be pleased, whatever you're inspecting."

"That's coming from Mr. Negativity, everyone," Mark laughed. "Put a red circle around the date. A miracle may have happened."

"Make two big red circles around the date if what he just said turns out to be true," Gwendolyn added.

"Hey, you're my wife. You're supposed to support me, here."

"I cook your food and keep your bed warm. Now you want me to carry you too? Would that be piggy-back or fireman's carry?"

When they got to the end of the alley, they discovered the covered walkway was a major thoroughfare between the bunkhouse and the other living quarters. It was wide enough for them to simply walk as a group. Where the bunkhouse was being built, there wasn't a whole lot of progress to be seen, but then, with everything else that had been done, it was tough to complain.

A branch of the walkway then went over to the stables, where their horses appeared to be in good condition. A couple of guys came up, offering to take care of saddling or anything else they might need. The main thing the group needed at the moment from them was to open the outside doors.

Mark added, "All of this supposes you did enough of a ramp for us to get out."

"It should be good enough," the one guy said with a grin. "We had it ready yesterday afternoon. We widened it some more since then."

After they got saddled and mounted, Lyle looked over at Mark. "You know when I had you start setting up a messenger route to McCook? We just might have to do that within Harlan if this kind of weather keeps up. I'm not even sure it's officially winter yet."

Gwendolyn and Rick ran into Dan over by the bunkhouse. He was away from everybody else at the moment.

"I think you scored points with the big dogs," Rick told him.

Dan tried to wave it off. "Having you in charge instead of Kevin and Duane is a real breath of fresh air."

Rick thought that was a popular and increasingly hollow refrain. Dan looked around before continuing. "Then there's how embarrassed John and I were. I have to admit what we did was really juvenile, and we're really sorry about it."

"I could say I forgive you. That might or might not be the case. You'll have to figure it out as we go. Whatever I do, I don't imagine Gwendolyn will forget any time soon. There is the old question of how many attaboys offset an awshit. Somebody told me one time that even if you have built up a huge amount of credibility, it doesn't make much to wipe it out. The other side of it is that we really do appreciate what all of you did for us these past several days."

"Thank you." Dan suddenly got a look of something like panic on his face. "Mr. Tahner and Mr. Lillard don't know about that, do they?"

Gwendolyn favored Dan with a predatory grin, and Rick shrugged it off. "They found out, but no names were mentioned. I didn't tell them. In any case, neither of them saw fit to pursue the matter. Evidently they've marked the case as being closed. That's not to say they wouldn't bring it up if you or John decided to have another mental lapse."

"I get your point. Did they say how our former bosses are doing?"

"They gave us the most current information they have, and think they need to get another update soon. Why?"

"I don't know. There's a feeling I get when one of them is in the area. I've had that feeling for an hour now. I came out by myself to talk myself out of the notion."

"That sounds like Mark and the way he gets a scratchy feeling when something's hunting him. He says it's saved him any number of times. Why don't you walk with us up the alley? Then you will have done your guard duties and dispel any problems in that direction."

"Works for me." Dan shouted inside that he was going for a minute. Rick thought it was interesting when Dan added that everyone should keep moving but be alert for problems.

When they got to the entrance to the alley going up to the house, Rick inquired, "Well, Dan, is that feeling going away?"

"No sir. If anything, the feeling has become more intense."

"So you're going with us. Do you prefer to be in front or behind?"

"I'll lead, if that's not being insulting."

"Not at all. Lead on, Dan."

Halfway to the house, there was a flash followed almost instantly by the crack of a rifle shot.

"This is my house. You can't come here unless I invite you or if Kevin says you can." That was Duane, all right.

All three hit the ground at the muzzle flash. Rick realized he hadn't heard the round go by them. Either it was a warning shot or Duane was as poor a marksman as what he'd heard Mark say that Kevin was. On the other hand, it didn't take an expert marksman to hit something down a lane only wide enough for two wheelbarrows. An advantage was that the candles along the tunnel didn't light the ground very well.

Dan called, "Duane, we're going back. We won't bother you. Are you a killer, Duane? Will you let us leave without killing us?"

All at once, they could hear Duane coughing and then sobbing.

"That sounds like the bullshit he did when he attacked me in the kitchen," Gwendolyn commented softly.

"We're a bit far for a hot fry pan to help at the moment," Rick said. "Let's turn around. Keep as far below the candles as you can."

The three made it back to the main tunnel without any more shots being fired. Once they arrived, Rick had an idea.

"Dan, why don't you and I go back up the tunnel? We'll stay low, and reach up, putting out candles along the way. The light in this main area should enable us to get back."

"What will that accomplish?"

"It will make anyone in the tunnel less of a target. I hate to suggest it after the work you guys put into it, but if Duane got back here, and maybe brought Kevin with him, we should give them the privacy they so desperately crave."

"You want to dismantle the tunnel?"

"Yep. Just as much of it as we can manage. Then, we can circle around and rebury the front of the house. Who knows, maybe we can reclaim the panels and supports for the covered walkway going to the outhouse."

Close to a dozen of the work crew was up around them by that time, everybody hearing the shot. Dan grinned. "I'm all for it, Rick. At the same time, what say we let a couple of the guys play hero for this part of it." He immediately pointed to two guys closest to the alley entrance. "You two heard what Rick said. Turn off the lights. The rest of you get ready to reclaim the panels and supports. While everybody is waiting, get away from the mouth of the tunnel. Who knows if that idiot might start shooting again?"

They watched the two work their way up the tunnel, pinching out each candle. They were soon as far as the three of them got when Duane took the pot shot at them. All at once, there was a weird sort of screech, followed by a door slamming.

"Dan, if that was Duane running for cover, they'll be able to shut down all the candles. Do you have a couple of good marksmen? We could send them up the tunnel to make sure nobody pokes their nose out the back door. We need a bunch of people to dismantle the walkway and tunnel, including the one going around the house. If there are folks who can do it, send them outside on horseback and rebury the front."

Dan grinned. "Now my feelings are improving. You heard what the man said, guys. One of you, roust everyone in the bunkhouse and get them up the tunnel, two with rifles. The stable crew will head to the front of the house. Whoopee!"

Rick, Gwendolyn, and Dan watched a parade of panels and timbers come out of the tunnel, and head toward the bunkhouse. After a while, one of the crew stopped and seemed to have something on his mind, but hadn't quite decided who to talk to about it. Rick took the bit in his teeth at that point.

"What do you have?"

"Uh, yes sir. The walkway between the back door and outhouse is completely dismantled. We pushed in the snow banks on either side. They'll have an interesting time getting out the back door, much less going anywhere now."

"That's pretty much what we were planning. Did anybody try to get out while you were doing that?"

"No sir, but here's the strange part. We heard a woman crying."

The three looked at each other for a moment. Rick thought out loud. "Duane got away from those plant people. He went to bust out Kevin, and little Susie came with him. She must not think this is paradise. Dan, what are your people doing on the front of the house?"

"They'll drag timbers at an angle, like the old highway snowplows. It should push the snow down into the walkway pretty well. We are already seeomg the temperature rise, so walking the horses back and forth will compact it into an icy mass. They'll have a good time trying to get out."

Rick nodded, but then shook his head. "Dan, you do realize that we'll have to dig their sorry asses out of there eventually."

Dan grinned. "We could just wait for spring."

"Remind me not to get on your nasty side. By the way, Gwendolyn and I need a place to stay until we get this sorted out."

"Right. Most of the guys already moved to the bunkhouse. I just need to encourage the few remaining, and the lower house will be yours. Would that be okay?"

Rick and Gwendolyn stared at each other. "That would be more than okay, Dan. Thank you so much."

After a while, they could see the tunnel going up the alley coming apart. Everybody agreed to leave a stub end of it so they would have a point to reconstruct the thing.

"Actually," Dan told them, "we had every intention of tearing it out as soon as possible anyway. We figured that if we could build it as a proper thing instead of a snow tunnel, it would be better for everyone. After all, there are no foundations or anything else. We know it has to come out when the weather warms up, but it can work until then, right?"

"Damn, you guys have been up to your eyeballs in this. It all sounds good to me. What do you think, Gwendolyn?"

"The covered walkway to the outhouse was awfully nice. I'd like to see that restored as soon as you could manage it. Speaking of which, is there a walkway to an outhouse near here? I could use a visit about now."

At the house, Dan showed them a closet. "There were quite a few women's clothes. Nobody knew what to do with them, so they all got put in here. I know you only have the clothes you're wearing, ma'am, and I have no idea whether these will either fit you or suit you, but you're more than welcome to go through them. If you don't mind men's clothing, we may have some that could fit you."

Gwendolyn seemed blown away by the thoughtfulness. Dan then looked at Rick. "We also have spare clothes that should fit you, Rick. I hope you guys are comfortable here until we can get you back into your own house. After those two being back in there, we should fumigate it."

"One of these days, Dan, you're going to have to explain your huge love for Kevin and Duane. It's quite remarkable."

"That would be on a day when you and I have an unlimited supply of booze. A great many descriptions might not be suitable for a fine lady's ears, if you'll pardon me saying so."

Gwendolyn grinned. "Thank you for the vote of confidence about my social status. Still, my shooting you the moon back at the other house should have taken care of the fine lady thing. It's okay if you just tell it to Rick. I'll dig out every sordid detail anyway."

Rick laughed. "Oh yes, Dan, we have to get you married. You'll find out just how educated you can become with a wise woman whispering in your ear. Did Nancy Rowley mention any other single ladies available?"

Gwendolyn looked at Rick and started giggling. "Nancy told me about your exacting specifications. I presume Dan would have similar restrictions."

Rick turned red, remembering that dinner, and Dan looked at both of them. "What specifications did Rick make?"

Gwendolyn gleefully ticked them off. "Any candidate had to be a member of the human species, female, an orphan, and between puberty and ninety-seven. Did I miss anything, Rick?"

Rick was nearly choking, but managed to respond, "Not that I recall."

Dan nodded. "Well, she came through on nearly all counts. Still, I'm puzzled. Where did the orphan thing come from?"

"I was not enthused about a proud papa nearby with a shotgun. I can refer you to Dennis Maguire if you're interested in how that works out."

"Still," Dan commented thoughtfully, "Susie's here now, unless there's another female in the deal. We won't know until we dig them back out."

One of the stable guys arrived breathlessly. "We backfilled the snow and compacted it like you said. We went around and did it so all the doors and windows are covered."

Rick suddenly had a thought. "Did they have any fires going inside?"

"There was smoke coming out of one of the chimneys. Not a whole lot, but they'll stay warm for a while. Was there wood inside the house?"

Rick shook his head. "A couple of pieces for the heating stove. I think five or six for the cook stove."

He looked at Gwendolyn for verification, and she nodded.

"The snow should insulate them pretty well. I suspect it'll be a cold night for them anyway. Speaking of which, how late is it?"

"It'll be dark in another twenty minutes," the guy from the stable said promptly. "The sun is near the horizon. Dan, the chores are all done."

Dan looked at Rick and Gwendolyn. "Would you be our guests of honor this evening? Our chow isn't fancy, but there's plenty of it. We also make better coffee than Rick does."

Gwendolyn made a sour face. "Thanks, even if it doesn't say much."

Later that evening, Gwendolyn looked at Rick as they lay in bed.

"Do you have any trouble sleeping in strange places?"

Rick considered that for a moment. "If I did, I'd never get any sleep. Not these days, especially. How about you?"

"Not really. Working for the Ragan families, I slept in any nook or cranny available. I remember reading Harry Potter books when I was younger. At the time, I thought it was just awful how they made him sleep in the cupboard under the stairs. Living in Ragan, I concluded he had it pretty good."

"How about now?"

"This is pretty nice." Her voice dropped to nearly a whisper. "The place is okay, but I really like the company."

"Somebody who actually thinks it's a good thing to be around me," Rick joked. "That's amazing."

She stretched over and gave him a kiss. "Well, that just shows how few people have good taste."

"Aw shucks, ma'am. I've got to say you're the nicest, sexiest girl I've ever seen or even heard of."

Gwendolyn giggled. "I appreciate that, but it only shows how little you've been around. Didn't you look at the sexy girls in the magazines?"

"Well, sure, but they were just pictures. You're the real deal."

The next morning, the two of them got moving at the same time, and soon had the kitchen warm. Gwendolyn rooted around and found enough to make a nice breakfast. They briefly discussed the situation, and decided that while the guys in the bunkhouse invited them for breakfast, they preferred to have a little quiet private time. They certainly hadn't seen very much of that lately.

A bit later, they wandered over to the bunkhouse, only to have quite a few guys try to give them a second breakfast. Dan was already at the stable. That furnished them with the excuse they needed to move on. In the stable, Dan was ready and waiting for them.

"I figured you guys would want to look at things at the main house. I took the liberty of saddling a couple of horses for you. Miz Forbes, I know you rode the broken down nag the last time. I put you on a gentle horse, but one that can actually cover some ground if it's necessary. Rick, I saddled the one you usually use."

"How's the weather holding?"

"Sunny and warm. Where the snow hasn't been packed, it's already dropped a noticeable amount."

A few minutes later, they headed out the door. Looking toward the bunkhouse, Rick could see a few exposed patches of roof. The snow was indeed melting quickly. Since the road was already packed, they made good time going around to the road and up to the main house.

Three guys with rifles sat on horses at strategic locations around the house. One had a good view of the front door and a second rider covered the back door. The third rider was at the end of the house, covering all the windows, and also in position to support either of the other two.

"Is there anything going on?" Dan asked the rider by the front door.

"The front door jiggled a bit a little after sunrise, but that's all. We quit seeing any smoke about the same time."

"We'll get you some relief in a little bit."

"No problem. It's a nice day, and we grabbed breakfast before we came out."

Suddenly the third rider called out, "Rider approaching."

Rick turned in the saddle, and saw a single rider coming at a good clip. As he got closer, Rick saw he was one of those in Vince's posse.

"I'm glad to see you guys are okay," he opened. "Duane smacked Charles in the head with a skillet and took off for Huntley. He joined up with Kevin, and they beat Dennis Maguire to within an inch of his life. Then they grabbed Susie and took off. Mark's helping them track the three. We're alerting the whole county."

Rick, Gwendolyn, and Dan all looked at each other. Finally Rick spoke up. "I think all three are accounted for. That's their refuge. We can't claim credit for finding them. They hijacked the house, and Duane shot at anybody coming near. Dan was able to immobilize them. Duane doesn't seem quite right in the head, frankly."

Dan guffawed and slapped his pommel. "Rick, you're talking like an old country boy. What happened to all that education?"

"The dust ate most of it. There must be a long Greek medical term to describe Duane's condition, but it wouldn't make us any smarter, so why bother? If you'd bring Vince and the rest of the posse over here, Dan might dig them out. They have run out of firewood, so they shouldn't fight being liberated very much."

The posse member nodded, but then Dan added, "Of course, as Rick's already observed, Duane just ain't right in the head. There's no telling what's liable to come out of there. I'd bring plenty of help, and all of them with weapons."

The guy, whose name Rick had never known, wheeled his horse around and headed back down the road leading to Harlan Ranch, the Lillard place, and Ragan.

Dan looked at Rick. "Should we tell those three what's coming?"

Rick shook his head emphatically. "Why encourage them to shoot holes in the house? They're almost certainly trashing the place anyway. Why egg them on?"

"That's a good point. Sealing holes in that house wasn't my personal idea of a good time. It will take that guy the rest of the day to round up enough guys to get the job done. What say we head on back?"

Rick agreed with that, and Dan turned to the sentry. "Keep an eye out for this posse. When they show up, send somebody back to get the rest of us. Like I said, we'll get you relief pretty quick."

The sentry touched the brim of his hat. "This isn't bad. If you could send us some lunch, we'd be okay. Of course, if we can get back for some hot food, that would be good, too."

Riding back around the property, Gwendolyn turned to Rick. "That may be the first 'all points bulletin' issued by this administration."

"It's definitely the first one for a purely internal matter. The thing with the dust and the one with the terrorists definitely qualified, in my opinion."

Chapter 12

Crime and Labor

Back in the lower house, Rick wondered out loud, "I wonder if we'll be able to go back to the so-called main house."

Gwendolyn stopped and looked at him. "Why wouldn't we be able to go back there?"

"It comes to me that the three might destroy the inside of the house just for giggles and grins. We might not want anything to do with it."

"I see your point, especially thinking about Duane. Maybe Susie could keep Kevin in line. She might not even want to be with them in there, after they beat her father like that."

Rick shook his head. "This whole thing went from straight-forward to a complete mess in a moment. I see what you're saying about Susie. She may have a whole new outlook on lover-boy Kevin now. Carrying his child makes her situation a whole lot worse. I'm starting to feel drawn toward Dennis Maguire's pseudo-religious stand in the matter."

"I hope you don't feel too drawn, Mr. Forbes. I might feel compelled to show you the mystical powers of a red-hot skillet alongside your head."

"It doesn't seem to have realigned Duane's thinking worth a damn."

"For all we know, he's thinking better now."

"Do you suppose he needed that kind of therapy a couple of times a day?"

"It's very likely, but he couldn't afford either the insurance or the co-payment if I did it."

Rick laughed. "There's no doubt in my mind. Still, would you mind if we had to stay down here?"

"I never got all that used to the other house. Wasn't there something about using this house for women training horses?"

"There's that, certainly. We've seen everything about that plan get messed up."

The rest of that day and a good part of that night, Rick worried and wondered what they could have done to prevent it. He also tried to figure out what they could do if the main house was no longer habitable. He wished he could up with better answers. Gwendolyn was keeping an eye on him, although she didn't say anything.

The next morning, during breakfast, Rick saw her getting set. "You're moping around like the weight of the entire world dropped on your shoulders. Lyle Lillard said you were the manager, but made it clear you are a trainee, doing on-the-job training. He's pleased with everything so far. Mark Tahner not only gave you a passing grade, he praised you. Now get that worried look off your face before you start having issues with this shiny new wife of yours. You remember you have one, right?"

Rick shook his head, walked around the table, and gave Gwendolyn a hug and kiss. "I don't know what happened to my priorities. Thanks for straightening me out. Thanks twice for not doing it with a skillet."

"You're very welcome, sir. Now, what say we wander on down the hallway, and see what's going on?"

What used to be the intersection for the tunnel going to the main house was easy to see this morning. The snow level dropped even more overnight, and clear sky was now visible through a hole at the end of the panels. Three guys were working to clear a ramp going up the alley toward the main house. They were able to see the roof of the main house easily, and there was still no smoke from either chimney.

Dan showed up then. "If you like, we can just walk straight up the alley instead of having to saddle up and ride around."

Rick looked at Dan as they started off. "This is much more peaceful than how the three of us found things the last time we tried this."

"It is indeed," Dan laughed. "At the moment, all the rifles are pointed away from us instead of at us."

"Did they ever find where his shot went?"

"Yeah, they found a hole in a panel about halfway between where he was standing and where I was. Kevin is a lousy shot. Evidently, Duane is even worse. Maybe he didn't want to shoot anybody. He only wanted to scare us."

"That may well be. Wow, it's almost shirt sleeve weather out here. Does anybody want to guess how long this will last?"

"The last weather report was long ago, back before the solar outbreak fried all the weather satellites. We decided talking about the weather isn't going to do us any damn good. It's all we can do to deal with whatever comes."

"You sound like an awfully smart man, Dan. Are you after my job?"

"Would it include living in the main house?"

"That has been the procedure."

Dan laughed. "I believe I'll pass. How do I avoid that promotion?"

The sentry on the horse guarding the end of the house was in frozen mud instead of snow. He glanced at them and touched the brim of his hat. His attention was elsewhere, and a moment later, he yelled, "Riders coming. A bunch of them."

At that point, the riders guarding the front and back of the house moved a bit toward the end, while the sentry who saw them coming wheeled his horse, and headed at a good clip around the property.

"It will be all hands on deck now, to clear a doorway for the posse," Rick commented.

Dan nodded. "That would be unless Mr. Lillard decides to just board up the place and leave it. Clearing a doorway is more likely. He'll want to talk to Susie Maguire at length. Getting any sense from the other two seems like a lost cause to me."

Rick slapped Dan on the shoulder. "We can all agree on that."

Lyle Lillard and Mark Tahner were in the lead, along with Vince. Rick thought it was interesting that the guy who'd brought the word the day before was back, too, and on a different horse. That meant the horse's normal rider was in Don Rowley's double-header, right behind the first horsemen. Maybe that should be horse people, since Adeline, Ellen, and several other women were there as well. Everyone had hunting rifles. Nobody looked like they were on a snipe hunt.

Lyle looked down at Rick and Gwendolyn. "You got to host some more folks, Rick. As you can see, they're really popular. What will it take for us to see them?"

"We've got a crew coming with ice chippers and shovels. It wouldn't do for the three of them not to make a proper entrance, even though it will be an exit in this case."

"Are you two going to be happy to get back home?"

"Time will tell."

It wasn't long before a work crew, armed with shovels and digging bars, arrived. Lyle Lillard decided the trio must have gone in the front door, so that was how they should come out. In addition, the people in the house might try to dodge capture if they opened the back door. Watching the workers, Rick could tell they knew exactly what they were there for and how to do it. An hour later, a second work crew showed up, relieving the first crew.

With the front door clear, Vince took over, and cleared everybody from the door. He had teams lined up by the doorposts on either side. Then Vince pounded on the door with his rifle butt.

"Kevin, Duane, Susie, come on out. We know you're in there."

After an interminable minute or so, the door opened slightly. It was Duane, and Rick could see he had his rifle in front of him. Lyle saw it as well.

"Duane, don't be stupid. Put the gun down and just come on out. You don't want to hurt anybody and neither do we."

Duane started to bring his rifle up to his shoulder. Thirty rifles now focused on him while the door drifted farther open. Duane suddenly went into that peculiar set of behaviors, first coughing violently and then sobbing. Vince kept an eye on the situation, and when Duane staggered forward a step, the deputy grabbed the rifle barrel.

Duane was still holding it, so when Vince yanked the muzzle of the weapon toward the middle of the open door, Duane stumbled out the door with it. A moment later, Vince had the weapon, and Duane was sprawled on the front step. Vince quickly pointed to the first two guys on the far side of the door. They stepped forward, grabbing Duane's arms, and dragged him clear of the door. At the same time, the line of posse members moved forward.

Vince nodded to the guy on the other side of the door, slammed the door fully open, and quickly ran into the living room. The other guy then ran in on the opposite side. The entire team was inside almost instantly. Rick could visualize where they were in the house as they yelled that one room after another was clear. All at once, there was a commotion in what had to be the main bedroom. In short order, Kevin came out the front door, a posse member holding each of his arms in a hammer lock.

Shortly after that, Vince and a posse member came out. They were pushing Susie in a gentler fashion. Rick couldn't decide if she looked more afraid or relieved. Maybe it was both. In a couple of minutes, the rest of the posse came out, sour looks on their faces and shaking their heads. Rick looked at Gwendolyn only to find her looking back at him.

"That's not a good sign."

She just nodded, and looked at Lyle Lillard, who was still mounted and gazing down at the three with an expression of extreme distaste. "Kevin, I was very specific when I told you how it would be. Duane, when we talked several days ago, you assured me you understood, and that working with the couple who know about our local wild plants was what you needed to do. Both of you messed up big time. Duane, you severely injured Charles. Then the two of you beat up Dennis Maguire. I am not even going to ask for an explanation from either of you, because there is nothing you could say. Vince, when you talked to the Maguire family, how old did they say Susie is?"

"Susie is sixteen, Mr. Lillard."

"That's not of age in any jurisdiction I know of. Susie, you're going home. We will keep an eye on your family, and if there's a problem, we will deal with it separately. Vince, have a couple of your people escort Miss Maguire home. Be nice if you can. Use restraints if you must. By the way, do any of these people have coats?"

Vince said a couple of words to two of his people. They dashed into the house, and came out, coats in hand, a few minutes later. Susie was handed her coat, and shuffled off dejectedly, accompanied by a couple of posse members. Lyle watched silently, and waited until she was out of sight going down the road. Only then he turned back to Kevin and Duane, both standing in front of his horse.

"Duane, I've heard the opinion that you need a shrink the worst way. We don't have any such animal. Rick, you're about the most educated person here, other than your bride. Tell me, in small societies of this size, what do they do?"

Rick was quite uncomfortable at so abruptly becoming the focus of everyone's attention. "I've read some tribes considered insane people to be under the control of either deities or demons. The way Duane acts would support the demons hypothesis."

"We'd have to get a shrink or a priest then. We have neither."

Rick heard Mark chuckle. "For shrinks, there are always shrunken heads."

"Indeed there are, Mark," Lyle returned. "That would certainly make the behavior cease. On the other hand, it is a rather extreme procedure, don't you think?"

Rick was aghast. Could Lyle Lillard be at all serious about that? Looking around, Rick saw a large number of the people there apparently wondering the same thing. Lyle was evidently measuring the mood of the crowd as well.

"Please pardon the poor attempt at levity," Lyle finally continued. "The first time I had to do this kind of thing, it was the cannibal leader, Willy. I banished him. We believe the dust got him in short order. The second was the terrorist who called himself Morgan Carr. He committed suicide rather than face us. Now, we have the other terrorist who tried to kill us with the last vial of Omega bugs and did kill his associate. There was no solution apparent, so he's a one-man chain gang."

"Should we put these two with him?" Vince asked. "Both these guys know things we'd just as soon our terrorist not find out."

"That's an excellent point, Vince," Lyle returned. Then he looked back at Rick. "Do you have jobs here where they could contribute to the solution instead always being the problem?"

Rick glanced first at Gwendolyn and then at Dan. "What do you think, Dan? Could we do something?"

Dan's eyes suddenly lit up. "Remember what they had you doing? You bet, there are lots of jobs around here. We have plenty of overseers, too."

Dan looked at his crew. "Hey, guys, we need to clear the snow from around the house. It looks like the inside needs a thorough cleaning as well. These two gentlemen just volunteered to do it all, especially the dirtiest, nastiest jobs. Watch them closely, though. If they get away, you're the ones who'll have to take care of it."

Mark looked down at Kevin. "What's the matter, Kevin? Usually, there's no way to shut you up. You don't have anything to say now. Why is that, I wonder?"

Kevin looked at the crew of workers coming for him, and then stared at the ground. "I'm so screwed," Rick heard.

Mark looked at Duane, whose eyes weren't focusing very well. Mark then looked at Rick, and Rick couldn't think of anything to do but shrug. Just as the crews claimed the two, Gwendolyn had something to add.

"Say, Duane, you insist that's your house and you're going to protect it. Well, now you get to hang around a little longer. Aren't you glad?"

Duane looked up at Gwendolyn. His eyes suddenly came into focus, and it looked like he might get violent again. Just as soon as the look passed over his face, though, he started coughing again. As they pushed him over to the house and handed him a shovel, the sobbing started. It got on Rick's nerves. The work crew immediately got in his face, telling him he could only change his diaper once an hour, and it would be quite a while before his bottle of milk was ready.

Kevin was functioning, but it wasn't nearly fast enough for the taste of the working crew. Frankly, the job would get done in a fraction of the time if they simply tied the two up and did it themselves. On the other hand, they were having a really good time.

Gwendolyn stared at the scene and then looked over at Rick. "Is what I'm seeing what they were doing to you?"

Rick sighed. "Yeah, pretty much. These guys may be nicer about it, if anything. Kevin and Duane had the nasty slant down to a fine art."

Lyle Lillard listened it, and shook his head. "I let this situation go altogether too long. Mark, was Kevin this way at Harlan Ranch?"

Mark shook his head. "No, he took pride in learning to do everything the very best way, and even spent a fair amount of time trying to figure out how to do things even better. I have no idea what happened to him."

"Some people get off track when they don't have a supervisor right there all the time," Lyle observed. Then he looked at Rick. "So how well do you work without a boss on your back all the time?"

"Time will tell. With Gwendolyn beside me, I'll be able to keep my mind on the job. That's, of course, when I don't have my mind on her."

Gwendolyn approved of that comment, and squeezed Rick's arm.

Dan looked around then. "Would you all like some lunch? I think we've got enough for everybody."

Lyle shook his head. "We've accomplished what we came to do. It looks like you've got plenty of ways to keep these two gentlemen amused. To keep them from temptation, though, Vince, keep a couple posse members here. Kevin and Duane, both of you look at me. Also, all you posse members, listen up."

The work crews got quiet, and the two looked at Lyle.

"The posse members have these instructions. If Kevin or Duane try to escape, escape, fail to cooperate with the work crews to which they are assigned, or generally become a nuisance, the posse members are authorized to shoot. They should not try for a fatal shot, but if that's what it takes to stop them, so be it. Are there any questions?"

Rick was astonished. He saw the posse members were surprised by the instructions, but fully supportive of it. Over next to the house, he saw Kevin's mouth move, and it looked like he was repeating what he said a short time earlier, "I'm screwed."

Kevin then spoke up. "Mr. Lillard, sir, how long will we do this?"

"Ah, you want a specific term that might reduce for good behavior and all of that? Consider it a variable sentence. We will look at a number of things. How long will Susie be pregnant? After the birth, how long will she need to care for the child? How long will it take for Charles to be right in the head? How long will it take Dennis Maguire to heal? Kevin, you will be here until the damage you've caused is gone. Beyond that, you will serve until I am convinced you not only can be a productive, functioning member of our society, but in fact already are."

That made sense to Rick. The message got through to Kevin. Rick saw Kevin's shoulders slump. Whether anything got through to Duane, Rick couldn't tell, since he just stood there staring with his jaw slack. Lyle touched the brim of his hat in Rick's direction, and wheeled his horse for home. Vince made an ad hoc schedule between his posse members, and took off, leaving two of them behind. The two conferred briefly, and took up stations on either side of the two work gang members. Dan's crew then started to work themselves, periodically harassing the pair.

"Would the two of you join us for lunch?" Dan inquired hopefully.

"We'd be delighted."

Rick took Gwendolyn's arm, following Dan around the house toward the mostly thawed alley. It was getting messy, but the mood was upbeat, what with the warm spell and all. The three ate together, and Rick got thinking about the situation.

"I don't want to see the inside of the main house until and unless it manages to become habitable. Watching the posse members gag as they went inside makes me disinclined to have anything to do with the place until then. Maybe you could give us updates every day or so about the house, and what you've found for our two laborers to do. I'd hate to hear that they're bored."

Dan laughed. "If nothing else, we can have them finish the fencing projects they had you working on. Whatever else happens, those two will not be allowed on any project they can simply sabotage. I read how the Nazis used slave labor to build armaments and defensive positions, and how those laborers messed things up every chance they got."

Rick considered Dan was someone he needed to keep a close eye on, indeed.

After watching them extract the three, Rick was certain that moving back in there was going to be later rather than sooner. Listening to Dan's ideas over lunch, it sounded like that date would be much later.

"You know," Dan told them, "those two are going to scrub every bit of nastiness from the main house. I'm debating whether to make them do it with toothbrushes."

"What about if women show up for training?" Gwendolyn wanted to know.

"We might have to build a separate bunkhouse for them. From what the guys in the work crew told me about what they've seen and smelled in there, it may not be possible to clean the main house. It's likely that we'll have to tear out all the plaster and dry wall, and redo it. Those two might have saved everybody a lot of aggravation if they used the internal structure of the house as firewood. That's all it's good for now. I'm not even sure if we want to put the wood in a stove."

"They did that much in a couple of days?" Rick was aghast.

"There were no sanitary facilities. They smeared it everywhere. What they didn't eat joined the nastiness on the walls, floors, and even the ceiling."

Gwendolyn shook her head. "You make it sound like we should have just left them in there. I'm amazed Susie survived the experience."

Dan shook his head sadly. "You saw as much of her as the rest of us. Pregnant and sixteen is not a problem I have a clue about. Having no support doesn't help. We need to expand our population, but babies having babies isn't the way to do it. Kevin cleaning the main house with a toothbrush won't cut it. He needs to lick that crap off the whole place. Since Duane doesn't have a mind to call his own any more, I can't say anything about him. Kevin, on the other hand, has no excuse."

"Damn, Dan, you're not only creative, you're vicious. Gwendolyn, remind me to keep an eye on his ass."

"Like he kept one on mine?" she asked sarcastically.

Dan's face reddened. "I have no way to assure you of my future good intentions about either of you."

Rick nodded. "That's quite true. Listening to your intentions for Kevin tells me I need to pay very close attention to everything going on around here."

Gwendolyn nodded, glancing at Rick, but now focusing totally on Dan, much to his discomfiture. Dan just gulped and looked off to the side.

Rick suddenly found he was reading the situation. He settled back in his chair, looking as comfortable as possible. "We need to discuss exactly what everybody's doing now, as well as what needs to be done before the next storm gets here."

Rick's action seemed to push Dan even further out of his comfort zone. Gwendolyn glanced at Rick with a slight smile before turning once again back to Dan, who visibly wilted under the combined attention.

"Uh, right, Rick. What do you want to know about first?"

"The public area of the bunkhouse looks good. Let's take a tour. Are any of the crews resting right now? I don't want to barge in on them or anyone having private time. I do want you with us, Gwendolyn."

They looked at nearly everything. Gwendolyn brought up points that Rick never thought about. It also seemed to be effective at keeping Dan from trying to sell what was there as being the right thing. Gwendolyn kept bringing up questions about why things were done a one way and not some other way. It had an additional effect, because Rick started to see shortcuts taken that should have been done better.

Later on, they inspected the horses and the minor bit of training being attempted at the time. If the weather stayed good for a few days more, they agreed conditions might permit a little outdoor training, which would be tremendously helpful for both the horses and trainees. The circuit took them back to the main house, where the snow was now cleared away from the outside. Their two chore boys were inside, under rapidly rotating close supervision.

Getting close to the open front door was all Rick could manage. Even from there, he could see Dan's description of the situation was not only accurate but fell short of reality. It was just awful. Gwendolyn managed to stick her head in the door and look around for a few seconds before pulling back. Rick's respect for what she could tolerate really jumped up at that point. The two finally headed back for what no longer looked like temporary housing after that.

As they got comfortable, Rick looked at her. "How could you stand that stench?"

Gwendolyn rewarded him with a knowing smile. "How long have women smelled the dirty butts they cleaned up? Honestly, I couldn't stand it, but I told myself I had to know just how bad it is now. That way,

I will be able to appreciate it all that much more when it's actually ready for real live people to be in again."

Rick had a sudden thought and chuckled, making Gwendolyn look at him strangely. "I just thought about making those families in Ragan who had you enslaved those months stay in the main house for a while. They'd love it."

Gwendolyn got thoughtful then. Rick got concerned, worried he'd said something really wrong. After a moment, she nodded.

"You know, Rick, that's exactly what they did to me. I hadn't thought about it that way, and they certainly never described it like that, but they really had enslaved me. That was involuntary servitude of the first water. Come to think of it, they did pretty much the same thing to you. Yeah, those Ragan families need to be here with Kevin and Duane. They won't be, but they need to be."

It was another great evening with his wife, and it seemed as though they managed to know each other a little bit better. Their lovemaking included the passion of previous times, but now somehow seemed a little more comfortable, as well. Later, lying comfortably together, Rick even brought it up.

"You know, Gwendolyn, if this is what married life is all about, I think I'm going to like a whole lot of it."

"What about when we have six brats, and three of them are raising hell?"

"I was the one everybody lectured because I consider the negative outcomes instead of having a positive attitude?"

Gwendolyn gave him a kiss. "You're such a bad influence."

The next morning dawned bright and clear. Gwendolyn informed Rick that she felt like staying home for a change. She sent Rick forth to dispense wisdom, justice, and favors. He found himself heading back to the main house.

The two current posse members responsible for babysitting their two delinquents were dismounted. They were trying to figure out how to both keep a good watch and stay out of the stench. For now, they took turns. The strategy was to take a deep breath, walk up to the house, look through a window or door, and return to fresh air as quickly as possible.

"Are they giving you any trouble?" Rick asked one posse member.

"So far, the only problem is your work crew getting too enthusiastic about encouraging them to work harder, faster, and better. Mostly, it is funny, but we had to slow the immediate supervision a couple of times."

"How long would they keep working if everybody got distracted?"

"They wouldn't be there longer than two seconds before high-tailing it for the deepest woods they could find. What they might do then is anybody's guess. Mark would be able to track them anywhere."

Rick shook his head. "It's your turn to be in the barrel. I don't envy you the job. Dan thinks we need to take everything down to the studs."

"From what I can tell, that's about right."

Rick didn't look inside this time. He headed back toward the other house, turning off toward the bunkhouse. There, work crews continued some of the projects discussed the previous day. That was reassuring, and something Gwendolyn would like to know about, he was certain.

Dan suddenly hustled up. Rick didn't know why he did it, exactly, but he looked at Dan and just grinned a little. "Your spy network must not be working today. I've been out and about a while now."

Dan really got flustered at that point, and Rick chuckled. "One thing I'd like to see is where our honored guests bed down these nights."

Dan got himself under control then. "They made you sleep on a cot in the hallway over at the main house. The guys in the posse said they had to have a place with shelter and heat as well as secure. We had most of this stuff anyway, and thought it was appropriate."

He led Rick to a corner of the public area behind a high-efficiency wood heating stoves. Dan opened a panel exposing hog confinements, stacked on top of each other, with a secure latch on the public side.

"We told them even hogs wouldn't live the way they had in the main house, so this was too good for them, but that's where they stay at night. Guys stay here by the fire, and the posse has people in here as well. We were originally going to store firewood there, but we've got enough other places for that. Did we do okay?"

Rick laughed. "It looks like poetic justice to me. Did the members of the posse say it was okay?"

"More than that, Vince inspected it and told me this was as secure as anything he could have found. He chuckled, so I didn't worry much."

"Since you've been chatting with deputy Vince, did he say anything about the McCook people down in Orleans?"

"They're settling in just fine, he says. You're one of the people they talk about as saving them. They figure if the snow is this deep here, with that intense belt of snow going up through McCook, they'd have died by now, because of their houses' roofs caving in if nothing else."

"If they want to build statues, they need to start with Mark, Lyle, and Don Rowley. It was Don who saved the lives of that woman Sammie and her four buddies by forcing them into the last wagon out. Did Vince say anything about Jimmy and Vickie?"

Dan snorted. "You're talking about Vickie, who is the godchild of everybody from McCook. She was not doing very well until Jimmy joined her. Since then, she's basked in all the attention, and her health has improved a lot. Everyone thinks she's pregnant, by the way."

"That was considered a given some time ago. Sensing such things seems to be a specialty of Stanley Peepul."

"Did you ever wonder why we suddenly have such a bunch of gifted people?"

"If you wonder that, Dan, then you also have to wonder why we also have such a bunch of yo-yo's. The way some of them talk, surviving the Omega dust means none of us can be average. What bothers me is that Kevin started out as a really nice guy, and a damn good horse trainer. What happened to him could happen to us, as well."

"Methinks the world has gone crazy, save for thee and me, and I'm getting concerned about thee."

"Yeah, something like that. Being with Gwendolyn has gotten me to focus. I still think we need to talk to Mrs. Rowley about you, Dan."

Just then came a familiar voice from behind him. "I'm glad to hear I've gotten you focused. I don't think you're focused really well, though, since I've got lunch ready, and you aren't home to eat it. Hi, Dan. Why aren't your crews doing lunch? I expected to have to fight my way through the door to get here."

"The time is getting on, isn't it? I'd better get everybody moving. It is odd when they forget to show up for lunch."

Dan hustled out to take care of business. Gwendolyn came up to Rick and gave him a lingering kiss. Then she looked at the cage behind the panel. "What's that?"

When he told her, she nodded and smiled. Then she shook her head.

"A hog confinement for some super pigs. That's great. At the same time, it's sad and sickening that we're back in that kind of business. What do you want to bet those work crews accomplish less than half of what they would have done without the two of them being there?"

Rick agreed with that. "In a sense, we've sunk to Kevin's level, which means he's won. Still, what else can we do?"

They walked, hand in hand, along the walkway toward the house. Just as they got to the opening for the alley going to the main house, Dan reappeared, poking his head inside.

"Rick, you need to see this. Maybe you should see it too, ma'am."

Rick and Gwendolyn looked at each other, mystified.

"Will lunch hold for a few minutes?" Rick wondered.

She shrugged. "I don't know why not. If it's burnt to a crisp, I'll have you stick around and make conversation while I do it again. What do you think of that?"

"Sounds like a plan. Let's go see what Dan found."

In front of the main house, everybody was in a circle. Dan led the way through what felt like a crowd, even though the mob was no more than two deep anywhere around the circle. Inside, Kevin and Duane were face-down in the mud, their hands tied behind their backs, and each closely attended by a posse member.

One of the posse members looked up as Rick arrived. "The work crews were getting ready for lunch. These two pilgrims didn't think we were paying sufficient attention, and made a break for it. You can see how far they got. Duane tried to snatch my rifle. I kept the rifle, but gave him the rifle butt. What do you want us to do with them?"

Rick walked over and looked at Duane. The posse member had butt stroked the opposite side of his face from where Gwendolyn nailed him. Duane's eyes weren't focused. Then Rick crouched down about three feet from Kevin's face. Kevin's expression was like what he remembered of seeing trapped animals.

"What should we do with you two, Kevin? Mr. Lillard gave you the best deal he could, and you two beat up a couple of guys to reward him. Now, after he gave you the opportunity to clean up what you fouled up, you're here, face down in the mud."

Rick sighed, standing up, looking at the posse member. "Everybody fought the feeling all this time. All we can do is to secure them as well possible. Then one of you needs to find Vince and see about the shackles they put on prisoners' ankles. We need to get some of those heavy-duty eyelets to put into the floor where they're confined at night. They have to be chained down wherever they are, but they still have to work."

The posse member nodded. "Mr. Lillard told the Taliban fellow that he should work as hard as everyone else. If there's anybody fed last or least, it will be him."

Dan looked around at the circled work crews. "You heard the man. We'll eat in shifts. Those not eating had better closely guard these two and be armed. You saw what happened when we got even a little sloppy."

Rick looked at a posse member. "You'd better double-check Kevin. He's far and away the most dangerous of the two."

The posse member nodded. Then he handed Rick his weapon. "Just in case."

The two posse members gave Kevin their full attention. Gwendolyn softly asked Rick, "Could you really shoot him?"

Glancing down at Duane, Rick saw his eyes were focused again. "I'll do what I need to do. Mr. Lillard said shoot to wound, but if the situation requires a fatal shot, that's okay."

Duane suddenly started coughing, and switched to sobbing after a few moments. It was all too predictable. Rick wondered if the cough and sob routine was an act. There was no way to test it that didn't include the likelihood of injury to Duane, so he just looked at Gwendolyn and shook his head. She mouthed back at him to keep his cool. While it was good advice, considering it was easier than following it. Fortunately, the two posse members finished with Kevin, and moved over to Duane. Rick took the couple of steps to get a bit closer to Kevin, who was now trussed up like the proverbial Christmas goose.

Rick was no more eager to get up close and personal with Kevin than a live mountain lion. Rick stood behind Kevin and backed up a step. The two men smelled really bad. Gwendolyn suddenly approached Kevin.

"Why did you do this, Kevin? Susie doesn't want you to be this way."

Kevin groaned, gritted his teeth, and struggled against the bindings. "It was mine. It was all mine. Just when I grabbed it, they took it all away. Old man Maguire told me to go away. Then he made me do women's work. I couldn't see Susie either way. I had the ranch. I gave Mark his marching orders and he was marching away. He really was. Then Rick plays assistant driver for Mark, and they both end up heroes. Lyle Lillard told me that I couldn't be a hero."

"Why couldn't you be a hero, Kevin?" Gwendolyn asked.

Rick stood there amazed. Kevin yakked like Rick was nowhere near. Kevin knew he was three feet behind his head with a loaded weapon. Didn't he?

"I had to train horses so Mark could be the big war hero. Then Rick comes sliding back to the ranch with everybody talking about what hot shit he is. I'm not stupid. He was coming back to push me out of a job. First I lose my girl, and then I lose my position. It was all too much. Well, Mark is nobody and Rick is nothing. I'll show them."

The two posse members were done with Duane. In addition, Dan had four armed crew members. Everybody listened to Kevin rant about his situation, and got an ear full. Rick was happy to hand the weapon back to the posse member. There was nothing he could think to say about what he just heard. Dan was not so taken aback.

"Kevin, old son, Mark will be overjoyed to hear your opinion. As for that person you just called nothing, he's going to have a nice lunch with his bride. Meanwhile, the young girl you knocked up is back home with her parents because she is a child. Meanwhile, there you are, all tied up, covered with mud and your own excrement. Yep, it's all yours."

Walking back for lunch, Gwendolyn commented, "Dan is no better than Kevin or Duane. He just hasn't gone over the edge yet. You do know that, don't you?"

Chapter 13

Players in the Penalty Box

Vince was concerned about his guys spending too much time around the smell of the house at Wagon Ranch, not to mention the people. His posse consisted of everybody in Harlan who could shoot and who had a horse. It was the basic militia concept. Since they all did it in addition to everything else they had to do, Vince didn't want to any of them to spend more time dealing with protecting Harlan than was absolutely necessary. Swapping people at Wagon Ranch frequently made good sense.

Heading for Wagon Ranch with two replacements, he ran into Mark and Lyle who were on their way to check on Rick, the fledgling ranch manager and penitentiary warden. Vince had no idea what he'd find, but didn't expect to see one of the posse members who was supposed to be guarding the two riding toward them in a hurry.

"Kevin and Duane made a break for it. We got them under control, and everybody at Wagon Ranch is keeping an eye on them. Rick asked me to get you, along with some manacles from the sheriff's office."

"You found me and you know where to find the jewelry. I hate the thought of getting back into that kind of business but you'd better bring them in case we can't come up with any better solution."

As the posse member moved down the road, Lyle looked at Mark, a grim look on his face.

"It looks like this will be something more than a social call."

The group moved on with more urgency then, arriving to find Dan trying to keep order as his group shouted imprecations at the two figures lying hog-tied in the frozen mud. Dan all at once became aware of the group's arrival.

"Would you mind getting Rick up here?" Lyle asked. "We can ride herd on this bunch, unless you think they won't listen to us."

Dan gulped but got himself together. "They had better listen to you, sir. I'll get Rick."

The two soon returned. Lyle looked at Rick and grimaced.

"We were on our way here when the posse member showed up to tell us about the escape attempt, as well as what you requested."

Rick was apologetic. "Having them in chains probably won't do us any good, but I'm at a loss to know what else to do with them."

"Tell me something, Rick. Have they made a positive impact on your operation?"

Rick shook his head. "Their presence has cut productivity to less than half what it was with them gone. Is that about what you've seen, Dan?"

Dan squirmed at the question, and it was a moment before Dan could answer. When he did, he started with his head bobbing up and down. "Everybody here just wants to train horses and riders. Trying to be a penal colony doesn't suit our talents at all. I was a little too eager to volunteer us to watch these two. The lads had a lot of personal issues with both of them, and each one of them wanted to get their individual problems settled while they could."

Lyle looked back. "Is that your observation as well, Rick?"

"That's more extreme than what I've seen, but in general it's about right. I asked for shackles, chains, and eyelets because I didn't know any other way to keep them from hurting somebody else. Gwendolyn brought up the fact that nothing we do is likely to make either of them into people we'd want to have around."

Lyle nodded. "I agree. We kept the man moving to get the items. They are at the jail in Alma. It'll be tomorrow before they get it here, though. Meanwhile, these two are wrapped up nicely for Christmas. Unfortunately, they smell awful, and I can't think of any recipient who would accept them."

Mark looked at Lyle. "You mentioned how Clay Williams has been looking for an apprentice. Duane seems like a stout type. If we could figure out appropriate security measures, he might be of some use there."

Vince leaned forward in his saddle. "The shackles and chains from Alma are hardened steel. Duane would have an interesting time trying to do anything to them with Clay's equipment. We'd need a posse member nearby in any case."

Lyle nodded. "That resolves Duane. What about Kevin?"

Now he directly addressed Kevin. "What about it, Kevin? What should we do with you, my boy?"

Kevin had nothing to say, but spread hateful looks all around him.

Mark raised his eyebrows after a moment. Vince wondered if the two of them hadn't come up with a fall-back position earlier. That thought was confirmed when Lyle nodded briefly and Mark spoke.

"There are a few people that Kevin wouldn't want to take on, either physically or mentally. That would be Tom, his wife Sammie, and the other snipers, as well as Stanley Peepul."

Kevin croaked, "You can't do that. The Peepul tribal members are cannibals. Those snipers are nothing but murderers."

"Would Tom or Stanley take him?" Lyle inquired. Vince was certain that was a staged question.

Mark smiled. "When I gave Tom and his bunch their new mission, I specified there would be additional missions. Keeping track of Kevin, the boy wonder, could be such a mission for them. Now, as for Stanley, I recall hearing that Stanley's hunters roam beyond their assigned hunting grounds. Stanley knows where his hunters go. He's aware that we know. Keeping track of Kevin might be part of his fee for poaching. Anyway, if anybody could tell whether Kevin reformed, it would be Stanley."

"You're right, Mark. Stanley's managed to do some amazing things with that band of thieves, misfits, and drug addicts. We'll give it a try."

Lyle now looked around at everybody gathered there. "Any of you with a personal vendetta against either of these two should take care of it now. They are both leaving, and won't see each other or any of you again. Rick, you have the main complaint, so you are first in line. Do whatever you need to do. As I recall, they dumped you off a miserable little cot and then proceeded to kick you."

Rick looked at the two tied up and covered with bad odors and cold mud. After gazing at them, he drew his thumb and forefinger across his eyes to the bridge of his nose. "They have to live inside their own heads. That is plenty of punishment. Anyway, doing anything to them now would prove I am as bad as they have been. I don't want that."

Vince saw a large number of the apprentices and wannabe wardens standing around, ready and eager to practice field-goal kicking on the prone bodies. When Rick said that, though, everyone suddenly took a couple of steps back. Lyle nodded approval.

"We may have a manager for the Wagon Ranch." Lyle looked toward the western horizon. "Another storm is coming. We'll get them to Ragan. We'll put them in the basement of the old schoolhouse. Rick, we'll need a couple of pack horses. Throw these two across their backs. We'll return the horses when the storm is over."

Rick nodded to Dan, who signaled in the direction of the opening in the walkway between the other house and bunkhouse. "Two horses are on their way," he reported.

The required horses were soon on hand and Duane and Kevin were aboard, but not in the classic riding posture. With their butts waving in the breeze, there was no way they would enjoy the ride. The biggest impact on Vince was when Rick showed a lot of class, taking the time and effort to ensure the two would stay in position, and not swing down where they could get hit by the horses' hooves.

Now, the wind kicked up, and small ice pellets made things difficult for everybody. Vince, the prisoners and the posse members headed to Ragan, with Mark and then Lyle each peeling off as they passed their roads. Five miles later, in the teeth of a near blizzard, they arrived at the old school, hauling their prisoners into the basement and depositing them in separate storerooms. The posse members were relieved to spend their time in an area that was warm and didn't smell bad.

It was impossible to be certain, but Vince figured he must be the last resident of Ragan still out in the weather as he headed for the stable. By the time he got his horse into a stall and took care of the additional animals pressed into carrying Kevin and Duane, the weather made it questionable whether he should even attempt the two-block hike to his house. The alternative was staying with Don and Nancy Rowley. They were nice folks, but he decided to get home. Stuck inside with the kids for several days would drive Beth crazy. He needed to be the calming presence. If he couldn't do that, they could both go crazy together. That's what marriage was all about, he thought.

Nancy Rowley bustled out from the living quarters, her husband in tow. "You aren't thinking of walking home with that storm, are you?"

"I feel like I need to, Nancy."

"Don will take you home in the sleigh. He insists, don't you Don?"

Don mumbled something under his breath as he shrugged into his winter gear. Vince didn't need an extensive law enforcement background to know who insisted. Don was doing him a favor, unwillingly though it was, so Vince went with him and helped get the sleigh and horse ready. Don kept up an ongoing unconscious monologue. It wasn't meant for anybody's consumption and did not reflect a great deal of happiness.

Nancy held the door open for them as they left, shouting, "Be safe!"

Considering the danger involved going anywhere under the current conditions, now approaching a white-out, Nancy Rowley telling them to be safe qualified as almost funny. Outside, Vince noticed the snow was finer than it had been. Also, the temperature was falling. It was no longer merely ice-cold. It was Arctic. Vince couldn't imagine what that might be about, not that anything about the weather had been normal recently.

His house was two short blocks off the main street. On a better day, Vince could have walked it in a few minutes. Now, it was as though they were lost in whiteness. Don was keeping as close to the buildings on one side as he could, although even then it seemed doubtful that he could possibly know where they were. After what seemed an eternity, they swung away from the buildings and made a wide U-turn. Amazingly, Don landed exactly at Vince's front gate. Vince shook his hand as he got out. Even being just a few feet from the front door, getting into the house turned out to be a major effort. Maybe Nancy was thinking about it the right way after all. Inside, he found Beth was astonished and gratified that he made it.

When the weather cleared a day and a half later, it failed to bring any kind of warming. The sun furnished brightness, but that was all. Harlan might as well have been in Antarctica from the way it felt. Duane's new assignment as an apprentice for Clay may not have been what Duane preferred, but at the moment, it seemed like a plum assignment. It was hard to complain about being on intimate terms with a fire and hot iron during weather like this.

The forge was in a large room behind the stable, and the stalls closest to it were the warmest. That area was a bit on the hot side, actually. The horses liked it a little cooler, and whenever somebody had to sleep in the stable, the back stalls were now the favored areas for people. In a way, those back stalls were now the Motel 6 of Ragan. Kevin would find his fate a bit less heart-warming, Vince thought, but Kevin's protests about both the Peepul and the snipers were overstated, at least at this point in time. In any case, they would take him later when Mark and Lyle could join the group going to Oxford.

Vince walked to the school and went into the basement. Four posse members brought out Duane. He looked appropriately miserable.

"You might not care for the restraints, Duane, but you were still more comfortable last night than you could have been in that house you helped ruin."

"It's my house. Kevin said so," Duane snarled.

"It was not Kevin's house. It never was his. He couldn't give you what he didn't have."

Duane resisted as the posse members pulled him to the stairway, so Vince went over and got in his face. He immediately regretted doing it considering the odor coming off the man.

"You have a choice, Duane. Go under your own power or we will drag you. I will guarantee the concrete stairs over there will leave some welts if we have to pull you up them."

Duane shivered and finally started to move. It was clear that he wasn't going to move any faster than absolutely necessary, almost like he thought his destination was an execution and not an apprenticeship.

Of course, once he tasted the bracing air outside, Duane might decide to pick up the pace a little. As it was, one of the posse members felt sorry for him and put a blanket over his shoulders. Duane didn't react then, but when they went out the door, he wrapped the blanket around himself as close as possible.

They took Duane through the outside entrance into the smithy. The abrupt transition from extreme cold to extreme heat made Vince gasp, and he was prepared for it. Duane predictably had a coughing fit. Clay looked at them like it was just another minor annoyance.

"Lyle says Duane can work as your apprentice, Clay."

"Bringing him in chains doesn't say much for his eagerness."

"I can't argue that point. Can you do something with him."

"If Lyle sent him, I'll do what I can. What do you have to keep him from wandering off?"

"We brought eye-bolts strong enough to keep a battleship in place. There is about ten feet of chain."

Clay pointed to a vertical timber strong enough to hold the entire building up by itself. The posse members tried hard to get the eye-bolts in. Finally, Clay came over and applied a combination of blacksmith arm and six-foot crowbar, finishing the installation. Vince thought that if Duane ever got to the point where he could unhook himself from it, he'd have gotten too strong to mess with in any case.

With Duane now attached to it, Vince kept one posse member there, sending the others home. Vince stood aside to see what would happen.

Duane showed passive aggression toward the situation. Clay told him that his first job was to keep the fire going. Duane responded by squatting against the wall. He didn't look at the fire or do anything. Clay went back to his work, ignoring Duane. After a while, the fire got too low. At that point, Clay took care of the fire. On his way back, Clay stomped on Duane's ankle.

Duane went into his outrage mode. Vince and his posse member prepared to go into action. At the same time, Clay was cool. He looked at Duane with a puzzled look on his face, like a horseshoe got up and protested the location of the nail holes in it.

Finally Clay said, "Everything in here has a purpose. You're on the floor. That means your purpose is to be a floorboard."

Duane really went into attack mode then. He jumped up, grabbed a piece of iron, and swung it at Clay. Vince and the posse member both grabbed their weapons, expecting Harlan's only farrier and blacksmith was about to be laid out on the floor.

Before they could do anything, Clay snatched Duane's wrist with one hand, stopping the swinging bar cold. At the same time, Clay grabbed his chin with the other hand, lifting him six inches off the floor.

Vince was well-acquainted with how strong Clay was, but was amazed at what he saw. Clay did it without getting out of breath. He then banged the arm holding the iron, and the bar clanged to the floor.

Clay now looked Duane in the eye, showing no emotion whatever. "As my apprentice, your first task is to keep the fire going. The only way you'll learn this trade is if you eat. The only way you'll eat is if you do the tasks I give you. Do I need to repeat that?"

Duane, nailed to the wall by Clay's iron grip, looked truly terrified. The smell arriving at his nose told Vince that Duane soiled his pants.

"I want to learn," Duane croaked. "I want to eat. I'll do it."

Clay released him then, and Duane went to look at the fire. After a moment, he started asking procedural questions about how high the fire should be. Vince decided Clay had a command of the situation, but left the posse member in case Duane got any other silly ideas.

Vince went out the other door into the stable. He wasn't surprised to see Mark and Lyle waiting. Vince briefed them about Duane's situation as Clay's new apprentice. They both thought it was funny.

"I wonder if we'll see as much humor in what we're about to do with Kevin," Lyle mused.

"Are you having second thoughts about it, boss?" Mark asked.

"The only other thing we could do is to exile him beyond the fog west of McCook and let him shift for himself. I'm not prepared to do that. Well, I'm not prepared to do that yet."

Vince had no doubt the exile option remained the ultimate sanction to Lyle. They collected Kevin and this time, he got to sit in a saddle. Shackles on his ankles ran through the stirrups and under the horse's belly. He went where the horse went. With his wrists cuffed behind him and the horse on lead, he had no control over that, either.

Lyle decided to go through Huntley on the way to Oxford, even though it was out of their way. Lyle wanted everyone in Huntley to know what was happening to Kevin. They made a special stop in front of the Maguire house. Dennis could not come to the door, but his wife and one of his daughters came out and screeched about how Kevin was a sinner beyond forgiveness. Kevin became jittery. Vince wondered if this was part of what Kevin lived with while doing Susie's work.

Finally in Oxford late that afternoon, everyone was cold. They were unable to get to the bridge, no matter how great their motivation to keep moving. A herd of cattle was there, and a short way beyond, Tom and his boys were there along with the Peepul deciding how soon they could get to any of them. Lyle and Mark carefully moved their horses through the herd and finally crossed the bridge. Vince and his posse members stayed back and kept watch on Kevin.

The conversation about livestock halted, and Mark reminded Tom that prioritizing critters for meat processing was only one mission, and that he had promised them additional missions. Vince fully expected a protest, but whatever Tom said was at such a low volume that Vince couldn't hear it. Wherever the conversation might have gone at that point changed completely because Stanley, the leader of the Peepul tribe showed up.

After hearing about the snipers' task to watch and reform Kevin, Stanley didn't rebut or argue the point. Instead, he observed all the ways that Tom would have to change how he did business and how priorities would, of necessity, have to change. Vince thought it was a telling point that all of the lowered priorities were things they did for Harlan rather than the tribe. For instance, they could not process cattle until other types of game were done. Also, trade with Harlan people would be put off for an unknown number of days.

There was more discussion, but Lyle looked back at Vince in a way that said to do something constructive. Vince nodded and looked at the drovers with the cattle.

"You'll need to build pens for the beef here. You're going to have to get feed and water for them."

The drovers nodded. That was what they expected to hear.

Vince turned to the posse members. "Two of you stay with Kevin. The rest of you help the drovers."

Lyle turned back to Stanley. "One reason we did this was that you are hunting beyond the areas we agreed on."

"My hunters stay inside those limits, Lyle. I know."

"I'm sure you would."

Lyle glanced back at Vince, who saw a new line of duty. He turned to the resident guard nearby.

"Gene, get the word out. The people they see east of Holdrege aren't tribal members. They must be terrorists. Shoot them on sight."

Gene grinned. "I'll get right on that, Vince."

The look Stanley gave Vince made him wonder how far beyond homicide and cannibalism the man really was.

Lyle ignored it. "We all agree then. Vince, bring Kevin across the bridge to meet his new instructors."

Vince nodded to the posse members, who were more than ready to get rid of a problem. They shortly had Kevin off the horse and on his feet. Vince dismounted and conducted the man halfway across the bridge. As far as he was concerned, the handoff could occur right then and there. Nobody rushed up to take him. Kevin looked ill. Vince leaned him against the bridge railing so he could barf into the dry stream bed that had been the Republican River long ago before it changed course.

Vince thought things should have happened sooner rather than later, but Tom and the sniper team just stood there, motionless. It was Stanley who made the first move. He walked across the bridge and looked Kevin up and down. Finally, Stanley turned, and advised Mark and Lyle that a decent outcome was highly unlikely. In spite of that, he would try.

Only then did Tom fix two members of his sniper team with a smile that was all teeth and no humor. "Congratulate yourselves, because I have just declared you fully qualified as drill instructors. Your first boot is this meat head. Your impossible mission is to turn him into a Marine."

Vince recalled the boot camp approach to rehabilitation. There had been good results, so Vince decided to be hopeful. At the same time, he considered the best prospects were those who actually wanted to be Marines.

The two newly designated drill instructors looked at each other for a moment. One shook his head slightly and the other shrugged. Then they stomped up to where Kevin was propped against the bridge guard rail, still in cuffs and leg irons. They tag teamed him, laying streams of verbal abuse far beyond what the military tolerated in the latter days.

Vince cringed, just listening to it. After a little bit, he saw what they were doing, and decided it was kind of funny. They were yelling at the guy who desperately needed the attention. It was the military version of what they heard at the Maguire house. Vince considered that might have as good a chance at giving Kevin religion as anything.

Kevin tried the tough guy routine, but the continued verbal abuse started getting to him. In addition, all the people standing there got a kick out of it. Before long, he stood on the bridge in a posture resembling attention. The snipers told Vince he could take off the restraints. While Vince did it, they yelled at Kevin about how comfortable he was wearing those pretty bracelets, and how he'd wish he was wearing them again."

Lyle and Mark joined Vince then. Lyle told them quietly, "Having a single drill instructor for thirty people was terrifying, as I recall. Two drill instructors on a one guy is beyond my imagination. Knowing both the drill instructors and their boss are certified killers gives the whole affair a dimension that boggles the mind."

The snipers got on either side of him, and marched him off then, whispering sweet nothings in his ears the whole way at full volume. Only distance reduced the harangue to tolerable levels, at least from Vince's point of view.

As they started back, Vince saw a rider charge up the bluff. He was carrying the news that tribal members east of Holdrege were now fair game. Lyle decided his attention needed to be on another subject.

"We need to let Rick and Gwendolyn know they are out of the prison business. It comes to me that his head must be spinning like a top by this time, with everything we've thrown at him. I have to say he's handled it pretty well. Mark and I have already gone over most of it. What do you think of Rick so far, Vince?"

Vince was never comfortable with that kind of conversation. It was one reason he was content to serve as a deputy under Sheriff Crichton even when the sheriff encouraged him to run for the office. It was also among the reasons he refused when Lyle offered him the leadership of Harlan County. Beth never agreed with his decision or rationale, but there it was and he was not sorry about it.

"When you offered Rick the opportunity to exercise instant justice, he wasn't fooled for a minute. If he had taken any physical action against Kevin, it would have been the last thing he did as the Wagon Ranch manager."

"You think you've figured me out, Vince. I still don't hear anything about Rick."

"He got the guys at the ranch on his side. That one guy, Dan, is a problem. He is not on anybody's side but his own. The rest of them seem like regular workers, but Dan is a manipulator. Again, that's more about Dan than Rick. One thing I'll say for Rick is that he does what he thinks is his duty. He'll do it come hell or high water."

"Does he regard ranch management as his duty?"

"He definitely thinks that is a duty. I believe he also thinks of his marriage as a duty. It's hard to say whether he'll come to think of it as something more than a duty at some point."

Lyle seemed to take that under consideration. Vince was relieved when he didn't pursue it any further.

They took the farm road north. As they approached the Harlan Ranch, where Mark lived, a rider approached them.

"Dan sent me to get you, Mark. Rick and Gwendolyn haven't come out of the house they're staying in, and we can't get any response from them. Also, with the snow piled up around the house, there is a definite odor. We don't know what it is."

Vince jumped in then. "We always knew there were drugs of some kind hidden on that place. We took in the best dogs and equipment, but could never find them."

"It appears we need to keep moving, although I'd really rather have a coffee break right now," came from Lyle.

"Did you try to break into the house yet?" Mark asked.

"We haven't done it yet. Dan said we should wait for you."

Lyle nodded. "I don't think the situation calls for us to make him wait one minute longer than necessary, gentlemen. Mark, you and I can take care of this. Vince, make sure Duane and Kevin are looked after properly. I'd like a daily report, if you can."

Now that was the kind of request Vince was more accustomed to handle. They all picked up the pace. In spite of now being on separate missions, the three stuck together until the State highway.

Chapter 14

Herbal Essence

Gwendolyn was waiting when Rick got back to the walkway. "Are we really out of the prison business?" she wanted to know.

Rick could only shrug. "I never knew we were supposed to be in that business. Unless something happens to send them back before they get very far, I would have to guess we're not going to have to worry about them until after this storm lets up. This time, there is no way I'm going to try to walk back to the main house."

"What if there's something I absolutely had to have?" she pouted.

"Then it would be my task to keep you so occupied that you wouldn't have time to think about whatever it might be."

Dan came into the walkway, and after glancing at the two of them, turned his attention to getting panels and reinforcing posts in place to cover what had been the entrance to the tunnel going to the main house. After that was done, he looked back at Rick and Gwendolyn.

"Rick, you were quite right about those two slowing us down to a crawl. I really hoped we'd have reinforced walkways in place before this storm. We're going to have to do it some other way now. Trying to build snow tunnels was just too much work."

"Do we have enough firewood to get through this?"

"I think so. Oh, ma'am, if you let me know what supplies you need, I'll make sure everything gets to you."

Gwendolyn smiled nastily. "Will you do it before I have to take real action to motivate you?"

"What you did already was more than enough for me. I saw what happened to Duane, and want no part of it."

"How about that? You might actually be trainable. When we see Nancy Rowley, I'll be sure to include that with your resume. Let's see, you have decent instincts, but rotten judgment and are kind of slow. Still, you might be trainable. She'll want to know that."

Dan turned red, which Rick could see even in the half-light of the walkway. He mumbled something that Rick didn't catch, spun, and hurried off toward the bunkhouse. Rick shook his head and looked at Gwendolyn.

"You just won't cut him any slack, will you?"

"Are you kidding? I could hear what was going on up there. If you hadn't said and done what you did, Dan and his buddies would still be trying to kick field goals with those two."

"Lyle Lillard and Mark wouldn't have let it go that far. I don't think they would have let me do anything in the first place."

"Probably not, but that wouldn't keep Dan from taking every lick he could get. There's one thing about Dan any prospective mate would have to know about. That sucker has a vicious streak."

They strolled on back to what Rick now assumed would be their home for quite a while. "You're absolutely right about him. Did you hear what they're going to do with Duane and Kevin?"

"Oh, yes, I certainly heard all of that. I saw Clay Williams when they sent me over to the Rowley place. Duane does not want to try the frypan to the head trick with him. Would they really send Kevin to the snipers and cannibals?"

"They all say that Stanley reformed that bunch of hopefully former cannibals. Mark's right, if anybody could figure out if Kevin is ever fit for prime time, it would be Stanley. What I've seen of him is truly incredible. As much as anything, I think they've given up on Kevin. Lyle and Mark must figure that if he runs away from Oxford, it will be some way other than into Harlan."

They were nearly to the house now. Gwendolyn stopped and looked at Rick. "Still, if Kevin's really gone crazy, he just might head back into Harlan."

"I can't argue that point," Rick replied, and opened the door for her.

"You're just going to hope their situation is finally resolved," she commented as she went inside.

"Let's just say there other are things I need and want to pay attention to," came as he was closing the door.

"Ooh, and what things might those be, pray tell?" she said, spinning around, and interlacing her fingers behind Rick's neck.

"The first of those things would be you. The second would be you. So would everything else on the list."

She gave him a kiss. "Poor baby. You have such a long to-do list. It must be just awful."

"Oh, it is. I don't think I could get to the end of that list, however hard I tried. There's just no end to how wonderful you are."

"Aren't you the romantic devil? This could be a long storm indeed. You'd better come in here with me and protect me, big strong man that you are."

Later, as they ate, the snow piling up outside turned everything into a twilight. "This could be a long winter, indeed. After all, winter won't even start until the end of this month."

"Would you mind being stuck here with me for the next three months?" Gwendolyn asked.

Rick grinned. "Ladies and gentlemen, there's a snark in the house. To quote Br'er Rabbit, don't throw me into the briar patch. Something just occurred to me. We should survey this place, just to make sure they didn't give us a house with peep holes all over the place."

"When I sent you out by yourself earlier, one domestic chore was to take a smoking ember around the house checking for any spots that might indicate holes in the wall. For what it's worth, the place is pretty tight."

Gwendolyn suggested they wander down to the bunkhouse once or twice each day. That would keep the guys from feeling a need to come up to the house for a welfare check. It would also be a helpful management tool, if Dan never knew when the boss and his lady might show up.

"In the meantime," Rick asked, "does our honeymoon keep going whenever you and I aren't out playing manager?"

Gwendolyn stomped her foot. "I never gave it permission to stop. It has to not only go on, but get better."

Rick grinned. "Yes, dear, I'll make a note of that."

"Note? I'll make you a note in a place you'll remember a long time."

"You say Dan is vicious. Now I see the comment came from personal experience, and I am well and truly terrified. By the way, how's that nasty old dragon?"

Gwendolyn now giggled and wrapped her arms around Rick's neck. "That critter quietly crept into his cave, all the way to the back."

"That old dragon just didn't know who he was messing with, did he?"

"The sucker never had a clue."

The house had its own outhouse and well. Both were on walkways separate from the main one extending to the bunkhouse. Rick and Gwendolyn emerged a couple of times a day, and there, by the front door, would be additional firewood as well as any supplies Gwendolyn said she needed the previous time they were out. It was pretty neat, Rick thought, to have all the privacy they wanted but still access to everyone and everything they needed.

The last storm lasted between two and three days. This one went well over three days, with the snow piled higher than anybody had seen before. In spite of that, Rick thought it was a very peaceful and nice time. Nearly all of that attitude was because Gwendolyn made sure it went that way.

One thing Rick knew about Wagon Ranch was that it had once been a dairy operation. As such, it had a massive grain storage facility. That included an enclosed tower for augers to transfer grain from one place to another. The tower was quite tall and had a small window at the top. That made it a dandy place to keep watch on the weather during these storms that covered all the windows and doors at the ground level.

A major piece of news whenever Rick and Gwendolyn did their promenade down to the bunkhouse was what might be visible from what they had taken to calling the crow's nest. Among other things, it gave them an accurate count of how many days it had been since the storm started. People took turns climbing the ladder to the crow's nest just to be able to say they had seen what was outside. Finally, the news was that the clouds were breaking up, and the sun was now visible.

Dan offered Rick and Gwendolyn the first look at the clear sky, and neither one of them wanted to pass up that kind of a deal. It was a rather long climb, but they made it, and the sun reflecting off all that snow was quite blinding. In spite of it, they soaked it up greedily. Rick, after his eyes got used to the brightness, looked around as best he could, but the snow was so deep that it was difficult to figure out where anything might be. Dan finally called them down so others could take a look, too.

"What did you guys think of the view?" Dan asked.

"It was really nice," Rick replied. "Looking over the pens, though, I couldn't help trying to overlay a vision of an arena. Frankly, it would be easier to skid the large timbers in over the snow rather than trying to do it over rocks and brush. You mentioned hearing about a place with power poles we could use for structure."

"One of the guys remembered the power company had a yard down in Alma, and that included poles. He wasn't really certain about the large hardware they used to attach the cross arms to the poles, but thought they had to have that kind of thing. All of that must be there somewhere."

"Alma? That's a long hard slog, Dan."

"It would be if we were going to drag them. The best idea I heard was to wait until the roads are actually clear. Then, we'll build rig to hang the pole between car wheels at both ends. The horses would hitch to the front set of wheels. We'd have to fabricate brakes."

"It sounds like you do have a plan. What are the chances that Don Rowley will make off with them before we can get there?"

"From what we've heard, old Don looked at them and scratched his jaw for quite some time. He finally computed the effort it would take him to rat hole them someplace was more than the contribution they'd make to his retirement plan. As far as we know, he's off chasing easier game."

"That's the Don Rowley we all know and love. Okay, then, we just might have something working here. Oh, what about those buildings they put up in various places? I think they call them clear span."

Dan nodded. "We looked at them. They all require a special concrete foundation. Other than that, they're wonderful. Do you have any idea how to move a specific size foundation over here?"

Rick laughed. "I wouldn't have a clue how to do that. Back when they did television shows about moving entire buildings, the one thing they never moved was the foundation. They'd build another one at the destination. What's the phone number for the local concrete company?"

"I tried calling. Nobody ever answered. Come to think of it, I could never get a dial tone. Maybe that had something to do with it."

Gwendolyn decided to get in on the act. "I wanted to order a pizza. I wondered why it never got delivered. Maybe that was the problem."

Dan shook his head, and took off on his next mission.

Rick laughed as Gwendolyn looked at Dan's retreating back. "I think you got him again, Gwendolyn. He's running from your rapier wit."

She grinned back at him then. "Well, he at least got the point. Do you think we'll see bare ground before another storm comes in?"

Rick put his finger over his lips. "We're not supposed to talk about things like that."

"That puts planning in a whole new light. If we are not allowed to forecast or even contemplate things coming, it puts the kibosh on your whole function as a manager, doesn't it?"

"I'm supposed to manage, whatever comes my way. It's something like married couples and babies."

She looked at him and smiled knowingly. "Is that what we've been working on lately? Why didn't I get the memo?"

Judging from what Gwendolyn did when they got to their little house, her complaint did not create a problem regarding the pursuit of the married couple project. If anything, it got things even hotter and steamier than ever. Rick didn't know what to think about that, except to consider that she might really want children.

Afterward, he decided it was time to broach the subject. "I take it you're not unalterably opposed to having a family," he finally said, not knowing how to say it any more delicately.

Gwendolyn giggled at that. "Mr. Forbes, with the current state of human civilization, there is only one way a girl could be certain of not having a family. Just in case nobody explained it to you yet, what we've been doing is most definitely not that way. Just out of curiosity, since you are a Forbes, are you on the Forbes 400 list ofw richest people?"

Rick laughed. "You and I are the first two on the only Forbes list I'm associated with. If you wanted 398 kids, we should have started much, much sooner."

She gave him a kiss. "You're such a disappointment. I thought you'd surely have billions of dollars to support me in the fashion to which I would like to become accustomed."

"If it's just dollars you want, we could run into town and make the rounds of the banks. I'm not sure what you could use it for, though. It won't even burn properly, so it's not much help in starting a fire."

"I was hoping for servants at my beck and call."

"We can call Dan and his buddies. They'd be glad to come down here and take care of whatever you would tolerate. I'm sure none of them would be trying to see anything improper."

Gwendolyn slapped his bare hip. "I'll bet they'd promise, anyway. I'd need quite a few skillets to keep them in line, and it would be far more effort than I really want to make right now. Do you know what would be really nice right now? I'd like to see a little sunshine coming through the window."

"You got to see it for five minutes, and you know what they say about too much exposure to the sun. I'd really hate to see anything happen to your flawless skin," he said, softly stroking her leg.

More quality family time ensued at that point, even though it would never have been accepted on broadcast television.

Sometime later, as they just lay comfortably together, Gwendolyn commented, "Isn't it strange, how we've gotten so comfortable with each other, and are busy pursuing children and a family on the one hand, but have never really bothered with the romantic end of it all?"

That made Rick think. "Everything people used to do to try to get to know each other no longer exist. I did take you for that one horseback ride. On the other hand, we've been attacked, shot at, and lots of other things many couples never experienced in their entire lives. I'm not sure what that says for how well we've gotten to know one another, but it seems like quite a bit."

"What kind of world are we creating, Rick?"

"Lyle Lillard seems to have concluded that people are going to do all the things, both good and bad, that people have always done. That's in spite of every effort we make to push the situation toward the positive. If we do everything we can to make things good, then hopefully our kids will be in a better position to do them even better."

"Our kids," Gwendolyn breathed. "That sounds awfully nice. We should work on our project some more, but I'm famished. Let's go see what we can find to cook. Come to think of it, the house got really chilly. Maybe we need to get the stoves built back up. You need a little time to recover anyway."

Rick shook his head. "I realized something. You never needed to worry about a dragon. I'm the one who needs to worry about the dragon, because you are the dragon."

"What say we get something to eat, and then you can experience what a fire-breathing monster I really am."

In spite of the chill, neither of them got dressed. Instead, they both just hustled some in getting some warmth back in the house. It seemed like wasted effort to get dressed when they both knew the clothes would go away again in a very short time. With the fire going in the heating stove in the living room, Rick took a chance and invaded Gwendolyn's domain. In the kitchen, she had the cook stove fired up, and was starting to cook. Rick turned a chair sideways to face Gwendolyn.

"That was one wild night. You know, I remember us doing a lot of things. It included many more things than we could have possibly done in a single night. On the other hand, any details seem kind of hazy. It's really strange. Is it possible there were strange weeds attached to the fire logs?"

Gwendolyn turned and looked at him. "It's strange you should say that. I was thinking pretty much the same thing. It is as though several days got compressed into a single night." She checked the food on the stove, and then walked over and straddled Rick's legs. She wrapped her arms around his neck, and pulled his face forward into her breasts. Just as she did that, a beam of light pierced his eye.

A moment later, Rick had pulled back from her a little, much to her displeasure. He stared at the upper left corner of the kitchen window.

"What was that all about?" she wanted to know.

"Do you remember when you said you'd like to see a little sunshine come through the window? Well, a whole bunch of it nearly blinded me. Look for yourself."

They both peered out the tiny open area at blowing snow and pale blue skies. Just then there was a firm knock on the front door. They both stared at each other.

"Who's there?"

"Lyle Lillard and Mark Tahner."

There was no mistaking Mark's voice. "We'll be there in a second," Rick yelled as they both sprinted for the bedroom to get dressed.

On the way back, Gwendolyn went back into the kitchen to check the food while Rick went to the front door.

"I didn't think they'd have the roads open for a day or two yet," Rick commented, opening the door.

"They've been open for a couple of days now," Mark replied, his face reflecting a combination of humor and concern. "We've been camped here for a day and a half now. Your people got concerned when you guys didn't come out for several days, and sent a messenger when the roads opened."

Mark's nose wrinkled, and he backed up a couple of steps. "We need to talk, but we shouldn't do it here."

Gwendolyn came to the front door, wrapping herself around Rick. "Come on in. We were just about to have some breakfast. I can make more."

Lyle shook his head. "It's the middle of the afternoon. We both had breakfast. We also had lunch."

Rick shook his head. "Really? I didn't think we slept that late."

"You missed the point again, Rick. The two of you went into that house more than three days ago. Nobody saw you any time since then. Whatever the two of you have been doing, it didn't include eating very much. Look at how loose your clothes are."

Puzzled, Rick saw that his pants were rather baggy compared to how they were when he'd just had them on before. Gwendolyn was checking her clothes as well, finally nodding her head. "Yeah, it's true. I seem to have lost between one and two dress sizes overnight. How could that happen?"

"Judging from the odor coming out of your door," Lyle informed them, "as well as how much you've both shrunk, it appears the two of you had non-stop sex for four days. I thought Mark and Ellen got carried away with their love life, but this is beyond belief."

Mark did a deep mock bow. "I am truly in the presence of greatness. I am not worthy."

Lyle raised his eyebrows at Mark. "No, you really aren't worthy, but we put up with you anyway. Leave the door open, and let's go to the bunkhouse. One thing will be to get the two of you some chow. We also have things to discuss."

They only allowed Rick and Gwendolyn back inside to get their boots, and made them walk in front of them toward the bunkhouse. Along the way, where Dan had put in extra panels and beams, there was now a spacious tunnel heading to the main house. Rick and Gwendolyn could only stare at it as they went by.

In the dining room of the bunkhouse, Dan did a Dr. Frankenstein impression, declaring, "They're alive!"

Rick didn't think the impression was all that good, and contented himself with simply nodding at Dan as Mark and Lyle steered them to a table in the corner. Witnessing the fact of their appearance not being unexpected, food began appearing almost immediately. Mark and Lyle just had coffee and watched the two of them. Rick thought they both still looked a bit amused along with a great deal of concern.

After Lyle and Mark looked at each other, and Mark opened. "Your crew performed extremely well. The moment the roads were open, Dan sent a rider to let me know about your situation. There's something strange about the air in that house. Dan mentioned it when he took us there the first day. Lyle and I both agreed it wasn't his imagination."

Lyle took over. "It's a good thing the work crew all moved to the bunkhouse. We've had the guys build the new tunnel over to the main house as a priority. They've torn out everything in the house, and have put in new walls. It isn't fancy, but it's clean. Mark and I slept there the last two nights. Now we're going to tear everything out of the lower house, as well. To make it a dormitory for women this coming spring, we would have to do that anyway. One thing is for sure. I cannot allow you two in that house again."

"Could there be something in the two houses making people do strange things?" Rick asked.

"That's our best guess. We can only hope that Kevin and Duane can manage to get beyond whatever happened to them. The fact that the two of you walked out of the house of your own free will is a positive sign. You'll both be going back to the main house, which was the point of the exercise anyway."

"Just out of curiosity," Gwendolyn put in, "when they were tearing stuff out of the main house, did they find anything in the walls other than the usual construction materials?"

Mark and Lyle looked at each other. "Yes, they did. It was almost like they used vegetation for insulation. Nobody could figure out what it was or how it got there."

Rick suddenly had a thought. "That couple in Ragan, Charles and Marcie, where Duane lived with for a few days until he went off his nut — maybe they can identify it. Gwendolyn and I knew we had a strange experience, and one thing we wondered was if there were herbs involved. At the time, the only thing I could think of was pot or something stupid like that."

"We'll have them keep an eye out for anything like that. It sounds to me like you are both functioning more or less properly now. Maybe we should head on up to the main house so you can see where you live now."

Gwendolyn shook her head. "I detect a common denominator here. We had no choice about moving out, and now we didn't get a choice about moving back. At least you let us put our boots on. That was not something Duane was likely to allow."

After they got into the new tunnel and a little privacy, Lyle told them about how it went with Duane. "Vince heard him say that he wanted to learn," Lyle concluded. "Nobody ever heard him say that before. Maybe there is hope for him."

Rick shook his head. "Duane understands logic after all. It just has to be expressed properly. Manhandling horses evidently equips a person to speak the language. I realize the risk involved with changing the subject, but Gwendolyn and I noticed the sun was still shining a short while ago. That means we've had several days of good weather. With both of you still here, nobody expects any more storms right away."

Mark grinned. "Damn, Rick, not only are your lights on, everybody's home, too. Nobody would call this weather 'good.' It is clear and the sun shines, but these conditions are more like Antarctica. It's just bloody cold, mate. We figure the snow storms are far south of us. Other than the sun being out, about the only good thing is that nobody's particularly worried about the terrorists attacking."

Rick thought about that for a moment. "I heard people talk about how the geese used to fly through here heading south in the fall, and north again in the spring. They were talking about how they missed seeing them last fall, and nobody seemed to know why they no longer went through here. Maybe it's because we now get the snowstorms going south in the fall, and north again in the spring."

Mark and Lyle looked at each other. Lyle finally commented, "That makes sense. It isn't welcome news, by any means, but it makes sense. Maybe the Canada geese and ducks found another migratory pattern to follow. Oh, were you at all interested in what became of Kevin?"

"My hand still twinges from him stepping on it. Sure, I'd like to know."

Lyle described what happened when they took Kevin to Oxford, and Gwendolyn reacted swiftly. "Doesn't that mean trouble finding enough food to get through the winter?"

Lyle shook his head. "Harlan is well stocked with supplies, even if Stanley doesn't send us one more bite. There is a lot of game in Harlan, and even more east of us. We have plenty of hunters and people who can process meat. We can even take care of the pig population. Everyone has accumulated ammunition and reloading equipment, along with extra weapons. Well, here we are, back at your once-again home."

Inside, the basic layout was the same. The two smaller bedrooms were a bit larger at the expense of the bathroom. In addition, there was a counter between the living room and kitchen. Gwendolyn approved that, commenting it updated the look of the place, and made it possible to heat the area more easily. She added, "I see we managed to keep the same cookstove. It is hard to mess up this much cast iron."

"There is that," Lyle replied. "Oh, to save you the effort of asking, we already sent for Charles and Marcie. I don't expect Charles, but Marcie should be here tomorrow. She can tell us about the organic matter in the walls. At least that's what we hope."

Rick considered that and asked, "It's hard to imagine a single cause for what happened to Gwendolyn and me creating such different effects in Kevin and Duane. I'll try to be open-minded on the subject."

"Having massive sexual urges and not being able to fulfill them might make some people crazy," Gwendolyn suggested. "The object of Kevin's lust was just out of reach. Duane is another problem, obviously."

"How is Gwendolyn now?" Lyle asked.

Gwendolyn started to reply, and then stopped to think. Finally, "I think I'm okay now. Still, I thought I was okay when something else was running the show."

Mark chortled, "Duane is certain that we're nuts and he's the sane one."

Marcie showed up the next morning, bundled up in the back seat of a sleigh pulled by a single horse. Don's carriage driver had the reins, and after dropping her off, went to the stable and bunkhouse. She seemed pretty much in control of herself, but Mark and Lyle treated her with kid gloves. Mark was one of the two who found Marcie and her husband, Charles, just after the dust came through. They saw the dust eat their friends just downhill from them. The two were basket cases for a long time.

Adding Duane's attack on Charles, nobody wanted to push her at all. That being the case, Rick decided he should keep everything on a low key as well. On the other hand, this wouldn't get the job done.

Gwendolyn solved it, coming out of the kitchen and going beside where Marcie sat. Gwendolyn put one arm on the back of the chair, and her other hand on the chair arm.

"How are you doing, Marcie?"

"I'm okay, I guess. Everybody is doing what they can for Charles. He was almost the Charles I married once more. That Duane person just grabbed a skillet and hit him with it for no reason."

"Oh, my. Did Duane say anything before that?"

"We were making breakfast. I was in the other room for a minute when Duane suddenly yelled, 'This sucks!' A moment came the awful sound of that pan hitting Charles' head. Duane stomped into the living room, the skillet still in his hand. He looked at me and then he looked down at the pan and suddenly started coughing. He staggered into his room and slammed the door. I ran into the kitchen where Charles was on the floor. I didn't know if he was alive, even. Then I heard Duane start sobbing, and then stop. Just after that, I saw him head for the front door, putting on his coat."

"How is Charles?"

"Nick Cotter says he should be okay. Charles has a headache that won't go away. He's also got a ringing in his ear. The worst part is that his balance isn't right, and Nick has nothing to help. It's a good thing I know of herbs for this kind of thing."

Rick saw Gwendolyn take that opening. "Speaking of herbs, when they tore the walls apart, they found organic matter. Could you identify it?"

"If it came from around here, I might. Hidden in the walls, it sounds like illegal drugs."

Lyle handed her a mason jar filled with stuff Rick couldn't imagine, much less identify. "What we want to know is if this stuff can have an effect on people if there is no fresh air or light."

Marcie suddenly understood. "You want to know if this could mess with somebody's mind, I take it. Well, let's have a look."

She closely examined it with the lid still on it, and then opened it. After looking at it, feeling it, sniffing it, and finally even tasting it, Marcie shook her head. "This was stuffed in the walls?"

Mark nodded. "We found it in all the interior walls. The outside walls had regular insulation. We're concerned another house on the far side of the corrals might be stuffed the same way."

Marcie considered that. "This is not a common plant. It isn't usually found around here. I won't annoy you with the official name. It is a mild hallucinogen. Before the dust, the amount you describe would have been worth a fortune. In the walls, and with normal sunlight and fresh air, you would never notice. Sealed in a room with it, the ingredients could take over a person's mind."

"Is there any way to predict the effect?" Rick wanted to know.

"It would amplify tendencies which already existed."

Rick pursued the thought. "If somebody was already shaky, it might push them over the edge."

"I think so. It is the kind of thing the CIA might have played with. This is the biggest stash I ever heard of. You say there might be another house full of it? What did you do with it?"

Mark and Lyle looked at each other. Mark finally said, "It went out the tunnel with the snow they dug out. It's under several tons of snow by now. Would there be a worthwhile use for it?"

Marcie smiled vaguely. "It could help my Charles. The amount in this jar is more than a lifetime's worth. I'd make a very dilute tea with a small amount of this with some other herbs."

Lyle considered that. "Would that be helpful for anybody else? Could you work with Nick Cotter on it?"

"Oh, I'd be happy to. If we could find someplace secure and dark for this, I'd feel a good deal better."

"What will happen to the large pile under the snow?"

"It's biological. When the weather warms up and melts the snow, it will rot, just like anything else."

Lyle nodded. "That's the perfect place for it, then."

There was a knock on the back door then. Dan was there. "Rick, we tore into the walls at the other house. It was just like we found up here."

He handed Rick a mason jar full of something like the other one.

There was no doubt about it, but Rick wouldn't take any chances. "Hang on a second, Dan. We need to get an opinion on this."

Marcie went through the same routine and finally nodded. "It's the same stuff. I'd ask to use this too, but one jar is more than anybody could claim has any legitimate use. Can we let this join the pile under the snow?"

Rick took the mason jar back to Dan. "You heard it here first. Get rid of it. Get rid of all of it. If there's a stick or a stem of this crap anywhere in the houses, you'll live in the stable."

After Dan hurriedly departed, carefully closing the back door, Rick heard Mark chuckle.

"Ooh. Tough guy."

Rick shook his head. "I didn't want him to have any misconceptions about the situation."

"You can't stand there, look me in the eye, and say that you didn't enjoy what happened to you."

Rick looked at Gwendolyn for a long moment and sighed. "Having sex until it kills me might be the preferred way to go. There might be one or two things I'd like to do in addition. Anyway, what's the point if I can't really remember it all?"

Gwendolyn nodded agreement with that. "It was an interesting way to drop a dress size. In spite of that, I wouldn't recommend it. Like Rick said, being able to remember that I had fun is all part of it."

Chapter 15

Frigid Days and Rowleys

Marcie leaned forward, her mouth hanging open. "Am I hearing this right? You were sealed in a room with with that stuff for days? It had that effect on the two of you?"

Gwendolyn modestly nodded. "Rick and I were just married. You can figure out what our tendencies were. It's a good thing that neither of us were into homicide."

"I suppose so," Marcie replied doubtfully. "Who else might have had a problem with it?"

Lyle looked straight at Marcie. "Duane was one. You had personal experience with that. Kevin is another. It must have impacted the rest of them, but it hasn't shown up in any antisocial sort of way."

Marcie got really nervous at that point. "I'm not so sure I want this jar now."

"If you don't want to take it, I fully understand," Lyle told her. "On the other hand, if you can do something good, it might offset some of the other things it did or might have done. At least, we'd be trying to put some weight on the right side of the scale."

"Okay," she said doubtfully, "I'll give it a try. I just need a pinch or two to see if it can help Charles. Please put the rest someplace dark and secure. Don't tell me where it is. The fewer people know, the better."

Gwendolyn rummaged in the kitchen a few minutes and returned with a jelly jar and lid. Marcie carefully transferred two small pinches to the jelly jar. Outside, they heard the sleigh bells. Dan decided that Rick's orders included Marcie's visit being done and sent it around. He was right, since Marcie was more than ready to get back to her husband.

As she left, they saw Vince ride up. Lyle looked at him and grinned.

"Timing is everything. Yours was perfect this time."

Vince glanced at the departing sleigh and gave Lyle a puzzled look. "I'm glad to hear it. I just came with my daily update on Duane. I see you rescued Rick and Gwendolyn."

"We have something else for you, too, Vince, but come on inside."

Vince shucked his coat and thanked Gwendolyn for the cup of coffee she put in his hand. "Duane only had a couple of episodes the past day, which is an improvement. He's starting to cooperate with Clay a little more. Time will tell if he's just waiting for an opportunity to coldcock him. My vote is to keep somebody on him at all times."

Mark and Lyle both nodded. "That's the right thing to do, Vince. Is there any word on Kevin?"

Vince nodded. "They send reports, and Kevin's training continues, featuring lots of pushups. Long runs have to wait for spring, assuming we have one. They took him into the meat processing plant for clean-up or something. The Peepul already knew about him, and advised that he needed to stay away from them because he was a nasty person."

"Coming from addicts and cannibals, that must have had an impact."

Vince snorted. "They reported his two drill instructors or whatever they are made sure it had an impact, asking how he liked being insulted by them. I don't think they put it that nicely. Was Marcie able to identify the organics in the walls?"

"She did identify it, although she declined to put a name to it. Both houses were stuffed with it. She said it would have been worth a huge amount. To me, it means they planned for this to be the next big street drug. Oh, and it was right here in Harlan County, Deputy."

Vince nodded. "We knew the people here were up to something, but we never knew what. They had show wagons, going a number of places around the country. It wasn't the usual places for their kind of rig, but nobody could pin it down. We knew they weren't the usual street drugs."

Rick had a thought. "Could they have been using the wagons and horses to bring it back here?"

"That's very likely. What they got never tripped any sensors. If they had it inside bales of hay or even in the wagons, nobody would have known. The most certain thing is that they were gone with their other rig, and got into some Omega dust. If they survived, they had no way back."

Lyle handed him the bottle. "Marcie said this much should be good for several lifetimes of positive things. She will work with Nick Cotter. In the meantime, put this someplace that's both secure and dark. When the snow lets you get to it, the ammo bunker by the Corps of Engineers at Rep City ought to do the trick."

"I can do that, Mr. Lillard. In the meantime, there are a couple of places I can use that would fill the bill."

"Good. Don't tell us where those places are. None of us need to know."

"It looks like transparency in government just went the way of the dodo bird."

"Dodo birds and government, at least as we knew it, belong together, Vince. Now, if you plan to give our terrorist guest a dose of it every few hours, that might be worth knowing. It might be interesting to see what tendency this stuff would bring out in him." Lyle chuckled and added, "Then again, maybe we wouldn't find it so interesting after all. Thank you for your report. We just gave Rick and Gwendolyn a general update on our two bad boys."

Rick found himself the subject of Vince's law enforcement scrutiny. "Are you and Gwendolyn really okay?"

"As far as I know. Would it help for Gwendolyn to demonstrate her hot skillet swing on your head?"

"No, I'll pass on that test. Mr. Lillard, if you and Mark think they're both okay, then I have to concur. They both are acting normally."

Mark grinned. "They are their abnormal selves."

With that assessment, Lyle and Mark decided it was safe to leave Rick and Gwendolyn alone. Rick was certain they both wanted to get home after such an extended amount of babysitting. The thing was, Rick discovered, that he felt uneasy with Gwendolyn. He thought he'd better get it out in the open.

"After all this, I'm confused about where you and I are."

Gwendolyn looked at him guardedly. "What do you mean?"

"Everything has been strange. We get married almost before we're introduced. We barely decide that we like each other when we suddenly find ourselves dealing with a combination of catastrophic weather and crazy people. We're still dealing with all of that when we get caught up in a drug-induced orgy. I'd suggest we try going back to square one, but it's entirely possible that's not an option at this point."

She nodded. "The fact that we agreed to be married is a large factor, and that happened before the episode with the walls full of weed. The other, and more substantive issue, is that I might have gotten pregnant with all of this. I suppose it's the last part you're referring to."

"I was thinking about the last part more than other things, but you and I managed to get through quite a few other things so far. Speaking of which, did all of this have any impact on that dragon of yours?"

"So far, so good. I'm astonished at how good I feel, considering what we just went through. How are you doing after finding out what pushed Kevin and Duane over the edge?"

"We don't really know what happened to them, Gwendolyn. I've got an idea. Tomorrow, we can solve Don Rowley's computer problem."

"Are you going to look in on Duane while you're there?"

"I don't think so. It would just be depressing. Come to think of it, you might not want to go. What if those Ragan families show up?"

"It won't matter. Nancy Rowley will be there. Posse members will be there. You'll be there. Lyle Lillard made his decision. All they can do now is make up a fairy tale that I was there voluntarily. If they do it in front of Nancy Rowley, she can show them up as liars. I don't think she would, though. She lives in Ragan and wants to keep her own cover story going."

That made sense to Rick. "Say, I've got an idea. Why don't we have a date? I'll take you out to the best place around here, other than your own kitchen."

"I like it. Our not showing now and then was what caused them to sound the alarms in the first place. By the way, did you know that we are at square one? We will always be square one for where we go next."

"That's brilliant, Gwendolyn. Can I quote you on that?"

"Absolutely."

They had a comfortable day and evening, just being together with no pressure to do anything. The next morning, Gwendolyn took her first longer ride. She settled into it after a while, but pronounced herself more than ready to get back on the ground when they got to Ragan. The first stop was the Co-op, where the owners were both willing and anxious to get rid of the computer, saying they never liked the thing in the first place. They even put it on a sled and pulled it to Don Rowley's place.

Don was taking a down day on Adeline Lillard's orders. That had nothing to do with his health. It was the health of the horses she worried about. Don was tickled to see the computer come in the door, and Nancy Rowley seemed even more pleased. To hear her talk, all Don did on these required down days was pace, fume, and fret. Having something to keep him occupied suited her perfectly. For Gwendolyn, Nancy Rowley was now her second mother as well as her match-maker and liberator, and the two were soon chatting about anything and everything.

Rick worked his way through the computer. Getting it to run was the easy part. Getting the software to function nearly stopped him cold, but he kept chipping away at it, and figured out enough functions so Don could keep track of his inventory. He was finishing the session, tutoring Don on what he had to do, and writing down each step for him, when a lady strolled into the office.

Rick wondered if that might be one of the infamous Ragan ladies.

"Don, dear, is Nancy around?"

Judging from Don's reaction, he either didn't take kindly to the lady or being called dear.

"She's in back, Delores," he growled.

Delores looked at Rick for a moment, and then headed on toward the living quarters, located behind the office. Rick's answer came a short moment later, when he heard Delores exclaim, "Gwen, dear, how lovely to see you. Oh, Nancy, I just remembered I left something in the oven. I must run. I'll talk to you later."

The lady then quickly strode through the office and back out the front door. Don just looked at her as she left and softly growled.

Rick couldn't help himself. "It really is like they say, Don, everyone causes happiness. Some bring it when they show up, and others when they leave."

Don laughed and slapped the desk the computer sat on. "Damn, Rick, you got that straight. Now, if this computer only worked like it ought to instead of how it does, things would be just dandy."

Rick nodded. "That would be a computer that would react to you like a person. They never got anything that advanced. Even if the world hadn't fallen apart, I don't think they could have ever done it."

"Well now, you're talking pretty smart for a computer guy."

"Being with Gwendolyn, some smarts rubbed off," Rick allowed.

Don just grinned. "That's not what I heard when you were here for dinner. By the way, did you know a guy you used to work with is in the back room, working as Clay's new apprentice?"

"Yes, I heard something about that." Rick elected not to pursue that subject any further than necessary.

"He's one strange dude. Vince has posse members in there all the time. Not only that, they have him chained to the wall. It's like he's got one eye in the middle of his forehead. He gets these spells where he is completely out of it. I always forget his name, and just think of him as Igor. There's been several times when Clay had to grab him with those big mitts of his, and pin him against the wall while he explained things. So far, that has straightened him out."

The four sat down to lunch not long after that. Gwendolyn looked at Nancy Rowley. "I hope being here didn't cause you any problems with the local ladies."

Nancy just smiled. "If I cared about the society stuff, I would have never lived in the country in the first place. The four families wanted to cultivate me. They thought that would give them an 'in' with Don. What they really wanted was to cultivate an easy way to get supplies and nice things hauled in for them. As Don accumulated things, they all wanted a piece of that, as well. The way to do that was to do anything to make us feel welcome. Then I found out they were doing nearly all of it with your labor."

"I just didn't want to cause a situation."

"Nonsense, don't worry about it a moment longer. If I needed any proof about who was getting things done, what you did to help me with lunch completely covered it. None of those old biddies could have begun to do what you did almost without thinking."

Rick thought he'd better ask before the thought left him. "So, Don, will you be able to do the inventory you wanted now?"

Don chewed on the question along with a bite of food. "Much as I'd like to say I need you to sit here and poke all this in for me, I do know you already have full-time employment. Anyway, if I used up much more of your time, Lyle Lillard would be over here to jump down my throat. More likely, he'd make me show up at his house, hat in hand, to receive a severe tongue lashing. I'll just work my way through this thing."

"I'll tell you what," Rick responded. "There's nothing to keep me from stopping by to say hello and seeing how things are going next time I get over here. Mrs. Rowley will doubtless require an occasional update on how her matchmaking is going. If you happen to be over near Wagon Ranch, be sure to stop in for a cup of coffee."

"That's right," Gwendolyn agreed. "We owe you guys lunch, at least. With the frigid weather that's settled in on us, I suppose lunch will be the only meal we could hope for until warm weather happens again."

Nancy Rowley picked right up on it. "Well, it's been a pleasure having the two of you here, and I'm so happy to know I played a small part in getting you two kids together. It's a pretty good ride back to your place, and like you said, it is just too cold for anybody to be out and about."

Don tagged along with Nancy when they went out to get their horses ready for the ride back. Rick thought it was noteworthy, at least. It might even be significant. It might even say something about keeping a happy home at the Rowley place. Rick led the way out of the old livery stable, and they mounted just outside the doors. The cold was incredible, and nobody spent very long with farewells.

Heading back, their horses seemed to know the barn was at the end of the road, and moved accordingly. As they got closer, the horses moved faster, and got to the point that Gwendolyn was barely in control of her horse. There was the combination of frozen hands and inexperience at work there. He kept an eye on her as she gamely hung on. When they got to the main house, Rick already decided what to do.

"Gwendolyn, go on into the house. I'll take the horses to the stable and come back through the tunnel. We can decide what to do after that."

She didn't say anything, but nodded as she slid out of the saddle. Rick waited until she got in the door before turning and heading for the stable. He found Dan was waiting with a couple of helpers. Rick figured Dan had somebody up in the crow's nest watching for them.

"Cold enough for you?" was Dan's question.

That struck Rick as a dumb thing to say, even if it was the obvious one. "Very nearly. I'm not sure it got above zero on the Fahrenheit scale today. If it did, I never knew about it. About the only thing positive is that it gave the horses pretty good footing coming back. I guess your man in the crow's nest ratted us out."

"Yeah, that's turned into a really handy thing to have. It's not the warmest place on the planet, but you already knew that. The guys take turns up there. None of them have decided whether it's easier to be up there taking it easy in the frigid air, or down here actually working. If you want to head over to your house, we can take care of the horses."

"That suits me. Take a look at that mare. She picked up a pretty good amount of snow in her hooves."

"Yeah, I see that. Thanks. We don't want anybody getting after us for causing one of the Harlan horses to go lame."

Rick picked up the pace as he headed for home. As he approached the bunkhouse, it became quite clear that Gwendolyn had already made the command decision about what they'd do next. She was standing by the door to the bunkhouse public area waiting for him.

"You must have spent at least ten seconds in the house before you headed over here."

"Was I there that long?" she asked, a totally innocent look on her face. "I didn't mean to take that much time. Could you ever forgive me?"

"I believe I could spend the rest of my life forgiving you. In return, it would be great if you ccould see your way to forgiving me every now and then."

He gave her a kiss. She returned the kiss with a smile that managed to melt everything that had gotten frozen on the ride.

"Gee, I guess I'll take that to mean I managed to say something right."

"Talk like that might let you take considerably more than that, Mr. Forbes."

"That seemed like a pretty successful ride and visit. I'm really proud of how you managed to hang on to your horse in spite of everything."

"I'm pretty well pleased, too. You really weren't interested in gawking at Duane. My being there gave Nancy a chance to put one of the Ragan ladies in her place. Lunch wasn't bad, either."

"I saw your hand in many of the things. Those were what I enjoyed the most. I should have offered to help. I could have made coffee."

"In a pig's eye. On the other hand, I have to wonder if you cook so badly on purpose, just to have everybody tell you to go somewhere else to park it."

"I'm not nearly smart enough to fake the way I cook, Gwendolyn. You can ask anyone here."

The moment they walked into the main house, Rick realized why Gwendolyn did not stick around. All the fires were out and the stoves were cold. He immediately got after the heating stove, knowing it would be a while before they could take off their winter coats. In addition, the temperature outside was dropping rapidly. It was a race between the fire and frostbite. At the moment, the kindling was the only thing burning, and frostbite was winning.

Gwendolyn was doing better with the kitchen stove, but Rick was certain there'd be much more warmth in the living room presently.

He had to do a better job of controlling the stove so they wouldn't have this problem. In the kitchen, Gwendolyn called. She opened the water reservoir on the side, and showed him how much ice was there.

"It's a good thing the water was only half full. We'll keep an eye on it. I'd hate to see it spring a leak."

Gwendolyn nodded. "That's what I was thinking, too. Will we be able to keep everything going if this cold keeps up very long?"

"I have no idea. All we can do is keep after it as best we can. I think I'd better make sure the heating stove has a really good log before we go to bed. If I get up during the night, I'll check it then, too."

"We're going to have to get the fire going first."

"It's going now. I'd better make sure the log caught."

The log had caught on fire, and the stove was beginning to radiate warmth, finally complementing the heat put out by the kitchen stove. The two of them soon cuddled together on the couch facing the stove.

"It's hard to imagine that winter hasn't officially started yet."

"I should be doing Christmas shopping, but there's a real difficulty trying to move at the moment."

"We'll need to move eventually. There's a bed in the other room. I imagine the room is already starting to approach someplace that people might actually want to spend the night."

Rick looked at Gwendolyn. "Do we have any bricks or stones around here?"

"We might. Why?"

"One time I read how people put bricks, stones, or things of that sort into the oven. Once they were heated up, they'd wrap them in towels and put them into the bed to get it warm before the people actually crawled in bed."

"That could be just about anything that would absorb heat, right?"

"I guess so."

"We can handle that. Rick, you're a genius." Gwendolyn gave him a kiss and headed into the kitchen.

Puzzled, Rick stood up and saw her grabbing the infamous skillet and other cast iron cookware, and putting them into the oven. Then she stoked the fire. Figuring that should work, he went over to the heating stove, and added more wood, rattled the grate, and did everything he could to get it burning really well. By that time, Gwendolyn had returned to the couch, and patted it invitingly. Rick cheerfully took the hint.

That night, Rick got up a couple of times to check the stove. He thought Gwendolyn got up too. Half asleep, he wondered if this was a preview of what being a new parent would be about. Then he considered the way things had gone, fathers would not be able to share the parenting duties like they had back in the days of bottles and formula.

For that matter, kids might not even wear diapers. Another chore would disappear, no doubt replaced by several others.

Shortly after breakfast the next morning, they heard a rider come up, followed quickly by a heavy rapping on the door. It was one of the posse members.

"Kevin managed to slip away from Oxford. They think he came back into Harlan. Lock everything as tight as you can. There are several more posse members coming here in case he tries to get in. I have to ride around and tell them on the other side. They'll need to send armed guys over here. Mark saw how you were with a weapon, and suggested we not arm you."

"Okay. Thanks, We'll lock up right away."

Rick closed and locked the door. Then he wedged a straight chair under the door handle. The two of them brought in as much fire wood as they could store inside. By that time, Dan showed up with a couple of his people plus the posse member.

"For Kevin to be out wandering around in these temperatures proves he's nuts," Rick commented.

"It proves he wants us to think he is, at least," the posse member returned.

"I guess Vince has put extra people on Duane, too."

"Vince did just the opposite. He set it up to make Kevin think he can bust his buddy out of there. It's a trap, of course."

"That's unless Kevin succeeds, and then we've got both of them to contend with. I should have aimed a few kicks at each of them while I had the chance. Since everybody else would have taken their turns, we might not have this situation now."

"I remember Mark and Mr. Lillard debating that very issue. If they came to a conclusion, I never heard it. You should know Mr. Lillard was firmly on your side. I don't know what Mark believed. It didn't seem like he was arguing from conviction. It was almost more like he wanted to see if Mr. Lillard really believed it, or if he was just saying it."

"How did Kevin manage to get away? It sounded like they had the two Marines on him constantly, and then the tribe all around him."

"I didn't hear anything about that. It takes a certain kind of person to be a prison guard. The situation gets boring very quickly, and then most people want to spend some time doing something else. At the same time, the prisoner has absolutely nothing else to do but to look around, find weaknesses in whatever holds them, and to take advantage whenever the cards happen to fall in their favor."

"What are you guys going to do when you find him?"

"We're supposed to capture him if possible. If somebody shot Kevin, and he died, nobody would pursue the matter very far or very long."

"I see your point," Rick replied. "With these temperatures, though, Kevin may find the weather a more formidable adversary than we could ever be."

"That would be something, to pull him out of a snow drift sometime."

"At the same time, guard duty until spring could be something of a difficulty."

The posse member shuddered. "You got that straight."

Chapter 16

Saving Susie

Rick, with no other function, watched as Dan went back and forth between the two sides of the ranch. He said runners would let them know if the watchers in the crow's nest caught sight of anything. Nobody saw anything lurking in the area. Rick couldn't imagine how Kevin could stay out of sight for the entire day since it never got on the warm side of zero.

Additionally, Dan arranged for his people to bring food over to the main house, so that Gwendolyn wouldn't have to use the cook stove for anything but a supplemental heat source. As he put it, there was no need to waste good firewood. Gwendolyn ignored his opinion, keeping the cookstove hot and everyone in coffee.

Late that afternoon, one of Dan's people scurried up the tunnel to let them know a rider was approaching at a good pace. The news was that Kevin went all the way across the county, and tried to get Susie from her parents' house. Susie appeared to cooperate with Kevin's plan. She had a number of bruises that couldn't have been from Kevin. Dennis Maguire was still bedridden from the injuries Kevin and Duane gave him before, so somebody else in the family did it.

None of it made any sense to Rick. "Where could they have planned to go?"

"Their idea was to go east. What they would do then, neither Kevin nor Susie seemed to know."

Gwendolyn leaned forward in her chair. "Kevin went to rescue his lady love, underage though she is. It appears Susie needed to be rescued. What was Kevin's attitude toward the military guys in Oxford? What did the military guys think of him? It's only been a short while."

The two posse members looked at each other, and the first one who came answered.

"I was usually at the bridge when they came with their daily reports. One of the guys would stay with Kevin while the other would go with Tom, their leader to give updates. They thought he was starting to get the idea of their program."

The latest arrival took up the other side of it. "When they picked Kevin up, he told them the hoo-ah guys in Oxford were crazy, but it wasn't too bad. He was more concerned for Susie. From what they said, he didn't say anything or ask about Duane."

Gwendolyn nodded. "You guys will think I'm crazy, but the Ragan families worked me awfully hard, and there was nothing resembling freedom. Still, they never abused me to the point you're describing as her situation. Maybe if Susie went over and helped them out, it would be a good thing for everyone."

Rick looked at her. "What do you suppose those fine ladies would say about your recommendation?"

"It would take them less than a second to decide it all made perfect sense. Does it make any sense to you, Rick? After all, it was you who decided not to push things with Kevin and Duane as far as most of the others were willing and even eager to go."

Rick smiled. "I'll go with astonishment and leave it at that for now. It sounds like something we could pass along to Mark and Mr. Lillard, though."

Rick turned to the newly arrived posse member. "I imagine they're reeling Duane back in. Don and Nancy Rowley couldn't have been all that comfortable, knowing they might be in the crossfire if anything happened."

That guy nodded. "Yeah, I imagine so. One of the other guys was taking the news to Ragan while I headed over here. The way they talked, Kevin might be more willing to stay in Oxford if he knows little Susie is in Ragan. The only issue will be if Susie gets it into her head to cook up something with Duane with a view toward springing Kevin."

Rick thought out loud. "If Kevin and Susie keep their noses clean, the Marines might give him a weekend pass now and then. The families in Ragan might even see fit to give Susie a little time off. As long as they're not trying to run off, why not give them a little time together?"

"That's a fact," everyone agreed.

Rick then looked at the second posse member. "It's getting late and it isn't good for your horse standing out there. Go around to the stable. Dan can find you a place to flop for the night. The great Kevin escapade ended in a peaceful way, so Gwendolyn and I can take the night off."

Dan looked at him. "Why don't you two come down for dinner, and save her from having to do anything more than be with you? I'd think that alone should be sufficient punishment for anybody."

Rick and Gwendolyn exchanged looks, and then Rick looked back at Dan who was now trying to draw his head down between his shoulders turtle style for protection.

"You managed a compliment, a nice gesture, and an insult all in the same sentence. We'll have to find a reward for that display. Oh, when I said 'we,' that was Gwendolyn and me. There's no mouse in my pocket. You guys go ahead. I need to make sure the fires in here will stay burning for a while. Walking into a sub-zero house last night is not a situation I'd recommend, but that happened to Gwendolyn."

Dan looked at one of his guys. "Take care of that little detail, and then come down for supper. By the way, you have a new job, making sure this place never gets that cold again. You got me?"

They still needed to dress for outside as they went down the tunnel. There was no heat in them. In spite of that, the tunnels felt noticeably warmer than if they had gone around outside. In the bunkhouse public area, the mood was good bordering on party hearty. On his own part, Rick had mixed feelings about the whole thing. If he'd stayed in one of the bedrooms instead of being exiled to the hallway, those herbs might have made him as bad off as either Kevin or Duane.

Later, back at the main house, they thanked the guy tending the fire there, and sent him on his way. Gwendolyn commented, "You never quite got into the spirit of the celebration."

"I guess not. What kind of crazy might I have been if things hadn't worked out like they had? Being with you made it a good crazy, if there's such a thing. Anyway, from what they said about Kevin, he wasn't acting crazy. He acted like any guy might who's in love. It was an honorable thing that he did."

After everything that had gone on, Rick found himself continually braced for bad things to rain on his head. If there weren't bad things, then something out of far left field would come. Maybe that did happen. It came in the guise of nothing happening over the next several days. Gwendolyn watched his stress with some concern.

"What's the matter, Rick? Can't you cope with a little life out of the fast lane? A couple of days when nobody's shot at you, kicked you, or drugged you, and you seem to be a total wreck. Why don't you try to relax? The day's still young, and there's plenty of time for the great deity of caca to rain on your head."

That made Rick grin, or at least try. "It's completely illogical, isn't it? There's part of me that keeps waiting for the next thing to happen."

Gwendolyn glanced out the front window. "What's that they say about being careful about what you wish for? We've got visitors. It looks like Vince and Lyle."

With everybody inside and somewhat defrosted, Lyle got the ball rolling. "Mark told me what you two came up with, and it makes good sense. I know you contributed most of it, Gwendolyn, and I thank you for the idea. Here's how we're going to do it. Kevin is in the basement of the schoolhouse in Ragan under guard. Rick, I want you with us. We'll scoop up Kevin, and head to Huntley. There, we'll get Susie, letting Kevin watch the whole thing, and take her to Ragan. What do you think?"

"Do you want me to go too, Mr. Lillard?" Gwendolyn inquired.

"I wasn't too sure about that part. How comfortable would you be facing those Ragan families?"

"The discomfort will be on their side. We'd better wrap up really well when we go."

"That's a good point, Mr. Lillard. Doing all of that is going to be a really long day. Should we do it tomorrow? Either that, or we could stay overnight in Ragan. It won't be at all easy on the horses."

Lyle grinned. "You know, I keep planning things as though we had decent conditions outside. You're exactly right, Rick. Will everything be okay here if you're gone a couple of days?"

"I believe so. We'll have to go through the tunnel to the stable. I'll let the guys know they need to keep some heat happening in here until we get back." Just then, there was a knock on the back door. Dan's lookouts had been on the job Dan advised there was no need for them to go all the way over there. He yelled down the tunnel to get two horses saddled and over to the main house.

"It won't take long. They most likely already have the horses ready to go, and were just waiting for the word to bring them around."

Lyle shook his head. "I don't get that kind of service, and they tell me that I'm in charge. Something's wrong here."

Dan grinned at him. "Just send a few of them over. We'll get them trained fast enough. After all, they're supposed to be apprentices from here, even if we hardly ever see them. Anyway, we'll make sure the house here stays warm while you're gone."

Rick nodded. "I'm sure Gwendolyn will appreciate it."

"Oh, and we'll keep an eye out. When you get back, we'll have people ready to take the horses back around, so you guys can just come in here. That's if you want to, of course."

"You're being awfully nice all of a sudden. You didn't happen to rat hole some of that weed from the inside of the walls."

Vince laughed. "If the stuff causes people to be nice, maybe we should have kept a ton of it. We could dump it on the terrorists, if nothing else."

Dan's grin kept on until Rick wondered if he was turning into the Cheshire cat. The two horses showed up, making Dan's prediction come true. Rick and Gwendolyn were ready to go, so the group hit the road in short order. Rick kept an eye on Gwendolyn. She seemed to do better at managing her mount this time. Of course, they were just going one way, which helped things a great deal.

In Ragan, Vince split off from the group as they came into town, and headed for home. The rest went to the schoolhouse. That wasn't for long, though. Vince showed up, informing Rick and Gwendolyn that his wife insisted on having them stay overnight with them.

Vince Sanders' wife, Beth, was a vibrant woman. When they arrived, she was buzzing around rearranging sleeping places for her three kids even as she was cooking a meal. The noise and commotion all seemed very good-natured, which all by itself reduced Rick's stress quite a lot. In addition, the three kids took one look at Gwendolyn and all started to giggle.

Gwendolyn went to Billy. He was the oldest one who Rick recalled was ten years old. "You are all having a good time," she said to him.

"We know who you are. You worked for that bunch of families a few blocks a few blocks from here. When they saw us, they'd try to hide you."

"Did you tell your parents about me?" Gwendolyn asked.

"Oh no, that would have spoiled the game," Billy responded.

"They know now, don't they?"

Billy shrugged. "When you went away, it was over. Our game was to see which of us could see you most often."

"Who won?"

Rachel, eight years old, raised her hand. "Billy was ahead for a long time, but I could sneak in places where he couldn't. Bobby didn't know how to be quiet and sneaky," Rachel said, referring to her little brother.

"Well, you all see me now. Does that count?"

Billy shook his head. "We all see you, but you see us, so it doesn't count."

Rick decided to join the conversation. "That's a pretty smart game, Billy. Are you going to be a Deputy like your father?"

"When Dad's done, there won't be any more bad people to catch. That wouldn't be much fun. Can I come work for you at Wagon Ranch?"

"You'll have to be a little taller, but I'm sure you'd be good at it."

Rachel ended up between Rick and Gwendolyn. Gwendolyn looked at Rachel and then up at Rick. She favored him with a certain smile, making Rick wonder if she thought there was not only a child in their future, but somehow knew it would be a girl.

Rick noticed Vince didn't talk about what he did on duty when he was with his family. Rick knew of people who tried to keep their lives in compartments. He supposed it was an individual thing, but since it was Vince's house, he found plenty to talk about beside what it was like to be the only lawman alive. Gwendolyn seemed to pick up the same vibration and also went with the flow.

That night in bed, Rick wondered about the situation to Gwendolyn.

"You may be right. On the other hand, we are part of the ongoing case. I cannot imagine him talking about the situation with us sitting there."

Rick chuckled. "I don't know how you got so smart, but I'm glad we're on the same side."

The next morning, they all met inside the old schoolhouse. It was fairly warm inside the building, at least. When they brought Kevin out of a storeroom, Kevin blinked and shook his head like he was trying to shake off some mental cobwebs.

He took one look and Rick and snarled, "You just can't get enough of seeing me get kicked around, can you?"

Rick shook his head, bewildered. "I'm here to help Susie Maguire get to a better situation. The only way you entered the equation was the hope that if you felt better about her situation, maybe you'd pay attention to what the Marines are trying to tell you over in Oxford. If you choose to think I'm the bad guy, there's not a damn thing I can do about that."

Lyle Lillard stepped forward at that point. "If Rick wanted to see you kicked, and if he wanted to kick you himself, he had every opportunity. He didn't do it, which tells me something about him. He is only here now because I asked for him personally and individually. Gwendolyn, his wife, volunteered to come along, but it was to help us with Susie. Gwendolyn thinks she can help us get Susie away from her family, and acquaint her with the families in Ragan Susie will work for."

Posse members, led by Vince, took Kevin up the basement steps. Rick looked at Lyle. "Kevin's actions looked honorable, but he talks like an asshole. What's up with that?"

"It may relate to how he thinks a man should be. Kevin's eighteen, and we got way ahead of ourselves when we put him in charge of the ranch. Mark forced my hand on that one, though. Didn't you, Mark?"

Mark was two steps in front of them as they started up the stairs, but turned to look back. "I suppose so. I could try to spread the blame, but if I had stopped to think as well as include others, I could have avoided the whole thing."

"Is it still one day at a time, Mark?" Lyle inquired.

"Yes, it is. Some days are tougher than others, but it feels a little easier as I keep going."

Lyle then looked at Rick. "Do you know what we're talking about here?"

"I know less than what I'd need to fully comprehend the situation. What I do know is far more than I really want to, though."

Lyle laughed. "What would I have given to hear you say that a month or two ago, Mark?"

Mark shook his head. "I have no idea what you would have given. There's no money. You control just about everything in sight, but nobody owns anything. We're all just squatters."

"Rick, did Mark talk like that when you two worked the evacuation?"

"Mark said a number of things. I don't recall much detail. The focus was on getting the McCook people to safety."

At the top of the stairs, Mark turned around, grinning. "One thing Kevin did I consider very worthwhile was to recommend you work with me, Rick. He said you were good at keeping your mouth shut, and that continues to be a strong suit for you."

At the Maguire house, Kevin and two posse members stayed on their horses. Everyone else trooped up to the front door, where Vince knocked with a good deal of authority. The door opened a crack, and an eye that Rick assumed must be Mrs. Maguire, peered out.

"We will see Susie," Lyle announced.

"She's not feeling well. She's in her room."

"I did not ask for references," Lyle replied. "We are here to see Susie, and that is what we will do."

"You have no right. This is our house," came the voice, and she tried to close the door.

It didn't happen because Vince was leaning on the door. The butt of Vince's hunting rifle also jammed into the opening. Vince beckoned a couple of posse members, and the three swiftly overwhelmed the token resistance inside.

As the party paraded through the house, the woman shrieked at them, "This is an outrage. She is our daughter. You have no right."

Lyle looked at her. "We are under martial law, and she is a citizen of Harlan. Ordinarily, we would have no right. In this case, you can rail on me all you want, but it won't change the outcome."

The door to Susie's room was evident by the fact that it was closed and also by the fearful looks focused in that direction by the rest of the family. Vince led the way to the door, and knocked softly. Not getting an answer, he opened the door, and let Lyle and Gwendolyn go ahead of him. At the doorway, Rick remembered the intervention on his own behalf. Susie had bruises on her face and arms, and was trying to deal with a bloody nose.

Gwendolyn immediately did what she could to comfort the girl. Lyle and Mark both took one look, and then glanced at one another. Lyle nodded to Vince, who organized how to get Susie out. Rick decided he'd better do something constructive, and suggested they see if there was a suitcase they could use for her clothes.

One appeared almost immediately, and Gwendolyn directed the packing of what she most needed.

The ride back to Ragan was marked by a completely changed Kevin. They put Susie on Kevin's horse, and from there on, it more resembled an honor guard than a security detail. The group went directly to the Stamford house in Ragan, where all four families waited for them.

"Susie Maguire will help your families as best she can," Lyle told them. "Right now, though, she needs several days to recover. In short, she will be a patient rather than an employee. I am authorizing Vince to check on her as often as he feels appropriate. In addition, I authorize Rick and Gwendolyn to visit her and do welfare checks whenever they or I feel such visits are needed."

Mrs. Stamford stepped forward. "We are more than happy to take care of her. If Gwendolyn and Rick would like to stay with us as guests, we'd be honored."

Chapter 17

Instant Parents

Rick was shocked at the offer, and looked at Gwendolyn. She didn't seem to have an immediate response either. Then he looked at Lyle, who seemed puzzled.

Lyle finally responded, "That's not be a bad idea. Vince, could you keep an eye, and make sure nothing gets to more than a dull roar?"

Vince nodded. "I can do that." He looked at Rick and Gwendolyn. "If you like, I can take your horses to a warmer place."

Rick nodded. "I suppose."

Off the horse, he looked up at Lyle. "At the risk of sounding like Mark, I'll have a hard time proving myself as a ranch manager if I'm never there."

"Don't worry about it, Rick. You'll have every opportunity to catch up. Wagon Ranch ran itself quite a while before we got you in there. It already looks one hundred percent better. You two keep an eye on Susie for me, and Vince will keep an eye on you. Does that sound okay?"

They grabbed their bedrolls, and walked onto the porch. Gwendolyn had a hard time with hers. It seemed unnaturally stiff. Rick offered to help, but Gwendolyn got it under control. Vince brought Susie beside them, and one of the posse members carried Susie's luggage. Kevin sat on his horse, looking forlorn. Susie glanced at him, but seemed far more concerned about everyone standing around her.

Inside the house, everyone headed upstairs. Rick and Gwendolyn got the first room, while Susie went next door. Their room faced the front of the house. Rick glanced out the window, and saw Lyle riding away.

"I'll make sure Susie is comfortable," Gwendolyn announced.

"What should I do?" Rick asked. "Do you want me to stand guard outside the door?"

"You can if you want," she replied. "I get the impression these folks want to make amends for what they did to me. Maybe they got carried away with what they did to me and are sorry now."

Gwendolyn did not sound like she believed her own words, so Rick gave her an insincere smile. "Maybe Kevin has seen the light and will be nice to everyone now."

Gwendolyn paused by the door and considered the situation. She nodded, finally. "You got that point, Rick. Still, we can hope, right?"

"If this bunch even looks like they are thinking about grabbing you, give the loudest yell you can. If that dragon shows any sign of coming back out, just remember you've got at least one friend nearby."

She walked over and gave Rick a kiss. "I will remember all of that. I'll be just next door and Vince is there, too. The important thing for Susie to realize is that she's got a friend nearby, as well."

"Maybe I'll hang out next door with you. It's good to get to know your neighbors, after all."

Rick stayed at the door while Gwendolyn went in. Susie just stared into space. When Vince or a posse member moved even slightly, Susie flinched, like they might hit her. She reacted that way to Gwendolyn, too, but after several minutes of Gwendolyn talking softly to her, Susie relaxed. A little after that, Susie gave Gwendolyn a hug. Rick was certain at that point that Gwendolyn was a remarkable person, indeed.

Vince and the posse members slowly slid toward the door, getting no reaction from Susie. At the same time, Rick decided he did the right thing by not trying to go any closer to the girl. Vince nodded to Rick as he followed his two people out the door and then stopped a couple of steps toward the stairway. He motioned to Rick.

"I'll get over here as often as I can. You'll need to make sure these people act like hosts and not slave traders. Remember, my place is only a couple of blocks away. I'll have posse members circle this block as often as they can. This entire situation doesn't sit right with me."

"I've been thinking many of the same things, Vince. I'll do everything I can to protect Gwendolyn. I'll do what I can for Susie, but she's her own situation, what with her family and Kevin and all. I guess he'll spend the night at the schoolhouse and go back to Oxford tomorrow?"

"That's the plan. We need to go now. I will stop by after dinner for a welfare check, and like I said, guys will cruise by here frequently."

"Thank you Vince, and thanks for having us over last night. We both really appreciated it."

Vince just smiled and headed down the stairs to where his two guys waited for him at the front door. After the three departed, Rick headed back to the doorway. Gwendolyn glanced at him and gave him a slight smile. Mrs. Stamford showed up a moment later.

"Will Susie be well enough to come downstairs for dinner, or should we bring something up for her?" she whispered to Rick.

Rick could only shrug and look inquiringly at Gwendolyn.

Finally, Gwendolyn softly said, "Susie won't be able to be around many people for a while. In addition, I'll have to stay here with her. If you could bring me up a bite, that would be nice."

The woman wrung her hands, pursed her lips, and then looked at Rick. "Perhaps it would be better if I brought all of you something to eat. I've got TV trays. The guys can bring chairs up, too. I wanted to thank both of you for staying with her a little while. I realize this can't be a comfortable situation for either of you."

She returned down the stairs, and Rick looked at Gwendolyn, who simply shook her head. It appeared they were all on strange ground.

Chairs and TV trays found their way upstairs. Plates of food were on their way, they said, and Gwendolyn got Susie to an easy chair in the room. Rick considered it an accomplishment when Gwendolyn had Rick sit inside the door instead out in the hallway. He felt more secure, having a wall behind him. Other than trying to smile the few times Susie glanced at him, Rick thought his best bet was to just keep quiet. That was something he knew how to do, anyway.

Susie did eat some. She reminded Rick of some of the horses Adeline Lillard said showed signs of abuse. In Susie's case, there was no need for conjecture on that point. It made Rick wonder if Kevin might have been abused, an abuser, or both.

When everyone was done eating, Rick quietly asked Gwendolyn if he could cross the room to get the dishes. Gwendolyn nodded, and everything was okay until he got within a couple of feet of Susie. She recoiled into her chair. Rick picked everything up quickly and retreated from the room. The Dennis Maguire school of parenting was not one Rick considered worthwhile. He saw why Susie tried so hard to get away from the situation.

Downstairs, the lady apologized both profusely and at length for not getting upstairs for the dishes. Rick thought she was far too apologetic to include any sincerity. These weren't people he wanted to be around any more than necessary anyway. As he got back to the stairway, Vince was knocking at the front door. The man was true to his word, that was for certain. One of the ladies scooted past Rick to answer the front door, so Rick simply waited, foot on the first step, and arm on the end of the stair rail.

Vince joined him as they went upstairs, saving their conversation for when they were farther from pointy little ears.

"Has there been anything out of the ordinary?" Vince wanted to know.

Rick told him about how he was able to eat in the room with Susie, but what had happened when he tried to get the plates. "Dennis Maguire must be a real winner," Rick finished.

Vince nodded. "I've seen that from time to time. You meet a guy who seems pretty straight, but when he's around women, and doesn't think other men will find out, he comes unglued. With the Maguire clan, the women weren't a whole lot better. That makes it really striking that Gwendolyn could manage to get close to Susie."

"Maybe all the men in Susie's life treated her that way, but at least some of the women didn't live to smack her around."

"Are you saying Kevin might be that way, too?"

"That's not my case to make, but it fits the situation. When they rode double over here, they didn't look like lovers."

Vince nodded. "You're right. Now that I think of it, her hanging on to him was more because she wasn't sure of her balance. That is a good observation, though, Rick. I'll mention it to Mark and Lyle. Will you guys be okay for the evening?"

"If they had illusions about anybody trusting them, you showing up again disabused them big time. Being okay for the evening may be a relative term anyway. I have a feeling that Gwendolyn is highly unlikely to ever make it back to our room tonight. That leaves me with dozing in a straight back chair. Whatever else our brave new world has given us, comfort doesn't appear to be on the list."

Vince snorted. "You could have gone back to Wagon Ranch, eaten with the guys, and had a whole bed to yourself."

"In the short time Gwendolyn and I have been together, far too many strange things have happened. I am better off in her company, even if uncomfortable, than anywhere else."

Vince smiled then. "You have this marriage thing figured out pretty well. My job includes looking in on Susie, so I should do that small thing. I will heed the warning about Susie and how she is with men at close range."

The deputy glanced in the room at Susie and Gwendolyn, and soon went back downstairs, where he exchanged a few brief comments with their hosts before leaving. Rick couldn't hear the specific conversation, but he picked up Vince's tone. He sounded totally professional. There was nothing either antagonistic or friendly. Rick thought if Vince talked to him that way, he'd know he was a subject in the eyes of the law, rather than neighbors.

The families got the same message, because a couple of them were upstairs shortly after Vince left, asking if there was anything they could do to make them more comfortable. Rick thought a camp cot would be awfully nice if they had such a thing. They did, of course, and Rick grabbed his bedroll and set up the cot just inside the door of Susie's room. Susie had collapsed in the bed, and Gwendolyn occupied the easy chair next to the bed, her feet propped up on an ottoman.

After some restless sleep, Rick suddenly came to, and found himself listening. He heard voices downstairs arguing while keeping the volume down. The tonal quality of the female was like a cat snarling just before attacking another cat. The male was like a dog subvocalizing a growl. Glancing at Gwendolyn and Susie in the moonlight, both appeared asleep. He got up, slipping into his boots, which were the only things he took off, other than his coat.

He went down the stairs as quietly as he could, wondering if the people in the kitchen heard him when the tread creaked. At the same time, he probably was just overhearing a family squabble. Rick thought it couldn't possibly matter. Whoever he heard was far more interested in making their point than in listening for anyone approaching. In the hall going into the kitchen, he now heard them speaking.

"We have to get rid of him," the woman's voice hissed. "There's no way we can pull this off with him here."

"We both saw how interested the big wheels are in the two of them," a man's baritone returned. "They're going to keep a watch on the girl, too. There is no way we can hide anything. For all we know, some of them are outside watching right now."

"Don't you see? It's easy. We just say he went back to the ranch. We stick his body under a snow drift somewhere, and if they ask, we don't know anything about it. Meanwhile, Gwen, dear, volunteers to stay to be with darling Susie. Later, they both are so happy being here that they decide to stay around. Of course, it's terrible about her husband being missing and all, but we all have to march on, don't we?"

Rick thought that if there was any doubt before, there sure wasn't any now. He leaned against the wall, still in shadow, folded his arms and said clearly, "So this is the hospitality that rural Nebraska is famous for. I can see why everyone is trying to leave."

There was a sudden dropping of china, and a rattling going on. The woman and her husband were suddenly out in the hallway, and Rick saw both of them had butcher knives.

"If it wasn't decided before, it certainly is now," the man growled.

Rick backed toward the bottom of the stairs and the front door. With no coat on, he'd quickly freeze if he went outside. He wasn't sure how much he was delaying the inevitable if he went up the stairs. In addition, Gwendolyn and Susie would suddenly be in the middle of it all. Rick didn't think either of the two coming after him were knife fighters. On the other hand, his own experience with self defense was nearly zero. He felt the end of the stair rail in his hand, and the couple were only a few feet away. He'd better figure something out quickly.

He suddenly heard the unmistakable sound of a rifle bolt going home. The couple heard it too. They all looked up to see Gwendolyn, with a hunting rifle braced on the bannister and pointed at the woman. The couple stared at her, wide-eyed.

"You old biddy," Gwendolyn snarled. "You think a couple of honeyed words can sell me back into slavery in this place? I figured something like this might happen and I packed for the trip. It made my bedroll heavier, but it was worth every grunt I made hauling it up here. Rick, I was going to suggest that you get your coat so you could find Vince or his posse. However, one of them is looking through the door right now. Why don't you let the man in?"

Rick opened the door, and the face in question belonged to Vince. Seeing the couple with butcher knives still in their hands, he drew his own weapon as he slid in the door.

"Drop the blades," Vince barked. "Do it now."

It was like they had both forgotten what they had in their hands, and nervously dropped them on the floor.

"Both of you, back up three steps and drop to your knees. Lock your fingers behind your heads."

They seemed in shock, but followed the commands. Vince took a couple of strides forward, and kicked the knives aside with his boot. Only then did Vince glance toward the top of the stairs. "You can secure your weapon now, Gwendolyn."

"They were going to kill Rick and throw his body in a snowdrift," Gwendolyn told Vince.

"No, we weren't," the woman protested. "You misunderstood."

Vince looked disgusted. "We misunderstood about you enslaving Gwendolyn. We misunderstood a minute ago when you came after Rick with butcher knives. We understood it all, folks. Here's something for you to understand: We aren't going to put up with this crap one minute longer. Letting them stay here was a test to make sure we had it right. I'm sorry to say that we did. Rick and Gwendolyn, I'm even sorrier we had to put you guys through this. This is not a place we want to leave Susie Maguire, not even a minute longer."

"What's the next step, Vince?" Rick finally got his voice back.

Vince favored him with a slight smile. "Mark and I got together with Lyle, and worked out the next step. These wannabe slave holders don't need to know any of it. All they need to know is that they're going to be cleaning their own houses from now on. In their appropriate free time, they'll also do some cooking and cleaning for the rest of Ragan. My kids filled me in on more of the situation that they saw over here. Nearly all of their stories fit in very nicely with what I've seen just now."

Rick went up the stairs, knowing that getting ready to go was only a matter of a few seconds. Mainly, he wanted to be with Gwendolyn, who just saved his life. For all he knew, Vince may have just saved Mrs. Stamford's life. Gwendolyn ejected the cartridge into her hand. Then she immediately cleared the weapon. It seemed clear she'd done that kind of thing before.

She was still carrying the rifle as she headed into Susie's room. Susie just stared.

"Susie, it turns out these are not good people, and this place is not right for you. Mr. Lillard has another place that will be much better. Are you okay with that?"

"I … I think so. Did Kevin give permission for it?"

Gwendolyn bent over and looked in Susie's eyes. "Don't worry about Kevin's permission. What you need to think about is what's best for you and for your baby. I bet it will be a beautiful baby."

Susie began to sob. "It can't be. Daddy says a baby conceived in sin has to be ugly and awful."

"How does your daddy know that?" Gwendolyn asked.

"He says it's in the Bible."

"Your daddy may say it's in the Bible, but I'll bet he'd be a long time finding where it's written. I'll bet he says it is also in there about having your mother and sisters beat on you when he can't or won't."

Susie nodded but didn't say anything. Rick was astonished at this bit of conversation, but was distracted when he heard the front door. There were several men's voices and then the sound of boots coming up the stairs.

"Are you guys ready to go? We have the sleigh out front, as well as your horses. Susie will ride in the sleigh. Save your questions until we get well clear of here."

Downstairs was the incredible scene of posse members hog-tying the two in spite of ongoing laments about various physical disabilities. Going out the front door, and seeing the sleigh as well as their horses, all saddled and ready to go, it occurred to Rick that Vince, Mark, and Lyle never had a doubt about how their little test would go. Come to think of it, Gwendolyn must have been tuned in to that test and knew where it was going as well.

Ah, yes, this was not a real emergency. It was only a test. If it had been a real emergency, there would have placards directing him to hide under the nearest urinal. That would be perfectly safe, since nobody ever actually hit it.

As they went past the Rowley place and the Co-op, Rick noticed Vince finally began to relax a little, and Rick thought it might be a good time to find out what was going on.

"So where are we going, Vince?"

Vince looked at him and grinned. "You're going home, of course. That is where Susie's going, too. We saw how the two of you circled the wagons around her, and how you protect each other. The main house at Wagon Ranch is the perfect place for her to be."

"What about Kevin? The whole point about taking Susie to Ragan was for Kevin to see that she would be okay."

"Kevin is a certified mad dog. Who knows what he'll do next? I've seen too many girls from abusive families end up with abusive husbands. It is time for that to end, my friend."

"We were wondering about Kevin when Susie asked if he had given permission for this."

Vince didn't reply, but it was clear to Rick that he had filed it in some massive law enforcement database. In the sleigh, he heard Susie begin to whimper, and Gwendolyn ordered a stop. She dismounted, handed her reins to Rick, and crawled under the quilts and comforters with Susie, who immediately became more relaxed and quiet. Vince and Rick just looked at each other Rick had no idea what Vince was thinking, but he was certain it didn't include any good will for either Kevin or Dennis Maguire.

When they got to Wagon Ranch, Dan Goble was true to his word. The main house was warm, and a couple of guys were on hand to take the horses to the stable. Vince looked impressed.

"The guys in the posse do many things really well. Still, having a homecoming like this beats anything I ever saw."

Rick shook his head. "From what Mark told me about the castle, they really did it right up there. Of course, those folks are all in Oxford now, organizing meat processing when they aren't training a recruit."

"Ain't that the truth, though? It's obvious you guys are in good hands now, so I'll get back to doing Lyle Lillard's bidding. Speaking of which, I owe both him and Mark a report about the fun and frolic we just had."

"Do you think he'd really back you on what you told those people?"

"If he leaves it up to me, that's exactly what will happen. He may well have something else in mind for them. Time will tell."

Inside, Gwendolyn took Susie to a bedroom and got her settled. Dan arrived at the house the same time.

"Did I do everything right?" he wanted to know.

"As far as I can tell, Dan. By the way, your eyes do not deceive you. Susie is staying with us, at least for now. Here's the deal: Everybody is to leave her alone, and I mean completely alone. Beyond that, everybody should stay as far away from her as possible. We will eat all of our meals here, until Susie is ready for something more."

Dan pursed his lips. "It's that bad, huh? Okay, we'll make sure you've got plenty of supplies. I guess you'll be making the rounds at some point."

Rick smiled. "Count on it, Dan. Anything new and astonishing?"

"It's bone-chilling cold. The horses are okay, and the guys aren't too snarly. We've still got hay, food, and firewood. Oh, we put together a map of solar-powered wells, as best we can remember them."

"What did you do with that closet where Kevin and Duane were staying?"

"We filled half of it with wood and the other half with food."

"I probably don't want to know how you gathered that much, but it all sounds good. I might come down the tunnel later, depending on what is going on here."

"We got it, boss. It is good to have you back."

"Hell, we were only gone overnight."

"Was it just overnight? It seemed more like several days, anyway."

Rick thought about it a minute, and finally nodded his head. "In that case, we'll say it was a year and call it even."

"Was Kevin a good boy?"

"Define good. He never hadw an opportunity to get out of line. They'll take Kevin back to Oxford after sunrise. With any luck, we can all do something besides worry about him. Maybe Kevin can go on to better things, as well."

"That's a bunch of wishes."

"You just got a bouquet of wishes. You'll want to get them into a vase with water as soon as possible, so they don't wilt."

Dan slipped out the back door, and Rick made the rounds, first checking the fire in the heating stove, and then the small maintenance fire in the cook stove. He finally went to the living room, where he waited for Gwendolyn to decide she could leave Susie alone. That was when an uneasy thought struck him. What if Susie couldn't bear to be alone, and Gwendolyn was the only one who could make her feel secure? Worrying about that would only make him crazy, and he'd had more than enough crazy lately.

Gwendolyn did finally come out of the bedroom, heading directly to the kitchen, where she stoked the fire and got some coffee making. When it was ready, she brought in a cup for both of them and collapsed on the couch next to him.

"The poor kid had it pretty tough," she told him. "First, it was her father, and then he started getting the rest of the family in on the act. She doesn't want to say it, but Kevin wasn't any better. Being stuck in this house with all the weed very nearly sent her over the edge. Susie may be a long time coming back."

"I noticed how she recoiled when I got close, and figured it had to be something like that. I warned Dan to keep everybody well away from her. I hope he got the point. How long can she go without you being right there with her?"

"That's the big question, and one that I'm trying to answer right now. At least she's giving me enough time for the odd potty break. Come to think of it, I should get her to the outhouse soon."

Rick looked at Gwendolyn doubtfully. "Will we have to housebreak her too? Could the mess on the walls in here have been from her?"

"Ugh!" Gwendolyn put down the cup and headed for the bedroom. A few minutes later, she helped Susie around through the kitchen to the back door. She looked over at Rick and mouthed, "It's okay."

The two women were not gone long. Taking an outhouse break in arctic conditions wasn't where anybody wanted to spend a second longer than they had to. After a while, Gwendolyn was back in, and this time fixed them something to eat. They sat side by side at the counter.

"This must be something like what it will be to have a new-born baby," Rick finally commented.

"The same thing occurred to me. That is one thing which keeps me going, knowing this is a rehearsal for our own. What worries me is that Susie not only has to get through her own problems, she's going to have a child of her own on top of it. I don't know the answer, but I'm sure that neither her family nor Kevin is the answer."

"I heard Mark's wife, Ellen, thought about having her baby without Mark. Lyle Lillard said absolutely not. He doesn't want anything to do with single parent families. This may be a case where there is no choice in the matter. Maybe something will turn up, though."

Gwendolyn reached over with a napkin and dabbed Rick's cheek.

Gwendolyn told Rick to sleep in their bedroom. She'd be with Rick when she could, and Susie when she had to. It wasn't great, but Rick thought it beat Kevin's deal of a cot in the hall and a kick from a boot for a wake up call. He stayed awake on the couch as long as he could, getting cuddles between whimpers from Susie's room.

By the next morning, Gwendolyn had been to bed a couple of times. She never stayed very long, though. Daylight found them sitting at the counter, leaning against each other. Dan knocked politely on the back door while they tried to get up enough energy to drink coffee. He took one look at them, nodded, and backed out the door. A few minutes later, two guys brought chow. Rick thought whatever it lacked in quality, it more than made up for in quantity. On the other hand, Dan's evident observation was well taken. They were both pretty draggy.

On the other hand, Susie shortly showed her face outside her room.

"Would it be okay if I get something to eat?"

Gwendolyn led her into the kitchen and sat her at the table, while Rick stayed on a stool at the bar. Rick's presence made her nervous, but she ate in spite of it. Rick couldn't decide whether she was becoming more comfortable with the situation, or if she was simply hungry. He couldn't recall her eating anything since they picked her up in Huntley. Okay, she'd eaten a bit at the Stamfords, but she certainly wolfed the food down now. At the same time, she kept one eye on him. Maybe the other eye was looking for an escape route.

She finally slowed down, and asked for permission to return to her room. Susie talked to Gwendolyn, but it appeared that she was really looking for permission from him. Rick smiled softly and nodded. That appeared to be the height of approval, as far as Susie was concerned. Gwendolyn was right there with her as she started to go into her room.

Susie turned then, and with downcast eyes asked, "Gwendolyn says you don't hit women. She also insists that you don't believe in it. Is that true?"

Rick cocked his head. "That is true."

"How do you keep everyone from being in sin?"

Rick didn't know where the answer came from, but it rolled out of his mouth. "God knows everything, so if beating will keep you from sin, it would always work. Your father believes in hitting women, but says you got involved in sin anyway. It didn't work, and I've never seen it written in any commandment."

Susie was puzzled. "That's what Gwendolyn told me. She said the commandment told us to love one another, not beat one another. I will have to think about this."

Rick nodded. "I think you should. You're among friends here. You no longer have to be afraid of anything."

Susie went to her room, then, and Gwendolyn smiled at Rick as she followed Susie. Rick guessed he didn't completely blow it. He decided to help out, and washed the dishes. Keeping the pan of wash water at the right spot on the stove, it never got cold, and it never got scalding, either. He then went out and brought in a bucket of water to add to the water tank on the side of the stove. As he was doing that, Susie and Gwendolyn came out, heading for the outhouse.

Susie looked at Rick in astonishment. "What sin did you commit that you have do women's work?"

Rick chuckled. "It isn't women's work. It's what needs to be done. I'm here and I can do it. Gwendolyn's with you. Why wouldn't I do it?"

"You're not doing penance?"

"If I left this for Gwendolyn to do, I might find myself doing penance of another sort."

Later, when Susie seemed to be reasonably settled, Gwendolyn came out and joined Rick on the sofa. "Your comments when we were headed out really got her. Susie couldn't stop talking about it. Her family has to be strange beyond belief. The really strange thing is that her mother goes along with it. If I didn't know better, I might wonder if they weren't really part of that terrorist group."

"From what I hear, the people we are fighting now may not be the same terrorists we fought in Afghanistan. Mark says they look the part and talk the part, but there's something different about them. However that might be, wild-eyed radicals resemble one another far more than any of them look like ordinary folks."

Gwendolyn snorted. "With a phrase mentioning some fictitious group known as ordinary folks, I could think you've gotten further into the rural lifestyle than you might want to think."

Rick grinned. "I remember Mark telling about some guy driving out in the country, and bragging about paying a hundred grand for his ride. A farmer wasn't impressed. When asked why, the farmer replied he had a ride that cost him a quarter million dollars, and he only drove it two weeks a year. It was his combine. These days, it's whether you're on a horse."

"That must mean I'm married to one of the big men in the county. How did I manage it?"

"Any girl who shows up with her very own dragon will always get my attention. What chance does a mere horse have against a dragon?"

Susie peered out her door just then, and Rick wondered how long she'd been listening. "What can we do for you, Susie?" Rick asked.

"I've never heard people talk like that. The closest was when Kevin was sweet-talking me. You two seem comfortable just being with each other."

Gwendolyn squeezed Rick's hand. "There's someone like that for you, too, Susie. For being comfortable together, Lyle and Adeline Lillard take the cake. They know each other so well that either of them knows in advance what the other is thinking. And, no, it doesn't come from them beating it out of one another."

"How do I get to be comfortable being with people?"

Rick looked at her. "Are you comfortable with Gwendolyn?"

"Yes, I am. She makes me feel secure. She also makes feel like I'm worth something."

"You should feel that way, no matter who you're around. You should feel that way even if you're not around anyone at all."

Susie took a couple of tentative steps toward them, and stopped, her hands clasped in front of her. Rick was reminded of comments from Adeline Lillard, along with Lyle and Mark, about horse training being excellent preparation for working with people. Right now, Rick could almost see an abused horse instead of a person.

Chapter 18

Kevin's Gang

It was soon clear that Susie did not have a horse's personality. She took a several small steps toward them. After a moment, she asked, "Gwendolyn, could I help you make the next meal?"

"Certainly, Susie. What kind of food do you like to make?"

"I don't know. I think I can make about anything."

Rick thought he'd take a chance. "Susie, could I ask you a question?"

"I think so."

"You said I was doing women's work. What would a man's work be?"

She paused, trying to think of an answer. Finally, "Recently, telling women what to do."

Gwendolyn frowned. "That was just recently. How was it before?"

"Daddy had a job, when we had electricity and gasoline, and people could drive places in an hour that now takes us two days on a horse. The company where Daddy worked closed, and he couldn't find work. Mommy worked at a couple of places, trying to keep things going. The electricity went away and Daddy just sat around. He got peculiar, and began telling us about things in the Bible none of us ever heard of. The funny thing is that with all the quotes, I never saw him open a Bible."

"That must have been the Gospel According to Dennis Maguire," Gwendolyn suggested softly. "You thought Kevin was your way out."

"Yes, I guess I did. Kevin acted like a real gentleman, so polite and everything. Then he had the job at Harlan Ranch. It didn't take long for everybody to know Harlan Ranch was the place to be, especially after the dust and big rain. Mommy had hope in her eye, and there was a sparkle in Daddy's eye as well. I thought I'd better get Kevin committed as fast as I could, and the big procession to get rid of the vial of Omega bugs seemed perfect."

Gwendolyn and Rick looked at each other. Gwendolyn said, "Susie, I'd love to have your help in the kitchen. Rick can be in the living room, so we can all talk to each other. Isn't it wonderful how they improved the layout of this house?"

Rick got up. "Now that you mention it, I really do need to go check on the guys. It wouldn't do for them to think the place would actually run without my personal supervision."

He headed into the bedroom to get his winter gear, and also give Susie and Gwendolyn a chance to get into the kitchen, where they could keep some separation from him. Anyway, it would give them a chance to have a more relaxed conversation for a while. As he walked into the kitchen and turned toward the back door, Gwendolyn came walking over to him and gave him a kiss.

"That's a good move, lover. Do me a favor, though, and don't stay gone too long. Okay?"

"When it comes to being separated from you, I'm always going to keep it just as short as possible. I saw you with that rifle. Somebody told me they had never handled one."

"I didn't want to make you nervous then. By the way, I hit my targets, and don't you forget it."

"I'm going to be sweating, no matter how cold it is. I'll be back in a flash. All this is to remind Dan he's not in charge. Not officially, anyway."

"It sounds like you've got your future all mapped out."

"Yeah, Mark referred to it as being a ROAD scholar. That was from his military duty. The letters in ROAD stood for Retired on Active Duty."

"So if you achieve that status, Mark would probably be able to figure it out."

"Yes, I imagine he would. Mr. Lillard would be on top of it, too. I should find a clipboard with some forms, so I can look official as I make my rounds."

"Oh, you should definitely look official. You've got to do that."

Susie cut in then. "The two of you make a joke out of everything."

Rick looked at her. "I wouldn't suppose Kevin ever tried to lighten the mood around you. I know he never did around me, but then, I was just the neighborhood punching bag."

Susie shook her head. "You always had Kevin running scared. He sent you off with Mark, hoping you'd screw up. Instead, you came back the hero, and he didn't know what to do. He was getting crazy anyway, but the fear of being compared to you really pushed him along."

"Now that's something I hadn't thought about. Kevin abused me and everybody because he was crazy. He got crazy because I wasn't clever enough to kill off a bunch of people evacuating McCook. What would he do to get back at me, I wonder?"

"Gee, I don't know. Kevin always thought of himself as the great leader of men."

Rick and Gwendolyn looked at one another. Rick finally shook his head. "I hate to think about it, but Stanley's tribe, the Peepul, is full of losers needing to follow somebody. Meanwhile, Stanley is trying to get them to think for themselves. Kevin might set himself up as Willy the Rat, version 2.0 and give them the Kevin plan. That plan would include taking you away from all of this, Susie. It would also involve vengeance against somebody with my name. I hope the snipers do a better job of keeping track of him this time."

Gwendolyn nodded, and looked at Susie. "We'll keep those hopes close to us. Meanwhile, it's really good to see you back among the living, Susie."

Rick nodded. "That's a fact, and while I've been jawboning, to use the local phrase, I have no idea if Dan and his people are among the living, and if so, what kinds of marvelous things they might be doing."

Down the tunnel, everybody wanted to know how Susie was doing. Rick quickly arrived at a standard answer. "Susie is doing much better, but she has to deal with people at her own speed. She no longer curls up into a ball when I'm in the room, but there's no need to push it."

Dan had the guys working hard on the other house, and managed to keep things going with no busy work. The place looked better than the last time he saw it. The insides of the other house had been torn out, and new walls were going in. Freshly sawn lumber smelled much better than that stupid herb, Rick thought.

Susie improved rapidly after that, even with several setbacks along the way. In a couple of days, Dan, as well as several of the crew were able to come into the house without her getting upset or apprehensive. Gwendolyn reminded Rick just how tentative this improvement was. The smallest thing could have her back the way she was, or possibly even worse. For the moment, at least, anything like the smallest thing she feared stayed away.

For his part, Rick was more than happy to see problems of any size staying away from both himself and Gwendolyn. It was amazing to be able to just get on with life, at least for a little while. At the same time, he was able to get to know this woman who was his wife. That was a really strange thing, indeed. Could this good life last? Probably not, so he figured he'd better concentrate on appreciating every last second of it. In this strange little scenario, Susie played the part of their sweet sixteen daughter.

What Rick viewed with particular dread was the prospect of posse members heading their way on a mission that included Kevin's name. The arctic winter they found themselves in still stung, but it had gotten to be a simple presence everybody dealt with. It had never been anything but winter. It would never be anything else, either. Supplies of hay, feed, rations, and wood continued to hold out. Dan's people found ways to get more wood.

It was sunny nearly every day, although the sun was just a bright light in the sky, and didn't warm anything. That brought the subject of solar collectors and water pumps back to the fore. The other issue was further discussion of getting the power poles up from Alma. There was no doubt they had to wait for a thaw to be able to set them, but at least they would be available for the construction of an arena.

Near noon one day, Don Rowley's senior driver showed up on top of the double-header. That sight had not been on Rick's list of signs of a coming apocalypse. However, in the wagons were more firearms and ammunition than Rick had any idea existed in the area. Dan's people arrived at the back door of the main house at the same time, having seen him coming.

The driver came into the house, pulled out and then recited from a carefully worded message. "This is from Lyle Lillard, Mark Tahner, and deputy Vince. Stanley Peepul sent word that Kevin is stirring up trouble with some of the Peepul tribe. Everybody is to be well-armed and ready."

He got another sheet of paper out of an interior pocket of his parka, and directed Dan's guys to bring in two rifles for every window, plus several spares. In addition, there were massive amounts of ammunition.

"Where will the rest of the load go?" Rick wanted to know.

"All the rest is going to the other side of Wagon Ranch, Rick. You can't believe the firepower going out around Harlan, and that includes the McCook people down at Orleans."

"With this, I believe we could win against a few spears."

"That's the thing. Stanley thinks Kevin is giving some of the tribe firearms. This could get really serious in a hurry."

Susie was off to the side, listening to all of it, but suddenly bent over, clutching her stomach. Gwendolyn and Rick looked at each other, and she mouthed to him, "I told you," just as she turned to help Susie.

"How many posse members is Vince sending us this time?" Rick asked quietly.

"He can't send any right now. He'll send as many as he can, as soon as possible. He understands your situation, but there's no telling what Kevin might do."

Rick just nodded. "Well, you'd better deliver the rest of your load."

After the driver left, Rick turned to Dan. "I know you need all hands on deck to unload those wagons, but right afterward, we'll need people in the tunnels and up here. Gwendolyn and I are not going to be able to hold off any kind of attack by ourselves."

"I got you, boss. I'll have our best people up to you as fast as we can. By the time those people in Oxford know Kevin's gone again, he could be knocking on our door."

Dan took off, and Rick walked over to Susie's door. Gwendolyn was talking to Susie, who was sitting on the edge of her bed. Susie looked up and saw Rick. Instead of recoiling, she smiled weakly, and said, "I'll be okay. Thanks for caring about me."

Rick grinned. "I'd come over and give you a hug if I thought you'd accept it."

Susie suddenly stood up and opened her arms. "I'll accept a hug from you right now."

Rick gave her a hug, even as he looked at Gwendolyn. She looked as amazed as he felt. Afterward, Susie decided it would be nice if they all sat at the table together for lunch. It appeared that what might have been a major set-back turned into a positive outcome in spite of everything. Rick was hesitant to push the issue, but as they sat down, Gwendolyn brought it up.

"Do you think you can talk about Kevin, at least a little?"

"I think so, Gwendolyn. Everyone here has been so nice to me, and then you doing all of this to protect me from Kevin and his strange ways. Rick, you act like a father should, while Kevin has become a lot like my father."

Gwendolyn nodded. "Many women are attracted to men like their fathers. Mostly it's a good thing. Sometimes, like in your case, it can be a real problem. You wouldn't want your child to deal with that for his or her entire life, would you?"

"Heavens no. Everyone is so serious about defending this place. I just can't believe it."

Rick shook his head. "I'd like to say that it's all to protect you. The fact is that everyone here is on Kevin's list of people he doesn't like. For what its worth, I'm right at the top of that list. I did find it interesting and worrisome that the warning about Kevin didn't come from the Marines who are supposed to be retraining and keeping track of him. It came from Stanley."

Gwendolyn nodded. "I wondered if you caught that." She thought for a moment and turned to Susie. "I'm really happy that you've come along as far as you have. Still, will you be able to tolerate more guys in the house? They'll be here to protect you, but they might not always act like they should."

Susie smiled. "You mean, they might start acting like I'm a regular girl or something? With both of you here, I'm sure nobody will get too far out of line. Thank you for thinking about it."

The stress level was high for everyone but Susie. As far as Rick could tell, she was almost dancing around the small house. Guys coming into the house at all hours of the day and night didn't bother her in the least. One really good thing was that Gwendolyn now felt like she could spend the night with Rick instead of having to be with Susie all the time.

As they got ready to go to sleep one night, Rick wondered out loud to Gwendolyn, "I'm glad Susie doing so much better. I almost wonder if she's doing too much better."

"I see what you're saying, Rick. It may be some over-reaction. With everything she's been through, this must feel like she's walking on air."

Early the next day, the alarms went around the place. They spotted a group approaching from Oxford. Gwendolyn looked at Susie. "Have you ever used a gun?"

"A few times. I didn't like it."

"Okay, your job is to keep track of everybody and bring them what they need, whether it's coffee, ammunition, or another rifle. Can you do that?"

She nodded. "Sure, I can certainly do that." Then Susie stared at Gwendolyn. "Do you use a gun?"

Rick answered, "Gwendolyn is a crack shot. She's the one who got us out of Ragan. Do you remember that?"

"Oh, my," was Susie's response. It was like she believed all women must be afraid of weapons. Rick decided he'd better concentrate on what was outside his window.

Some of the guys claimed military experience, and introduced them to the idea of each person having an area to concentrate their fire. It was obvious that ammunition was going to get very hard to find eventually, and whatever ammunition they did find would be less dependable as time went on. "Don't mess with them. Just take them out with one shot," was the advice, and Rick thought it made sense.

Suddenly, he heard a couple of shots from the stable. Additional shots followed a few minutes later, this time from near the other house, or maybe the bunkhouse.

"Is everybody ready?" Rick called softly. He got a chorus of, "Yeah," in return.

A head popped up momentarily, but disappeared before he could draw a bead on it. It was like an old computer game. He recalled it was called 'Whack-a- Mole.' The difference was, of course, that this was the real thing, and Rick knew it.

"They're checking us out," one of Dan's people muttered under his breath. "They want to see if they can draw our fire so they know how many are here and how alert we might be."

Gwendolyn growled, "If they give me enough time and target, I'll be sure to let them know."

All at once a rather skinny raggedy guy jumped out from behind a snowdrift, and ran toward the front door of the house. He was waving a switchblade knife, and yelling, "We are Peepul!"

He was in Rick's area, and Rick followed all the instructions they'd given him. He concentrated on center of mass, controlled his breathing, and was amazed when his rifle suddenly fired. The guy was at the line the military fellow claimed was ten meters away. Unlike the movies, where getting hit by a rifle threw people all over the place, this fellow just ran out of gas and collapsed not much more than an arm's length from Rick's position.

There was another big difference from the movies. Rick did not feel either victorious or manly. It didn't feel like he'd done much of anything at all other than to reduce the threat a bit. Several 'Whack-a-Mole' heads appeared and withdrew. Then somebody came to the back door. There was a double knock followed by Dan's voice.

"Our guy in the crow's nest signaled the west gate with a mirror. As far as we can tell, the posse should be on its way. Are you guys okay?"

"We're all breathing, at least for the moment," Rick softly called back. "The other folks have one less person available to threaten us with. Does that constitute okay?"

"It sounds pretty good to me. It'll take the posse a while to get here, so keep on keeping on."

"You do know that I'm here with a weapon and a rotten attitude. If you lay any more old song lyrics on me, I may have to put you out of my misery."

"I got that loud and clear. I'm out of here."

"Hey, is that you, Rick?" That was Kevin's voice coming from behind a snowdrift.

"Yeah, Kevin, I'm here, no thanks to you. Aren't you supposed to be doing your duty down in Oxford?"

"I got tired of that. I just dropped by with some friends to settle some debts and collect my woman."

Rick kept an eye out the lower corner of his window. "You have it wrong. All the debts are ones you owe, and there isn't enough money to pay for them. Why don't you just lean back, take a load off, and soak up the sunshine? It's such a nice balmy day."

"Do you think I'm dumb enough to stick around until Vince's bunch gets here? The debt I'm here for is going to be paid, and I will be back to collect it. Don't go away, now."

It got quiet then. Rick couldn't imagine being out there in that cold. He was freezing with the cold coming in through the window he opened just barely enough for firing. A few minutes later came another light knock on the kitchen door.

"The crow's nest reports all or most of the bunch has taken off at an angle away from the road. Everyone at the other end is still holding their positions, but it looks like we're clear for now," was Dan's report.

"That's good to hear," Rick called back. "Like your guys, we'll hold our positions until it's certain they're gone. What do you think they were really after, Dan?"

"I think the horses would be the first target. Whatever score Kevin fancies he needs to settle with you would be a high priority. If he knew about Susie being here, I think he'd have hit a whole lot harder and I don't think he'd have left nearly as fast. Thinking about it, I'd better bring more people up here."

"I only heard a few shots from the other end. Were they just checking us out?"

"Beats me. It sure didn't feel like a real attack. It was only harassment at most."

"Kevin might feel there's a score to settle concerning him being shackled in that storeroom just off the bunkhouse."

"There is that, certainly. Wait a minute. I hear something from down the tunnel. Hang on a minute while I check it out."

"What do you think it is, Rick?" came from Susie.

"The best bets are either that the posse is coming or that Kevin is returning. I'll hope for the posse, but let's get ready in case it's Kevin."

Rick blew into his hands, and flexed them several times, trying to make sure they'd still function if he needed them to. Suddenly, Susie was pressing a hot cup of coffee into his hands. That was far more effective. His hands were cold enough that the cup almost felt scalding at first. A moment later, there was another knock on the kitchen door.

"I've got two guys to help out," came Dan's voice. "Send them in," Rick replied.

He was ready to keep the position, but found that he was one being relieved at that point. Gwendolyn was the other. Everybody crowded around the window to look at the body outside, face-down in the snow. Rick's shot made an ugly exit wound. Other than knowing the individual was not Kevin, nobody had any idea who it could be.

Rick, meanwhile, already saw more of that body than he wanted, and was happy to carry the cup of coffee closer to the stove. After a minute or two, he opened the kitchen door.

"Any word on who's coming?"

"They're mounted, which is a good sign," Dan responded. "We're still trying to get a positive identification on the riders."

Rick thought for a moment about asking as to whether anybody else managed to reduce the odds, but decided it didn't matter and just sucked down some coffee. Gwendolyn joined him then.

"Are you doing okay?" she asked.

"I'm doing better than the other guy. We'll have to wait a while to know much more."

There was a faint voice outside, and Dan immediately relayed it. "It is the posse. Do you want to stand down yet?"

Rick shook his head. "Not until they're actually outside the door. Why take any chances? Tell everyone down the tunnel to stay alert until we find out what's going on."

"You got it, boss. I'll tell them myself, and then come back."

Rick finished his coffee, and pulled on enough winter clothes to last for a while talking to the posse. Gwendolyn decided to join him meeting them as they pulled up in front of the house soon after. Vince, Mark, and Josh were leading them. Rick told them the basics of what happened. Mark stayed mounted, but rode around and checked on how Kevin's bunch had been situated. Then he rode around to look at the body. He dismounted, and turned it over.

"I think he was one of the meat cutters," Mark commented.

Vince looked at Rick. "You say they headed off the road, but your impression was that they were heading for Ragan?"

"That's what Kevin gave me to believe. He said he'd be back to settle our debt, whatever the hell that might be."

Mark and Josh looked at each other, and then at Vince. Mark finally nodded. "Rick, we need to get you and Susie out of here. Gwendolyn, you should come as well. Get Susie ready to travel. We'll also take some of your people. You are all going to the Lillard place. We can defend it reasonably well. We'll give you some posse members, just in case. How is Susie?"

Gwendolyn looked at Mark. "She's doing very well, considering the situation. We'll get her ready. Did you all want to come in and warm up?"

"We'd love to, but we need catch up with Kevin's bunch. If they're slogging on foot through deep snow, we should be able to beat them to Ragan."

Vince, meanwhile, was conversing with three posse members. He finally turned around and told Rick, "These three will be with you guys."

Rick nodded. "We'll meet them at the stable. Tell them to bring their horses on in. We may be a couple of minutes getting organized here and walking over there."

"You guys be safe," Josh added.

"Good hunting," Rick called as they got their group turned around and headed out. Several arms went up to acknowledge the wish.

Back inside, Susie looked at them. "They said we have to go?"

Rick nodded. "I'm afraid so. It will only be for a little bit, until they can get Kevin and his bunch corralled. They're taking us to the Lillard place. If anywhere is safe, that would be."

"You need to get your things, dear," Gwendolyn told her. "If you need more warm clothes, let me know and we'll see what we can find."

Going down the tunnel, Gwendolyn and Susie took the lead, while Rick and Dan discussed how they could defend Wagon Ranch. There really wasn't much of a change, other than a few less defenders on hand. Hopefully, Kevin would be too busy trying to stay away from Vince and Mark to concentrate on the Wagon Ranch to any great degree.

"If Kevin knows you aren't here, he might skip it," Dan speculated hopefully.

"Kevin knows I was here. He might figure out that Susie came over here as well. How are you going to convince him? Invite him in? Take him on a tour?"

"I see your point, and I knew that was the case. I was just trying to get a little hope into it."

"For hope, concentrate on the possibility that Vince, Mark, and Josh can get to Ragan ahead of Kevin and company. Really concentrate on them being able to round that bunch up sooner rather than later. If they make it back here in spite of all your hopeful thinking, then concentrate on center of mass when they're too close to miss, but still too far from you to do any damage."

"That sounds like wisdom to me. Where'd you get it?"

"One of your people said it. He's the one who claims to have some military experience."

"I know the guy. Maybe I should find him and take him on a tour of the place. He might be able to suggest some things we can do better."

"There you go. He's still at the main house, if that saves you any time."

"I think I'd better take care of that right now. Stay safe, boss." Dan spun around and headed back up the tunnel toward the main house. Meanwhile Susie and Gwendolyn were deep in conversation as the trio approached the intersection with the main tunnel.

Rick thought he'd pick up the pace a bit, only to almost run into the two women who abruptly stopped. He soon saw why they had stopped. Facing them with rifles were two of the guys working for Dan.

"The three of you, turn around and go back to the main house," the one guy growled.

"They said we need to go over to the stable," Susie gasped.

"That's not going to happen anytime soon. Right now, you're going to do what I tell you."

The rifle barrels didn't waver and the eyes behind the weapons looked very serious. The three duly turned and trudged back the way they came. None of it made any sense. Rick knew for a fact that when they got to the main house, Dan and the others guarding the place would simply turn the tables on these guys once more.

Approaching the back door, one rifleman yelled, "We got them."

Just that fast, the door opened. Their military advisor was standing right behind it, rifle at the ready. "Come on in. There's somebody who wants to see the three of you."

As they went into the living room, Susie took one look at who was there, and grabbed onto Gwendolyn in fear. Kevin was lounging on the couch while one of the other guys who'd been there to protect them now held a rifle barrel to Dan's head.

"Susie, my love," Kevin smirked. "They said you were going to be a servant for those families in Ragan. It appears they decided that wasn't degrading enough, and stuck you here with these two. Rick, old buddy, we had some fun times, didn't we? I think we should have some more. Your bride there has plenty of practice being a servant, so she can be Susie's maid. That Mark is one clever devil. Sending the Peepul to raid Ragan and Huntley won't give him anything like enough entertainment, so we need to leave."

The three then headed back down the tunnel, with their two new friends ahead of them, and with Kevin, Dan, and the others behind. At the intersection, they headed toward the stable, but turned off just before getting there, entering a tunnel Rick had seen on many occasions, and had been told was where they took the snow when they were digging the tunnels. It was wide enough for one wheelbarrow, and had bays every twenty feet or so for wheelbarrows to pass one another.

A heavy wooden door was at the end, and the two riflemen pulled it open, exposing a deep gully they'd used to dump the snow. It appeared there would be room to dump quite a bit more snow, should the need arise, but that didn't seem to be part of the plan for the moment. They followed a narrow path along the side of the gulch. Rick realized there had to be communication between Kevin and his buddies at Wagon Ranch leading up to all of this. To judge from the trail, there had been quite a lot of it.

"When did this get here?" Dan wondered aloud.

"Shut your yap," Kevin told him. "Save your breath. You're going to need it. We've got a long way to go."

The trail wandered down, routing around snowdrifts and staying out of sight of Oxford. At the bottom, it wasn't long before they saw one of Stanley's hunting parties. Stanley also soon appeared, standing in front of them. Rick was suddenly hopeful this whole catastrophe would end right then and there.

"Let them go," Stanley said quietly.

"They go with me or they die. While they're gasping their last, we'll shoot you. We'll take out your hunters while we're at it. What kind of philosophical bullshit are you going to spout now?"

Stanley didn't say anything. He made a small gesture on either side of him, and the hunters suddenly disappeared as though they had never been there. A moment later, Stanley was gone as well. If it weren't for his bootprints in the snow, Rick would have had a hard time believing Stanley had ever been there. It appeared their last best chance of getting away from Kevin left with him.

"Move it," Kevin ordered roughly.

The cold was soaking through Rick's boots, and he kept flexing his fingers, trying to keep circulation going through them. Nothing helped a lot. As long as they kept moving, the continuing exertion helped his physical condition somewhat. The down side was that every step took them farther from any possible salvation. Worse, they kept moving west. Rick recalled all too well from the runs to Arapahoe, that meant they'd go into worse weather. None of them were dressed to be out in this kind of temperature for more than a short while. In spite of it — or maybe because of it, Kevin kept them stumbling on.

They soon ran out of trail, but Kevin kept pushing them on. His means of motivation were just like always. The favorites seemed to be yelling, cursing, and slapping them. It became evident that Susie couldn't go much farther, and Kevin finally relented and directed everyone into a farmhouse. There, they were able to build a fire. Kevin was careful to keep Gwendolyn inside under guard, while Rick went out with another guard to find wood. It was interesting that a farmhouse picked almost at random happened to have a wood-burning stove. Not only that, the stove was a new high-efficiency model with a cooking surface. The house actually got warm.

The warmth did not equate to comfort for anybody except Kevin. Rick had no idea what Kevin thought would make him comfortable, but it included getting up close and personal with Susie. On her part, Susie looked as miserable and terrified as anyone possibly could. That didn't seem to have any impact with Kevin, who drug her into a bedroom as soon as the frost melted off the walls. What Rick heard then would have been considered rape in every jurisdiction back when law and order meant anything.

When he dragged her off, he left instructions with his cohorts that Rick and Gwendolyn were to make something to eat. He advised them not to get too close to Gwendolyn if she was anywhere near a frying pan. Then he laughed his head off as he pushed Susie through the door. Rick and Gwendolyn exchanged glances, where Kevin's status as an asshole was a given. Rick again wondered if he shouldn't have given Kevin a good kick in the head back when he had both the opportunity and the permission.

Dan kept his head down through all of this. Rick wondered if Kevin was deciding which side Dan might be on. He didn't let Dan have a weapon, but Kevin didn't send him to do so-called women's work, either. As he thought about it, Rick was increasingly uncertain which side Dan was on, as well. Dan was doing what Dan always did, which was to look after his own interest. If they lived through this, Rick considered Dan's status would be a topic of conversation with Mark and Mr. Lillard.

Kevin came back out of the bedroom later. Susie didn't. In addition, Kevin was in a foul mood, muttering something about cold fish. That, Kevin thought, might mean Susie adopted Gwendolyn's strategy of being completely passive. Several minutes later, Susie came out, fresh bruises visible on her face. Rick suspected she also had bruises elsewhere, but Gwendolyn would have to tend those.

Gwendolyn and Rick served everyone else, and then had to sit on the floor with their plates. Gwendolyn broke the silence.

"Kevin, when are you going to get Duane?"

"Duane has gone totally nuts. He can't go in one direction for more than a minute. Then he goes on a crying jag. That really weirds me out." Rick paid strict attention to his plate. There was too much he could say, and nothing he should say. What Kevin thought was weird would have been when Duane would get some measure of sanity periodically. Kevin was just consistently nuts.

Chapter 19

Trail of Tears

The next day, Kevin steered them on a southwesterly course. After several hours, they got to an area that Rick recognized as the road for McCook. Glancing around, he even knew they were more than halfway to Arapahoe. There wasn't anything to mark this as being the road other than the fact that it was clear, and extended on beside the trees that he knew marked the Republican River. The walking wasn't any easier, as far as that went. It wasn't like anybody had plowed the road in a long time.

Evidently the packing they had done, along with the traffic along it, did help a bit. Rick wasn't sure. It was likely that none of it mattered. Despair knocked at his door. Rick tried his best to not let it in. He kept telling himself that if there was any way to help Gwendolyn, he would never recognize it if he gave up. Susie was having more troubles than either of them, and in spite of her being the object of Kevin's passion, he was as likely to yell at her to get her butt moving as anybody else.

They got to Arapahoe before dark. The massive snows had slid off the solar panels on the roof, and the batteries appeared to be pretty well charged. There was a supply of wood inside, so Rick and Gwendolyn were able to get the place warmed up sooner rather than later. The well still functioned, as well, although Rick had no idea how it had managed with the arctic conditions. Gwendolyn reported there was food in the refrigerators, and it was still good, even if it had to be defrosted first.

After supper, Rick heard Kevin tell his buddies about where they were going. It was the dry zone beyond McCook. It would take two days to get to McCook at their present rate, and with much heavier snow toward McCook, Rick thought four days was far more likely. He didn't think Susie would survive the trip. She had already switched off her mind, and was just an automaton stumbling along, more or less obeying whatever Kevin demanded. If there could be a dead person still walking, she was it.

The guys in Harlan would probably need several days to resolve all the tribal members running amuck. How long would it take them to realize that Kevin was not among them? He had disappeared altogether, would be all they would know. As far as he could tell, nobody even saw them go out that stupid tunnel toward the gully. Presumably, the posse members who were waiting for them in the stables would get somebody to investigate why they hadn't shown up. Maybe they would have gotten the alarm out at that point.

The other question was why Stanley made no move to rescue them. There had been the single comment from him just before every one of his tribe including himself disappeared. Rick had no idea why things had gone that way, but they were in a very narrow place, and things looked as though they could get a whole lot worse. Rick had trouble finding anything to give so much as a glimmer of hope.

In addition, Kevin personally escorted the two of them out to the service room. "You two are now the hired help. Anyway, I've taken a look, and you aren't going anywhere."

He unnecessarily shoved them inside, and they listened to the sound of things being shoved in place to prevent the door from opening. They were at least able to start the stove in the room. There was a pretty good supply of wood there, along with matches. There were beds, which beat sleeping on the floor like they did the previous night.

"We'd better get what enjoyment out of this that we can," Rick told Gwendolyn. "It may be a long time before we see anything this good again."

Gwendolyn looked at Rick, a pleading look in her eyes. "Won't the people from Harlan be looking for us?"

Rick couldn't find any hope to give her. "If they were looking, they would have found us by now. It's not like we're moving fast. With us in this room off the service bay, they would have the perfect way to get us out of here. I don't see any sign of them."

"Aren't you supposed to be telling me anything at all, trying to make me feel better?"

"You'd know if I lied to you, even if it was a lie you wanted to believe. You survived those families in Ragan. You also got away from those weirdos on the road. If there is a way to get you out of this, I'll do it, whether it gets me away or not. I told you before that I would not allow you to be anybody's slave, and I meant it."

Gwendolyn gave Rick a hug. "That was the nicest thing anybody could ever say. It was way more romantic than promising me the moon. On the other hand, what makes you think I'd leave you to Kevin's less than tender mercies? As I recall, half of why you and I got married was to put an end to that, too."

"We'll do what we can do. If Kevin is serious about going beyond McCook, that will make us the first people those terrorists meet if they send more of their people to take care of us. From what Mark said, the next time they come, it probably will be with everything they have, just to make sure they finish us off. Six hundred lunatics will roll right over the few people I see here, and you can just bet that Kevin is not about to hand us weapons. I don't know which side Dan is on. Kevin doesn't know either. Dan may not have decided. Susie will be more a hindrance than help to anybody."

The lights suddenly went out, and the two felt their way over to a full-size bed. As they cuddled, Gwendolyn suddenly commented, "It must really bother Kevin that you and I are together. Whatever he wants to have with Susie simply isn't there. He'd get more satisfaction from a blow-up sex doll."

"We'll need to keep an eye on Susie. The way she's going, it's almost as if she wants to die."

Gwendolyn was silent for a while after Rick said that. "What can we do?"

"If I have to, I'll carry her. She doesn't deserve any of this. Just the short time she's been with us, I've found myself starting to think of her as a kid sister."

"It's that way with me, too. Nobody had better mess with my sister," Gwendolyn growled

For Rick, the situation was darker than the storeroom they were in. He could hear faint noises through the insulated wall. "They are messing with her. It's happening right now and there's not a damn thing we can do about it."

The next morning, Kevin roared through the door, maybe hoping to kick Rick around some more. They were already up and built bedrolls from blankets and sheets of plastic in the room. They put together three bedrolls so Susie could have something, as well. In addition, they both were on the far side of the room, and Kevin would have had to get past several beds and a hot stove to get to them. It was too much trouble, so he looked at them from the doorway.

"Why don't you have coffee ready? We need to have breakfast right now," he snarled.

"The door wouldn't open," Rick observed.

"That's just how it was supposed to be, and don't you forget it. Just in case you get any bright ideas about escaping, your little lady will die if you try. You'll die, too. You get me, asshole?"

"You're coming through crystal clear."

"Those Harlan people had better not mess with me. I'll kill them, too."

Rick considered Mark's opinion of Kevin's abilities with a weapon, which went that he might be able to hit the broad side of a barn, but only if he was inside the barn at the time. Kevin's buddies were another matter, especially the one who claimed to have military experience. Of course, considering those supposedly on their side were the four snipers, currently in Oxford, who were supposed to be watching Kevin in the first place. Whatever their abilities lacked in babysitting, they should be able to handle a weapon.

None of that came out in his reply. "We'll get the coffee going, Kevin."

Kevin could find no fault with that comment, even though he tried hard to find something. Finally, he barked, "Well, move it, then," and backed away from the door just enough so they could get out. Inside the Arapahoe Inn's public area, the heating stove was going full blast but they had to rebuild a fire in the cook stove. That didn't do more than slightly slow Rick and Gwendolyn. Before long, coffee was perking, and breakfast was cooking.

One notable absence was again Susie Maguire. After everyone had eaten, Kevin pushed back his chair so hard that it caught on an uneven piece of floor tile and tipped over. That enraged him even more, and he stomped over to the room he'd occupied with her overnight, screaming to get her lazy ass out of there that very moment. He yanked the door open, and as hard as he did it, Mark thought it was a good thing for Susie that it opened outward, since she was just on the other side of it.

Seeing her, even Kevin should have given her a break from verbal abuse. In addition to the previous bruises, Susie now had a black eye, a number of additional bruises, and several cuts, as well. In addition, she shuffled forward bent over, and clutching her stomach. Rick glanced at Gwendolyn for confirmation of his own suspicion, that Kevin must have punched her in the stomach. Now, Rick really wished they'd gotten out of the main house sooner, to get Susie to the safety of the Lillard place.

Susie was obviously in no condition to go anywhere, but Kevin didn't care. As they were all herded out the door, Susie fell going over the threshold, landing face-down in the snow, not moving. Kevin's solution was to go over and kick her. Yesterday, Rick was sure he would end up carrying her eventually. That time came sooner than he had any idea. He figured it would be an awful day, but even his worst nightmares were swiftly turning into hopelessly optimistic expectations.

Rick picked her up as gently as he could while Gwendolyn took the bedrolls, and they started moving through this strange world. It would have looked like the North Pole if it weren't for the trees here and the Arctic Ocean there. As they moved ahead through the snow, Rick wasn't even sure Susie was alive. Finally she moaned, which seemed to be a good thing under the circumstances. At the same time, Kevin was screaming at them to move faster.

Dan finally ventured to say, "Hey, Kevin, you're from McCook. I guess you know everything about that town, don't you?"

"I know the place sucks. It sucks as much as Harlan. Nearly every sucker in McCook is dead now, so maybe it doesn't suck quite as much. Some of those who suck the most are still alive and living in Harlan now. That part really sucks."

Rick remembered a joke about a guy asking a local about the town ahead. The local asks about the town he just left. Whatever the guy said about that town also went for the next town.

Kevin was seventeen or eighteen from what everybody said. There was no way in hell he should have been given the management of a ranch dedicated to training new riders and horses. Rick felt no confidence that he had enough on the ball to do it. Now, he was never going to get a chance to do anything besides stumble through increasingly deep snow on his way to a frozen hell.

For his part, Dan apparently decided the act of keeping some warmth inside his mouth by keeping it closed was a more desirable situation than sending Kevin off on a rant in some new unpredictable direction. Rick still couldn't figure out whether Dan was really a buddy of Kevin, or if this was just his way of trying to keep the inevitable pain down to a manageable level.

For that matter, why were these other guys supporting Kevin? The two in front were in it voluntarily, as far as Rick could tell. What did they expect to get for their efforts? They had seemed reasonably sane. They had to see that Kevin's train had left the tracks, and there was no way they could wind up anywhere desirable. Okay, revise that estimate about the two seeming sane. Willingly following a visibly crazy person was in itself a crazy thing to do.

Meanwhile, Rick's arms and hands had become numb from the cold. The day before, when he was able to swing his arms and flex his hands, he could keep some circulation going. Now, carrying Susie, who was nearly dead weight, he couldn't do any of that. If there was any warmth from her body, he couldn't feel it. Rick didn't know how much longer he could do it. It was certain that Kevin wasn't about to have any of his guys do it. Even more evident was the fact that Kevin himself wouldn't do it. Why should he? After all, he caused it.

Maybe Kevin had some shred of conscience left. Maybe he just didn't feel like going any farther. Whatever the motive, he redirected them to a farmhouse near the road. This one, they found, did not have a wood-burning stove. Rick placed Susie on a sofa as gently as he could manage under the circumstances while Kevin raised hell with the world in general about the situation.

For the moment, at least, Kevin wasn't concentrating his wrath on Rick. His presumed buddies now got the brunt of it. That was something of a reversal in behavior, and made Rick even more uneasy. Kevin also wasn't after Susie to any degree, but there was no sport in it since she no longer reacted to anything. Maybe Kevin saw it that way. Maybe he was coming from another direction altogether. Last fall, his motivations seemed completely normal. Could his mental balance be returning? That would be a great deal to ask, Rick knew.

Suddenly, Kevin stopped, and stared out one of the windows of the house. He ignored everyone and everything else. A couple of moments later, he jerked around to the guy claiming military experience.

"I saw movement out there. Those damn Peepul may be trailing us. Get out there and check it out."

The guy, whose name Rick couldn't recall, grabbed his rifle, made sure his coat and gloves were as weather-tight as possible, and headed out the door. Kevin continued to watch through the window. Just the body heat in the house seemed to make things a little less frigid. The additional fact that Kevin was, for the moment, ignoring them, made the feeling of comfort move into something like a positive area.

Rick helped Gwendolyn get Susie into a sitting position. They sat tight against her on either side. Gwendolyn tried to rub circulation back into Susie's arms and legs. There was no way Rick would even consider trying that. He did not want to give Kevin any reason to accuse him of trying to get too familiar with his supposed girlfriend. Everybody sitting together helped everyone, at least in theory. In any case, Rick was still trying, unsuccessfully, to get his own circulation going, and Gwendolyn seemed to understand the situation.

All at once, Rick saw Kevin jump. Just after that, he heard a yell and a single gunshot. Kevin looked around wildly, trying to figure out what to do next. Suddenly, he twisted around to Rick. That was the first time in several minutes that Kevin even acknowledged Rick's existence.

"Rick, get your butt out there and find out what happened to my man. Remember what I told you. If you try to run, I'll shoot your bride. I'll also shoot you. You hear me?"

Rick headed outside, following the only bootprints from the house. Two-thirds of the way to the road, there was a ten-foot high snowdrift, and the tracks led around the edge of it. Then he saw the rifle as well as blood in the snow. There was no other sign of the military guy. Just then, Stanley appeared at the far edge of the snowdrift. After looking at him for a moment, Stanley motioned for him to come. Rick had no intention of testing Kevin's threat, especially after what he'd done to Susie. Rick shook a finger in a negative gesture that Kevin wouldn't be able to see.

Stanley nodded, but then pointed to the rifle, at the same time mouthing, "Do It."

Rick went around and picked up the weapon, purposely holding it backward, upside down, and away from his body. He hoped it would demonstrate to Kevin that he posed no threat. He carried it back to the house in that way. Since he didn't get shot along the way, perhaps the message was received in a more or less coherent fashion.

Half a step inside the door, Kevin ripped the rifle out of Rick's hands. "What happened out there?"

Rick opted for an edited version of the truth. "I have no idea what happened. Just beyond the snowdrift, I saw the rifle and some blood in the snow. I didn't dare go any farther because I didn't want you to think I was running. I did not see your guy."

Kevin studied Rick intensely. Rick was still too frozen from the trek to use his facial muscles anyway. He couldn't have shown emotion if he wanted to.

Finally, Kevin grunted. "You and your wife were trying to help Susie. I could see that. See if you can help her a little more."

When he resumed his place next to Susie, Gwendolyn looked over at him. Rick glanced at her and blinked several times. Suddenly, Susie glanced up at both of them. After a brief period of eye contact, she put her head down again and seemed to sigh. Rick wished he could let them know, but had no way to do it. Soon, Gwendolyn got up, and opened a bedroll, carefully leaving the plastic on top of the blankets to use as a vapor barrier. Rick thought it felt pretty good.

Rick dozed off, and sometime later, as it got dark, Kevin patted his shoulder. It almost felt like a friendly gesture.

"Keep Susie where you have her. She's just a damn lump in bed — an icy, nonreactive lump at that. See if you can get her acting like a live person."

Rick was astonished. Somebody who didn't know better might think Kevin could act like a real human being. He must have been capable of acting sane long enough that the Marines in Oxford thought they could give him some room. The current situation showed what that kind of an assumption bought. Rick thought he'd take advantage of whatever breaks came his way. For the moment, being halfway warm and the offer to leave him alone for the night, was as good as he could expect.

Knowing Stanley was out there lent a ray of hope to the situation that Rick did not want anybody to see on his face. He covered his face and tucked his feet up to defrost them if he could. Rick had a feeling only warm weather was likely to do that, and who knew if any of them would survive that long? On the other hand, Stanley already dispatched several groups of terrorist fighters. The question was why he hadn't taken any more aggressive action than what they'd seen.

If Kevin made his guys do guard duty overnight, Rick never knew since he played turtle under the covers. In any case, he found himself awake and peering out from under the covers to see it was first light. Kevin's people were all up, and Rick thought it must mean something to see that Dan inherited the military guy's rifle. Which side was Dan on? It was still anybody's guess. Maybe nobody could break the code because Dan didn't know either.

There was nothing for breakfast. All they could do was to suck on some snow.

Anything nutritious would be frozen rock-hard, and would break teeth in the process of consuming it. On the positive side, Susie seemed able to walk, at least for the moment. Rick had no doubt he would have to resume carrying her very soon.

They wound their way out to the highway, such as it was. On the way, they passed the place that Rick and the military guy had gotten to the previous day. Kevin stopped and stared at the frozen blood in the snow, as well as the imprint of the rifle. There was nothing to tell Kevin that anything happened other than what Rick reported, and after a few moments, they started moving again.

Rick thought he'd better get as much circulation to his arms as he could while he still had the opportunity. With that in mind, he was swinging his arms and flexing his hands with every step. Kevin was no longer yelling at everybody to move faster. Rick was having an ongoing debate with himself as to why that might be. The main conclusion was that Kevin no longer had a reason or plan. He only had a direction.

After a half hour, Susie began to stagger. Rick and Gwendolyn were on either side of her, and immediately moved next to her, supporting her. Susie managed to keep going another unsteady ten steps. Then her legs buckled altogether. Rick was ready for it, and caught her. He picked her up without missing a step. At least he wanted to tell himself that.

Kevin stared at the whole thing, not seeming to comprehend what was going on. Rick couldn't imagine that being a problem today, after he hauled Susie the entire previous day. The small group came to a complete halt while Kevin tried to wrap his head around the situation. Finally, he shook his head and started them moving again.

This erratic behavior struck Rick as a larger potential problem than his consistently harping on everyone. The way it was going, he might pat somebody on the back one moment and shoot them the next. This was the fourth day of their very own trail of tears, and the way Kevin was going, it was likely that nobody would survive the experience.

Knowing Stanley was somewhere in the area should have given some reassurance. The trouble was that Stanley was somewhere while Kevin was within dead bang range. That gave little hope, even if Mark didn't think Kevin was much of a shot. In addition, while he was certain that Kevin was completely off his rocker, Rick had no plan of checking to see if he'd suddenly gotten stupid as well.

The two riflemen in front suddenly stopped. Rick had gotten into the one step in front of the other routine to the point that Gwendolyn had to grab his shoulder to stop him. When he focused on the situation, Rick saw Stanley was standing in the middle of the road twenty yards in front of them. The two riflemen both had their weapons pointed directly at the large man.

"Release the three," Stanley said, not in a loud voice, but one which carried without any effort to them.

"I told you what would happen if you got in my way," Kevin snarled in reply.

"The situation is not what it was when we last faced one another," Stanley calmly replied.

"The only thing that's changed is that there are two rifles aimed at you while mine is aimed at this worthless Rick person."

"It seems strange that you would shoot the only means Susie has of getting anywhere. Not only that, but the way your rifle barrel is shaking, any shot you take at Rick would almost certainly kill Susie as well. None of that has to do with the change to the situation I spoke of. The hunting party you insulted is here with me. In addition, there are others. I direct your attention to the snowdrift on your right."

There was an entire field of snowdrifts in that direction. Out of the corner of his eye, Rick saw Kevin's head jerk around anyway. A moment later, a shot rang out from that group of snowdrifts, and Kevin yelped, releasing the trigger on his rifle to cover his ear. After a moment, he brought his hand down and looked at the blood on his palm.

Kevin screamed, "You shot my fucking ear!"

Rick heard Tom the sniper's voice reply with almost a chuckle, "That was your ear lobe. I just pierced your ear. Now you can wear jewelry and be all stylish. The next shot goes somewhere guaranteed to give you enough pain to forget about shooting anybody. Everyone with a weapon is targeted. My whole team is here. Drop your weapons or be martyrs for no reason, with nobody to celebrate your supposed sacrifice."

Dan and the other rifleman in front of him looked around nervously. Their rifles both dropped on the snow in front of them. Rick glanced behind him, where Kevin and the others also let their weapons drop at their feet.

Tom's voice sounded off again. "Rick, take Gwendolyn and Susie, and move straight toward the river. I don't want you guys in anybody's firing lane."

They followed the instruction, and as they turned toward the side of the road, Rick thought he could see far-off movement on the road. At the moment, though, there was closer movement, as the Peepul hunting party magically appeared from all kinds of unlikely hiding places. Most quickly retrieved the rifles. At the same time, others assisted the three off the road, brought rocks, and created a fire pit right where Rick, Gwendolyn, and Susie were. A fire was soon going, and Rick started to feel some warmth coming off of it.

At the same time, the movement Rick noticed up the road turned into the carriage, very low-slung on its skis. Several outriders were with the carriage cum sleigh. The Peepul hunting party saw it as well, and started prodding Kevin's group farther ahead, until they got close to Stanley, who hadn't moved. Stanley directed Kevin and his buddies to sit on the ground with their backs facing inward. Kevin was given the privilege or punishment of facing toward the fire, but far enough from it that he would not be able to feel it.

Curiously, the passenger area of the sleigh was set up like a tent, and as it drew up to the small fire, the vet stuck his head out of the tent flap, instructing them to get Susie inside. She tried to stand but couldn't, so Rick picked her up and carried her to Harlan's equivalent of advanced life support. Gwendolyn followed Susie inside, and Rick was invited to go wait by the fire, where two of the hunting party were making coffee. Tom and his snipers came to the fire, as well.

The scene was quiet except for occasional groans from inside the tent rigged as an ambulance. Rick tried to come to terms with what just happened. Finally, Tom pressed a cup of coffee into Rick's hands. After warming his hands on the cup, he sipped a bit of it and looked at Tom.

"I figured we were going to die out there. It really seemed close after Susie collapsed from the beatings Kevin gave her, I thought our little trail of tears would be both short and nasty."

Tom nodded. "I can see why. It took a while for the posse to figure out what happened. Then they signaled west gate. The word got down to us soon after that, and Stanley took one of his hunting parties out to verify the situation. We'd have gone then, but Lyle Lillard sent word that we needed to coordinate to do everything at the same time."

Rick stared at Tom over the rim of the coffee cup. "Get everything done? Kevin nearly killed Susie."

"We weren't too happy about it either. The hunting party shadowed you guys the whole way. Stanley said they were itching to take Kevin down. It got tense after that night in Arapahoe, when it was clear that Kevin got really nasty with her. Watching you carry her the whole way yesterday bugged everybody."

Rick got madder by the moment. "Merely being bugged would have felt good, especially toward the end of that day. What was going on that made the lords of Harlan think they needed to do more than rescue an innocent young girl?"

"The tribal members with Kevin created far more aggravation than they should have been able to cause. The posse was gathering them all up. Mr. Lillard has this thing about shooting mad dogs, even when they're running around biting people and frothing at the mouth. The posse is marching the lot of them this way."

"I'm happy for that, but what did it have to do with Susie? Kevin grabbed Gwendolyn just because she was with me. Everybody suffers because they are dead set on having a complete package?"

"Yeah, well, you can discuss that with them. There's no way you can make me defend what I don't agree with."

Gwendolyn climbed out of the carriage then, a somber look on her face. She seemed to be fighting the urge to return to the ambulance even as the warmth of the fire invited her. She joined Rick and warmed her hands.

"How's she doing?" Rick asked.

"Susie's resting, and seems fairly comfortable. Whatever that jackass Kevin thought he was doing, she lost the baby, what with the beating he gave her. He hit her a number of times in the stomach. The vet doesn't think he damaged her internal organs, or at least not very badly. The problem is that he has no way to know for sure."

Tom growled, "After you get done talking to them, I think I'm going to have some words, too. There's just no excuse for that. I should have taken him down instead of simply getting his attention. Nobody would cry."

That thought didn't give Gwendolyn comfort. "Give me a weapon, and I'll make sure he never messes with any woman, ever again. A round through the groin, each knee, and both elbows ought to take care of his situation just fine."

Tom shook his head. "That's what happens when it gets personal. I try to be professional at all times."

"It needs to be personal. That way, Kevin gets to live with the hate and disgust as well as the few rounds I'd use. Let me at him."

"Tempting as it is, we'll wait here by the fire. The last messenger said they were force-marching the tribal members. I think they had some thoughts about what they wanted Stanley to do with them, too."

Rick shook his head. "From the sound of it, you guys and the Peepul are more like the kind of folks I'd prefer to hang around with. Harlan can't protect its own people, but at the same time, they give orders far and wide."

One of the hunting party pointed down the highway toward Harlan. "That's them," he announced.

The hunters may have once been drug addicts, but they certainly had keen senses. It was another minute before Rick saw and heard the incoming group. They were coming slowly. The reason became clearer as they approached, as there was a group of twenty on foot, who appeared to be in restraints. They had to be the tribal members who followed Kevin. Mark and Lyle were up front, of course. Suddenly, the very sight of them filled him with disgust.

Rick said softly to Gwendolyn, "A few days ago, this sight would have excited me. I'd have kissed their boots. Any more, I can't even stand to look at them. There's no way Susie could have lived much longer. The way Kevin was going, neither you nor I would have survived very long, either."

Gwendolyn nodded. "Lillard decided he's the local deity. Everything he does or says just has to be beautiful and wise. It all adds up to the best possible solution to whatever the situation might be."

"That would be the world from his perspective. It doesn't look that way where I'm sitting. From here, it looks like there's been a great deal of misery for no reason at all."

"I find myself agreeing with you, Mr. Forbes. If we ignore them, would they just go away?"

"They came for the adulation of the vast throng of people, and they will not leave without it. It doesn't matter. I'm still six stages beyond cold, although the coffee has helped."

"I don't see a great deal of excitement or relief here," came the voice of Lyle Lillard above them, still on his horse.

"If you want excitement, go check Susie in the carriage," Rick didn't bother to look up, but adjusted where he was squatting. He then added, "Sitting in the snow does nothing for any feeling of relief."

Nobody said anything, and Rick finally did look up at Lillard. "You say how you don't want any deaths, but I count two so far. The only thing the one did wrong was to be conceived, and that fetus had absolutely no say in the matter."

"Why is Dan with Kevin's bunch?"

"He took the rifle when Kevin offered it. When Stanley stepped into the road, he was immediately aiming center of mass along with the other guy. Dan made a choice, and there he is. For all I know, he may have been the one organizing Kevin's sympathizers at Wagon Ranch all along."

"Wait a minute, are you saying that Susie lost her baby?" Gwendolyn looked up at Lyle with narrowed eyes. "That is exactly what Rick said. The vet thinks Susie will live, but there is no doubt that her challenges are far greater than what he's willing to say. For your information, Mr. Lillard, I refuse to go or be any place that freak has any chance of getting anywhere near me."

Rick nodded. "It was kind of you to offer me the position of ranch manager, but after due reflection, I have to decline the honor. At the moment, the safest place for us appears to be with the group of snipers."

Lyle and Mark exchanged glances. "Let's resolve Kevin's situation, once and for all. Then, we need to get you to someplace where you can actually warm up."

Chapter 20

Rescue, Hold the Gratitude

Vince and the posse members herded the tribal members down the long road from Harlan. He noted the carriage was on the shoulder of the road, and the snipers were huddled around a small fire just beyond it. Vince had to look twice before he realized the two people with them were Rick and Gwendolyn. Both of them were in really rough shape, looking more like the tribal members they were driving past them at the moment. It seemed incredible the two of them had gone so far downhill in such a short period of time.

If he had trouble recognizing the pair, what the two of them said to Lyle was nothing short of astonishing. The worms just turned into a pair of grizzly bears. Vince had to agree that Rick had more than enough cause. Lyle's entire plan on how to clean up the mess that Kevin created never had a good feel to it. Even Mark had reservations about it. On top of it, Lyle broke off the conversation so fast that Vince wasn't sure Lyle really heard what Rick and Gwendolyn said. It was very strange. The way Rick and Gwendolyn stared at the departing Lyle was pure hostility. Vince listened to their conversation as he helped the posse move the knot of tribal members to join Kevin's group.

Rick growled, "Did you hear him apologize or give any indication that he understands the situation, Gwendolyn?"

"I didn't hear a word, Rick. Tom, it didn't seem like he was about to give you an opportunity to contribute to the conversation."

Tom shook his head. "There was no point in trying since he wasn't going to listen to me. To Lyle, I'm just the joker who managed to lose his lovely Kevin child. The fact that Kevin was the monkey on his back, and the fact that he tried giving him to me is beside the point."

Rick attempted a smile, but it showed up as a grimace. "Who's in charge of making sure all monkeys stay on the back where they belong?"

"Every time I've tried to sort that out, I get informed that it's not my business and keep carrying those damned monkeys."

"You make it sound like we're brothers from different mothers, Tom."

"How is it that you're suddenly talking like you're in the military, Rick? Here, have some more coffee. We're about to finish this pot so I'll start another. I have a feeling we'll be here a while."

Vince kept his group moving toward Kevin's bunch. When the tribal members arrived, Lyle told Vince to unshackle them. When they did that, Lyle looked at the group. "You and your friends have been a pain for quite long enough, Kevin," Lyle informed him. "It appears you're headed for the area beyond McCook where there isn't any snow. We've decided that's fine, but you won't be taking any prisoners or slaves with you. In addition, you will not take these weapons. I'm certain you'll find more, wherever you end up. Stanley already agreed to have one of his hunting teams accompany you."

Stanley, standing on the far side of the group, now put in his piece. "If you stay on the highway and go straight through McCook, and into the fog beyond, you will not see my hunters. If you turn back or try to take some other way, you will see my hunters, but it will only be momentarily as they kill you. Do you have any questions?"

Stanley paused for a moment, and then continued, "Good, stand up and start walking. It is the only way you will be able to stay warm. While my hunters would prefer to take game, dipping their spears in your blood would not bother them at all. Ask the former tribal members traveling with you if you have any doubts. For you who were of the tribe, know one thing: you are no longer Peepul. Now go."

Vince flashed back to what he'd heard of the old Peepul chant: "We are Peepul. They are animals." Stanley just demoted the bunch with Kevin to animal status, according to that. If any of them strayed off the road, Vince guessed he would find out if the Peepul had truly left their cannibal ways behind them.

The former tribal members never sat down, and simply waited for Kevin to get up. He did, briefly touching his earlobe. Vince saw a fresh notch in it, probably courtesy of the snipers. It was no longer bleeding. "Let's go," he growled. Dan and the others were soon tracking behind Kevin, with the tribal members bringing up the rear. Nobody from the group looked back as they trudged down the road.

Vince marveled as the hunters faded from view on either side of the road. He knew the hunters could go faster through snow than Kevin on a hard surface. Vince took several posse members and followed at a distance. Nobody said they were part of the deal, but there was no way Vince would leave this half done. In any case, they weren't that far from McCook.

To give Kevin and his gang credit, they did nothing but walk the entire way. There was no conversation between any of them. Vince tried to check body language to see if he could determine anything that way, but if there were any messages, they were well-buried beneath misery and fatigue. The snow kept getting deeper. By the time they hit McCook, the only things visible were occasional rooftops. It was a real push to get through the snowdrifts in the city. After getting through the place, Vince couldn't imagine the snow zone ending.

They stumbled into a wall of fog, where the level of snow dropped rapidly. The fog got even thicker, until Vince had to strain to make out footprints in the snow right in front of him. The strangest part was that the temperature rose a degree every few feet. At the same time, the snow disappeared. It was a truly strange experience. His horse now dealt with semi-frozen mud, evidently caused by the dense fog. What trees they passed dripped water. Finally, the fog began to thin, and before long, the entire group was again visible. Soon after, the horizon became visible, and Vince saw the stories were true.

The skies ahead were clear, with a soft dry southwesterly breeze. Where everything had been white, now it was light brown. While that was nice, the trade-off was that everything was dead. Everyone stopped at that point. Stanley strode out of the fog. He glared at the exiles, like Zeus about to launch lightning bolts.

"You can go north or south. We will allow you into the fog to get water. If you go to the snow, you will die. You are not Peepul. You are not even animals, so you can stay out here where neither Peepul nor animals live. I showed that you should make your own plans. You refuse to make your own plans because it takes effort. Instead, you follow one whose plan is to kill without cause. Now, you can live without reason."

With that, Stanley turned around and headed back into the fog. Vince compared Lyle's recent decisions with Stanley's actions. He now wondered who should lead Harlan in the future. He didn't ponder long, and before Stanley completely disappeared, Vince urged his horse after the man and his posse members followed closely.

They got to Arapahoe at dark. Inside, the fires were going. The vet, Nick Cotter, was sitting at the counter while Mark and Lyle were at a table in the corner in earnest consultation. Susie, Rick, and Gwendolyn were nowhere to be seen. Vince couldn't imagine Susie being very far from Nick since he was the closest thing to a medical specialist in the area. Vince wandered over next to Nick.

"This isn't the celebration anyone expected, Nick."

"No, it isn't. I guess you heard Rick's initial comments to Lyle."

"Yeah, and from the look of it, things haven't improved since then."

"There was only thing everybody could agree. That was the fact that it would be warmer if the two of them rode back here in the carriage with Susie and me."

"That doesn't sound like a victory for anybody."

"It wasn't. Rick and Gwendolyn checked for any available housing in Oxford. There is nothing habitable. Tom and his bunch live in what were apartments over a couple of stores. Nothing else could hope to hold out the weather."

"That leaves Rick and Gwendolyn with a real dilemma. It looks like Lyle appreciates the situation."

Nick nodded. "The lack of housing was the only reason they agreed to go along with anything Lyle proposed. Second, while it wasn't warm inside the tent we created on the carriage, it was a lot better than outside. The way they talked, the temperature in the carriage compared to the house they stayed in the previous night. At least there were plenty of quilts for them to get under. Susie was asleep, so I looked at them and put a finger to my lips. Rick and Gwendolyn crawled under the quilts without a word."

Vince smiled thinly. "At least they weren't screaming imprecations at Mark and Lyle."

"They weren't screaming. I'll give them that much. They did keep it quiet, but I couldn't ignore a conversation a couple of feet away. Rick told Gwendolyn, 'I feel like a complete idiot, making brave statements and then turning around and following the directions Lyle Magnus gives to the letter.' Gwendolyn replied, 'We had no alternative, Rick. Should we have stood in the snow throwing a fit? How about trying to walk back to Arapahoe? Neither of us is fit to travel right now, and everybody knows it. Lyle Magnus. Lyle the Great. I like it. In any case, we can stand on principles a whole lot easier if we wait until our toes aren't about to freeze and fall off.'"

"They managed to keep a sense of reality, anyway. Do you think Mark or Lyle heard what they said?"

Nick snorted. "They got the gist even if they didn't hear the details. The two of them have been huddling ever since we got here. As a matter of fact, they are looking this way right now. It looks like they want to include you. You'll have to tell me about Kevin's stroll into exile later."

"I'll do that." Vince turned around, and sure enough, Mark and Lyle were beckoning him.

"I presume Kevin is now out in the drylands."

"Yes, Mr. Lillard, they are out there. The drylands don't look inviting. I suppose they'll wander the edge of the fog until they find shelter."

"I presume you're aware that Rick and Gwendolyn took issue with how we handled this."

Lyle's face showed as much strain as Vince could ever recall. As the chief of law enforcement, it wasn't his job to make Lyle feel good. It was his job to give as much straight-forward information as possible.

"That is correct. I am also aware that a large number of people around Harlan share their opinion. They all think we should have freed the three hostages immediately, and pushed the tribal people into the drylands as they were found."

"Is that your professional opinion, deputy?"

"Yes, it is."

"What Stanley proposed doing included a significant amount of risk to the hostages. It included the almost certain death of the entire group."

There it was — Lyle was unalterably opposed to the possibility of killing people under any circumstances. Vince felt compelled to add the consequence of that approach.

"I understand that what he proposed carried the same kind and quality of risk as when his hunters took out the terrorists. As it is, you now have a group nursing intense hate toward all of us, and actively plotting revenge. For all we know, they might support or even join the terrorists now."

Lyle wearily leaned back in his chair. "Everybody is ganging up on me now. For all I know, Adeline is on your side as well. It may be a good thing for me that she isn't here now. However it might have been, we need to do what we can for Susie Maguire. We also need to get Rick and Gwendolyn back on our side."

Vince shook his head. "Nick is doing his best for Susie. As for the other two, why are you suddenly adopting all this talk of 'we?' The only reason they're here at all is because they couldn't find anyplace else to live right away. The minute this arctic weather breaks, they will almost certainly be gone. If they think it's worth their time to stick with a larger group, they might go with the McCook bunch. There's also the possibility they might head out for wherever they think would be a happier place."

"I do thank you, Vince, for neither referring to it as 'the imperial we' or inquiring about the mouse in my pocket. I have a question, though. Would they consider going back to Wagon Ranch?"

Vince shook his head. "There would have to be many changes to Wagon Ranch before they would even visit the place, much less live there. Dan was evidently a large part of the problem. For all I know, he may have orchestrated the entire plot. With him not around, they might eventually reconsider it. Do you have any other possibilities in mind?"

Mark spoke up then. "We've been talking about them taking over Harlan Ranch. Ellen and I would move to Wagon Ranch, and I'd take over the active management. Would they buy that?"

"That would have a better chance," Vince agreed. "There are two main weaknesses: it is in deepest Harlan, and not far from the Lillard place. At the moment either of those considerations could be a game ender. I won't guess what they might say now. I haven't been through what they survived. I'd have to add that they just barely survived it."

Everybody helped put together a meal. When it was ready, Mark knocked on the couple's door. Susie wouldn't eat with them. Nick took a thin broth into her room as they were coming out.

Vince noticed Rick's aggravation didn't get in the way of his appetite. Vince figured it was connected with not eating the previous day, as well as playing pack mule. He and Gwendolyn sat at a table separated from the rest, and Lyle instructed everyone to leave them alone. Vince kept track of them in his peripheral vision in good cop style. Rick was taking in everything even while gobbling.

Vince figured Rick was analyzing how accurately Tom reported the situation. Did Tom know the whole story? On the other hand, Tom and his three guys were present and accounted for. That meant they heard what Lyle said about his side of the situation. Vince thought it interesting the snipers had not been part of the escort for Kevin and company as they went into exile.

After everyone finished eating, Lyle gathered himself together and headed over by the heating stove. There, he finally looked at Rick and Gwendolyn.

"Are the two of you feeling better?"

Vince saw Rick was in no mood for geniality. It was hard ass time. "We feel better. To feel worse, we'd be dead. I've still got aches and pains, so I assume I'm not dead. Knowing we went through all of this, when you could have stopped it any time doesn't fill my heart with gladness. What Susie went through really pisses me off, especially knowing one word from you could have saved her all of this anguish."

Vince saw Tom listening closely, and nodding when Rick said that. Lyle saw it, as well. Mark pressed his lips together tightly, cocked his head to one side, and sighed.

"Do you understand that we were chasing tribal members all over Harlan? Every one of them was dead set on cutting as many people as they could."

"Kevin bragged that they were all pawns. Their sole purpose was to distract you from his real goal, which was to snatch the three of us. Kevin considered the entire group only as sacrifices in his chess match with you. His gambit succeeded brilliantly since you went for it, chapter and verse."

"You talk as though he won. He lost, or didn't you notice?"

"I understand you gathered all the tribal offerings Kevin sent. What irritates me is that while you had your round-up, Stanley and Tom were not allowed to do what they could have done and wanted to do days earlier."

"The whole thing needed to be done at one time. Don't you see that?"

"What I see clearly is that Stanley and Tom could have gotten the three of us out at any time. They could have secured Kevin and company at their leisure, and let their butts sit in the snow while you worked on the big reunion. Your immense knowledge and understanding ought to have let you see all of that and more."

Lyle was clearly and uncharacteristically flustered at that. "I don't like your attitude."

"My attitude is not the issue. What you like is also beside the point. Your judgment concerns me right now."

Gwendolyn broke in then. "I just had a vision of what would have happened if your plan continued. Susie, Rick, and I would have died within a mile of where you caught up to us. If that happened, Tom and his snipers would have wiped out Kevin and his gang."

Vince glanced at Tom, seeing him briefly nod like that outcome would have been obvious.

Gwendolyn was not done. "When your group got up there, Stanley would have had you release the tribal members from the shackles, but he would not say anything or march them anywhere. They would die with pig spears through them right there."

It was as though Gwendolyn was in a trance, looking at a future that never quite happened.

"Your dream of a better future would have died in the middle of the road to McCook, Mr. Lillard. From that point, there would not have been any trust or people working together. The terrorists would come with warm weather. They would finish the job."

Gwendolyn simply stopped there, daring Lyle to say something. Vince thought it was a bit anticlimatic when Rick added, "We caught a break with the terrorists, both at Harlan Dam and with the two solar buggy attacks with the Omega dust. Your luck obviously has its limits and your judgment calls could wipe out the entire community. It makes going back to Harlan something we are in no hurry to do."

Lyle let the ensuing silence run an incredible time before he finally nodded. "It has gotten to where my wife, Adeline, is the only one with enough balls to call me when I screw up. Both of you are right, and I do apologize for everything you went through. That is in particular since you shouldn't have gone through much of it at all. You and Gwendolyn are precisely the people we need in Harlan. What I have to do now is to make it possible for the two of you to come back. Not only that, but you have to feel comfortable doing it."

Vince saw Mark steel himself to say something very distasteful. Was this the thing they mentioned about Harlan Ranch?

"Lyle," Mark commented, "one thing really necessary is for them to go somewhere besides Wagon Ranch."

Lyle nodded. "You're right, Mark. In addition, we need somebody who can put Wagon Ranch back together. Here's what I'll offer, Rick. You, Gwendolyn, and Susie can live at Harlan Ranch. It is far from where anybody comes into the county. Mark can get Wagon Ranch back on its feet. Rick, you can do special training with horses and people. Also, both you and Gwendolyn can work on computers since Harlan Ranch has electrical power."

Vince knew there was an fly in the ointment. A major player, namely Ellen, was not in the game. They were giving away her house. That made it a great deal less than a done deal. At the same time, Gwendolyn held Rick's hand in a very supportive fashion. She was behind whatever he did, at least for now.

"That might be an acceptable temporary expedient," Rick said after consideration. "There are a couple of points. Mark never stuttered when he talked about whose house it was, and I don't see Ellen here. We will not go to Wagon Ranch. Until we know Ellen and Mark are out of Harlan Ranch, we stay here. There is also no way Susie could travel right away, and she stays with us."

Lyle looked at Nick. "You're our medical expert. How's Susie doing?"

"She had a close call. If we can transport her with the carriage set up as it is, I think a couple of days would be enough unless there's another problem that hasn't shown up yet."

"We can appreciate that. If our wives were here, they'd give us even more appreciation for what could be involved. Gwendolyn, as the only woman here who can talk about it, what do you think?"

"A couple of days sounds right. The trip has to be slow and smooth. When we get to Harlan Ranch, she'll need plenty of time to recover from all of this. She was on the way to a full recovery before this happened. This has all been a real trial, but she's tough. We're hoping for the best."

Rick and Gwendolyn came out of their room for breakfast, ignoring Mark and Lyle. As the pair got ready to leave, Lyle advised they would send word when the house was ready. Vince followed them outside, and bade farewell to Mark, Lyle, and several posse members.

People staying included the carriage driver, two snipers, Vince, and several posse members. The snipers and posse members did security. In addition, the posse members cooked and kept the place warm, although Vince pitched in, as did Nick when he had a spare moment. There was no way Kevin and his bunch could get by Stanley's hunters. On the other hand, it wasn't a good idea to get complaisant.

That afternoon, Susie got out of her room, making it to the nearest table. Vince couldn't tell whether she decided living was either possible or desirable. Sitting at the table seemed positive since she could see a little sunshine peeking through the massive windows. A few minutes later, she tried to stand up on her own, but after several attempts, finally accepted assistance.

Gwendolyn spent a great deal of time with Susie. As the day wore on, Nick spent less time with Susie, and Gwendolyn was with her more. Vince heard Gwendolyn was as animated and upbeat as possible, far more than she could have felt. There were ongoing monologues about having a house with running water and electricity.

When she came out of the room, she told a different story.

"She is listless. I'm afraid she's close to giving up. I don't know what to do."

Vince asked Nick, "Is it something physical?"

"Not that I can tell, Vince. Her body is healing as well as I could hope. Her spirit is another thing. The combination of her family and Kevin came close to breaking her. I could keep her sedated, but that wouldn't help the real problem."

Vince looked around then, and something occurred to him. "Do you suppose that Arapahoe is the problem?"

Everyone stared at him.

"This is where Kevin beat her so badly. All those memories can't help her at all. She might even be continuously re-living that night. Everything since then may just seem like no more than a dream. Well, the forced march would qualify as a nightmare, but would pale in comparison to what she went through in this very building. Come to think of it, what room did she stay in?"

Gwendolyn was horrified. "That is the room she was in with him. We have to move her out of there right now. Could we use the manager's apartment behind the kitchen? It would be as far from what she recalls as possible."

"Let's do it," everybody agreed.

Being in a different place did have an impact, although overt signs of improvement were a while coming. Gwendolyn stayed with her a long time. Everyone not otherwise occupied, hung around the service bar hoping something good would happen. They could all hear Gwendolyn going on about how good things would be. Vince couldn't imagine how she could keep up the line of patter like that. He also thought she poured it on a great deal thicker than he supposed could possibly do any good, but he'd often been mistaken when it came to estimating what might have an effect on a woman.

Gwendolyn finally came out of the room behind the kitchen. She had a bright smile that rapidly evaporated, leaving a combination of fatigue and despair. Rick wrapped an arm around her and guided her into their room.

Nick waited a few minutes, and then went in to see how his patient was doing. Most of the guys wandered off after deciding the look on Gwendolyn's face was sufficient reporting for them. Vince, on the other hand, decided to wait it out. He poured another cup of coffee, added more wood to the two stoves, and sat on a stool at the service bar.

It was Vince's experience that people often needed space to think about what was going on. It was quiet for quite a while. Vince finished one cup of coffee. The coffee pot needed an additional start, which he furnished. Vince was halfway through another when he began to hear low conversation from the room. Not long after that, Vince looked through the sheet that served as a door and saw Nick sitting there. He emphatically waved Vince over to him.

A window high in the wall gave let in enough daylight for Vince to see Susie studying him.

"I remember you," she said softly. "You're the policeman who took me from home."

Vince nodded.

"Is Kevin really gone?"

"He is really gone, and so are the people he was with."

"Everyone told me he was gone before, but he came back. He told me everything was my fault. Then he said he would cure my problems, and that my father didn't go nearly far enough. I don't remember much after that. I couldn't walk very well, and I hurt all over. Maybe that was my fault, too. He said we were going where there wasn't any snow, but now I'm here and he is gone. Gwendolyn keeps telling me stuff, but none of it makes any sense."

Vince now felt the call to act like a professional law enforcement officer, even though he mostly saw his own kids instead of Susie. Vince wanted to give her a hug and tell her it would be all right. At the same time, he was well-aware that Gwendolyn had been doing that very thing and right now Susie needed something she could think of as a reality check.

"What you just said is a large part of what happened, Susie. Kevin beat you badly. You lost your baby from the beating. Kevin made you walk anyway, and when you couldn't walk, Rick carried you. You stayed in an unheated house the next night. Stanley, his hunters, and the four snipers got you away from Kevin and his gang. We sent them where they wanted to go. Stanley's hunters will kill them if they try to come back. We are staying here for a day or so. They agreed for you to move into Harlan Ranch with Rick and Gwendolyn, but Mark and Ellen have to move out first."

"They're doing all that for me?"

"It is the safest place for all of you right now."

"I need to think about all this. Could you leave me alone, please?"

Nick was still be the door, and gave a fatalistic shrug. Vince joined him.

When they got to the pass-through going into the dining room, Nick commented softly, "This is where she makes it or she doesn't. Are you a betting man?"

As they waited and hoped, Vince considered very unprofessional things about Kevin. A couple of posse members sat with him. One of them brought up the very subject he'd been dwelling on.

"If the posse helped watch Kevin, that would be good, wouldn't it?"

"I expect it would. Stanley might think that was neighborly of us. He might even process a little more meat for us."

"That's what we thought, too. If Kevin or his friends had accidents while the posse was watching, would there be an investigation?"

Vince had to control his expression to keep from cracking a grin. "I don't think anybody would cry much. As long as it was an accident, the gang is too far away for any of us to try to investigate. Just between us, if an accident happened to Kevin and caused him a great deal of pain, some people might think it was karma at work. Others might term it divine retribution. At the same time, we would have to be sure there was no human help with it. Lyle sent them into exile, and whatever happens to them out there is their own problem."

The two posse members both nodded solemnly, but there was no doubt in Vince's mind they just came to an agreement having nothing to do with the words they spoke. This was a return to ad hoc justice of the most primitive sort. With no prison they could use, it would have to serve. Nobody could do what Kevin did to Susie and walk away. He didn't care what Lyle said.

Susie's face suddenly peered through the doorway. "Is there anything to eat? I'm starved."

Gwendolyn prevented a stampede at that point by striding over to her. "We have some cornbread, and we can heat up some stew. What would you like?"

Rick scrambled over, checking the fire and stuffing an additional piece of wood in the cookstove. Two posse members checked the bank of refrigerators to see what might be available. As it turned out, some broth and a few morsels of cornbread were all she could handle, but the prognosis was now positive.

Gwendolyn talked quietly to Rick. Rick finally walked over and knelt beside Susie's chair.

"Susie, do you know what you mean to Gwendolyn and me?" he said in a soft voice. "You are our little sister, and we won't let anything happen to you, not ever."

Vince thought Rick was really pushing it. At that point, Rick glanced at Gwendolyn. Vince was surprised when she encouraged him to keep it going.

"Kevin is gone far away. Stanley's whole tribe and the Marine snipers are no longer trying to reform him. They are going to keep him away forever. He won't be able to bother you again. Not only that, but we're going to a better home with electric lights and a well full of water. All you have to do is turn on a faucet, and out comes fresh water. What do you think of that?"

Vince considered that if nothing else, Rick was confirming what he told her a short while before. Susie looked at him without cracking a smile. "I think that for a big brother, you are really full of it. Still, it sounds like fun. Are there unicorns?"

"I don't know about really truly unicorns, but if you want one, I'll attach a horn to one of the horses. Would that be okay?"

That was when Vince decided that Susie would be just fine. The posse members headed toward the kitchen to start some lunch. Just then they heard a single rider come into the service area. Vince wondered what the message might be. He couldn't imagine that Harlan Ranch could be ready for them this quickly. It turned out that was exactly the message. They could leave for Harlan Ranch whenever Susie was ready. Vince could only shake his head as Susie and Nick discussed them leaving the next morning.

Chapter 21

Harlan Prison

That afternoon, Susie wanted to eat every few hours. Once again, Rick and Gwendolyn agreed that caring for Susie was a dress rehearsal for caring for a newborn. The difference was that Susie could and did tell them exactly what she wanted. Another difference was having a whole crew of people trying to keep up with her cravings.

The next morning, everyone agreed they should take food with them in the carriage. Rick and Gwendolyn would ride with Susie inside the tent erected over the passenger section. The difficulty was that eating in a carriage jouncing over the uneven surface was a guaranty of spills, and lots of them. At the same time, the trip became a mobile picnic. Rick didn't know if Susie was playing a part. Maybe she was reacting to the miserable times she just had. Since she managed to eat quite a bit along the way, Rick decided it didn't matter much.

By the time they reached Oxford, they were out of food. Rick stuck his head outside the tent. "Stop at the meat processing place. See if we can get something ready to eat for Susie."

The meat processing plant had lots of food but no way to cook it. The Marines cooked bacon, ham, and side dishes quickly. In an aside, Tom again advised there was no place in Oxford where they could stay.

As they started to move again, Rick apologized to the driver. "I'm afraid there's grease on the seats."

The driver, who also got a snack wasn't concerned. "There's a lot to clean up on this rig. A little bacon grease is the least of my worries. If we have to use it for another wedding, it will take everyone in Harlan a week and a half to get it in shape again. Finding another carriage might be easier."

By the time they jolted their way up to Harlan Ranch, they created more coffee spills, crumbs, and additional grease spots. Rick felt guilty in spite of what the driver said. Looking outside the carriage's tent, Rick saw Mark's and Ellen's horses, both saddled and tied to the front porch column. Rick thought it was strange this deal went together so easily and quickly. At the moment, he had visions of getting screwed. There was nothing he could do about it at the moment, but it would definitely go toward their original decision to leave Harlan.

Mark leaned out the door and beckoned them in. "We kept the place ready for you guys. Ellen prepared quite a lot of food."

Rick and Nick both helped Susie into the house, even though she gamely tried to walk on her own. Gwendolyn gathered up the bedrolls and followed them. Since the carriage stopped right by the front steps, it was only a few feet into the house. Mark stood by the door, shutting it the moment Gwendolyn got into the house. They got Susie into the guest bedroom, where Nick did one more check on her physical well-being.

"How are you feeling, Susie?"

"I'm doing much better. I don't know what was the matter with me back there. I'm so sorry for being such a pain."

Nick nodded. "I think you'll be fine. I'll check on you tomorrow."

He came out of the guest bedroom, and Rick commented, "I think the guy driving the carriage would like to get home. In any case, thanks for coming along. It really helped for you to be there."

Nick stopped and stared at Rick. "First you raised hell with Lyle and now you thank me. You're a person we'd better watch out for."

Mark came up then. "I believe both of you are right. By the way, Nick, are there any restrictions on what Susie can eat?"

"Whatever she wants to eat should be okay. You'd better not give her too much at a time, though."

Nick headed out the door, and a minute later, they heard the carriage take off.

"Rick, Ellen made you guys something to eat. They did their best at Arapahoe, but they really weren't cooks. By the way, you now have three apprentices. They are not the normal, run-of-the-mill guys. In addition to wanting to get in line to learn horsemanship, they also want to join the posse. All are crack shots, and part of their duty is to protect you guys."

"Just as long as they aren't related to Dan."

Mark chuckled. "I sure hope not. I interviewed them in depth. After I got done with them, Lyle interviewed them some more with Adeline looking on. Everyone is pretty comfortable with them. If you get any idea otherwise, let me know right away."

Rick shook his head. "My reactions don't count. I thought something was amiss with Dan, but I didn't get concerned until the fourth day after we were kidnapped. That was too late for meaningful action. By the way, is that food I'm smelling?"

Mark nodded, slapping Rick collegially on the shoulder. "I believe Gwendolyn and Susie are already in the kitchen. Maybe we should catch up. There might be real food to enjoy."

Rick found that was the case. It was strange, sitting in Ellen's and Mark's kitchen, eating their food, while knowing the house was theirs to live in for a while. There was something he just had to know.

"Mark, how long will we do this switch-around routine?"

Mark shrugged. "We'll play the game this way until Lyle says we do it some other way. Just in case you're curious, I fully plan on outfitting Wagon Ranch with solar panels and refrigerators."

"That was on our list of things to do," Rick replied. "An arena was the first priority. Training could continue in spite of the weather."

They discussed some of the ideas for building the structure. Both Ellen and Gwendolyn commented about parts of the ideas. Finally, Mark and Ellen agreed they'd better get to their new home if they didn't want to ride in the dark, which promised to be even more frigid than what it was anyway. Ellen made a point of showing Gwendolyn where everything was stored, and then they were gone into the late afternoon.

"I'm still trying to persuade myself that what we agreed to do was the right thing," Rick commented as they watched Mark and Ellen ride off.

Gwendolyn agreed. "What's really strange is how quickly Ellen agreed to this, or that she agreed to it at all. She's not known for going along with any program that's not hers. On the other hand, what I've heard about their relationship, both with one another and with the Lillards is nearly the stuff of legend. Do you remember what Mr. Lillard said when he showed up right after Mark and Ellen did their strange little version of a marriage ceremony with us?"

"Yeah, I do remember that. One thing we'll have to figure out is just how much truth Lyle can stand at a time. I don't think anybody can take too much of it unmixed with bullshit, especially if we're talking about the one running the show."

"Well, now, aren't you the killjoy."

"Stumbling through snowdrifts while carrying somebody makes me a bit snarly, I suppose. It's just luck that we caught old man Lillard at a weak moment."

"So if he asks you something, are you going to just tell him what you think? I think I'm hearing you say that you'll need to schmooze now and then."

"That's the usual rule, isn't it?"

"How does he propose for everybody in Harlan to just get along with one another, anyway? It is his prime objective, but there's never any talk about how he plans on getting there."

"Anybody who doesn't go along with him and his program takes a walk in the snow. They could volunteer to be part of Kevin's gang."

"Ah, so if two people don't get along with each other, that's personal. However, if either of those two people don't get along with Lyle Lillard, they go down the road."

"That would be my suspicion."

"You've been a killjoy twice in a single minute. Your job is to make me feel secure and wanted. Didn't you know that?"

"Well, what say we make sure there's enough wood in the stoves. That way, I can concentrate on doing my real job. Speaking of jobs, where's Susie?"

"She went in her room. I'll check on her while you check the stoves. That way, I can fully appreciate and evaluate your efforts to make me feel secure and wanted."

Later, they cuddled on the couch. Gwendolyn suddenly untangled herself from Rick.

"Do you know what day it is?"

"I don't have a clue. It must be late December. It might even be early January. Why?"

"I think today is Christmas, Rick. Merry Christmas."

Rick had his doubts about that. It didn't feel like Christmas, but if Gwendolyn wanted it, who was he to argue? He had a sudden flashback to dashing through the snow, both with and without a one-horse sleigh and shivered to think about the reality. "Merry Christmas, whether it is or not. It looks like you got a home for the holidays. I'd have put a bow on it if I had realized what day it was."

"That's okay. You can give me a kiss and that will make it just fine. In any case, thank you very much. For a great present, Susie got a new life. That's an excellent gift for our little sister."

"It's not the gift she was hoping for, but we'll make it be the best gift we can."

"There you go."

As Gwendolyn pulled Rick down onto her, he thought this was the best Christmas he'd ever had, even if this might not be the exact day. Another song came to mind then, about how the weather outside was frightful, but the fire was so delightful.

For several days, Rick had no urge to do anything staying close to Gwendolyn and keeping an eye on Susie. Being with his wife was a joy and Susie appeared to be doing amazingly well, considering everything she had been through. After a few days, though, he began to get fidgety, to the point that Gwendolyn suggested several times that he go check around Harlan Ranch. Just like at Wagon Ranch, he needed to see what was going on. There was also a question as to whether the apprentices, so called, were doing anything more than just guard them.

He was only a few feet out the door when one of the apprentices headed out of the bunkhouse toward him. The man didn't try to tell him anything, but just stuck a few feet diagonally behind him. The stock still at Harlan Ranch all appeared to have been cared for adequately, and the fences were in good shape. The thing that made Rick really uneasy was that the guy was carrying a rifle. That wasn't like someone trying to be sure the boss was happy with how the chores were done.

Rick finally spun around and looked at the guy. "I'm getting nervous with you following me around. What's the deal?"

He didn't even blink. "Our orders are to make sure nothing happens to you. Wherever you go, one of us will be with you. At the moment, I'm assigned to be your bodyguard."

"The only danger to me is from you at this moment. The horses around here are more interested in hay and fresh warm water than any possible action against me. What if I decide to take a ride?"

"My instructions are to do everything possible to discourage you from such a thing."

"In other words, we're prisoners. What crime did we commit that we're being held like this?"

The guy got very uncomfortable then. "Mr. Lillard and Mark said they wanted to be more certain about the situation with Kevin and his gang. There was something about the group staying where they were supposed to be."

Rick snorted. "They weren't concerned about Kevin's gang when the tribal members were roaming inside Harlan. Susie, Gwendolyn, and I were the only ones concerned about Kevin then. I didn't say that quite right. It wasn't concern so much as a question of how soon we would die, and how much torture and pain we could stand in the meantime."

"They said that subject might come up. I must request you return to the house, and stay there until Mark and Mr. Lillard come to talk to you."

"Just out of curiosity, when was Christmas?"

"It was two days ago, the day you guys came from Arapahoe."

Rick grunted, and decided he might as well go back to the house and share the joyous news with Gwendolyn and Susie. He needed to tell Gwendolyn, and then they could jointly decide how much to share with Susie.

"Remember how we were Kevin's prisoners? Well, it seems that we're still prisoners. This time Lyle and Mark have us locked down. It's far more comfortable than stumbling through the frigid waste, but this is a prison and we are prisoners."

"How is staying at Harlan Ranch being prisoners?"

"We can't go outside the house until Mark or Lyle show up to tell us otherwise. I still wish we could have found a place to stay in Oxford with Tom and the snipers."

"You saw the snipers' lousy living conditions when we stopped there. Everyplace else looked twice as bad. It would have made that unheated house seem like luxury. Here, at least, we are warm. Did I mention there is food? How about the electricity? In any case, what is our alternative?"

"That has been the question all along, hasn't it? At no point did we have any alternatives. Mark and Lyle pushed us along, and with Vince's help, gathered up Susie as well. In the thing with the four families, we were never more than bait. The fact that you smelled a rat and came prepared to deal with them was the only unexpected part. The plan was that they were supposed to be our saviors. In return, we were to be duly appreciative."

"Rick, do you suppose they had some idea the thing with Kevin training under the snipers wasn't going to work?"

"If they already knew what would happen, why would they go along with Kevin's plan like they did? It is hard to imagine that they figured out there was an inside man coordinating the whole thing. That's exactly what Dan was doing, using the two former military fellows as his front men."

The two of them looked up then. Susie stood in the doorway. Rick shuddered, knowing any chance to work out a better way to tell her about all of it just flew out the window. The worst part was that Susie appeared to be in shock.

"When I was still trying to figure out if it was worth it to stay alive, I remember you guys talking about all of this but none of it mattered. Now I'm hearing it again, and it matters a lot. When they came and took me away from my family and home, they said it was for my own protection. Nothing they've done since then has been for anyone's protection but their own. What kind of people are running the place?"

Gwendolyn was the first to react. "That is exactly what we're trying to figure out. In addition, it seems that we simply swapped one form of incarceration for another. The three guys they said were here to protect us are keeping us from doing anything beside sit here in the house."

Susie shook her head. "My own family kept me locked up. They slapped me around, all in the name of keeping me from what they were pleased to call sin. Kevin liberated me from you two, but his goal was to have a punching bag. At least nobody is talking about sin and my bruises may fade. I guess it isn't so bad, compared with the other situations. On the other hand, there are a few things I'd like to do besides sit around being safe, warm, and fed. It all feels like the cattle in the feed lot."

"We all agree about that, Susie," Rick observed. "What Gwendolyn and I have been discussing is to do whatever we need to in order to get through this winter. Meanwhile, we can get together and plan what we can do when the weather warms up enough that we have some choice in the matter. Going west is not an option, with Kevin and his bunch out there. We don't have to decide anything right away."

Susie agreed, and a minute later, decided she was hungry again.

The only trips outside the house were to the outhouse, where even the apprentices cum security people decided they didn't need to hold anybody's hand. Rick spent the next three days quietly going crazy. Then came a quiet knock on the door. It was one of the guys with the security detail on duty at the time.

"Mr. Lillard and Mark Tahner said to ask if it would be okay if they came for a visit today."

"It's nice of them to ask," Rick told him. "Since when does the warden need the prisoners' permission? They are coming, one way or another. You can duly note to them that I have a bad attitude."

"I think they were hoping for a more positive response."

"The prisoners are duly grateful for the warmth and food. The fact that nobody has physically beat any of us lately is a positive note. Now, since we're losing a bunch of heat out the door, I'm closing it. Don't take it as a personal insult."

The guy muttered something and turned back to the bunkhouse. Rick closed the door and went to tell Gwendolyn and Susie. Since both of them were in the kitchen, the update was short and to the point.

"They have returned to the belief that we should worship at their feet and continually thank them for what they barely got around to doing."

It wasn't long before the exalted visitors arrived. None of the three were inclined to throw rose petals. On the other hand, they did nothing that Lyle or Mark could find particularly discourteous. In addition, cups of coffee were offered. After an extended period of silence, Lyle opened.

"I hoped that you would get past your little snit in a few days."

Rick didn't know what to think of the phrase Lyle used, other than the certainty that it didn't and couldn't fit the situation.

Gwendolyn stepped in then. "You make it sound like our experience with Kevin was no more than a bad hair day. The three of us nearly died. Susie did lose her baby. You should know that none of us will get over it any time soon. That is in addition to our current situation — being held incommunicado, having nothing to do, and physically restrained from going anywhere is driving all of us crazy."

Mark stared at Gwendolyn. "What are you talking about?"

Now Rick had something to say. "I was to do something Lyle called special training. With that in mind, I went out to look at the horses and almost immediately found a man with a rifle prodding me back toward the house. The only time they let any of us out of the house is when we go to the outhouse, and I don't think they like us doing that. I'm sure they'll appreciate functioning plumbing as soon as you can manage it. Then they'll nail the doors shut."

Rick thought a look of nervousness passed over Lyle's face. At the same time, Mark stared at him. "Boss, this was not what we talked about."

"This seemed the best way to keep everyone safe while preventing wild stories from making the rounds in Harlan."

"For controlling wild stories, that horse already left the barn." Mark turned to the three. "Posse members most likely added to the rumor mill, if you're interested. At the moment, they haven't exaggerated the stories too much. The story goes that Stanley brought the Kevin show to a halt before Lyle wanted. Lyle's plan was for him to wait until the posse pushed the tribal members up to you before taking action."

Rick shook his head. "From what I saw of that mob shambling down the road, they'd have been a long time catching us. They were moving the same speed that we were. That's part of what you said, Gwendolyn."

"Stanley said that was one of the reasons he did it there. The other was the probability that the three of you would have been dead within a mile."

"I don't know where you got your vision, but you were on the same wave length as Stanley," Rick observed.

Lyle broke in, "We might have caught up to Kevin's group sooner than he thought, too. I didn't want to endanger you with an ill-advised action. Kevin could have killed you. I couldn't take that chance."

"That's funny," Rick growled. "We were dying with our salvation right by us, but they couldn't act because we might die. You decreed Harlan too small to have jails and prison guards, but here we sit, sealed in a house with jailers on hand twenty-four seven to make sure we don't hear or spread any rumors. That makes so little sense I wonder if you've been sniffing the herb they stuffed in the walls at Wagon Ranch."

Lyle looked at all of them. "Mark, I hoped you would be on my side in this, at least while we were here. That isn't happening, so my concern is where we go from here. Nobody, including me, likes where we find ourselves now. Before we leave, I'll give the three out in the bunkhouse new instructions, to help the three of you any way you want. Nobody's going very far until the weather breaks. If these conditions continue much longer, it wouldn't surprise me to see polar bears moving in."

Gwendolyn looked at Lyle suspiciously. "Are you saying that we will now have the situation you told us we would have back in Arapahoe?"

"I don't have any special training for you to do, Rick. That means you'll have to figure out some way to make yourself useful. If Mark can use you over at Wagon Ranch, that's between the two of you. Frankly, I'd prefer you stay away from there until we can be more certain about Kevin staying away. If you can figure out a way to do computer work, that would be okay, too."

Mark agreed. "Having you show up now would just confuse things, and believe me, things are already more confused than I want to admit. I already sent a couple of guys back to Ragan when they couldn't figure out who was supposed to take care of things. As for Kevin and his bunch staying beyond the snow, they tested the system. The first guy got some bruises. The second guy found it a terminal experience, and was sent back to Kevin rather the worse for wear. The gang buried him in the desert a little way beyond the fog."

Rick asked, "Are they moving around much?"

"They keep sending people north and south along the edge of the fog. Stanley thinks they are seeing what might be available. He is also certain they are trying to outflank his hunters. He says there is no way that will happen."

"We accomplished a couple of things," Rick said as they watched the two ride away. "The problem is that everything is same as before. The fact that we can travel doesn't mean anything if nobody wants to see us and if there isn't anything we can do while we are out there. That means we're still pretty much stuck here."

Rick noticed the two women looking at him and decided to add, "That being the case, I can't think of two people I'd rather be stuck with."

"That was a decent save, but a long way from being a good one," Gwendolyn advised.

"Gwendolyn told me how you two nearly met last spring at a car accident. If you had gotten together then, what would you have done?"

Rick had to think about that a while. "At the time, there was still electricity sometimes. More to the point, there was still hope. We might have been able to team up since our specialties were complementary. The question would have been whether to get to someplace with more tech. What brought that up?"

"Why don't you guys do that now? You have electricity, so you could pursue it. I'm not just thinking about computers. Wouldn't it help Vince, the posse, and the gate guards if they had some communications? Kevin's plan might not have worked at all if everybody in Harlan could talk to each other. They could bring their radios here to recharge. Maybe Don Rowley could use some, too."

Rick snorted. "You know, that just might keep us on the right side of the situation. That could also be a plan for us to follow whether we stay in Harlan or try someplace else. On the subject of radios, Mark told me one time about how the President went to Offutt Air Force Base. There's a bunker where he might have survived. He might even be there now. We might pick up signals from Offutt with shortwave equipment. I don't know much about that kind of thing, but between us, we should be able to figure it out."

Gwendolyn considered that. "I remember the increasingly strange pronouncements coming out of the Oval Office, and that was before the Omega outbreak. Especially with the insanity around here, I'm not at all sure I want to know what he's saying now. On the other hand, this would certainly give us an idea how cooperative our bodyguards and former jailers have become. They might just decide that we are people they want to cultivate rather than irritate."

After a brief discussion about strategy, they concluded the next step had to involve the feminine approach. Gwendolyn got into her parka and took a walk to the bunkhouse. One point in her walking over there was to demonstrate how much easier it would be if they could have used a radio to call the bunkhouse. The subject of getting radio gear to check for other survivors was one they decided should not come up at this time. That would be their private project.

Susie went into the kitchen and prepared a few snacks. It wasn't long before Gwendolyn returned with all three of the current security detail. They sat in the living room with coffee and refreshments. It turned out that finding stashes of technical equipment was easier than they could have imagined. Most local places had been surveyed, and electronics were ignored except for solar or wind generators. A couple such places were not too far away. In addition, of course, there were the stores in the surrounding larger towns.

The next day, they all set out to collect what equipment they could. Fortunately, the farm wagon based at Harlan Ranch was still there, along with the necessary horsepower. Rick was familiar with the rig and the horse, having driven both in the McCook evacuation. Several of the houses were occupied, and those living there were more than happy to part with the assortment of electronic boat anchors and paper weights laying around. Most had been relegated to storage buildings. Time would tell if many were functional.

Whatever the condition of the gear, it gave a way to occupy their time. More than that, it would be something that Lyle and Mark should actually buy into, whenever they heard about it. Rick was in no hurry for that, but he was quite certain that every time they got a new set of bodyguards, the outgoing ones briefed Lyle on what they saw and heard. Even if he wanted to, Rick would not have been able to keep them from spilling their guts to the big man.

By the next day, Rick found some communicators that functioned and were on compatible frequencies. He knew of some with a range of up to thirty-five miles, but these weren't that kind. Five miles would be the best they could do, and that would be under the best conditions. The Lillard Place was about five miles away, but it was on the far side of a ridge. These radios would not be able to call there. West gate and the hill above Oxford might be a good spot for them. Currently, mirrors and bonfires were the only available signal devices other than a horse and rider.

The other issue was how long they could go between charges. Rick concluded that if the things passed so much as a single critical message, the whole project had to be considered successful by those involved. On the other hand, they might come to depend on a lash-up of radios. Then, if a single message failed to get through, some would claim the whole project was a complete waste of time. In other words, things would be like they had always been.

In addition, he found a couple of multi-band receivers. They should work, but needed an active power source. The other thing they would need was an antenna. That created a problem for keeping that end of the project quiet. Rick then considered that he could rig an antenna in the attic. He recalled some folks doing TV antennas that way back in the day. It would give some privacy while giving them an opportunity to see if anybody was broadcasting.

He procured some wire appropriate for the occasion. It was called horse wire, and was like heavy-duty barbed wire, except there were no barbs on it. He crawled up in the attic and created a loop which he hooked to the receiver, kept in the master bedroom. For privacy, he used headphones. It didn't take long before he picked up signals. The words sent a shiver up his back.

"This is the President of the United States. I am issuing the following Executive Order."

There followed an incoherent rant which changed subjects every sentence and a half. The Presidential tirade was on multiple frequencies, and Rick couldn't find any other transmission in the time he had it on. He immediately brought both Gwendolyn and Susie in to listen, with the speaker at a low volume.

Chapter 22

Maybe a Better Way

Several days later, as he watched Lyle and Mark ride up to the house, Gwendolyn informed him this was now the new year, and actually a couple of days into it. Rick couldn't decide whether to be gratified or concerned, and finally elected to accept the information as basic trivia. There was no change in the ice cap gleaming outside, and certainly no break in the sub-zero temperatures. When they came in, Rick handed them two of the communicators.

"These will communicate with each other. The batteries should keep them going for a while, anyway. I thought the posse and gate guards could use them. I'm sure you guys will want them for command and control, if that's what you call it, Mark. I'm hopeful to find at least a few longer range devices. Getting them may have to wait until I can get to Kearney or somewhere like that."

"That is a great thing you've done, Rick," Lyle told him. "I have a radio at my house, but the only place it ever communicated was with the Harlan Sheriff's Office in Alma. There's nobody down there now. I'm surprised that you're going to so much work, considering your opinion of our county."

"It's what I do. This wasn't the only project I worked on. Come on into the bedroom."

Everybody crowded into the small room and after checking outside for their guards, Rick turned on the receiver. He had it on one of the Presidential frequencies, and the man himself came up at mid-rant. It included advice about putting tape around windows and staying indoors to avoid the deadly dust. Then he rambled on into other topics, like the need to beware of awful barbarians roaming the streets and countryside. It wasn't long before everybody agreed they heard enough, and Rick switched it off.

"If there are other stations broadcasting, I haven't found them. He never says where he is located. From what you told me, Mark, I presume he is in the Offutt bunker. That means a group of survivors is less than two hundred miles from here. From what I've heard, I'm in no rush to connect with his bunch. Still, with survivors there and McCook, it raises the possibility of quite a few people in various places."

Lyle looked at Rick doubtfully. "How many people know about what you've found?"

Rick motioned around the room. "As of now, just the five of us in this room. I didn't tell anyone about my additional project, and hid the antenna in the attic so nobody outside could see anything. I usually use earphones. That is also why the radio went in here. If anyone came in, we could shut the door to the bedroom without anybody wondering about it. Anyone with a radio and a battery could have picked it up, but that would have become public knowledge in short order."

"After what you had to say about my keeping a little information off the board, I thought it entirely possible that you already took it to what passes for a newspaper in Harlan."

"I draw a distinction between this kind of information and what you were doing. With this drivel, somebody would undoubtedly attempt to follow what the radio says. Since the so-called guidance contradicts itself at every point, it would hurt or kill us all. What you were doing could and did cost lives. Considering what is coming over the radio, the only choice is to ignore it."

"We agree on that, at least. Could you keep anything else you find out between our little group, at least for now?"

"I have no problem with that. Do you have any problem with me casting a wider net for electronics?"

"You could go farther afield, but people have been doing that for a while now. I'll check with Don Rowley. He could have his people pick up electronics for you. The tradeoff would be you having to supply him with communication. You know how he likes to manage every little detail."

"That would work. It would not be popular with his crew. The reason they would hate what I'm doing would be why Don Rowley would want them."

Lyle chuckled. "I believe that's exactly right. Thank you for getting some communication happening. Mark and I will test them on the way back. Would you stand by the unit here while we do that?"

Their treasures in hand, Mark and Lyle headed back. He listened to radio chatter between the two of them. They did periodic radio checks with Rick, who did his part with his boots off and a cup of coffee beside him. He found it a visceral pleasure listening as the frigid temperatures began to effect them. The signal became weaker as they got to the top of the grade. At that point, Mark stopped while Lyle continued home. Rick quickly lost Lyle's signal, but kept in contact with Mark. Mark, in turn, was able to communicate with Lyle. If nothing else, strategically placed people could relay messages.

The other part of the equation was knowing how privacy in Harlan just evaporated.

A couple of days later, Don Rowley drove up with a freight wagon full of electronics of every description. Gwendolyn stood in the doorway behind him looking at it.

"Rick, this is where our partnership needs a little distance. I didn't want that other stuff in the house. There is no way in hell you're turning the place we live into a warehouse and a work shop."

Don grinned at Rick. "That sounds like the noises Nancy made when I started bringing too many treasures home. What would be your next choice for them?"

"Are you telling me that we're in the same business now?"

Don smiled widely. "We are in complementary trades, it seems. All of this came from my warehouses. My crews haul it in from time to time, and I hadn't gotten around to getting rid of it. Lyle says you have a use for it. The deal is that I will get half of any two-way radios you manage to get running."

"I can handle that, Don. We'll put all of these in the shed next to the bunkhouse. The three guys in the bunkhouse are going to have to rearrange things, because that's where I will do my repair work. First, though, they can bloody well get off their cans and help us unload your wagon."

"Are you the same timid soul who offered to go to work for me a while back?"

"We didn't have anything to talk about, so there was no reason to flap my gums." Rick suddenly remembered Tom saying the same thing not long ago. Maybe they were brothers. Then he continued, "Now you've dumped a wagon full of stuff on me. Some of it might have salvage value. We have that in common for the moment. Another thing is the weather, and it isn't getting any warmer."

Don looked at Rick like he had never really seen him before. "You're making sense, Rick. I think I ought to be afraid."

The wagon was soon unloaded and Don got down the road. That was when the three bodyguards discovered their part of the story had just begun. Three beds were shoved to one side of the room and the rest upended against the back wall. A workbench and stool came inside on the opposite side of the room, next to the door into the shed where all the equipment was stored.

"You guys ought to get involved with this. Lyle and Mark tell me you are candidates for the apprentice program. The thing is that I don't have any horses. That means reviving these radios is the current job. What do you say?"

They didn't have much to say about it, and set to work under Rick's direction. There was a notable lack of enthusiasm. Two days later, when a new set of bodyguards appeared, Rick saw that word about the radios got out, and the new guys were very interested in getting their hands on any new toys. The new guys weren't as good with weapons and had nowhere near the same enthusiasm for ranch work. That combination of traits suited Rick just fine, as long as their lives didn't come down to the new guys' marksmanship.

In addition to interest, two of them knew more about the radios than Rick. It wasn't long before they took over the job. That suited Rick since his priority projects were in the house. He knew them in order. The highest was Gwendolyn, followed by Susie. The scanner was more a matter of interest than a priority. Still, every hour or so, Rick went out to the shed to see what was going on, and if there were any other items he might play with. A couple of things caught his eye on an early trip. One was a high-end laptop computer. The other was a scanner. Both were still sealed in cartons. The scanner could work on several bands he couldn't get on the other receiver. Available bands included military. He hauled both back to the house.

Going every hour became a few times a day. Rick forced himself to go out to the bunkhouse periodically to see how things were going. The three went through equipment at a prodigious rate, and true to the agreement, divided functioning radios so Don could get his share. Rick could tell they knew the estimable Mr. Rowley quite well. Neither pile was identified, leaving Don to decide which pile he wanted. He couldn't decide whether to be amused or disgusted.

True to form, Don came by the next day to see what he could snag, and took the pile of radios that appeared fractionally larger. Rick tried putting on a show to make Don think he was stealing the best equipment anywhere. The truth of it was that Rick was totally indifferent. Vince showed up a little later, and was grateful to have radios for some of his posse. To show his gratitude, Vince left full-fledged posse members with radios to give Harlan Ranch some more realistic firepower.

The next day, posse members without radios showed up, and hung around, waiting to get communications. Anybody attacking Harlan Ranch now would need a great deal of firepower, if they weren't bent on suicide. As word got around, the bunkhouse became the unofficial posse annex. It had all the conveniences of home (and more than most) along with the best communications around.

Rick had mixed feelings about seeing his radio shop turn into the police station. At least, when he went to the house, they pretty much left him and his ladies alone. That was a positive since he devoted what time he could to the new scanner in the bedroom, trying to find anyone out there.

The obvious answer was that survivors without electrical power or technical expertise would not transmit anything. Not receiving anything meant little. Rick worked his way through frequencies in something like a systematic fashion. In the area identified as military by his radio, Rick started to pick up artificial sounds. It sounded like transmitters being keyed periodically. He decided to stay a bit longer in this area. Just about when he was ready to give up and move on, the scanner stopped on an open microphone.

"Alpha Two Seven, status check."

A moment later on a nearby frequency, came, "This is Alpha Two Seven. Rations, twenty-one percent. Water, seventeen percent. Other consumables are twelve percent. Mechanical systems are status yellow. The air filters are still clogged. All personnel accounted for. Over."

That had to be a military organization. They had both power and communications. From the chatter, it wasn't clear if they knew it was okay to leave their bunkers. At the same time, he now had something to report to Mark and Lyle the next time he saw them. It wasn't ten minutes before a knock came on the door. It was one of his radio apprentices.

"We assigned one of the channels for the exclusive use of command," he told Rick as a preface. "Mark just called in on it, and he is on his way out here with Mr. Lillard."

There was, Rick considered, something to be said for advance notice. Having those two simply show up could be a real drag. On the other hand, having them not show up was an even bigger drag. Rick figured he'd take it for what it was worth and keep moving.

When they showed up, he took them on a tour of the radio shop and posse annex. With what Mark called a command inspection done, they adjourned to the house, where they sipped coffee and Rick described what he'd heard on the scanner.

Turning on the scanner and going to the same range of frequencies produced no chatter, though there were several instances sounding like somebody keying a transmitter. Lyle and Mark both became thoughtful, and after a few minutes, Lyle turned to Rick.

"We need Vince in on this conversation. Can the guys out in the bunkhouse get him on the radio?"

"They can, or you could initiate the call yourself. Use channel three."

Rick thought it might have been a half hour before Vince was close enough to call directly. Lyle invited him to come by, and mentioned he should spend more time at Harlan Ranch since his posse was there. Nothing more was said, and Vince didn't pursue the matter over the air.

Once in the house and brought up to speed, Vince considered the situation. "There is no way we should attempt to contact the Presidential radio stations. As for the military sites, I agree they are surviving missile bunkers in the western part of the state. Trying to break into their net will only get us grief. There is absolutely no reason we should tell any more people than necessary about this."

Just then, Vince's radio beeped, and he answered it. After a short conversation, Vince looked at all of them.

"Lookouts in Oxford report storm clouds coming from the south. Everyone should get to wherever they want to spend the next several days. We may see a break in the arctic conditions. There may be a pile of snow before that, though."

That was pretty much the end of the conversation. Mark and Lyle both took off then. Vince hung around, finishing a cup of coffee he was working on.

"Shouldn't you be heading for Ragan, Vince?"

"Yeah, first, I need to have a word with the posse. Out of curiosity, are you three happy with your current situation?"

"Is this Vince asking, or is this Lyle asking with Vince's mouth?"

"It's me asking. You should know that wif Lyle asks me about it, I'll probably tell him."

"Speaking for myself, it's nice to have a function everyone thinks is useful. As for whether I'm pleased with Lyle Lillard, nothing has changed. We'll stick around until the weather gives us a break. We'll decide then what we'll do and where we'll do it."

"Personally, I hope you guys stick around. It's nice having somebody willing to call Lyle's bluff. Just between us, the business with your rescue involved really poor decision making at his end. I'd better head for home before the storm gets here."

Vince handed Rick his coffee cup, got his coat on, and slid out the door. After he left, Rick turned to see Gwendolyn and Susie both looking at him.

"Did I mess up?" he asked.

A slight smile crossed Gwendolyn's face. "He asked where your mind was, and you told him. With his cop mind, you probably scrambled his circuits big time. As far as I'm concerned, it confirms you're a nerd. Best of all, you're my nerd."

The End

Bruce I. Schindler

This Reality and Every Other

The Dust & Cannibals series, so far, is set in a place both exotic and remote. The Marrakesh Express gets nowhere near it. Even in far-off Kathmandu, this place seems a world away. Its inhabitants call it Harlan County, and describe it as being in South-Central Nebraska.

People fly overhead on their way to important destinations. They are within a few miles, but cannot know what is just below them. Others drive past or through with no idea something magical happened. A veil over the area makes most people choose not to see.

In Harlan County, it is a short distance between this reality and every other reality. Some inhabitants cross over routinely, and come back with strange tales, spun as though they are the same world as ours.

When I was younger, I listened while the old guys told their stories around the fire. The tales were long, involved, and as kids will, I nodded off periodically. Some details are a bit fuzzy, but I pass along the stories as faithfully as I can.

I came to Harlan County for love, and found it. I got much more, finding a friend, a muse, and a goddess. That alone was more than enough, but more blessings came: horses waiting impatiently for more hay and a macaw loudly demanding pizza. There is also our Shih Tsu, a psychic dog who projects her thoughts, making me do as she wishes.

Life before Harlan County now seems less real than all the other realities about which I write. My main indicator about the real world comes when the horses, macaw, and dog make their needs known.

In this world, I find pleasure in sharing these stories. Since there is no way to give escorted tours, they say I must call them fiction – science fiction. You and I know they are real.

Bruce I. Schindler